THE
STARDUST
IN THE
ASHES

AMBER D. LEWIS

Editor: Andi L. Gregory

Back Cover Art and Map Design: Ben Lewis

ISBN (Print Paperback) 979-8-9874915-0-8

ISBN (Print Hardback) 979-8-9874915-2-2

ISBN (ebook) 979-8-9874915-1-5

For Business Inquiries visit www.amberdlewis.com or write to 4359 Wade Hampton Blvd, #282, Taylors, SC 29687

The Dark Sea

Isle of Atroxmorte

Château des Chamans

Summer Palace

Paravlia

Aleahya

Balan

Vanaar

Gleador

Finjon Mines

Koshima

Yomori

Heldonia

Ging Tu

Takuma

Silver Mines

Muldainah

Hundon Valley

Forduna

Hyati

Luma

Character Pronunciation Guide

Alak:	æl-ik (Al-ick)
Aoibhinn:	ā-vēn (Ae-veen)
Astra:	æs-truh (Ash-truh)
Bram:	bræm (Bram)
Brock:	bräk (Brawk)
Cadewynn:	kad-u-win (Kad-uh-win)
Caedios:	kā-dē-us (Kay-dee-us)
Cal:	kæl (Kal)
Ehren:	eh-ruhn (Air-un)
Felixe:	fē-liks (Fee-licks)
Jessalynn:	jes-u-lin (Jes-uh-lin)
Kaeya:	kī-yuh (Kie-uh)
Kai:	kī (Kie)
Kato:	kā-tō (Kay-toe)
Kiera:	kē-ehr-u (Key-air-uh)
Lorrell:	lor-rul (Lore-ul)
Luc:	luk (Lewk)
Makin:	māk-in (Make-in)
Mara:	mär-uh (Mar-uh)
Nicolette:	nik-ō-let (Nik-oh-let)
Nyco:	nī-kō (Nie-koe)
Pascal:	pæs-kæl (Pass-kal)
Pax:	pæks (Paks)
Ronan:	rō-nin (Roe-nin)
Sama:	sam-u (Sam-uh)
Sobek:	sō-bek (Sow-beck)
Tola:	tō-lu (Toe-luh)
Yoon:	yön (Yoon)

Place Pronunciation Guide

Kingdoms

Ascaria:	æs-kâr-rē-u	(Ass-scare-ree-uh)
Athiedor:	æ-thē-u-dōr	(A-thee-uh-door)
Callenia:	ku-lin-ē-u	(Kuh-len-ee-uh)
Gleador:	glē-u-dōr	(Glee-uh-door)
Naskein:	næs-kēn	(Nas-keen)
Oyrain:	ɔɪ-rān	(Oi-rain)
Paravlia:	Pu-rav-lē-u	(Puh-rav-lee-uh)
Portia:	pōr-šu	(Pour-shuh)

Gleador Provinces

Aleahya:	æl-u-hī-u	(Al-uh-high-uh)
Balen:	ba-lin	(Bah-lin)
Gingtu:	gēng-tu	(Geeng-too)
Hundan Valley:	hun-dun	(Hun-done)
Heldonia:	hel-dō-nē-u	(Hell-doe-nee-uh)
Jakuma:	jæ-kü-mu	(Jah-koo-muh)
Luma:	lü-mu	(Loo-muh)
Vanaar:	væ-nār	(Vah-nair)

Key Cities

Beaurac:	bü-rac	(Bü-rahck)
Forduna:	for-du-nʌ	(For-due-nuh)
Hyati:	hī-ya-tē	(High-yah-tee)
Koshima:	kō-shē-mu	(Koe-she-muh)
Yomori:	yō-mōr-ē	(Yo-more-ee)
Mullidain:	mul-u-dān	(Mull-uh-dain)

To all the shippers out there. May your happily ever afters come true.

AUTHOR NOTE

This story contains some material that may be upsetting to some readers including talk of infertility, reference to past abuse and abusive situations, reference to past suicides and suicide attempts, grief and mourning, PTSD, brief suicidal thoughts, slight homophobic references, and bouts of depression and anxiety.

View more details at www.amberdlewis.com/content-warnings or at the back of the book following the Acknowledgments.

"THE STARLIGHT IN THE SHADOWS" RECAP

KEY PLOT POINTS

Part One: Apart (Astra's Events)

- Astra, Bram, Ehren, Makin, and Cal are on the Isle of Naskein while Kato fled to Athiedor with Alak.
- After a brief meeting with Master Arcanis, Ehren decides they will head to the Hundan Valley in Gleador. He also agrees to activate portal stones on their journey.
- Bram gets upset when he learns Astra will be made Court Sorceress and the two break off their engagement.
- Astra is made Court Sorceress during a formal ceremony and the crew leaves Naskein the next morning.

- When they arrive in the Hundan Valley they are met by the head of the Valley, Jessalynn, who is Ehren's half-sister.
- Ehren meets up with Nyco, a spy he had in the Valley.
- The crew is integrated into life in the Valley and given jobs. Ehren sorts official papers in library, and Astra joins him for a little while. They discover the story of Caedios and his fall into the darkness.
- Astra joins Kai, a wolf shifter, on night guard duty and the two bond.
- Jessalynn agrees to support Ehren and offers an escort to Koshima. Ehren, Cal, Astra, and Bram leave the Valley with Sama, Kai, and Nyco.

Part One: Apart (Alak's Events)

- Kato resides in Brackenborough, the village where Alak's aunt lives.
- Using wisping, Kato takes his group of magical recruits to Periola to bring Lord Wallish to his cause.
- Ian is suspicious of Alak, but Alak plays his part well.
- Lord Wallish is hesitant to join Kato, but after a meeting with his council agrees to join Kato under several conditions. Kato and Lord Wallish sign a treaty that can be broken if Kato doesn't get all the Clan Lords on his side or if Astra can match his offer.
- Kato takes everyone to the pub to celebrate, and

when Alak sneaks away, Aine follows him. She magically drugs Alak and tries to take advantage of him. Alak calls on Felixe and escapes in a haze.

Part Two: Closer

- Astra and Ehren are welcomed to Koshima by King Naimon and given three adjoining rooms. They meet with the king and he agrees to fund their cause, but withholds his armies for now. He invites them to join him at a masquerade ball celebrating the god Oryus.
- Alak wakes disoriented at a strange location. While looking around, he spots Astra and uses his illusion magic to hide himself before approaching her. The two dance and kiss before Alak fills her in on what is happening with Kato. They share one last dance before Alak wisps back to Periola with the help of Felixe.
- The day they are to leave Clan Wallish, Lord Wallish pulls Alak aside and asks him about Astra. After some persuasion, Alak fills Lord Wallish in and Lord Wallish admits he would rather choose Astra's side.
- Kato and crew wisp away to Clan McDullun, but the lord is away. They spend time in the village, and Alak catches glimpse of the old Kato as he shows his magic to children playing in the street.
- Lord McDullun proves to be harder to convince than anticipated. After the official meeting with

Kato, Alak hangs back and recruits Lord McDullun—who requests to be called Ronan—to Astra's side. The two become friendly and Alak confesses that he has connections to Astra because they are bond-mates.

- Meanwhile, Astra's group make plans to head to Callenia. They activate an old portal in a garden before spending the day enjoying the city. While talking with Illyas, King Naimon's Court Mage, Astra discovers she killed everyone in the attack in Brackenborough and it upsets her. Illyas gives Astra a bracelet with a Syphon Stone to store magic and Ehren a ring with a similar stone.

- A letter arrives from Alak informing Astra that if she shows up at a meeting of the Clans arranged by Kato, she may able to sway things in their favor. Astra and Ehren make a plan despite Bram's reservations.

- The group leaves Koshima, escorted by some Gleador guards. They stop at the abandoned city of Jasaltine. Astra explores an old magical mine and finds a couple small pieces of Luvgim. Ehren activates another portal and they head into Callenia.

- Once in Callenia they stop in another abandoned city that used to belong to a magical order. They reactivate another portal and are ambushed by Callenian soldiers on the way out. All those with magic unleash it on their attackers, killing hundreds, and Astra wisps them away to safely.

- Astra has a breakdown due to all the lives she's

taken, and Ehren comforts her. Ehren uses a
spell to help her sleep so the dead won't haunt
her dreams.

- Alak helps Kato set up a neutral meeting place
  for the Clans. The Clan leaders arrive and Alak
  is forced to socialize and entertain them.
- When Lord Wallish arrives, he brings news of
  Astra's escape from the king's men, and the other
  Lords begin questioning whether or not they
  backed the wrong twin.
- The day of the treaty signing arrives, and Alak
  sends for Astra via Felixe. Before the meeting
  can start, Astra appears with her magic on
  display. The lords are impressed and sign her
  treaty instead of sticking with Kato. Astra uses
  her magic to protect the lords so they can escape.
- Once done, she wisps away, but she doesn't go
  far. Alak find her in his room. They kiss and
  Alak tells Astra that he loves her. They're
  interrupted, and she's forced to wisp away before
  she can respond.
- Astra rejoins Ehren and crew, and they continue
  their journey toward Hounddale, Bram's home.
- Kato is furious and sets out to find who betrayed
  him. When he discovers it was Alak, he drags
  Alak before him. He then reveals that he has
  freed one of the Dragkonians. The Dragkonian—
  Akaash—reads Alak's mind and confirms his link
  to Astra. They torture Alak to bring Astra.
- Astra collapses, feeling Alak's pain through the
  soul bond. She wisps to his side and confronts
  the Dragkonian and her brother. Using a spell

put into her Syphon Stone by Ehren, she frees
Alak and they wisp away, using up almost all of
Astra's power and energy.

Part Three: Together

- Astra wakes from a nightmare to discover that
  Hanna and Healer Heora have joined their
  group, led there by a young Seer named Pip.
  Thanks to their help, Alak is unconscious but
  alive. He also has scars that will never heal.
- When Alak wakes up, he's sore but healing
  quickly. After resting some more, he's introduced
  to the newcomers in the group. He discovers
  Astra in Ehren's tent, asleep. He assumes Ehren
  and Astra are together, but Ehren corrects him.
  Ehren asks what really happened with Isabella,
  and Alak shares some of the story. Ehren agrees
  to trust Alak completely and leaves Astra in his
  care.
- When they arrive in Hounddale, Alak is taken
  aback by how much Bram's sister Diana looks
  like Isabella. During dinner Alak steps outside to
  escape her attention. Ehren joins him and admits
  he also sees the similarities between the two
  sisters. In the middle of their conversation, Alak
  screams out in pain.
- Astra rushes outside and Kato appears. He used
  a dark magical symbol carved in Alak's back to
  track them. He steals Astra away and Bram
  blames Alak.
- Kato locks Astra up so he and Akaash can drain

her magic to free more Dragonkonians. Astra passes out and meets with Aoibhinn in the in-between. Aoibhinn tells Astra that Kato is possessed by Caedios and that the only way to win against him is to kill Kato. Astra insists she'll find another way.

- Meanwhile, Ehren comes up with a plan to rescue Astra. He calls Bram and Alak together and gives them the Syphon Stones and Luvgim filled with magic. The two reluctantly agree to cooperate, and Alak wisps them to Astra by following the bond.

- They find Astra in a dark room and go to free her. Kato, Akaash, and Fionn show up and they fight. They manage to free Astra and escape, but Alak is very weak. They follow Felixe and inadvertently enter the realm of the Fae.

- A Fae named Elidyr takes them to a Healer in his village. The Healer heals Astra and Alak, and they rest and recover.

- Alak wakes first and goes out to explore the village. He finds a Fae named Hycis who takes him to Bram. While he's talking with Hycis and Elidyr, a Fae named Fenian brings Astra to them. During conversation, the soul bond gets brought up and Astra learns Alak has known about it all along.

- Astra rushes away and Alak chases after her. They talk about the bond and Astra admits she's in love with Alak and wants to complete the soul bond ceremony. They kiss and Bram finds them. Bram storms off and Astra goes after him.

They talk a bit before she rejoins the Fae and Alak.

- The Fae tell them about a berry that can kill the Dragkonians. They agree to contact Astra once the berries are ready.
- Astra and Alak are taken away and prepared for the bond ceremony. They meet in a Fae glade and swear an oath in blood. Once the words have been said, they both fall into a dreamworld where they fight their worst demons in order to find each other. When they wake they consummate their bond.
- The next morning, the Fae give Astra some of their magic for her Syphon Stone before leading them back to the human realm. Kai finds them and leads them to their camp. Everyone's relief is short-lived when they realize an attack on Embervein is imminent.
- They rush to Embervein in time to see the attack begin. Astra wisps Ehren into the palace. He goes off to find his father while Astra hunts down Cadewynn, who is in the hidden library room with people she helped rescue. Astra wisps everyone to the forest where Bram and Healers are waiting.
- Astra storms through the castle and finds Ehren locked in a battle with his father. Kato shows up and challenges the king, who he then kills. Ehren is shocked and Astra convinces him to go to the forest with his sister and mother while she clears the castle.

- After a brief confrontation with Kato, Astra rushes through the castle, recruiting soldiers to help everyone escape. When she reaches the courtyard, she discovers Alak, Cal, Nyco, and Makin have arrived. Makin dives in front of a Dragkonian to protect Cal and dies.
- Feeling defeated, Astra wisps away with Cal, who's holding Makin's body, and they join the others in the forest. Astra's magic is weak but she helps the Healers with whatever tasks she can.
- Later, she finds Cal and convinces him to eat while he tells her about Makin. She then goes and finds Ehren, who is having a breakdown. They cry and comfort each other, and Ehren promises to join her to get some sleep soon.
- Astra finds Alak and they lie down next to one of the fires, joined shortly after by Ehren and Cal.
- They burn most of the dead, but Cal insists on digging a grave for Makin. Ehren is broken, lost, and desperate for hope.

KEY PEOPLE

- **Astra**: twin with starlight magic
- **Kato**: twin with fire magic; went rogue
- **Mara**: Astra's best friend
- **Pax**: Kato's best friend
- **Bram/Captain Bramfield**: Prince Ehren's Captain of the Guard
- **Ehren**: Crown Prince of Callenia

- **Healer Heora**: Healer who helped Kato and Astra
- **Hanna**: Healer Heora's granddaughter; Healer in training
- **Pip**: Seer who joins Hanna and Healer Heora
- **Alak**: Syphon with illusion magic
- **Felixe**: an adorable Fae Fox who can wisp at will and turn invisible; Alak's familiar
- **Cadewynn/Winnie**: Princess of Callenia; Ehren's sister
- **King Betron**: King of Callenia who hates magic; Ehren's father
- **Makin**: member of Ehren's Guard; close with Ehren and Bram; chosen to guard Astra
- **Cal**: member of Ehren's Guard; close with Ehren and Bram; chosen to guard Astra
- **Nyco**: talks to insects and spiders; spy for Ehren and part of his Guard
- **Kai**: wolf-shifter who grows protective of Astra; from the Valley
- **Sama**: gentle Syphon from the Valley
- **Niall**: Alak's cousin; has shadow magic; dangerously pro-magic
- **Kayleigh**: Alak's cousin; has telekinesis; seamstress
- **Caitlyn**: Niall's fiancé; an empath who can see auras
- **Ian**: Niall's friend; strong in spellwork
- **Aine**: Niall's friend/ Ian's sister; has metal attack magic; interested in Alak

- **Fionn**: Niall's friend; specializes in spellwork and potions without needing ingredients or spell books; poisoned Astra
- **Master Arcanis**: Head of the Order of Naskein
- **Aoibhinn**: the goddess of magic
- **Caedios**: Evil counterpart to Aoibhinn
- **Jessalynn:** Ehren's half-sister; leader of the Hundan Valley
- **Kaeya**: Jessalynn's Captain and partner
- **Brock**: Jessalynn's Lieutenant and partner

View character profiles and art, maps, and more on my website: https://www.amberdlewis.com/storytelling

PROLOGUE
CADEWYNN

When I was ten years old, my good friend died overnight with no real explanation. At least, I think of her as my friend, even though she was a few years older than I was. Her name was Isabella Bramfield, and she was kind.

Before her, I had no real concept of death. Her death snuck up on me like a quiet shadow and still haunts the corners of my mind.

Now, I have a much more realistic expectation of death. My father, the King of Callenia, is dead. He was killed by a man I once thought my friend. Many loyal soldiers are also dead. Some I knew, others little more than strangers. My brother is alive, if you call his current state living. The shadows that haunted the corners of my thoughts after Isabella died consume his. He's quickly becoming a ghost of his former self.

Mother isn't helping. I know she mourns our father, but she blames Ehren for his death. She's far too stubborn to admit she's wrong, and I hate her for it. She's never exactly been a role model for me—which is dreadful to say about one's mother—but I hope I can be better. Ehren defended our father, even after our father shunned him, leaving him no choice but to flee Callenia. I don't want to speak ill of the dead, but a little piece of me feels my father deserved his fate. Though, if I could take some of Ehren's pain from him and bear it myself, I gladly would.

Now, I am on my way to Gleador. Ehren says it's for my protection. If I am in Gleador under the protection of King Naimon, I may outlive this war. I wanted to protest when he told me, but he's so broken I was afraid I would shatter what remains of his resolve. So here I am, off to Gleador with my mother. I have the protection of my brother's Guard, Nyco, as well as Sama, a girl from the Hundan Valley.

I've been stored away in my library for nearly as long as I can remember. Books can only take me so far, and I'm ready to do more. I may not be able to lift a sword in battle, but I can recruit those who can. Ehren sends me to Gleador to keep me safe, but I go with the intention of finding a way to win this war.

Part One:
Fallen

CHAPTER ONE

ASTRA

A cold breeze wakes me from my dreams. I blink and look around the room enough to register that it's morning, but I have no desire to rise from bed yet. I glance at Alak curled up beside me, my eyes falling to the jagged scar on his lower back. Several Healers have examined it, assuring us that whatever dark magic once lay there is long gone, but it still makes me uneasy. I force the fear away and burrow further under the covers, snuggling closer to his warm body.

Alak sighs in his sleep and shifts closer, turning over. I take advantage of his new position to rest my head on his bare chest, the steady, calm thrum of his heart comforting and familiar. He shifts again, this time enough I can tell he's waking. I press in closer and his arm tightens around me.

"You awake, love?" he asks, his voice gravelly from sleep.

"Mmm," I mumble, grinning against his skin but not bothering to open my eyes.

"Don't you have a kingdom to help run?" he teases.

"I need a few more minutes," I whisper, draping my arm

across his waist and slowly tracing my finger along the waist-band of his pants.

Alak inhales sharply and arches into my touch. I slide my finger just barely beneath the band and his breath catches. Warm desire surges down our bond.

"Don't start anything you don't plan on finishing," Alak purrs.

"I'm sure I don't know what you mean," I reply with a grin.

In a rapid flash of limbs and blankets, Alak wraps his arms around me, flipping me over. I squeal as I land on my back and grin up at him, his body braced above mine. There's a mischievous glint in his emerald eyes—a glint that tells me clearly what he has in mind, even if I couldn't sense his every intention through our bond. He, likewise, can sense my very positive reaction.

"You know exactly what I mean," he says, lowering his lips to mine.

I bite my lip and meet his eyes as he pulls back. "I think you need to show me."

Alak's eyes flash with desire as he grins. "Oh, I intend to."

Alak's lips are almost to mine again when a loud huff from the floor of our room gives him pause. A second huff that sounds more like a growl has him flopping back to his side of the bed.

"Seriously, Kai?" I yell, sitting up in bed to glare at the large gray wolf stretched across the rug at the foot of our bed. "I know you have your own room."

Kai opens one of his piercing gray eyes long enough to acknowledge me before closing it again. I collapse back on my pillow and turn to face Alak.

"You know, lots of people do all sorts of things in front of their pets."

Alak's rich laughter fills the room. "Aye, love, I'm sure they do, but those pets aren't likely to be able to kill them in two forms."

A grunt from Kai on the floor indicates he agrees with Alak. I roll my eyes and push back the covers.

"Fine. If we're not going to do anything fun, I suppose I better get the day started."

I sit up, swinging my legs over the edge of the bed, and stretch. My bare feet hit the cold floor and I immediately jerk them back up. Using a touch of magic, I reach out my hand, palm down, and warm the floor. When I set my feet down again, they're met with the perfect temperature.

I plod across the room and throw open my wardrobe to choose from an array of dresses. When we had to flee Embervein, we didn't have much. There were several servants and citizens we helped evacuate who didn't have anywhere else to go. Many of those people accompanied us here, to the northern Summer Palace, to serve in whatever capacity they could. While I'm sure our castle is more under-staffed than normal, we have a decent amount of help, including seamstresses, maids, and even Cook with her kitchen crew.

I grab a simple dress and duck behind the changing screen in the corner of the room.

"I don't know why we have that stupid screen," Alak mumbles. "I've seen everything already."

I laugh, but Kai's throaty growl is reminder enough of why we have the screen. I pull off my nightdress, discarding it on the floor, and pull my dress over my head as someone knocks on the door. I peek around the edge of the screen and glance to Alak, who's now sitting up.

"Were you expecting anyone?" I mouth.

He shakes his head and I shift my eyes to Kai. His head is raised, ears perked up on full alert with his eyes locked on the door. Obviously, he wasn't expecting anyone either. A second knock follows, this time accompanied by a warm, familiar voice that makes me relax.

"Astra, Alak, are you awake?"

I duck back behind the screen and finish dressing as I call out, "Yes, Cal. You can come in."

The door creaks open, followed by the heavy sound of boots. Kai huffs, presumably lying back down. I straighten my hair and pop out from behind the screen.

"Oh, there you are," Cal says with a smile when his eyes find me.

I return his smile but jump straight to the point. "Any change?"

All brightness immediately fades from Cal's face as he shakes head. "Not at all. He wouldn't even let the servants enter this morning with breakfast. I don't think he ate at all yesterday." He glances quickly at Alak then back to me. "I don't mean to interrupt your morning again. It's just, well, you told me if he was still—"

I cut him off with a wave and nod. "I know."

I close my eyes for a moment before walking to the nearest window, looking down at the sad, disarrayed castle grounds below. As much as I hate to admit it, they're a perfect representation of the kingdom and the prince in charge.

"I'll do what I can." I turn back and look at Cal. Worry etches every line of his face. "I promise."

Cal nods and licks his lips.

"Anything else?" I ask, praying that there's no news, given all recent news only seems to be bad.

Cal shakes his head. "Nothing of note. Though, I only have the word from the night guards. I haven't been to the kitchen yet."

"I'll head down there and check in."

"Do you have to, love?" Alak whines from the bed. "It's cold in the bed without you."

The tips of Cal's ears redden slightly as he glances away. Kai lifts his head, stretches with a wolfy groan, and leaps into the bed, transforming into his human form in midair. Alak cries out, rolling to the edge of the bed. I burst out laughing as Kai tucks a hand behind his head, looking over at Alak with a grin.

"There, problem solved," I say as Alak frowns and mumbles, "This is not what I had in mind."

Cal laughs and shakes his head. "I guess you'll be a bit more careful what you wish for in the future."

Alak rolls his eyes. "Only with Kai around."

Kai's grin widens as he props himself up a bit more on the pillow to look over at me. "Let me know if you need help."

I nod. "I will. I suspect that unless there's some unknown disaster waiting outside the castle gates, today will be more of the waiting game we've been playing for weeks now." I glance back at Cal and add, "If I can get Ehren up, we'll convene in the Meeting Hall after breakfast."

"And if you can't?" Cal asks, his voice so quiet I barely catch his words.

I meet his eyes and swallow. "I'll find a way."

Cal holds my gaze for a beat before nodding once. "I'll make sure everyone is ready."

"Thank you."

Cal gives us all one last parting nod before slipping out of the room. I take a moment to gather my thoughts before I pluck up my boots and sit down on the edge of the bed by Alak. His fingers trace lazy circles on my back as I lace my boots.

"You know, love," he says, his voice low, "it's not your burden alone. You don't have to be the one to fix everything."

I sigh. "I know."

"Do you?"

I tie the last lace with a tug and twist to look down at Alak. He's watching me in that careful way he does when he can tell I'm near breaking. I meet his eyes and nod.

"I do. I know. I just . . ." I let my voice trail off as I glance away.

"You just have to be true to your nature."

"Ehren was there for me when Kato abandoned me, and I don't know what I would have done without him. He held me together." Alak's guilt spikes through the bond. I turn back to him quickly and place my hand on his. "You were there for me in a different way."

Alak looks away with a sigh but weaves his fingers with mine. "I know. I still hate that I wasn't there for you those first few days." He looks back up at me. "I know I did what I had to, what I felt was right in the moment, but . . ." He drops off with a sigh.

"It was the right thing," I insist, squeezing his hand. "You helped me in a way no one else could but—"

"—you still need to be there for Ehren, to repay the favor," Alak finishes for me.

I look down at him and offer him a tight-lipped smile. "Yes. And because he's one of my dearest friends and it's my fault he's—"

"Hey," Alak says sharply, sitting up. "None of that. You are not responsible for Kato's actions."

"He's right," Kai jumps in. "None of this is your fault."

"Deep inside, I know that, but I still can't help but feel a little responsible." Before either of the men can argue with me again, I stand, pulling my hand from Alak's to straighten my dress. "Either way, I have things to do."

"I love you, Astra," Alak says as I approach the door.

I turn to him and force a smile I know doesn't go all the way to my eyes. "I love you, too."

Kai glances between us and rolls his eyes before flopping onto his side and pulling the covers over his head, jerking them off Alak in the process. Alak cries out, trying to yank them back and Kai responds with a growl halfway between human and wolf. With a smile, I leave the boys to fight over the bed, closing the door behind me.

The halls are quiet—often too quiet. It looks like a palace, and we do our best to make it feel like a palace, but something is missing. It falls short in some way. Then again, maybe it's not what's *missing* but rather what's here that shouldn't be—the overhanging cloud of despair, depression, and looming demise.

I round the corner and pause before a large ornate door. The royal chambers. I raise my hand to knock but can't make myself complete the motion. So many mornings since our arrival I find myself outside this door. Some mornings I can get through a little, and others . . . My hand drops to my side as I sigh and shake my head.

"Breakfast first," I mutter under my breath before I turn and walk away. "It'll be easier on a full stomach."

While the halls of this castle may feel like they're filled with ghosts, the kitchen feels alive. When we first arrived, everyone seemed equally lost. We'd been on the road for weeks, dodging Dragkonian sentries and fighting to survive. The castle provided protection and a chance at living again, but in those weeks we'd all forgotten how to live. Cook fixed that. She gave the servants and refugees work to do and helped them find purpose. She gave the rest of us hope and established a routine we could work with. Most importantly, she established relations with the nearby village of Oxwatch.

"What news?" I ask, sliding onto a kitchen stool amidst the flurry of early morning activity.

"Well," Cook replies, punching down a loaf of bread, "I hear tell there's to be wedding of a village girl today. The whole town's a-twitter about it. It seems to be quite the affair."

She plops the bread in a bowl to rise before turning away to scoop a large spoonful of eggs onto a plate. "It also seems that one of the women of the town gave birth last night to a little boy. He's good and healthy." She adds a couple pieces of crispy bacon to the plate and sets it down in front of me. "And Old Man Jenkins swears it will rain today."

I grin and take a bite of my eggs. "Nothing magical then?"

Cook shakes her head. "Nary a whisper."

I breathe a sigh of relief and sink into my breakfast. Cook knows I can't eat until I know what's happening in the local village. The castle is protected by a fairly strong protective charm, meaning people can't just come and go with news without being invited or guided into the castle by those given admittance. The downside to this arrangement is that no news drifts in on its own, so we rely heavily on the news Cook and the other servants receive from the village as they do their daily business.

Cook slides a cup of coffee in front of me. I thank her and take a sip as she smiles, watching me for a moment before turning back to her work. I quickly down my breakfast and coffee. When I stand, fresh determination swells in me. I know what I have to do. I ask Cook for one more cup of coffee. She arches an eyebrow but complies without question. Before I can hesitate a moment longer, I sweep through the halls, coffee in hand, back to the royal chambers. I take a deep breath before knocking. There's no answer, which isn't unexpected. I knock again, harder this time.

"Go away," a hoarse voice calls back. "I don't need anything."

I swallow, steeling myself before placing my hand on the doorknob and turning it slowly, afraid it's locked. I release a sigh of relief when the door pushes open. When I step into the room, my heart sinks. All the curtains are drawn, drowning the room in stale darkness.

"I said I don't need anything," a voice mumbles from the bed.

"Fine," I reply with a shrug as I close the door. "I guess I'll drink this coffee on my own."

The blankets on the bed shift as Ehren sits up, his eyes finding me. My heart breaks looking at him. He's a whisper of his normal self, unkempt and unshaven. He hasn't changed or left his room—likely his bed—in days. Even as he takes me in, there is no life in his eyes. He's broken and drowning.

I force a smile and approach his bed, holding the coffee out to him. "Do you want it?"

Ehren eyes the mug for a moment before shaking his head and glancing away. "No."

My heart aches as I set the mug on his bedside table. Ehren lies back down, turning his back to me as I fight tears.

"I think it's time."

Ehren doesn't even turn to me as he says, "It was time two weeks ago. I can't do this, Astra. I just . . . I can't let everyone down again."

I swallow and close my eyes for a moment. I step forward and slide onto the bed behind Ehren, wrapping my arms around him. He tenses under my touch, relaxing a second later. I press my forehead against the back of his neck. He slides his hands up and places them over my arms, linking his fingers with mine.

"I want to, Ash," he says after a moment, his voice catching. "I want to get up. I want to help. I simply can't find it in me to do it. I don't want to fail everyone again. The pressure is too much."

"You only fail when you fail to keep trying. You haven't failed anyone, Ehren."

"Tell that to my father," Ehren says, his voice barely audible. "Tell that to my mother. Tell that to M-Makin."

His voice breaks on the last name, a small sob escaping his lips. I squeeze him tighter.

"There are thousands of people out there who still believe that you haven't failed. Though, if Makin were here, he'd be the first to tell you that you didn't fail him."

"How do I go forward?" he asks through tears.

"I'm glad you asked, because I have a plan."

He shifts, turning his head so he can see me out of the corner of his eye. I offer a weak smile.

"A plan?"

"Yes. First, we are going to lie here for ten minutes and wallow in our miserable failure. We'll pity ourselves and wonder what else we could have done to save lives. We'll consider every way we've let down our friends and screwed up."

"And then?"

"And then," I say, the corner of my mouth turning up into a half-smile, "we get up and try again."

Ehren turns away, but I continue.

"We stop pitying ourselves, and we simply try, no matter how hard it is. And you will get out of this bed and take a bath, because quite frankly you smell horrible."

Ehren makes a small sound that almost sounds like a laugh. It encourages me to keep going.

"And then you're going to get dressed and come down to the Meeting Hall so we can decide our next move together. We will go over the correspondences, maps, everything. You're the best at constructing plans. You have the mind for it, and we need that mind now more than ever. And, of course, along the way we'll eat."

I feel more than hear Ehren's deep sigh. I wait, barely breathing, as he considers my words.

"Fine."

My heart lurches and I can't hide my smile as happy tears well in my eyes. "Fine?"

Ehren nods and tilts his head to look at me. His eyes meet mine and I can see how lost he is. But he's trying. He's *trying*.

"I won't make any promises, but I'll give it a shot."

"That's all I ask, Ehren." I give him a small squeeze. "That's all any of us are asking."

He flips over so we're lying face-to-face. He presses his forehead to mine and wraps his arms around me, holding me close. We lie there for at least ten minutes, probably more, before I slide from the bed. I stroll to the nearest window and throw the curtains open, rich sunlight flooding the room. Ehren flinches away and raises a hand to shield his eyes.

"All right," I say, moving to the next window. "Rise and shine."

I march around the room and open every curtain, including those leading to his balcony. Ehren scoots to the edge of his bed, letting his feet hover over the floor but making no move to stand. I pick up his coffee and use my magic to warm it before passing it to him.

"Drink," I command, spinning and heading into his washroom the moment the mug is in his hands.

I run a bath and lay out clothes and other things he'll need. As I exit the washroom, I catch him take a few tentative sips of his coffee before downing the whole mug, a little of the grayness leaving his features as hints of life return.

"Now, go wash up, maybe trim that thing you call a beard, and meet me downstairs in no more than an hour. Got it?"

Ehren eyes me over the top of his mug, his lips turning up slightly at the corners. "I thought only the prince gave orders."

My heart flutters with relief at his near-smile, even if it's lacking its usual carefree warmth.

"Yeah, well then maybe you shouldn't have made me your equal, hm?"

His eyes brighten a touch more. "I'll keep that in mind next time I need a Court Sorceress."

I grin and turn toward the door, pausing to look back at Ehren. "I'll have some breakfast sent up."

Ehren shakes his head. "No, if I feel up to it I'll eat when I go downstairs."

I nod. "Sounds good." I meet his eyes for a minute before adding, "We can do this, Ehren. Together."

He manages a tight smile and small nod before I close the door, leaving him alone.

CHAPTER TWO

EHREN

Ten steps. That's all it will take me to get to the washroom. Ten damn steps. And yet, those steps seem almost insurmountable. It's not the steps themselves. Not really. It's everything that comes after. If I take those steps, then I have to wash and dress. If I wash and dress, then I have to face the others. My hands tighten around my coffee mug. I don't know if I can face them. In their eyes, I see my failure. Death haunts their faces as a constant reminder of how I let them all down.

No. It's just ten steps. I can take ten steps. I can start here.

I stand. In some ways, that's the hardest part, but I do it. I take a deep breath and cross the room, pausing in the doorway of the washroom. Steam curls from the tub, caressing the air with the scents of fresh oils and soaps. Astra laid everything out. Soap and a washrag lie within reach next to a large, fluffy towel. She even laid out clothes.

With a sigh, I cast off the crumbled mess of an outfit I've been wearing for days and sink into the hot water. It's almost odd how a little warm water can ease my worries. I still feel like I'm staring at the world through a dark, dense cloud, but some of the weight lifts from my shoulders. For a few moments, I relish the warmth of the water. My limbs feel heavy—far too heavy to lift and wash—but eventually I find the strength I need. I scrub the dirt and sweat from my skin and wash my greasy hair. The movement and simple feeling of being clean almost invigorates me. Almost. I still can't quite glimpse my former self, but I'm a step closer.

When the water cools to a less comforting temperature, I rise from the tub, wrapping myself in the towel. I start to dress, pulling on my pants, but pause, staring down at the shirt in my hand. My crest blinks up at me in gold thread. It's the crest of a crown prince. It's a reminder of who I'm supposed to be and how much I fall short. I crumple the shirt and cast it aside as I stride into the main room.

I stand in the center of my room, lost for a moment. I glance to the bed. I want to hide from the world and curl up beneath the covers. I want to forget who I am and who I'm supposed to be. But I also want to stop hiding. I want to go and find Astra. I want to help her rebuild my kingdom. She shouldn't have to do everything alone. It's not her responsibility. It's mine and I'll be damned if I force her to bear my burden.

I turn and examine my reflection in the floor-length mirror in the corner. I'm a disheveled prince of a broken kingdom and I every bit look the part. Can I even come back from this?

A knock on my door breaks me from my thoughts. Did Astra send up breakfast after all? I'm not sure I can eat it if she did.

"Come in," I call out.

AMBER D. LEWIS

As the door creaks open, I walk over, scooping up my discarded shirt, my back to the door. I'm about to slip it over my head when a voice stops me cold.

"I don't mean to intrude," Cal says, his voice hesitant but steady. "I wanted to check and see how you were coming along."

I swallow, my hands scrunching the fabric in my hands. I don't turn around. I can't look at him. Every time I do, the world around us fades, and all I can see is Cal, on his knees in a dark forest, covered in blood that isn't his own, weeping over a broken body. I—I can't face him.

"I'm fine," I say, my voice far too harsh. I squeeze my eyes shut and try again, softer this time. "I'll be down in a few minutes."

I turn to Cal with great effort, my movements too stiff to be considered natural. He takes a step toward me, moving directly into a golden ray of sunlight shining through a window. The light catches his eyes and makes their brown glow in a way that steals my breath. It takes me off guard and for a moment the world seems brighter, better. But then he takes another step and the illusion of happiness vanishes. His face is etched with concern. I avoid his eyes, glancing off to the side.

"Please let Astra know I'm nearly ready," I manage, turning and slipping the shirt over my head.

"Ehren . . ." Cal pauses, thinking better of whatever he was going to say and says instead, "I'll let her know."

Without another word, he leaves, shutting the door behind him. I'm alone again. I take a shuddering breath and glance in the mirror. Fully clothed I look a bit less disheveled, but I still don't look like the prince I should be. I find enough energy to comb through my hair, but I can't find the strength to trim my beard. That will have to wait for another day.

~

LEAVING my room feels like a breath of fresh air. I'm not sure how we managed it, but the castle looks and feels like home. The windows are clean and usher in fresh, warm rays of light. While my childhood memories of the Summer Palace aren't necessarily my favorites, I did have many good moments here. A smile threatens to break out as I recall running down these halls, hiding from my Governess. The smile fades, however, when I almost plow into a young servant girl turning a corner. She looks up at me with wide eyes, and I feel a surge of fresh guilt. Why is this girl here? Is she one of the many displaced servants that had to flee Embervein? Did we recruit her somewhere along the way? How many people has she lost to this war?

Before I can overthink her presence too much, the girl offers a low bow and scurries off. I sigh and resume my path to the Meeting Hall. When I arrive, I hover outside the door, peering in like an imposter, eavesdropping on a different world.

The Meeting Hall was the room where my father would hold his most important conferences. It's born witness to some of the most crucial treaties and hosted many prominent dignitaries and nobles from all over the continent. The ceiling stretches high, etched with golden flowers. The far wall is made of gold-rimmed windows with random panes of colored glass framed by silk curtains. The other walls bear intricate tapestries and paintings depicting Callenia in all its glory. A long oak table stretches down the center of the room, surrounded by specially crafted chairs that always seemed to impress any of father's honored guests no matter their status.

While many aspects of the room remain the same, much has changed. For one, the people seated around the table are vastly different. When my father sat at the head of the table, he sat with men of honor and titles. Everyone was stiff and serious, no matter the topic of conversation. Everyone who sits around the table right now is casual and laid back.

The most out of place people around the table are Hanna and Pip. I had no idea they would be here. They look so young compared to the members of my Guard that make up the majority of the presence in the room. Pascal and Lorrell, a pair of brothers with sharp features and bronzed skin, have been in my Guard for a little over two years. They're little more than a year apart and look like almost mirror images of one another. They recently returned from Oyrain, bearing no good news. Bram sits near the brothers, chatting with Collin, a lanky blond-haired, blue-eyed member of my Guard. Of those scattered around the room, Bram belongs the most. He sits tall, almost at attention, his captain's uniform immaculate. Across the table from him is Alak, who seems the most out of place after Pip and Hanna. He's leaning back in his chair at an angle, one leg slung over the arm of his chair, using wide hand gestures to talk to Astra who stands near the head of the table. Astra smiles down at him, shaking her head, but amusement shines in her eyes.

When my father would use this room, he sat at the head in a chair that was nothing short of a throne. As I glance past Astra now I'm almost startled to see that the throne is gone, replaced by two regal chairs, sitting side-by-side.

"You came," Cal's voice says from behind me, making me jump.

I straighten my shoulders and turn to face him. The image of him with Makin's body threatens to rise but I push it back. I attempt a smile, but it refuses to come.

"Of course."

Cal eyes me for a moment, something unreadable in his expression. I'm relieved when Alak draws my attention.

"Morning, mate!" Alak calls out, grinning from ear to ear as he swings around in his seat.

Astra's eyes meet mine, bright and welcoming, as she crosses the room to me.

"I'm glad you came," she whispers, quiet enough that no one else hears.

"Me, too," I reply. I glance around the room, everyone's eyes watching me warily, like I could break down at any moment. "Is everyone here?"

Astra shakes her head. "Almost. We're just waiting on Kai. We can go ahead and take our seats, though." She floats across the room, and I follow. She gestures to the ornate chairs. "Take a seat."

I feel like a fraud as I sink into the chair on the left. I place my arms on the armrests, my hands clutching the ends as Astra takes a seat next to me. I look out across those gathered, afraid to meet their eyes, focusing instead on the papers scattered on the table in front of me. I pick one up, looking it over. It bears the official seal of the Court of Ascaria.

"What's this?" I ask, tilting the paper toward Astra.

Her eyes flick down to the letter in my hands and a shadow crosses her face.

"Ah," I say before she can answer, tossing it back on the table with a frustrated flick of my wrist. "More rejections."

Before we fled Embervein, I poured my heart out in letters to our allies. I begged and pleaded for their help. So far, my efforts have proven to be pointless. Not one of our allies, other than those that already promised help, have stepped forward. Their replies are almost all the same:

We understand the situation in which you find yourself, but we regrettably cannot assist you at this time. While we send our sympathies, our land is also much changed by magic, and we have our own challenges to face. Best of luck.

They may not all use the same words, but the sentiment is the same. We're on our own with no help coming.

The room shifts and I look up as Kai enter, a couple other guards trailing behind him. Everyone still standing settles into their seats. This is a regular meeting, I realize. I'm the only one in the room that doesn't know what to expect. Guilt stabs my gut. I should be the one running these meetings, not a guest sitting in for the first time. Astra reaches over, placing her hand on my knee. I glance over at her, meeting her eyes.

"Are you okay?" she whispers, tilting her head.

No, I'm not okay. I want to run. I want to go back to my bed and avoid those stares. I want to drown in my guilt. I take a deep breath and release it slowly.

"You can do this," Astra says, giving my knee a squeeze. "I promise. Remember, I'm here for you. Equals."

I smile softly and nod. "Equals."

Astra removes her hand and turns her attention to Kai, who has taken a seat on the other side of Alak.

"Report?" she asks, bringing the meeting to its start.

"Everything is secure," Kai replies without hesitation. "I checked in with the border patrols and guards and no suspicious activity has been reported. The wards are also still in place."

Astra nods and turns her attention to the next person.

One by one they go around the table, everyone contributing their bit. They share news from the village, different guard points, rumors, and anything else they find pertinent. It's a lot of information, but it seems like it's the same conversation they have every morning. I find it hard to focus and my thoughts drift. I shouldn't be here. I have nothing to contribute. I should . . .

"That's up to Ehren," Astra is saying.

I blink and look over at her. She's watching me, her eyes shadowed with concern. I have no idea what they're talking about, but I obviously need to say something. I clear my throat and look down the table at all the eyes on me. I meet Bram's gaze and he gives me a half-smile and an encouraging nod.

"There are many things I need to consider," I say, shifting my eyes to meet Alak's. He smiles encouragingly and I go on. "I know I haven't been as present as perhaps I should've been, but I'm here now."

I don't even know what I'm saying, but somehow the words are tumbling out. My hands fall to my lap and Astra reaches over and places a hand over mine as I continue.

"I have failed many of you, but no more. We are moving forward. Together." I feel my confidence rise and I stand. "I will make a plan, and we *will* find a way to take back my throne. An imposter has stolen my kingdom and I refuse to cower in fear." I meet the eyes of every individual one at a time, my eyes lingering on Cal's for just a bit longer. "I cannot replace those who have been lost, but we will avenge them." I tear my eyes away, looking back at Alak. "Together."

The room falls silent as I sink back into my chair. The air has shifted. Dozens of eyes still watch me, but they hold less judgment. I glance over at Astra, who wears a genuine smile.

After a moment she turns her attention back to everyone else.

"Any more news to share?" she asks. When everyone responds by shaking their heads, she stands, saying, "All right. We'll touch base again later."

Slowly, as if woken from the haze of a dream, everybody rises from their chairs. A few of them offer me a parting nod before exiting. Astra stands and I stand with her, but Bram remains seated, watching me.

"See, that wasn't too bad, was it?" Astra asks, nudging me with her shoulder.

My mouth twitches, a smile threatening to break free. "I suppose not." I take a deep breath and shake my head. "I don't know where to go from here, though."

"You make your plan," she says, like it's that simple.

Alak walks up behind her, looping his arm around her waist.

"You're going to take him to the library, aren't you, love?" he asks, kissing her cheek.

Astra grins, leaning into his embrace. "If that's what Ehren wants."

I roll my eyes as a real smile creeps onto my face. "Why am I not surprised you have everything I need all nicely arranged in the library? Let me guess—the entire history of Callenia is laid out in easily accessible records?"

Astra laughs. "It's not like that. I, well, I needed a place to organize all the correspondence and everything. It'll be easier to show you. Would you like to head there now, or do we need to find you something to eat first?"

I shrug. "I'm fine for now."

She arches her eyebrows skeptically.

I glance away and run a hand through my hair. "I need to feel useful more than anything."

Astra nods. "All right, but you have to promise me you'll eat something soon."

I offer her a weak smile and nod. "Cross my heart."

Alak leans forward and plants another kiss on her cheek. "I'll meet up with you later, love. I'm going to make the rounds and check on the illusion wards."

"Okay. I'll catch up with you in a few minutes."

She presses her lips to his and I feel a surge of jealousy. No—loneliness. I glance away, feeling like an intruder. When I look back up, Alak winks at me before sauntering away.

"Well, shall we go?" Astra asks, her eyes sparkling.

I nod and she links her arm with mine, guiding me through the castle. We cross a few servants, but they don't shrink away from Astra like they do me. They meet her eyes with bright smiles. She knows most of them by name. I don't know any of them. I'm drowning in fresh guilt by the time she throws open the library doors.

The library here isn't nearly as grand as the one in Embervein. It's one large room, stretching maybe two stories. Bookshelves line every wall, save for the far wall which consists largely of narrow windows. The middle of the room is a collection of furniture, mostly chairs, that look sad and unused. Astra ushers me to the corner of the library, stopping beside a desk covered with papers.

"I've tried to arrange all the correspondence into stacks," she explains, gesturing to neatly arranged piles of letters.

"These"—she points to the tallest stack—"are from your Guard, soldiers, and spies with information you've requested. I've sifted through some of it, trying to make sense of everything, but I really don't see things the way you do. Hopefully, you'll find something in their words I missed."

She moves on to the next stack, placing the letter from Ascaria on top as she speaks. "These are from the leaders and official liaisons of our allies. You've already read most of these, I believe, except for the new letter from Ascaria and the one from Illyas that arrived with Cadewynn's letter."

"Cadewynn wrote?" I ask, raising my eyes from the desk to meet Astra's.

She nods and gestures to an unopened letter sitting on its own. I lift it, my finger tracing the familiar handwriting curling across the front.

"You didn't open it?"

She shakes her head. "No. She wrote us each separate letters, so I didn't see the need. Her words are for you alone."

I swallow and nod to the last stack. "What are those? Who are they from?"

Astra follows my gaze. "Oh, those aren't really letters, more general notes from around the kingdom. I've been recording all the little bits of gossip and rumors, hoping to use the information in a productive way, but so far, I haven't found anything." She looks back up at me. "Any questions?"

I shake my head, letting my eyes wander over the desktop. "No, I don't think so."

"Well, then, I guess I'll leave you be," she says, offering me a weak smile. "If you need anything, let me know."

I nod and she starts to leave, hesitating in the doorway.

"I'm serious, Ehren. If you need me, just call."

Something in me warms as I meet her eyes. "I promise."

Once she's gone, I collapse in the desk chair. Cadewynn's letter suddenly feels heavy. My fingers feel numb and I have to close my eyes for a moment and block out the world. I take a few deep breaths and try again. I break the seal and let my eyes drift over the page.

My Dearest Brother,

I am writing to let you know that mother and I arrived safely in Koshima. King Naimon has been very kind and accommodating. I tried to speak with him on behalf of our kingdom, but he keeps brushing me aside. I will not give up or be put off. I will do everything in my power to gain more aid. Illyas seems sympathetic and I believe he will be an excellent ally.

I hope you are doing better than when I left. I hated leaving you in that state. I know it is a lot for you to take on, but you can do this, Ehren. I love you and I believe in you. We may not know what will come next, but we will get there.

All My Love,
Winnie

Her words bring me a little comfort, but I still feel so overwhelmed. I wish I had a tenth of her confidence. All I can do is take it one step at a time, starting by catching up on everything I've missed. I lean forward and pluck up a letter from the first stack. Here goes nothing.

CHAPTER THREE

ALAK

I t's bloody cold this morning, and I regret not grabbing a cloak. I rub my hands together to warm them a little before reaching out to touch the magical barrier surrounding the palace grounds. I close my eyes and let the magic flow through me, careful not to Syphon it away. I smile as I pull my hand back. It's still strong. We're still safe for now.

With a sigh of relief, I stuff my hands into my pockets and make my way back to the side garden entrance, pulled by the bond. I'm barely two steps inside when Astra sweeps around the corner toward me. She meets my eyes and smiles. My heart skips a beat as I cross the distance between us and draw her into my arms.

"Did you get Ehren all set up?" I ask, looking down into her mesmerizing amethyst eyes.

"I did," she replies, her eyes bright. "He's still struggling, but I think he's going to be okay."

I lean down and brush my lips across hers. "That's good."

She lifts her lips to my mine and kisses me again. My breath catches and I pull her tighter against my body, returning her kiss hungrily. She doesn't fight it, but pushes the kiss forward, slipping her tongue into my mouth. My heart beats wildly, wishing we were near a bed. Moments like this, the bond between us is so strong with need.

A servant stumbles into the hallway at the end opposite us, making Astra jerk back with a sharp gasp. The servant flushes a deep crimson and scurries off, but the moment is lost. Astra's cheeks tinge pink as she draws away, sliding her hand into mine.

"We have work to do," she says, pulling me down the hall. "We need to be ready for whatever plans Ehren comes up with."

"Oh, I have plans of my own," I whisper, my lips brushing her ear as we turn the corner. "And I can promise they involve no one besides us."

Astra's blush deepens but she can't hide her wide smile as she turns to me. "You're horrible, Alak Dunne."

"Aye, love. That's why you love me." I grin, swooping in for a kiss.

She laughs and returns the kiss. "I do love you. I love you so very much."

My heart skips a beat at her words. She's told me she loves me at least a hundred times by now, but every time it feels like a dream. I still don't feel like I deserve her and, despite the undeniable strength of our bond, I'm afraid she'll wake up any moment and see I'm not who she thought I was.

"Master Alak?" a voice calls down the hall, drawing me from my thoughts.

I turn and find a servant rushing toward us.

"Yes?"

31

The servant steps up to me, holding out a letter. "This arrived for you this morning."

I take it and glance down. It's simple parchment sealed with the official rose and thorn seal of Clan McDullun. I grin and thank the servant before he scampers away.

"Who's it from?" Astra asks, eying the letter with unabashed curiosity.

"Ronan," I reply, breaking the seal. "Which means we have word from Athiedor."

Astra brightens but her face sinks into a scowl when we discover that the letter seems . . . lacking. It's no more than a few scrawled lines.

Alak,

Well done on your wards! Since I was unable to locate you and your hidden palace, I have settled in Oxwatch at a lovely little tavern and inn called The Raven's Wing. The mead here is nothing compared to mine, but it's more than tolerable. I've brought news and supplies. Come find me whenever you're ready to let me past your secret barriers.

—Ronan

I grin and pass the letter to Astra. She takes only a moment to read before she hands it back, grinning.

"This is good, right?"

I nod, licking my lips. "I think so. I hope so, at least. I should probably go meet with him immediately. Fancy a trip into town, love?"

She looks up at me and scowls. "I want to go, but I think I should stay here in case Ehren needs me. Plus, one of us should stay inside the wards to ensure their full strength."

I nod and press a kiss to her forehead. "I understand."

Without warning she throws her arms around me and buries her face into my chest. I wrap my arms around her and hold her close. I can feel her emotions through our bond as clearly as if they were my own. She's optimistic but scared. She's under so much pressure. She wants me near, but understands I need to go. After a moment, she draws back and smiles up at me.

I brush my lips across hers. "Feel better, love?"

She nods, tucking a stray strand of hair behind her ear. "I think so." She glances past her shoulder toward the front of the castle. "You shouldn't keep Lord McDullun waiting long."

I nod. "Aye, but I'm most definitely grabbing a cloak first. It's bloody freezing today."

Astra laughs as we walk. She helps me locate my cloak and escorts me to the front entrance of the palace, watching me with longing as I walk away. I can feel the bond tugging the farther apart we get; it's a struggle to put distance between us. In some ways, being farther apart is easier on the bond. Often, when we're in the same room, there's this over-whelming need to acknowledge the bond through touch. It doesn't even have to be any sort of intimate touch. We're just drawn together, searching for the feeling of completeness the bond brings. When we're apart, like we are now, it's less of a dominating feeling. I still want to go back to her, and she's still drawn to me, but it's easier to ignore so we can focus on other things.

The walk into Oxwatch isn't long, taking maybe twenty minutes. My hands are nearly numb from the biting wind by the time I arrive, despite using magic in an attempt to warm them. The Raven's Wing is nestled in the heart of town, which is lively and awake this time of day. Most of the villagers recognize me from my previous visits, giving nods of greeting as I weave through the crowd. We never really announced our presence and our illusion spell keeps anyone from getting too curious, but I have a feeling they know my purpose and whom I serve.

When I throw open the door to the tavern, I spot Ronan right away. He's sitting at a table in the corner, a nearly empty plate of food and a mug of coffee in front of him. He looks up and grins at me as I saunter over to his table, plopping into the seat across from him.

"I see you got my message?"

I grin. "Naw, I just like to hit up the tavern first thing every morning."

He laughs and shakes his head.

"So, do you come bearing good news or bad?"

Some of the amusement leaves his face, but his eyes still shine. "Right to the point I see. Well, I can't really say it's one or the other. It's all a bit . . . gray, I'm afraid."

"Well, that's better than all bad, I suppose." I sigh.

"Indeed," Ronan says, throwing back his mug and draining his coffee. "Well, I do have a bit of good news. I brought you something."

Ronan's eyes twinkle with delight as he grins.

I arch my eyebrows. "You brought *me* something?"

"Well, you, Astra, and others. It's kind of a group gift."

I glance around. He has nothing with him. "Where is it?"

Ronan laughs. "Outside." I look at him skeptically and he laughs again. "I can show you now, but perhaps I should gather my things first? Of course, that's assuming I'm permitted inside your wards."

"Of course you're allowed in." I grin. "Unless you mean to cause trouble."

He chuckles. "I didn't want to presume, and I make no promises." Mischief glints in his eyes. "I'll pack my things and meet you outside in ten minutes?"

I nod, rising from the table as he pushes into a standing position using his cane. "That sounds fine."

I head outside while he goes up the staircase in the corner of the tavern. I'm lost watching a group of children kicking a ball around when Ronan comes outside, a couple bags slung over his shoulder and another larger pack in his hand. I offer to help with his luggage, and after a moment of hesitation, he allows me to take the largest bag before leading me around the back of the tavern to where he boarded his horse for the night. When we enter the stable, I stop short, my eyes falling on a speckled brown horse.

"Fawn?" I gasp, tears welling in my eyes. I look over at a grinning Ronan, my voice a hoarse whisper. "How?"

"Well, when I was running correspondence between the Clans, I stumbled across the fact that you had to, once again, leave your horse behind. I couldn't in good conscience keep a man and his horse separated when there was something I could do about it."

I'm struggling to find the words to show my appreciation when another horse catches my eye. And then another.

"Y-you brought all our horses." I blink at Ronan in disbelief.

"I did. You and Astra provided an alternative for me and saved my Clan. It's the least I could do." He holds my gaze for a moment before clearing his throat and glancing away. "Well, shall we get going?"

I nod, still feeling like I'm in a dream as I mount Fawn. With the help of a stable hand, we lead the horses out into the street. I'm a little surprised that Ronan traveled all this way with six extra horses in tow and no help, but he insists it wasn't any problem at all thanks to his warding magic. Once we clear the village and the prying eyes and ears, I turn to Ronan.

"Is there any news you can share with me now, or would you prefer to address Astra directly?"

Ronan shrugs. "I can do both. It doesn't matter to me." He looks over at me. "What about Prince Ehren?"

I sigh and focus on the road ahead. "Ehren is . . . developing a plan. He may sit in while you talk with Astra, or he may just have her relay the information."

Ronan nods, weighing my words, and I hope he doesn't see them as proof of Ehren's weakness. Ehren is strong— stronger than I'll ever be. He's just struggling right now.

"Well, as you can imagine, much of Athiedor is unhappy that Kato took the crown with such ease. Many feel like we backed the wrong person. If we'd stuck with the original treaty, Athiedor could very well be free by now," Ronan says.

I shake my head. "But, surely, people can't support the way Kato took the crown?"

"No, most of them are terrified of Kato. They are very against his alliance with the Dragkonians. However, they do fear Kato will seek revenge for their betrayal."

I swallow, nerves twisting in my stomach. "Are they . . . Do you think they'll try to ally with him again?"

Ronan shakes his head firmly. "Naw. While a couple of Clan leaders feel that maybe they should have stayed with Kato, the general consensus is to throw support behind Ehren as agreed. The Dragkonians won't be satiated with getting Kato a crown. They'll want to rule the continent, and that terrifies every single Clan leader enough to keep them in line. We'll do whatever we can to overthrow Kato and get Ehren back on the throne. I have details from each of the Clan leaders laying out exactly what each Clan can provide in the war."

War. Even though it's been a war for some time now, hearing the word still sends chills down my spine.

"Do the Clans have any specific complaints or concerns?"

Ronan laughs, but it's a harsh, joyless sound. "I think some of them have more complaints than anything. One of the biggest is, of course, compensation for losses. Despite Astra's show at the treaty meeting, some of the Clan leaders still have doubts that Ehren will be able to provide the necessary funds."

I glance sideways at Ronan. "Do you have doubts?"

I expect him to keep his eyes forward, so I'm pleased when he meets my eyes.

"I want to make sure that my people are taken care of in every aspect, but as it stands, neither you nor your bondmate have given me any reason to doubt you."

I offer him a weak smile and nod. "Good. Because out of everything we have, money is the one thing we have enough of."

"Really?" Ronan asks, arching an eyebrow.

"Aye. Not only has Gleador sent funds, but a few other allies have sent some resources. It also seems that Ehren's father, despite his faults, kept a stock of jewels and coins at the Summer Palace. We have money, but that alone won't win the war."

"Naw, it won't."

Ronan falls silent as we approach the barrier wards. I can

feel the tingle of magic. To me, it's welcoming, but to guests like Ronan it's much stronger. I cast a little magic his way to help counteract the spell, but his eyes still go a bit glassy as we pass through. Once we're on the other side and riding toward the palace stables, Ronan looks over at me, blinking.

"That is powerful illusion magic. Is it yours?"

I grin. "Aye. A bit of my magic and Astra's mixed together."

Ronan lets out a low whistle as we enter the stables and dismount. "I knew bond-mates were strong, but your magic is something else entirely. To be able to maintain that level of magic is quite the feat."

I nod but don't get a chance to reply before Peter, the stable boy, approaches. At first, he looks like his downcast self. While I was able to help him escape the siege on the castle in Embervein, his brother, who lived in the city itself, didn't make it. When Peter sees the extra horses we have in tow, he brightens, his eyes going wide.

"Is that Captain Bramfield's horse?" he asks, approaching Solomon. "And Dauntless, as well?"

I nod. "Aye. Lord McDullun of Clan McDullun is our guest and he brought the horses along with him from Athiedor."

I notice Ronan wince slightly at the use of his formal title, but he offers Peter a charming smile regardless as he dismounts.

"My horse is named Pixie," Ronan says, offering the reins to Peter.

I glance sidelong at him. "Pixie?"

He laughs. "Aye, Pixie, and don't ask where I got the name. It just came to me. I meant to rename her, but somehow the name stuck."

I look over at his horse and grin. "Well, Pixie, welcome to the Summer Palace."

I glance fondly at Fawn, not ready to leave her yet, but I do have things to do besides hang out in the stables. I rub her neck affectionately and place my forehead against hers.

"I'll come back and catch you up later, Fawn," I whisper. "I promise."

Fawn gives me a huff and a nudge. I turn back to Ronan and find him watching me with gentle admiration. Color rises in my cheeks as I glance away.

"Fawn has been the one constant in my life."

Ronan offers me a soft smile. "I'm glad I could reunite you."

I return his smile and gesture toward the castle. "Shall we go find Astra?"

Ronan nods and I lead him inside. I don't need to ask anyone where she may be. The bond knows. I follow it, embracing its strength the closer I get to Astra and her magic. She's in one of the side gardens looking over the notes in her journal. She senses my approach and raises her eyes to meet mine, a smile on her lips. She glances over at Ronan and stands, walking toward us.

"Lord McDullun! I'm pleased we get to meet again in less formal circumstances," Astra says, inclining her head.

Ronan grins and raises her hand to his lips, giving her a quick kiss of greeting. "The pleasure is mine. And please, do call me Ronan."

Astra smirks, sliding her eyes to me. "Maybe kisses really are an Athiedor tradition."

Ronan arches an eyebrow and glances sideways at me. I avoid his pointed look, finding the bush nearest me incredibly interesting.

"Well, Ronan, do I want to know why you came?" Astra asks after a moment, a shadow covering her normally cheerful disposition.

Ronan nods. "I bring mostly good news that I believe you may find helpful."

"He also brought our horses," I add, meeting Astra's eyes.

"Luna?" she gasps, looking at Ronan who nods. "And Solomon and Dauntless?"

Of course she knows their names. I smile.

"Aye. They've been well cared for, but they wanted to come home. Well, at least as much of home as possible right now."

"Home is more people than a place, so I think the horses have made it home." She turns her gaze to me, her eyes bright. "We should tell Bram and Ehren immediately. I know they miss their horses."

I offer her a tight smile. "I can go and let them know. Why don't you take Ronan into the library and talk? I'll have tea and biscuits sent in."

Astra shakes her head. "No, Ehren is in the library crafting a plan. I think it might be best to leave him alone for now. We can go into the Meeting Hall or one of the lesser meeting rooms."

"The Meeting Hall sounds fancy," Ronan says, his eyes twinkling. "I rather like the idea of being thought important enough for a meeting in such a room."

Astra laughs and my heart warms, a smile curling on my lips.

"The Meeting Hall it is, then," Astra says. "If you'll follow me, I'll show you the way."

I step forward and give Astra a quick peck on her lips. "I'll catch up with you in a bit."

She pulls me in for one more lingering kiss that makes me want to do very different things than arrange for tea and biscuits. When she draws back, mischief and desire linger in her eyes.

"Don't cause trouble," she mutters, turning away to lead Ronan to the Meeting Hall.

"When do I ever cause trouble?" I call after her, grinning wickedly.

"Daily," she responds, not bothering to turn around. My grin grows.

As soon as she turns the corner, the call of the bond weakens a bit, but I ache to follow her. I want to go with her, but I do have other things to do. With a sigh, I head toward the kitchen. It doesn't take but a minute to find a servant to prepare the tea and biscuits for Astra and Ronan. Once that's arranged, I head off to inform Ehren and Bram their horses are home. I have every intention of going to Ehren first, but stumble into Bram as I round a corner. He rears back, glaring at me with pure and utter hatred.

"Morning, mate!" I say with forced cheer.

"I don't have time for you, Alak," Bram growls, trying to brush past me. "I have more important things to deal with."

"Look, mate," I say, catching his arm.

He spins to face me, eyes flashing as he jerks away.

"Don't touch me."

I hold my hands up in surrender. "It's not like I want to go around touching you, but I have news that may brighten even your day."

Bram crosses his arms and glares at me. "What news?"

I take a deep breath, reminding myself we're on the same side. "Lord McDullun has arrived. He's currently in a meeting with Astra, but he brought more than information. He stopped in Brackenborough and secured our horses."

Some of the anger and tension leaves Bram's face as his shoulders relax and his lips part. "What?"

"Your horse, Solomon, is in the stables."

Bram blinks slowly, as if he's waking from a dream. "Solomon? He's . . . here?"

I don't bother hiding my smile. Bram and I may not get along most of the time, but at least we share a mutual love and appreciation for our horses.

"Aye, mate. He's back. As is Dauntless. Peter is caring for them, but I thought you might want to know. I was just on my way to tell Ehr—"

"I can do that," Bram cuts me off. "I will tell Ehren."

I open my mouth to argue but figure there's no point. It really doesn't matter who tells Ehren. I shrug and nod.

"All right. I guess I'll go take care of other things."

I offer Bram a parting nod and saunter toward the Meeting Hall. At least now I get tea and biscuits.

CHAPTER FOUR

EHREN

I'm in the middle of a letter when there's a tentative knock on the library door.

"Enter," I call out, not bothering to raise my eyes from the paper as the door creaks open.

"It is good to see you up and about," Bram says.

I lift my eyes to his and offer him as much of a smile as I can muster. "I'm trying."

He approaches me in long strides, his eyes shining. "You will get back to normal, soon. I know you will. Nothing ever keeps you down for long."

I'm inclined to argue I've never faced anything like this before, but instead I offer him a nod, setting the letter on the desk with a sigh. Bram glances down at the disheveled stacks of letters and scowls.

"Any new information?"

I shake my head. "No. I don't think so, anyway. I'm still trying to catch up with everything. It's . . . a lot. Thankfully, Astra organized everything, so it's a bit easier to sort through."

Bram clears his throat and glances away. I wince. Sometimes I forget that Astra's been a bit of a sore subject with him lately.

"Anyway," I say, eager to shift the conversation. "Were you seeking me out for anything specific?"

"Oh, yes, actually," Bram says, a smile spreading across his face. "Lord McDullun arrived and he brought our horses from Athiedor."

My heart stops for a moment. "Dauntless?" I ask, almost breathless. "Dauntless is here?"

Bram grins and nods. "Yes. And Solomon. He said they are well cared for and they are in the stables now. Perhaps, if you would like a break, we could go for a ride. Get some fresh air."

I inhale slowly and run a hand through my hair. Fresh air could be good, but I'm already so far behind. I shake my head.

"Not right now," I say, and Bram's face falls slightly. "I have a lot to do. Maybe if I make good progress today we can ride tomorrow. I'd like to see the outer wards and protections we have in place."

Bram relaxes and forces a smile. "All right. I will hold you to that." He glances back toward the desk. "Do you need help?"

I shake my head. "No."

Bram nods. "I will let you get back to work, then. I will tell Dauntless you will be by soon."

I force and smile and nod. "Thanks."

With one last nod, Bram turns and leaves. I glare at the desk of letters. Letters that are full of depressing things and little hope. With a sigh, I resume my work.

At first, the stacks of letters feel entirely overwhelming.

They bring nothing but bad news that I want to avoid. But I power through. I decide to focus less on the collection as a whole and more on the individual piles and letters themselves. There's a sense of satisfaction watching each stack grow smaller as I wade through their contents and it's much easier to handle. Mid-way through the stack from my Guard and spies, I'm struck by a thought that has me turning back to scan previous letters.

I search through the drawers of the desk until I find ink and a scrap of parchment. I rapidly scrawl the names of cities and locations mentioned in the letters and see a pattern forming. After several minutes I step back and look down at my notes. I'm not imagining it.

I barely dare to breathe as I locate a map and spread it over a table, weighing the edges down with books so it lays flat. I mark the paths and cities, adding to my scribbled notes as I go. I'm so deep into my work, I don't notice Cal enter the library until he speaks.

"I brought you lunch."

I jerk my gaze from the map and swallow hard. Cal stands mere feet away, a tray of food in his hand. I straighten and glance away, fighting to breathe evenly as I press my hands firmly to my sides to keep them from shaking.

"You can set it anywhere."

Cal doesn't move. I slowly force my gaze to meet his. His jaw is clenched.

"You need to eat. You haven't eaten a proper meal in days."

"What does it matter?" I snap without meaning to. I shake my head. "I . . . I'll eat soon. I'm just . . . I'm in the middle of something."

I gesture weakly to the map and notes scattered across

the table. Cal nods and moves stiffly to set the tray down on the least cluttered corner.

"The food's here when you need it." He glances away for a moment, his hand folding into a fist at his side. He slowly raises his eyes back to mine, his expression heavy. When he speaks again, his voice is soft and has a hint of something close to desperation. "Please eat."

He turns and walks away with purpose, his boots echoing against the silence. He pauses a few feet from the door.

"I'm sorry," he says quietly without turning.

My thoughts swirl as bewilderment overwhelms me. Why is *he* apologizing?

"What?"

"I'm sorry," he repeats, his back still to me. "It's my fault Makin's dead, and I know you blame me."

I feel as if the air has been sucked from the room. I squeeze my eyes shut and try to make sense of his words.

"I don't . . ." I trail off, shaking my head in an attempt to loosen the thoughts flooding my brain, but they're all tangled together in a muddled mess. "Why would you think that?"

Cal turns to face me, tears glistening in his eyes, emotion written on his every feature.

"Cal," I choke out, taking a stumbling step toward him. I have an overwhelming need to comfort him, but I freeze. He doesn't want my comfort.

"He died saving me," Cal says, a tear slipping free. "If I'd been paying attention, he'd still be alive. It's my fault you lost a trusted member of your Guard. It's my fault you lost a friend. I only wish you could forgive me long enough to look at me."

I stare at Cal, not blinking, barely breathing, my heart pounding so hard against my ribcage it's almost painful.

"I know it's my fault. I just . . ." His voice breaks off in a sob. He composes himself, taking a deep breath, and continues. "Losing Makin made me lose a piece of myself, but I thought I could heal and move forward. But I lost you, too. Because of my own foolishness and carelessness, I lost both of you. If you want to reassign me so you don't have to bear my presence, I understand. It'd almost be easier for me that way. Makin is a ghost, dead and gone, but you're a living ghost that haunts me every day."

"Cal, that's not . . ." I struggle to find the words, taking several steps toward him. "Makin's death wasn't your fault. I don't blame you."

Cal lifts his eyes to mine. "Then why won't you look at me? Why won't you speak to me?" His voice is thick with desperation that shatters my resolve.

"Because it's *my* fault Makin's dead!"

I don't mean to yell, but I do, my voice echoing off the library walls. Cal's face rearranges into an expression of confusion, his mouth falling open as he watches me. I swallow, glancing away as tears burn my own eyes, and clench my hands into fists at my sides.

"It's *my* fault Makin is dead, and I am so very sorry. I'm your prince and I failed you. I can't look at you because every time I do, I see you holding Makin's body and I . . . I can't handle it. I know you must hate me. I—"

"Ehren," Cal says, so softly I barely hear him as he takes a step toward me. "I don't hate you. I could never hate you."

I lift my eyes and meet Cal's. "How can you not hate me? It's because of me that you lost your best friend. I hate myself for what I let happen."

"You weren't even there in the courtyard. How can you be to blame?"

"That's exactly it!"

Damn it. I'm yelling again. Something about Cal makes all my emotions unravel. I take a deep breath and try again, my voice still raised, but I manage a semblance of control as more words rush out.

"I wasn't there. I should've been by your side. I should've been fighting with you and defending my kingdom. But I ran. I was safely stored away in the forest, far from the battle. If I'd been there, maybe I could've done something, anything. But I wasn't. I failed you, and now, Makin is dead."

I break off into an uncontrollable sob, falling to my knees, my hands covering my face. I don't even realize Cal has crossed the room until he gathers me in his arms.

"I don't blame you," he whispers, pulling me against him so I'm practically in his lap. "You had just witnessed your father's murder. Your crown had been stolen. You needed to get out to ensure that you would live to take back the throne. You needed to be in the woods with your sister and mother. Makin's death is not your fault."

I draw back and look into his eyes, mere inches from my own. "You really don't blame me?"

Cal forces a small smile, releasing me from his hold though I don't move away. I rock back on my heels, our knees pressed together.

"No," he says softly, lifting a tentative hand to brush a tear from my cheek with his thumb. "I could never blame you. Makin died for a cause he believed in, and I can promise you he wouldn't want either of us to feel guilt for his death."

I take a deep breath and nod. A shadow flickers across his face and he glances away.

"My offer stands. If you need to reassign me so you don't have the constant reminder of Makin hovering around, I'll go wherever you need me," Cal says, refusing to meet my eyes.

"I need you here," I say, the words rushing out. Cal's eyes snap to mine and a smile creeps onto my lips. I reach out and take his hands. "More than anything I need you here with me."

Cal looks like he's barely breathing as he asks, "Are you sure?"

I nod. "There are few people I truly trust with my life as much as I trust you. I want you by my side through this. If you can forgive me—"

"I already told you there's nothing to forgive," Cal cuts me off.

I shake my head and glance down at our hands still clasped between us. "You can say it as much as you want, but I can't make myself believe it. I can't even forgive myself, so I definitely don't expect it of you." I raise my eyes back to his. "I can try, but it will be a struggle. Having you here, supporting me, may help me learn to forgive myself and . . . heal."

"I'll stay by your side and help you however I can," Cal says firmly, giving my hand a gentle squeeze. He glances over at the table where I've been working. "I can help you now, if you'd like. That way you can eat your lunch and not lose any time." He looks back at me. "Unless you'd rather be left alone."

I pause, considering his offer. Part of me wants to be left alone to wallow in silent self-pity, but there's another part of me that longs for company—Cal's company. I swallow and force a smile.

"I think I could use the help."

His eyes are bright and his smile sincere. "All right. Why don't you eat while you explain to me what it is you're planning."

I nod, reluctantly releasing his hands as we rise. I head over to the tray of food while Cal stands over the table staring down at the map in confusion.

"What are you tracking, exactly?" he asks, picking up my scrambled notes and scanning the paper.

"Well," I say, talking over a bite of bread, "the messages from my Guard as well as other spies and people from around the kingdom keep mentioning their villages being ransacked."

Cal raises his eyes from the paper and meets mine with a nod. I take a couple more bites of food and wash it down with a swig of mead before continuing.

"Even with their villages essentially gone, they speak of reuniting with others, but in most cases it's not just family and friends reuniting, but soldiers. A few of the letters even mention groups of displaced soldiers leading people to refuge."

Cal nods along for a moment, his forehead furrowed as he tries to piece together my words. "That makes sense that people fleeing would be seeking refuge."

I nod, swallowing a big bite of food. "That's what I thought at first, but"—I move around the table to next to him—"if you start to look closely at all the different times it's mentioned, it sounds like they're looking for specific places."

"What?" Cal says, his eyes going wide. He glances back down at the paper in his hands, his eyes scanning wildly before lifting his gaze back to me, a smile breaking out across his face.

"You think they've set up refugee camps and people are gathering together to protect each other."

I nod. "Yes, but more than that." I wipe my hands on my pants and cross over to the desk, sifting through the letters until I find the one I need. I take it over to Cal and hand it to him.

"Start at the first line of the second paragraph," I instruct, nodding to the paper.

"'Two of the brothers said that they were headed toward the pass to find the instruction they needed to protect their family from future attacks. The older brother was proud of his skill with a sword, but the younger brother kept talking about how he could finally be useful as a soldier with magic alive,'" Cal reads aloud.

He pauses and reads a few more lines to himself before raising his shining eyes to mine. "They're forming an army of magic and non-magic soldiers working together."

I nod, grinning. "I think so. At first, I didn't see how it all connected, but situations like those brothers were mentioned over and over again. On their own, they didn't mean much, but side-by-side with all the other reports, I think it's an army. At least one, maybe more."

Cal nods, setting the letter and my notes to the side as he looks down at the map. "I assume this"—he gestures to my map—"is you trying to figure out where the army is."

I step to Cal's side with a nod, staring down at the map with him.

"I'm close. I've found a relatively distinct trail in the letters. I'm marking down the locations and whether the people mentioned were looking for refuge, other soldiers, or both. It's possible there are multiple camps where people can go, depending on their needs, with one main camp that attracts the majority of refugees and soldiers. I'm not quite sure. Either way, I want to unite my people with magic and non-magic working together, so if I can find these camps, find these armies . . ."

I let my voice trail off as I look up into Cal's shining eyes.

"You can win the war," Cal finishes, his voice full of awe.

I laugh. "Maybe not the war. Not yet. But I'd love it if we could get in a punch or two."

Cal looks startled for a moment before a grin spreads across his face, crinkling the corners of his eyes. I tilt my head and laugh again.

"Why are you looking at me like that?"

The tips of Cal's ears tinge red as he glances away. "It's been too long since I've heard you laugh." He looks back up, his eyes locking with mine. "I've missed it."

My breath catches in my throat and my heart picks up. I'm lost in the swirling brown of his eyes until he jerks his gaze back to the map on the table.

"So, what else do you need to figure out in order to make this work?"

I clear my throat and force my eyes back to the table, exhaling slowly. "Well, I'm only about halfway through the letters. If I can pinpoint the locations a bit better, I can send someone to see if my theory is correct and potentially recruit the soldiers we need."

Cal nods. "How can I help?"

I step away and gather the remaining letters from the desk. "If you'll help me find all the references so we can map them, I think I can formulate a plan by morning."

Cal grins and holds out his hand for some of the letters. I split the stack in half, giving him some and keeping the rest for me. We settle down at the table with the map and get to work. With Cal's assessing eyes scanning each letter, we move quickly, covering the map with marks. We're nearly done when Cal pauses, scowling at the letter in his hand.

"This isn't from one your Guard or spies," he says, passing the letter to me. "It's the letter from Ascaria."

I swallow and stare at the paper in my hand. My fingers suddenly feel numb and heavy. I take a shaky breath and force myself to look at Cal.

"It must have gotten into this stack on mistake."

"Have you read it?"

I shake my head.

"You should."

"I don't want to," I confess, glancing away. "I can't take any more defeat right now. I'm so close to finding a way to help my kingdom. I can't face the rejection from Ascaria right now."

"It's not a rejection. Not really."

I raise my eyes to Cal, brow furrowed. "What do you mean?"

I scoop the letter up and scan it. Cal is right. While the letter starts off with their general regrets and condolences, they never outright refuse help like the other countries have done. They simply state that they understand the urgency and need for aid but 'are unable to leave the kingdom for a proper discussion at this time.' I look back up at Cal, my eyes bright.

"They didn't deny help," I marvel.

"Do you think they'll send the aid we need?"

I shrug and look back at the map, my mind spinning fast as the pieces of a plan click into place.

"I'm not sure, but I think I may be able to make this

work. Let's finish this project first. Let's find the makings of an army, and then we'll make a plan to secure more allies."

Cal grins. "Sounds good to me."

Cal and I sink back into our work, but everything feels lighter now. For the first time in weeks, I feel a glimmer of hope.

CHAPTER FIVE

JESSALYNN

I sign the bottom of my letter with a flourish. Most people assume I don't enjoy the minutia of leading and that I hate having to keep up appearances and diplomacy between the other provinces of Gleador. They assume I'm a woman of action. And, well, they aren't entirely wrong. There are few things I love as much as a heart-racing, blood-pumping, one-on-one fight, but I also find enjoyment in the more diplomatic matters. There's a special sense of satisfaction to keeping everything in balance. Not to mention, I'm damn good at it.

I set the letter to the Province of Aleahya to the side and reach for the next. Ah. Heldonia. Of all the provinces, Heldonia tends to be the most tedious to keep relations with. They seem to think that housing the main silver mine for the entire continent makes them special, especially now that magic has returned. I sigh and break the seal, ready to dive in, but I'm interrupted by a knock at my door. I glance up to Kaeya standing in the doorway. At her feet licking its paw is her familiar, Nila, a tiny spotted wildcat the size of a kitten who typically prefers to stay hidden with her camouflage magic.

"Come to give me a little distraction?" I flash her a smile as I lean back in my chair.

Kaeya scoffs, rolling her eyes as she saunters into the room, Nila trailing along behind her. "No, I have a messenger from the caves who claims we have visitors approaching."

I straighten, my body going on full alert. I scowl, though, when I realize that Kaeya still seems relaxed. She's not worried.

"Were we expecting someone?"

Kaeya tilts her head and meets my eyes, almost a challenge. "We should have been."

Great. She's talking in riddles. I love her to death but sometimes I wish she would just come out and say things directly. I sigh, tapping my fingers on my desk in irritation.

"Send the messenger in."

Kaeya arches her eyebrows.

"Did you want a 'please'?" I add.

Kaeya sighs, scooping up Nila and mumbling "You need a snack" as she exits the room. She returns a few minutes later with Nila perched on her shoulder, one of the cave guards following her in. Like most of the citizens of Southwestern Gleador, he has browned skin and jet-black hair. I reach into my brain, searching for his name. With so many guards and soldiers in my service, it's difficult to remember them all, but I still try.

"I hear you have news, Kabir?"

Kabir's eyes widen slightly at his name, but he recovers quickly. "Yes, there's a small party approaching the Valley through the cave pass. They should be here within the hour."

"And . . ."

Kabir scowls. "And what?"

I sigh and push to my feet. "And are they a threat? Who are they? What do you know?"

"Oh," Kabir fumbles, glancing down for a moment. "It's, uh, Sama returning."

"Sama?" I say, my eyes brightening. I won't admit it to most people, but I've missed having her around. "Good. She's needed here. Is she alone? I can't imagine my brother would send her back on her own."

Kabir shakes his head. "No, that Guard, Nyco, is with her."

My eyes flash. Seeing as how Nyco was previously sent to spy for my brother, it's more than bold for him to return. Though, I have to respect the balls he has to do so.

"They are also accompanied by the princess."

I still. "What princess?"

Kabir swallows and looks suddenly nervous. "Princess Cadewynn of Callenia."

The heat of anger rises in my chest. I grind my teeth to keep from shouting at the poor messenger. It's not his fault that he brought me bad news. He still eyes me like I could explode at any moment. I wave him off, feigning disinterest.

"You may go. Make any preparations necessary for their arrival and inevitable stay."

Kabir nods and scurries from the room. Once he's gone, I turn to Kaeya who watches me with cautious amusement from the back wall of my study.

"Why is Princess Cadewynn coming to *my* Valley?" I snap.

Kaeya shrugs and pushes away from the wall. "Who knows? Maybe Ehren sent her as a sign of good will."

I shake my head, my fury barely contained. "He would know better. She has some hidden motive, but I won't let her trick me."

Kaeya places a gentle hand on my shoulder. "You don't know there's anything nefarious about her presence. Let's not jump to conclusions, *Jaanu*. She may have a very good reason to come here. After all, her kingdom has been taken over by a lunatic."

I inhale slowly. Kaeya's words and term of affection help to calm me, but only a little. I won't be entirely calmed until I've spoken with the princess myself.

"Fine. I'll feel pity for her until I know to feel otherwise, but I won't openly trust her, either."

"Very wise, *Jaanu*," Kaeya says softly, pressing a kiss to my temple. Her eyes drop to the letters on the table. Nila seems to take this as an indication to leave Kaeya's shoulder and leaps to the desk in one smooth move as Kaeya asks, "Do you need my help here?"

I shake my head. "No, I'm almost done with these—Nila, stop that!" I scoop up the small wildcat and pull her away from playing with my quill. "If you could intercept the princess and her caravan and escort them to me personally, I would appreciate it. Also, take this thing."

I lift a wriggling Nila and Kaeya accepts the feisty beast, cradling her to her chest and pressing a kiss between her ears. She whispers something affectionately to the cat too quietly for me to hear, earning an eye roll from me.

"Do you want me to bring them here or the usual room for diplomatic meetings?" she asks, turning her attention back to me.

I pause, considering my options. Sama would know for sure that any other room could be seen as a slight against a visiting princess. Nyco, while less aware of how things work in the Valley, may still catch something is amiss. As much as I have personal reasons to dislike the delicate princess, there's no true reason why I shouldn't treat her with the same respect I would other visiting royalty.

"Take them to the meeting room," I reply at length.

Kaeya straightens and, even with Nila playfully batting at one of her braids, she's the perfect picture of a respected captain. "I will see it done."

Once she's gone, I settle back in my seat, picking up the letter from Heldonia. Suddenly, putting up with them doesn't seem so bad. I struggle to concentrate, getting much less done than normal, until a messenger pops in to let me know my guests have arrived. I tuck the letters away safely in a locked drawer before wisping outside the meeting room door. I pause a moment before entering to collect my thoughts. When I throw the door open, I swagger in, exuding much more confidence than I feel. Sama lights up, her brown eyes bright and welcoming. The Guard next to her seems far less sure, shrinking back in his seat a little. At least he has enough common sense to know he's not welcome. My eyes are drawn, however, to the third member of their traveling party.

Princess Cadewynn is everything I thought she would be. She looks like a delicate porcelain doll, easily broken, with bright, sky-blue eyes and golden curls. She's the kind of beautiful that ridiculous men fight wars over, and a piece of me hates her for it. She sits primly in her chair, with the kind of grace that can only be perfected inside palace walls.

"So," I say, as flippantly as possible, "I expected Sama to return eventually, but you other two are a bit of a surprise. Care to share why you're here?"

"I have come to ask for your help," Cadewynn says without preamble.

I meet her eyes with a hard glare, but she doesn't back down or flinch in the slightest. Instead, she matches my gaze with a fire I didn't expect.

"My help? Didn't I already have this conversation with your beloved brother?" I say, struggling to keep my voice even and nonchalant.

"Precisely," Cadewynn says. "You promised aid and now the time for aid has come."

I plop into my seat and fold my hands on the table, tilting my head as I survey the princess.

"Your brother sent *you* to ask for troops?"

Cadewynn grins in a way that unsettles me. Nothing that fierce should be on a face that delicate.

"On the contrary, Ehren has no idea I'm here." My eyes widen, betraying my surprise, but Cadewynn barely reacts. "I am here of my own accord, seeking aid for my kingdom. I suppose you know the most recent events?"

I shrug. "I've heard a few things."

"Well, allow me to catch you up and fill in any gaps in your knowledge," Cadewynn says, her voice venom-lined. I sit a little straighter as she continues. "My father has been slain and his throne stolen by someone I once thought a trusted friend. My kingdom is being destroyed and torn apart by the most evil race of creatures to ever exist. My people are dying. My people are being tortured. My people need help, and in order to help them, I need you."

She speaks with such fire and fervor I'm rendered nearly speechless. Nearly.

"And what do you expect me to provide? I may be able to

offer a few more soldiers for your troops, but I will force no one. How much aid do you expect?"

Cadewynn waves me off. "I don't want just your troops."

I tense. "You want my gems?"

She shakes her head. "No, I want your help to recruit the other provinces."

I laugh. I can't help it. She stills, her mouth in a firm set line, clearly unamused.

"And why, little princess, do you think I would be any help recruiting the other provinces?"

Cadewynn locks her eyes on mine. "Before we came here, we went to Koshima. I made my case before King Naimon but I got essentially the same response Ehren received. King Naimon is willing to provide funds, but he will not force the hands of the provinces to provide troops. He is hesitant to reach out to even present the idea of war."

"He's a logical man," I reply. "Did you expect him to do otherwise?"

Cadewynn shakes her head. "I did not. Likewise, you cannot expect me to sit back and let the people of my kingdom continue to suffer until I have exhausted every resource to help them. That's why I am here."

I arch my eyebrows and study her face for a moment. Her features are like carved stone, her gaze serious and intense.

"What exactly do you expect from me, then? I have no sway with the king."

"While at court I had the opportunity to talk with the Court Mage, Illyas, as well as a representative from one of the Northeast provinces. It appears that you are held in the highest regard and are very well respected across Gleador."

Her words take me by surprise and I can't hide my shock. Amusement flickers across her face for a brief moment.

"You didn't know?"

I shake my head. "I . . . I knew I had some respect, but . . . what is your point?"

Her amusement vanishes as quickly as it appeared. "I want you to use your pull with the other provinces to help me find additional support. We need more than gems and gold. We need soldiers. We need weapons. Please, Jessalynn, I need your help."

I take a deep breath and exhale slowly. "Even if my influence is as great as you suppose, why should I use it to help you? I promised to offer some aid from my own resources, and I'll hold to that promise. But why should I go above and beyond?"

Cadewynn stands, her eyes locked onto mine. "Because you are a decent person." I scoff but she continues. "You can pretend that you don't care about Ehren, but he's still your brother."

"Half-brother," I correct.

"Brother. And I am your sister." I flinch and open my mouth to speak but Cadewynn doesn't give me the opportunity. "I was a toddler when my father cast you out. I had no influence over his decision. It was not my fault. Any grudge you hold against me because of the actions of a dead man are foolish. For the sake of Callenia—for the sake of the world—I ask you to look past the mistakes of a foolish king. If we are unable to secure the throne of Callenia, the disease of the Dragkonians will spread. They will not be happy with the power they gain from one kingdom alone. I know; I've studied the histories. I know the path this will most assuredly take. Perhaps you may be able to rally forces and save your precious Valley if you refuse aid and Callenia falls, but I beg of you, please help me save both."

Before I can respond, Cadewynn moves around the table with the fluid grace of the Fae. She drops to her knees, lifting her bright blue eyes to me in supplication.

"Please, Jessalynn, I am begging you. I have no sword nor magic I can use to use for my kingdom, but I will not let that stop me from doing everything I can to save my people."

I'm without words as I look down at the princess in front of me. Everything about her emulates her desperation, but there is no weakness in her. I have severely underestimated her. Most royals and nobles will barely say please, let alone kneel before someone who's below them on their social ladder. This girl will lay down her life for her kingdom, I have no doubt. I rise from my seat and stand over her.

"Get up," I say, offering her my hand.

Cadewynn swallows and eyes my hand like it's a snake. "Does this mean you will help?"

I sigh, resting the urge to roll my eyes. "It means you should get up. Now, take my hand."

She reaches out hesitantly but places her hand in mine. I pull the princess to her feet and she meets my eyes without fear. This girl doesn't need me. How the king managed to resist her charm and fervor, I have no idea.

"I need to think over the logistics, but I will seriously consider your plea. I'll do what I can. There are many things I need to think over and consider before I can commit to anything. In the meantime, please relax and enjoy yourself. I'm sure you had a long and trying journey, all things considered." I pause, turning my attention to Sama, "I suppose you don't mind sharing your space with the princess?"

Sama's eyes brighten. "Not at all!"

"Very well then," I reply with a nod. "I'll not keep you waiting for a reply. Sama can show you around as needed. You are all dismissed—except you, Nyco. You stay."

Everyone exchanges quick glances before shuffling from the room. Soon, Nyco, Kaeya, and I are the only ones remaining.

"Don't hurt the boy," Kaeya says quietly, her eyes shining as she places her hand on my shoulder.

I bite back a grin as I turn my attention to Nyco. "Why exactly did you return to the Hundan Valley? You can't pass as a spy anymore. Isn't your place by your prince's side?"

Nyco looks intimidated only for a moment before he straightens to his full height and meets my eyes, lifting his chin defiantly.

"I wasn't going to send Sama and Winnie across Gleador on their own. I'm trained to serve and protect, and I knew the path we needed to take. I'll return to Ehren's side when the time comes, but for now, I serve Princess Cadewynn."

I nod, studying Nyco for a moment. "Why didn't Kai return? He also knows the way and he belongs here."

A smile twitches on the corners of Nyco's lips as he says, "I wouldn't expect Kai to return any time soon, if at all."

I arch an eyebrow, curiosity swelling in me. "Kai? Brooding, grumpy Kai? We are talking about the same person, right?"

Nyco relaxes a bit, his grin growing. "Kai will be by Astra's side until she casts him away, I can promise you."

I frown. I didn't expect Kai to take to Astra this much when I forced them together. I knew they were meant to meet, but I did not foresee him becoming so attached. Nyco is watching me with far too much interest. I school my features and wave him off.

"You may go."

Nyco gives me a parting nod but doesn't say anything as he flies from the room. Once he's gone I turn to Kaeya.

"What do you make of Kai and Astra? Surely, he's not . . ." I let my voice trail off.

Kaeya gives me a half smile. "Kai is a wolf shifter. They are loyal and devoted to their pack. It seems as if Kai has found his new pack."

"Well, I suppose there's no undoing it now that it's done. At least maybe he's happy now."

Kaeya nods and watches me for a moment before she asks, "Are you really going to help the princess? Help your brother build an army?"

I meet Kaeya's eyes and let my shoulders drop. "What would you do?"

Kaeya cocks her head in thought. "I would do it."

"You would?" I ask, a little surprised at her easy acquiescence.

Kaeya nods. "The girl was right—the way your father treated you has nothing to do with her. She loves her kingdom and you respect her for that."

"I suppose," I sigh, dropping into a chair. "Part of me really wants to leave them all hanging, but the better part of me knows that they would be there for me if I ever needed it. Damn those Montavilliers! They'll be the death of me."

A smile plays on Kaeya's lips as she walks over behind me. She places her hands on my shoulders and massages them gently. I roll my neck into her touch.

"What will you have me do?"

"Well, I won't force my people to go to war, but I will accept volunteers. Coordinate efforts with Brock and see what type of army you can raise for my dearest brother.

Once we have a better grasp on the numbers, we can decide how to split it up. Of course, we want to make sure that we leave enough trained soldiers behind not only to guard the Valley but also to defend it when necessary. At least we have the advantage of centuries of magical knowledge on our side."

I roll my neck again before shaking Kaeya off and standing to face her.

"Either way, we're going to war," I say, meeting her eyes.

Kaeya doesn't even blink as she says, "But we will not go easy."

I grin. "No we won't. We may even win."

CHAPTER SIX

EHREN

The morning sunlight shines through the window, reflecting off the mirror as I trim my beard. I have no desire to completely rid myself of it, but I need to do something to make myself feel more regal. I have a lot to make up for and looking the part might give me the boost I need.

I step away from the mirror to my wardrobe. I'm already dressed in the finest tunic I have, but I need my crown. I lift it from the shelf. It's an unwelcome weight. Even though this crown is a simple circlet, it dredges up the memory I try to push away to the back corner of my mind. I'm no longer in my room. I'm back in Callenia in the throne room watching my father's crown tumble from his head as he falls, never to rise again.

"It's over," I whisper, squeezing my eyes shut, willing it away.

A sharp knock breaks through my thoughts, bringing a welcome distraction.

"Come in."

I turn toward the door, crown in hand, as Astra steps into the room. Her eyes go to my bed first before going wide and sweeping toward me.

"You're out of bed!" she cries, her eyes shining as she smiles. "And you're dressed and everything!"

I grin wickedly. "Disappointed? I can disrobe a little if you'd rather."

"Oh, hush," she chides, but her smile doesn't fade.

I laugh and place the crown on my head. It's heavier than I remember.

"Is there a meeting this morning?"

Astra nods. "We try to gather every morning."

I swallow and nod, fighting the urge to glance away. "I'd like to be there again. I think I have a plan."

Astra's eyes brighten. "You do?"

I duck my head and smile. "No need to act quite so shocked."

She laughs and shakes her head. "I'm only surprised you put something together so quickly, but then again, plans have always been your strong point."

"I think I'm going to trim up my beard a little more so I look a little less ragged and then I'll be down, if that works."

"Of course it works. You're the prince. Don't you know everything revolves around you?" she teases with a wink.

I throw back my head and laugh. "I know. I'm at the center of everything."

She grins and makes her way across my room to the door. "I'll make sure everyone is present. Fifteen minutes?"

I nod. "Perfect."

She closes the door behind her, leaving me alone. Without her there distracting me, I'm tempted to spiral again, but I force myself to stay on track, trimming my beard before heading downstairs.

Like yesterday, the Meeting Hall is filled with our misfit crew. Astra sits in one of the chairs at the head of the table, a page of notes in front of her. Alak sits to her right, his arm slung over the back of his chair as he's twisted to face a man with reddish-brown hair on his left that I don't recognize. The others sit scattered around the table, casually chatting.

"Good morning," Cal says stepping up behind me.

I smile and turn to face him. "Is it a good morning?"

Cal's entire face brightens as he smiles. "From where I'm standing, the morning looks pretty good." He pauses, pulling his gaze away to glance past me into the room. "Full house in there today, huh?"

I nod and swallow, nodding to the stranger next to Alak. "Am I supposed to know who that man is?"

Cal laughs. "I only met him yesterday afternoon after I left you in the library. That's Lord McDullun."

"Oh. From Clan McDullun in Athiedor?"

Cal nods. "The one and the same."

Great. I really didn't want any extra faces in the audience today, but I suppose I have to adjust. Cal must read my distress because he furrows his brow in concern.

"Are you okay?" he asks quietly, placing a gentle hand on my arm.

I take a deep breath and meet his eyes, forcing a smile. "I'll manage."

With another deep, fortifying breath, I stride into the room toward Astra. She looks up from her paper and meets my eyes with a wide grin.

"Ehren, may I introduce you to—"

"Lord McDullun," I cut in, putting on my most charming smile and offering Lord McDullun my hand.

His eyes shine as he clasps my hand, giving it a hearty shake. "Ah, I see my reputation proceeds me."

I laugh, but it's forced. "A bit, I suppose. I do regret that this is the first time you and I are meeting, but given all our current circumstances . . ."

"Aye, I agree," Lord McDullun says with a nod. "I hear you're quite the planner. I suppose you'll be sharing some of those plans this morning?"

Astra shifts awkwardly behind me and I hear a ringing in my ears. Lord McDullun's tone is easy and casual, but his gaze is hard and assessing. He threw his lot in with a broken prince, but I can't let him know that. No, I need to put on my mask. I need to pretend that I'm capable of the task in front of me. So, I force another smile.

"Indeed. I have a plan to move forward."

"Ehren really is the best at crafting plans," Astra jumps in, placing a hand on my arm.

I look over my shoulder and offer her a smile that is weak but genuine. Astra meets my eyes for a moment, returning my smile, before she lifts her eyes past me to whoever entered the room.

"Kai's here, so I suppose we can start now, if everyone is ready," Astra says.

I nod and take my seat next to her. Everyone else settles in, their eyes flicking toward me. My heart starts to race and my mouth feels suddenly dry. I take a shaky breath, clenching my jaw. My hands start to tremble, so I grip the edges of my armrest to steady them. Without glancing at me, Astra places her hand over mine as she smiles at the others gathered. She gives my hand a slight squeeze and my nerves fade a bit.

"We have a lot to get through today so, Kai, let's start with you."

The meeting launches and we go around the table, sharing bits of news. The wards are secure, but more villages have been attacked. Nothing of note is happening in Oxwatch, but nerves are high. Hanna relays that Pip has a bad feeling but nothing specific to share that's actually useful. The only new bit of information comes from Lord McDullun, who stands when it's his turn to talk. He has a strong, commanding presence I envy. A presence I used to have.

"Athiedor is banding together to provide troops and supplies toward the cause of uniting magic and non-magic and taking back the crown."

He proceeds to outline the exact numbers from each Clan, along with other ways the Clans are willing to help. When he sits, Astra nods and turns to me. I swallow and rise from my seat. All eyes bore into me. I can feel the judgement and wariness. What made me think I can do this? I'm no leader. Not really. My eyes meet Cal's. He's seated at the far end of the table next to Bram. He holds my gaze and gives me a reassuring nod. A smile presses on my lips as I take a deep breath, some of my fear dissipating. I can do this.

"I have reviewed the correspondence from Ascaria, and I realized that they did not outright deny us aid. They did, however, hint that they'd like a visit to discuss a potential alliance. I believe it is in our best interests for me to go directly to Ascaria to meet with the royal family. I believe we can form a stronger alliance with them that will put us one step closer to gaining a positive foothold in this war."

I take a deep breath and look around the table. No one is arguing. In fact, many of them are nodding in agreement.

"When do you plan to leave?" Bram asks.

"I plan to sort everything I can today, so I can leave first thing in the morning," I answer turning to him.

Bram nods. "I can arrange a detail. We probably won't want to take too many men, to a keep a low profile, but—"

"No," I cut him off.

Bram pauses, scowling. "No? You want a large detail?"

I shake my head. "I mean you won't be coming with me. I'll take two or three of my Guard but that's it."

Bram looks uncomfortable. I can tell he doesn't like that he's not going with me, but he also doesn't want to argue publicly.

"I have something else I need you to do," I add in quickly. "I've looked over all the correspondence we've received from every angle. I believe that many of the soldiers from destroyed villages and others seeking refuge have been banding together to form an army, possibly multiple armies, of magic and non-magic people working together. As you know, it's been my intent to create such an army, so if we can find and recruit those soldiers, we are halfway there."

"So," Bram says, understanding dawning. "You want me to follow the trail and find these soldiers and bring them back here? You want me to find and train an army?"

I nod. "Yes. There's an old training fortress not even a full day's ride from here. You can bring the soldiers most ready for battle to that fortress or divide them up as needed. We'll train them to fight using their magical abilities side-by-side with weapons."

Bram nods. "All right. I suppose I can do that. How many men do you want me to take?"

I pause, readying myself. I know Bram isn't going to like what I'm about to say next.

"Just one. You know soldiers and weapons, but you know nothing of magic. I need you to take the one person with you who has actually trained others in magic."

Bram furrows his brow in confusion. "Who—" His eyes go wide and he shakes his head. "No. Absolutely not. No way in hell."

"I'm sorry, Captain Bramfield, but I'm afraid this is a direct order. I need you and Alak to find, recruit, and train our army."

"Mate, no," Alak murmurs, staring at me in wide-eyed horror.

I glance toward him and notice Astra gaping at me in shock, a look almost like panic on her face. Alak reaches toward Astra, linking his fingers with hers. Guilt surges through me and I glance away, picking a random spot on the wall behind them to hold my attention.

"I'm sorry, but I need you two to work together. You're the only two I can trust to get this done. You two succeeded in freeing Astra from Kato, so I know you can do this."

"That was for Astra," Bram snaps, his voice tight. "And only because I had no choice in the matter."

"Please," Alak says, his voice breaking. "I don't mind working with the captain, but you know about the bond. You can't separate us. Please, don't."

I meet Alak's eyes and something in me nearly breaks from the desperation I see there. I feel my resolve shake slightly until Astra speaks, her voice barely a whisper.

"It's because of the bond you're splitting us up, isn't it?"

I meet her eyes and nod. "I'm sorry, but yes. You two can communicate across any distance and be by each other's side in a moment's notice. It won't be for long, I promise, but I need a way to stay in contact."

Astra nods but a flurry of emotions war behind her eyes.

"So, I'm to stay here, then?" she asks.

"Yes. I need someone here whom our allies will see as my equal. We're still waiting on letters from potential allies as well as more information from the allies we have secured. I need you here to lead while I'm away in Ascaria. I think I've found a spell that will allow me to check in with you on occasion."

She nods. "Very well then."

I lift my gaze to Lord McDullun, who's watching everything with cautious interest.

"Lord McDullun, I don't suppose you would be willing to remain here for the foreseeable future as an official representative of Athiedor? With Athiedor on the verge of being free, I'm sure they'll respond better to one of their own Clan leaders when it comes to certain issues."

"Aye, Your Majesty," Lord McDullun replies, inclining his head. "It would be my honor to serve you in such a capacity."

"Very well, then." I let my eyes drift over the remaining members in the room. "Does anyone else have anything they wish to bring forward or discuss?" Several people shake their heads. "Good. Then, I suppose we're done for the day. I'll take two or three volunteers to accompany me to Ascaria. Everyone else will remain here for the time being. Captain Bramfield and Alak, you should be ready to leave first thing in the morning as well."

As soon as I'm done speaking, everyone shifts, eager to be out of the room. Bram pushes to his feet, making firm eye contact with me and shaking his head before he storms from the room.

"He'll adjust as always," Astra says softly, placing a hand on my arm as she stands.

"I really am sorry about splitting you and Alak up," I say, turning to Astra. She glances away, nodding. "It won't hurt you physically, will it?"

"It will in a way," Alak answers. I glance toward him and he continues. "The bond is, in many ways, physical and distance can be . . . uncomfortable."

I look back at Astra and she meets my eyes.

"We'll manage," she says quietly, attempting to convince herself as much as me.

I reach out and take her other hand. "Ash, if you need me to find another way . . ."

She shakes her head. "No, we can make it work." She forces a smile. "It's a good plan."

"Except for the part where I'll be alone with Bram for gods know how long. How do you know he won't murder me and blame it on Kato?" Alak mumbles.

I sigh and release Astra's hand. "I'll take care of that, but you need to talk to him, too."

Alak's eyes go wide. "Me? What can I say that I haven't already?"

"The truth. He needs to know the truth."

Alak looks confused for a moment before he starts shaking his head. "You can't mean . . . No. I don't— I can't do that."

"I won't force you to do anything you're not comfortable doing, but I really need you on this mission, Alak. I don't know how well you two can work together with the way things are between you. If you feel you can't do it, you can't mend this fence, I'll find another way. Let me know by this evening. If I don't hear otherwise, I'll assume you've found a way to make it work."

Alak sighs and nods, running a hand through his hair. "I'll see what I can do."

I place a hand on Alak's shoulder and offer him a weak smile. "That's all I ask." I look past Alak at Lord McDullun. "I'll be in the library most of the day, sorting details for my journey. If you'd like to stop by and discuss any concerns you have, please do so."

Lord McDullun smiles. "I may take you up on that offer. I'd like to get to know you on a more personal level, if you don't mind."

My smile is almost genuine as I reply, "I'd like that."

I give a parting nod to Alak, Astra, and Lord McDullun before leaving the room. I need to find and talk to Bram. I can't stand the thought of someone else mad at me. I turn the corner and nearly plow into Cal.

"Oh," he says, stumbling back with a startled grin. "I was hoping you'd be out soon, but I didn't want to interrupt. I know Alak and Astra can't be too happy."

I shake my head and glance away. "No. It seems all I can do lately is disappoint people."

"Hey," Cal says, reaching out and taking my hand in his. I look up into his eyes. "Your plan is a good one. It's logical and laid out well. You're a good leader, Ehren. Even Bram and Alak see that." Cal seems to realize he's holding my hand and releases it with a jerk, his ears reddening as he glances away. "On another note, I was wondering if you've chosen who will accompany you to Ascaria."

I shake my head. "Not yet."

"Well, I know that perhaps the sight of me every day isn't

what you want, given the circumstances, but I'd be willing—"

"Yes."

Cal's eyes widen as they snap to mine. "What?"

I smile, nothing about it forced. "If you're volunteering to come with me, the answer is yes. If you can put aside what I did—"

"You didn't do anything. I told you."

"—then I would love to have you along. I trust few people as much as I trust you, Cal. I'll be going into possibly hostile territory, and I need someone who is trained and skilled."

"Ehren, I will follow you wherever you go and protect you with my life."

My heart constricts and I stumble away from Cal. "No. No, please, don't say that." I shake my head, placing my hands over my face as I struggle to breathe. "No." I manage a strangled gasp. "I can't— I can't lose anyone else."

"Ehren," Cal says softly, pulling my hands from my face and drawing me closer so we're mere inches apart, his eyes searching my face with distress. "It's okay. Take a deep breath."

"Please, Cal, take it back. Take it back," I plead, my voice breaking.

Cal closes his eyes for a moment, opening them slowly as he says, "I lost my best friend because he gave his life for me. What kind of friend would I be if I weren't willing to do the same? But I understand. I . . . I will serve you to the best of my ability and make sure we both come home alive."

I smile and nod my head, drawing a slow breath. "That's better. I just—I can't . . ."

Cal gathers me into his arms and I sink into his touch.

The terror gripping me calms. I wish we could stay this way for a while, but all too soon he's releasing me and taking a step back.

"You've got this, Ehren. I promise. We'll get through this together, you and I. I promise."

I swallow and nod, feeling like a weight has been lifted. I hold Cal's eyes for a moment before glancing around.

"Do you know which way Bram went? I need to clear the air with him a bit."

Cal shakes his head. "I didn't see where he went, but he's been spending a lot of time in the Eastern Garden."

I arch an eyebrow. "The Eastern Garden?"

"Yes. It's the least tended so not many people visit it. I think he likes being alone with his thoughts."

"Ah, I see. Well, I guess I'll start there."

I turn and begin walking away but Cal calls after me.

"Ehren, you know I'm here if you need me. Always."

My smile is genuine and warm as I glance back at him. "I know. And I know I'm a mess, but if you ever need me, please, reach out."

Cal nods and smiles, his eyes bright. I offer him one last smile before I wander off in search of Bram. Cal's instincts prove to be accurate, and I find Bram wandering alone in a half-dead garden. He sees me approaching and tenses, but doesn't make any move to put distance between us.

"I didn't realize you had taken up tending gardens," I tease, stepping to his side.

He doesn't speak. He only shrugs and looks away. My heart sinks a little.

"Bram—"

"How could you?" he says, his eyes snapping to mine. He doesn't even try to mask the betrayal and it stabs like a knife to my heart. "You know what Alak did, and yet you are pushing us together like this? Why, Ehren?"

I sigh and rake a hand through my hair. "Alak didn't kill Isabella."

Bram shakes his head, clenching his jaw as he looks away. "He was responsible and you know it."

"No, he wasn't."

Bram looks back at me and takes a step back, his jaw set and his eyes flashing. "How can you say that?"

"I don't know the whole story, but I know enough to know that you need to talk to Alak. I can't share a story that isn't mine. Work this out. Please."

Bram glances away. "Fine," he says through clenched teeth. "I will give him one chance to explain." He meets my eyes, his gaze hard. "One."

I offer Bram a weak smile. "That's all I ask. Now, how about we take a quick ride and you show me the wards and everything we have set up? I've been longing to take Dauntless out since I found out he returned."

Bram relaxes a touch, his eyes brightening. "That sounds good."

His smile is forced, but it's a step in the right direction. We all have a lot of healing left to do, but at least we're on the right path. At least, I hope we are.

CHAPTER SEVEN

ALAK

Astra has a few things to take care of this morning after our meeting, but as soon as she wraps everything up, we lock ourselves in our room. And by lock, I mean we throw up magical wards galore so not even Kai can bother us. If Ehren is splitting us up, we need to make up for any time lost. Our day is spent exhausting every carnal need. Our bond surges and soars, strengthening with every kiss and caress. I'm not sure how we keep it up as long and often as we do, but we finally surrender to sleep sometime in the late afternoon.

When I wake, it's night, but I'm not sure exactly how late. I glance over at Astra. She's still deep asleep. Her bare back is exposed, her hair spilling across her pillow. I reach out and run my fingers down her shoulder. She reacts only slightly, shifting into my touch, but she doesn't wake. With a sigh, I ease from the bed and slip on my pants. We barely paused to eat all day and I need a snack. Astra doesn't stir as I cross the room and slide into the hall.

The castle is quiet, which makes me believe it's even

later than I first suspected. When I get to the kitchen, I expect to find it empty, so I nearly jump out of my skin when I come face to face with Cook. She chuckles and cocks an eyebrow.

"I, uh, I wasn't expecting anyone to be in here," I mumble, avoiding her eyes.

"Another minute and you would've been correct." She chuckles. "I was just making sure everything was ready for tomorrow's meals and for those traveling tomorrow. You're one of them, aren't you? One of the travelers?"

I nod. "Aye, I am."

Cook eyes me for moment. "Well, I would suggest you get your sleep, but I happen to know food was sent to your room a couple times today. I imagine you're hungry from exerting so much physical energy on draining activities."

Red rises on my cheeks as I nod. Cook laughs, her eyes twinkling.

"Believe it or not, I understand. Well, find what you can," she concedes, gesturing to the kitchen behind her. "There's a pot of nettle tea near the fire that should still be plenty warm and there's a tray of biscuits on the counter and cheese in the larder. Just clean up any messes."

I nod, a little surprised by her generosity. "Thank you."

She gives me a parting nod before shuffling away. I cross the kitchen and fill a cup of tea and grab a few biscuits before settling down at the table in the center of the kitchen. I'm nearly done when I hear footsteps in the hall. I jerk my gaze up to find a figure frozen in doorway.

"Why are you here?" Bram asks, his voice cold.

I wash down a bite of biscuit with a swig of tea before replying. "I was hungry, and this is where we keep the food."

Bram nods and turns to leave. "Why don't you have a cup of tea with me?"

Bram turns to me, frowning. "Why would I do that?"

I release a long sigh. "Look, mate, we're off tomorrow for gods know how long. Can we at least try to mend the fence before we go? Please? Just have a cup of tea with me, and if you still hate me when we're done, then so be it."

I'm sure he's going to leave. He stands there for a minute, staring at me without blinking. It's . . . unsettling.

"Fine."

I startle, my eyes going wide. "Really?"

Bram shakes his head as he steps into the kitchen and goes to the cupboard to get a cup. He takes a seat next to me and I fill his cup for him.

"Don't expect this to fix everything," he says, his voice almost void of emotion. "I am only doing this for Ehren."

I nod, licking my lips. "I'll take what I can get."

We fall into an awkward silence, and I wonder what exactly I thought would come from having tea with Bram.

"So," he says at length, "tell me what happened with Isabella."

I freeze and my heart starts racing. I slowly shift to meet his eyes. His gaze is set and firm. I can't read what he's thinking, what he's expecting.

"I . . . What about Isabella?" I ask quietly.

"Did you . . . ," he starts, but he can't finish. He shakes his head and pushes away from the table, turning his back to me as he goes to leave. "Forget it. This was a mistake."

He's almost to the door before I find my voice. "I loved your sister."

Bram spins to face me, his eyes flashing. "Why did you kill her, then?"

I wince, an all too familiar pain stabbing my chest. I cup my hands around the tea, squeezing it tightly as I stare down into the amber liquid.

"I didn't kill her, Bram. She did that. I may have been somewhat responsible, I know, but she made the decision herself."

I pause and raise my eyes to Bram and I start. In all the time I've known Bram, I've only seen him show raw emotion a handful of times. Right now, it's written all over his face, tears brimming in his eyes.

"Tell me what happened, then," he says, his voice rough.

I swallow and nod. "I will. I'm just not sure where to start. It would help if you could sit back down. You hovering like that is . . . intimidating."

Bram walks stiffly to the seat he just vacated, his eyes locked on mine. Even though it's dark, I can see the specks of gold in his brown eyes. My heart stops and I take a shuddering breath, glancing away.

"What?" Bram snaps.

"It's your eyes," I confess, staring back down into my tea.

"What about my eyes?"

"You have the same eyes—you and Isabella."

"What?" His voice is barely a whisper. I glance up and he's staring at me in utter bewilderment. "We . . . have the same eyes?"

I nod. "You didn't know?"

Bram shakes his head and glances away. "No. I . . . I never really thought about it, I suppose."

"When I look into your eyes, I see her. Ehren does, too, I think."

Bram shakes his head harder, shifting uncomfortably. "No, that's not . . . no."

I laugh bitterly. "Trust me, mate, I wish it wasn't that way." I exhale slowly before continuing. "Anyway, I loved your sister from the moment I met her. Or at least I loved her as much as my fifteen-year-old self could. I had very few bright spots in my life and Isabella outshone them all. She was beautiful and kind. She grounded me. She felt like home."

"Home?"

"Yes. At least, what I expected home to feel like. I spent years of my life being unwanted, being told I was worthless, but all of that seemed irrelevant when I met Isabella. For the first time in my life, I saw a future I wanted—a future that revolved around Isabella. In order to make that future happen, I had to change. I couldn't be a nobody relying on the mercy of a sympathetic prince. I had to make something of myself. I had to prove myself. So, I got a job. I figured if I could save up enough money I could provide for Isabella and become a respected member of society. But I got paid practically nothing. Everything felt so hopeless."

I take a breath, staring down into my tea, struggling to push down the rising emotions.

"That's when Dylan offered you the wager, isn't it," Bram says. It's not really a question, but I nod anyway.

"He did. At first, I only had to kiss Isabella in front of you. That was easy enough but then, the next task . . ."

I trail off and shake my head. Bram stiffens beside me and I jerk my eyes to meet his.

"I didn't do it, Bram. I swear to it. I went to your sister's room that night to see where things would lead—I won't lie about that. I wanted to sleep with her. She was attractive and I was a fifteen-year-old boy. I wanted—"

"I don't require all the details," Bram cuts me off sharply.

I nod, swallowing hard. "Fine, but you need some details. I went to her room and we . . . kissed. It was leading somewhere, but I stopped it. Isabella wanted to continue, but the time wasn't right. I couldn't do that to her—using her to win a bet. She was my world, my everything. I respected her and I loved her. I ran from her room and a servant saw us and assumed. It was all a misunderstanding.

"I didn't know what to do next, so I hid. I'd been hiding all my life, so it came naturally. I struggled with what to do. I wanted to fix things, but I didn't know how. I've never been good at fixing things, only breaking them. I hated that I broke her heart; I broke along with it. I was miserable."

I stop, tears trailing my cheeks. I can't look at Bram, so I focus on the tea that's gone cold in my cup. I take a shaky breath as more tears slip free.

"By the time I gathered the courage to face Isabella, it was too late. I went to her room, but . . ."

I break off in another sob as the image of her body strewn across her blood-soaked sheets flashes in my mind. I squeeze my eyes shut, bowing my head. I can smell the blood even though I know there's none nearby. I struggle and fail to control the tears until I feel a hand on my shoulder. I open my eyes and look over at Bram, tears on his own cheeks.

I swallow and manage to find my voice again, but it's quiet and hoarse. "It shattered everything in me seeing her. A maid came in and I hid. I had to see you and Ehren find the body. I lost everything and everyone—the love of my life and my friends—in the span of a few minutes. I couldn't handle it. So, I ran. I knew you'd kill me before I had a chance to explain, and I couldn't bear to see your disappointment if you left me alive. I ran out of fear and because I thought if I could put enough distance between me and Embervein I could start over."

I pull my eyes away and lift a trembling hand, turning my wrist upward. It's dark, but I know Bram can see the scar as I allow the illusion to fade because he inhales sharply.

"You . . ." He looks back up at me, bewildered. "Why?"

"I didn't want to live in a world without Isabella, a world where all my friends hated me."

"How are you alive?"

"Someone found me. A Seer. He saved my life and assured me I had a purpose. I didn't believe him, but I was curious enough not to try to end my life again. I live with the scars, both physical and emotional. Not a day goes by that I don't miss her. Sometimes, I wonder what would have happened if she had lived. Would I have married her? Or was our love the kind of young love that's fierce but burns out quickly?"

"What about Astra?" Bram asks, his voice unsteady. "Do you love her as much as you did Isabella?"

I meet Bram's eyes. "My love for Astra is all-consuming. It's the kind of love that moves mountains and drains oceans. I will die for her and sacrifice every part of me to make her happy. If she had truly wanted you over me, I would've been content with that. It would've hurt like hell and made it hard to go on, but I would have done it. For her."

Bram nods and glances away. For several moments thick silence fills the air. When Bram finally speaks, his voice is low.

"I believe you. Every word. I am sorry I have been holding a grudge against you."

"I don't blame you," I say quickly. "When Isabella died, you needed someone to blame so you could move on and heal, and honestly, I was okay with being that person. I hated that you thought less of me, but I understood."

Bram shakes his head. "It wasn't right, and I am sorry." He takes a deep breath and rakes a hand through his hair. "I don't know exactly how to move forward, but I promise to try. I don't have many friends, either, and I think . . ."

I grin. "Bram, are you saying you want to be my friend?"

Bram scowls, his mouth tightening into a firm line that wants to be a smile. "I am not promising anything."

My grin widens. "Whatever you say, best mate."

Bram frowns as I laugh. "I did not agree to that . . . term."

I laugh harder as I stand. I feel like a huge weight has been lifted, and I can breathe freer than I've been able to in years. I clap a hand to his shoulder and look down at him.

"I sincerely appreciate whatever friendship you can give me," I say. "Now, get some sleep because we have a journey to start bright and early in the morning, mate."

Bram nods but doesn't stand. I don't push him, figuring he needs a few more minutes alone. I head back upstairs and slip into my room. Astra is still asleep as I slide back beneath the covers. She shifts, moving closer to me. I wrap my arms around her, drawing her close as I press a kiss to her temple.

"I love you, Astra," I whisper. "You are home to me, now and forever."

CHAPTER EIGHT
ASTRA

I wake before Alak. His arms are curled around me, holding me tightly. An ache fills my chest at the thought of waking up without him once he leaves on his mission with Bram. I'm also worried about my nightmares returning. Ever since we completed the bond, my nightmares have almost completely vanished. I don't know what I'll do with both Alak and Ehren gone.

I shift, pulling the blanket closer around me. Alak stirs behind me, and I turn my head to see if he's waking up. Two sleep-filled emerald eyes blink back at me.

"Morning, love," Alak murmurs, smiling softly.

"I didn't mean to wake you," I reply, rolling over so my body is facing his.

He presses a kiss to my forehead. "I suspect I'd have to get up soon anyway. I doubt the good captain wants to wait too long to be on the road."

"You're probably right."

A roguish grin snakes onto his face. "Unless, of course,

you have other activities that involve us staying in bed but not sleeping."

I laugh. "We did that all day yesterday."

His grin widens. "Your point?"

"My point"—I laugh, throwing back the covers and sitting up—"is that we really need to get you ready to go, since we did little of that yesterday."

Alak scoffs and rolls onto his back, lacing his fingers behind his head as he watches me walk across the room. "As if you didn't make sure I had every little thing packed and ready to go before we did anything fun yesterday."

I flash him a grin. "It wouldn't hurt to double check and make sure you have everything. You also may want to take a bath. You may not get another chance for a while. I know that's what I'm going to do."

Alak jerks into a sitting position, his eyes sparking with interest. Desire rushes down the bond as he says, "You'll be in the bath with me?"

I laugh. "As long as you actually bathe."

Alak leaps from the bed, charging toward the washroom. "Say no more, love. Time for a bath."

Bath time consists of a lot of not bathing followed by quickly washing up. In all honesty, I could use another day like yesterday, but I know that Alak needs to help Bram. When we finally finish with our bath, we head back into the main room and dress.

"I talked to Bram," Alak says, sitting on the edge of the bed putting on his boots as I braid my hair.

"When?"

"Last night. I woke up and went down to the kitchen for some tea and he showed up."

I tie off the end of my braid and turn to face Alak. "What

did you say?" I feel a tremor through the bond similar to pain. "You don't have to talk about it."

Alak shakes his head and forces a weak smile. "We just talked everything through."

The pain is still there. Quiet and subdued, but there.

"You talked about Isabella, didn't you?"

The bond is heavy as he meets my eyes and nods. "Aye, love. We did. Everything isn't magically fixed between us, but we're a step closer, I think." I glance away and he rises from the bed, striding to me and placing his hands gently on my shoulders. "I love you so much, you know that?"

I meet his eyes and smile. Even if I couldn't feel the strong surge of love now coursing through the bond, I see it in the depths of his eyes. I nod, pressing a soft kiss to his cheek.

"And I love you."

Alak laughs, dropping his hands as he shakes his head. "I still don't know how I got so lucky."

I grin but don't get a chance to reply before a knock on the door interrupts.

"Are you decent?" Cal calls through the door.

"Unfortunately," Alak calls back, his eyes sparkling with mischief as I playfully smack his chest.

Cal opens the door and steps into our room. One look at the shadows crossing his face and my heart falls.

"Ehren?"

Cal swallows and nods. "He was doing so well."

I take a deep breath. "Good days won't erase the heaviness bearing down on him."

Alak presses a quick kiss to my temple. "Go check on him, love. I'll look over my bags and meet you downstairs."

I nod and follow Cal out of the room.

"I'll wait out here," he says when we reach Ehren's door.

I give Cal a quick nod before I knock on the door and slip inside without waiting for a response. Ehren stands shirtless, staring into the mirror, his face dark and grim. He doesn't even glance at me as I close the door and cross the room to stand behind him.

"How are you?"

Ehren's jaw tightens but he doesn't pull his gaze from the mirror as he answers, "I don't know."

I place my hand on his arm. "Look at me."

He takes a shuddering breath before slowly blinking and turning to meet my eyes.

"I thought I could do this, Ash," he says, his voice trembling. "But I don't know that I can. I'm not cut out to lead. I see that now. What if I get to Ascaria and they see right through my mask? What if they can tell I'm not the leader needed to defeat Kato? What if—"

"Stop," I say gently, raising a hand to caress Ehren's cheek. "You are stronger and more capable than you give yourself credit for. I believe in you, Ehren."

"You're the only one."

"You are very wrong. This castle is filled with people who believe in you and support you."

Ehren shakes his head, glancing away. "No, this castle is filled with people who believe in *you*."

Something in me cracks at his words. My shoulders drop and my hand falls from Ehren's face as I turn away.

"Maybe they shouldn't believe in me, either," I confess, my voice barely above a whisper.

Ehren's eyes snap to me and he reaches out, turning me back to face him. His eyes scan my face.

"You can't mean that."

"Why not?" I reply, glancing away from his penetrating gaze. "Yes, I have magic, but right now even my magic can't save us. I looked through the letters dozens of times and never saw what you saw right away. You are meant to lead. I know you are, Ehren. And you're wrong. These people are rallying around you as much as I am—some even more so. Cal is out in the hallway right now, worried about you."

Ehren's attention jerks to the door. "Cal's out there?"

"He is, because he believes in you. Like I believe in you and Alak believes in you and Cadewynn believes in you. The list goes on and on. Even Ronan was impressed by your plans yesterday."

Ehren drags his eyes from the door and looks at me, his brow furrowed in confusion. "Who's Ronan?"

A smile twitches on my lips as I reply, "Lord McDullun."

A glimmer of the Ehren I know disperses some of the shadows as he says, "You're on awfully casual terms aren't you?" He pauses, arching his eyebrows. "Does Alak know?"

I laugh. "Yes, he is aware. He calls him Ronan, as well."

"Interesting," Ehren drawls, brightening slightly as he waggles his eyebrows.

"It is nothing like that, and you know it!" I cry, my eyes shining.

Ehren smiles and it's not entirely forced, warming my heart.

"Thank you, Ash,.."

I smile softly. "Any time."

I turn to leave but Ehren stops me with, "How do you do it?"

I turn back to him, tilting my head in confusion. "Do what?"

"Face your demons."

My breath catches in my throat. I could try to deny I have demons, but Ehren knows as well as I do that would be a lie. Blood-soaked battle fields haunt my dreams any time Alak isn't sleeping by my side. I have a father who disowned me and a mother who didn't fight for me. My own twin brother turned against me. I have demons. So many demons.

"I take it one moment at a time," I confess at length. Ehren cocks his head, studying me. "Sometimes, I focus on making it through the day. Other times, I just need to hang on until the next breath. And the next. And the next. And so on and so on until it gets easier. It's less difficult when I try not to bear everything myself. Having Alak and you and Kai helps me so much."

Ehren nods. "One breath at a time?"

I nod. "One breath at a time."

He inhales deeply, releasing the breath slowly. "I can do that."

I offer him a smile. "You can."

I hesitate only a moment before I go to leave again. This time, he doesn't stop me. I glance over my shoulder as I slip out the door. He's brighter, the shadows not so obvious.

"Is he . . . ?" Cal asks as the door closes behind me.

"He's getting there." I pause before adding, "You should probably go in. He needs you."

Cal's eyes widen with surprise. "Me? Why would he need me?"

"Because being alone makes it harder to make it to the next breath sometimes, and being around someone you love makes it easier."

Cal holds my gaze, and something in his eyes tells me

he's turning my words over carefully. After a moment, he nods.

"All right. I can't do what you do for him, though."

I shake my head. "No, but you can help him in a way only you can."

He studies me for a long minute. "Ehren's lucky to have you."

I smile weakly. "We're lucky to have Ehren. Now, get in there."

Cal nods and knocks on Ehren's door as I brush past him down the hall. I hear Ehren tell him to come in as I disappear around the corner, heading downstairs. I make my way to the kitchen, which is a chaos of motion. Cook spots me immediately and has a mug of steaming coffee ready by the time I get to her.

"Morning, dear. Breakfast?" she asks, offering me the coffee.

I shake my head as I accept the coffee, taking in the bustle of activity. "Not this morning. I'll grab something later. You seem busy."

Cook nods. "It's a bit busy, but I'd rather be busy than idle and twiddling my thumbs."

I nod my agreement as I sip my coffee. I feel Alak's magic before I hear him.

"Fancy meeting you here, love!" Alak says, sweeping into the kitchen behind me.

Cook's eyes narrow at him as she says, "Captain Bramfield already got the food for your journey, if that's why you're here."

Alak nods. "That's exactly why I'm here. But you're sure he took my food as well? He didn't toss my portion away when he thought you weren't looking?"

Cook looks less than amused and doesn't reply. She huffs and shakes her head, moving deeper into the kitchen. Alak turns to me, kissing my cheek as I drink my coffee.

"You almost seem like you love that coffee more than me," he teases.

I wink. "It's a toss-up."

Alak's rich laughter floods the kitchen, and several of the staff turn curious eyes our way.

"I would say I'm offended, but I understand," he says. "I'm going to head outside."

"I'll meet you out there in a minute."

Alak nods and disappears. I make quick work of my coffee before heading out to the front courtyard of the castle. Several Guard members are lingering nearby with the horses prepared for travel. Bram stands next to Solomon while Alak chats with Ronan next to Fawn several yards away. Dauntless stands nearby with three other horses, two of which have Guard members—Pascal and Lorrell, if I remember correctly—holding their reins, but Cal and Ehren are nowhere to be seen. Bram catches my eye and raises his chin in greeting.

"Are you ready?" I ask, walking over to him.

Bram arches an eyebrow. "Ready for a road trip with Alak? I don't really know if anyone can ever truly prepare for that."

I laugh. I feel a wave of relief when I realize that the former hostility that used to lace his words when talking about Alak is gone.

"As long as he doesn't try to sing the entire time, you should be okay," I say. Bram smiles and shakes his head. "I heard you two talked last night?"

Bram sobers as he nods. "We did. Did he share the details?"

I shake my head. "Not really. He just said you cleared the air."

Bram bobs his head absentmindedly, letting his gaze drift to Alak. "That we did. I don't know how much it helped, but at least I think we can move forward now."

I place a hand on Bram's arm and he jerks his eyes back to meet mine. "Thank you."

He smiles softly and inclines his head. "Of course."

I glance over at Alak as he laughs at something Ronan said. He's so carefree, and despite the fact he's survived well enough on his own most of his life, I can't help but worry. The stakes are so high, and I don't know how I'll go on should something happen to him.

"I will take care of him," Bram says, as if he can read my thoughts.

I turn back to him. "Really? You'd do that for me?"

Bram nods, placing his hand over his heart. "I swear it. I will watch over him and make sure he comes back to you." His gaze softens as he drops his arm, and something very close to a smile presses on his lips, though his eyes contain a hint of sadness. "I will always do anything for you, Astra. I know what Alak means to you, and if protecting him is what you need from me, then it is the least I can do."

I swallow, emotions rising up in my chest. "Thank you, Bram. That . . . that means a lot."

He nods once but doesn't say more, largely due to Ehren striding into the courtyard with more confidence and bravado than he's shown in weeks. It's the mask he wears, but maybe if he wears it enough, it will become less of a mask and more of a reality.

"Everyone ready to go?" Ehren asks, scanning the crowd.

"We're ready!" Pascal says, nodding to his brother.

"Good," Ehren says, shifting his eyes to Bram. "And you?"

"Ready as I will ever be," Bram says, forcing a tight grin.

I hide my smile as I cross to Ehren. His mask falters for just a moment.

"Are *you* ready?" I ask quietly so no one else overhears.

Ehren smiles. It's weak but genuine. He glances over his shoulder at Cal, who is attaching a bag to his horse.

"I'll be okay." He turns his gaze back to me. "Will *you* be okay here, alone?"

I nod and force a smile. "I have Kai and Ronan."

Ehren's eyes search my face. "That's not what I meant."

I swallow and glance away toward Alak. "I'll miss him, but we'll manage. We can stay in contact well enough." I look back up at Ehren. "And thanks to the dream walking spell you found, I'll be able to communicate with you."

Ehren nods. "Right. Just make sure when you go to sleep, you keep the spelled feather under your pillow so I can reach you."

"I promise. I am a little concerned you're not taking anyone with magic on your journey."

Ehren shrugs and glances toward Pascal and Lorrell. "They're good fighters, if nothing else, but I don't want to take anyone with strong magic into Ascaria. I don't know their current views on magic, but according to records they weren't accepting of magic when it was active before."

"I know, but it doesn't lessen my concerns any. How long will you be gone?"

Ehren's eyes sparkle. "You miss me already, don't you?"

I laugh and shake my head. "I'm just trying to plan."

"Well, we are a day, maybe two from the mountains, and then it could take anywhere from four to eight days to cross the mountains depending on what kind of conditions we meet."

"We should probably get on the road," Cal says, walking up behind Ehren.

"All right," Ehren says with a nod and a false smile. "Let's do this."

The travelers mount their horses, and my heart contracts as I watch Alak on Fawn. He looks back at me, and I sense the arc of pain down the bond. This is not going to be easy. I take a step back, falling even with Ronan as the riders spur their horses forward. With each clip of Fawn's hooves, my heart aches more.

Everyone starts heading back inside, but I remain in the courtyard, staring in the direction Alak left. I feel the exact moment he rides through the wards. It's not the first time he's crossed them, but I know this time he won't be right back. A hot tear slides down my cheek as I press my fist over my heart.

"Are you okay?"

I peel my eyes away from the road and turn to face Kai. He stands just inside the door, watching me, his face etched with concern. When he sees the tears on my cheeks, he quickly crosses the distance between us and gathers me in his arms. I bury my face in his chest as a sob breaks free.

"He'll be back before you know it," Kai whispers, holding me tightly. "You'll see. It won't seem like long at all."

I pull back and look up into Kai's gray eyes. "What if something happens?"

"Nothing will happen," Kai says gently.

"You don't know that. War's everywhere. Kato knows what Alak means to me, and Alak betrayed him. He won't hesitate to kill him."

Kai sighs, pulling his gaze from mine to look toward the road.

"There are many things about this world that I don't know, but one thing I know for sure is that it would take a lot more than death to keep Alak from coming back to you."

"Death seems pretty final," I whisper, my chest tightening at the mere thought.

Kai's lips turn up into a sad smile as his eyes meet mine. "Somehow, I think it's something even you two can conquer. Now, staring at the road isn't doing anyone any good. Have you had breakfast?"

I nod, stepping back out of his arms. "I had a cup of coffee not that long ago."

Kai scowls, crossing his arms. "Coffee is not breakfast."

"It is when you drink it at breakfast time," I argue.

"It can be a *part* of breakfast, but it is not substantial enough on its own to take the place of an entire meal."

I sigh and roll my eyes. "Fine. Then, no, I have not had breakfast."

Kai slips his hand into mine and pulls me toward the door. "Well then, how about we fix that?"

I grin and follow him inside. I may have to wait a few weeks before Alak returns, but at least I won't be alone.

Part Two:
Rising

CHAPTER NINE

JESSALYNN

"You're sure that many people volunteered?" I ask, staring at Kaeya in utter disbelief. "That's nearly the entire army."

Kaeya nods. "I am aware. I double checked all the numbers with Brock. It seems that people are eager to use their skills and not remain sitting idly by when there's a war going on."

"But they realize that the war hasn't come to us yet? That they'd be fighting for Callenia?" I press.

"Yes."

"And Brock is okay with losing this many people? He's likely to be the one in charge of the army while we're away."

"So you still want me to accompany you?" Kaeya asks, tilting her head.

"Yes, that hasn't changed," I reply. "As long as you don't mind, that is."

"I don't mind."

I study her for a moment and narrow my eyes. "What aren't you saying?"

A smile plays at the corner of her lips. "What do you mean?"

"Kaeya, I know you. You're not saying something. Out with it."

"Fine. I can understand exactly why every volunteer is so eager because I am also looking forward to the prospect of battle."

I quirk an eyebrow at her. "Really?"

"Really," she says, her eyes bright. "I didn't spend all those years training to be the best of the best to run a small army that never sees any action."

"Is it really so horrible living in peace?"

Kaeya rolls her eyes. "That isn't what I meant. I only think if there is a war that could destroy lives, people like me with fighting skills need to stand up against evil and bring it down."

"I suppose I understand," I concede with a sigh. "So, how many people will we leave behind?"

"Enough to defend the Valley should we be attacked, but we do have magical wards that protect us. Brock is working out the exact numbers. We should be able to provide decent aid."

I nod, processing the information. "So maybe enough for two troops? We could send one directly to my brother and the other somewhere else. Koshima, maybe?"

"Do we want to take any soldiers with us?"

I consider her words for a moment before shaking my head. "I don't think that'll be necessary. You and I are well-trained, and I'm sure Nyco will be willing to accompany the princess, giving us another talented sword. Sama can join us, if she's willing. A Syphon is always useful."

Kaeya nods. "With that small of a travel party, we can

make good time. We can also wisp occasionally as needed, putting us in danger less often."

I smirk. "You make it sound like the provinces are all safe, welcoming places."

Kaeya barks a laugh. "I know far better than to believe that, but at least we expect the ambushes there."

"That is a valid point." I give her a sigh of resignation. "All right. I guess we have a plan. Go confirm the numbers with Brock and set everything in motion. I'll let the little princess know the details. We'll leave in the morning. "

Kaeya nods and leaves without another word. She's always been more for action than words, anyway. I hesitate only a moment before I go off in search of Cadewynn. She's been here barely a day and already has half the Valley under her charms. The sooner I get her out of here, the better. I head to the quarry first. I don't find Cadewynn, but I do find Sama working.

"Hey, Jess!" Sama grins as I approach.

I offer her a cocky smile. "You missed your work so much you started it back already?"

"I like to feel useful," she replies with a shrug.

"Did my dearest brother find a way for you to be useful those weeks when you were away?"

Sama shifts uncomfortably, avoiding my eyes. "If you had needed me here, I would have returned."

"You were fine to go with him," I say with a flippant wave, doing my best to hide my guilt at making her ill at ease. "I simply wanted to make sure you were treated well."

Sama still looks a little unsure, but she brightens slightly. "Ehren is a good man."

I fight the urge to roll my eyes. "So I hear. Speaking of

Ehren, do you happen to know where Cadewynn is? I have things I need to discuss with her."

"Are you going to help her?" Sama asks, her entire face glowing.

Gods. What kind of power do Ehren and Cadewynn have over these people? No one is that amazing. I glance away, doing my best to appear bored.

"I suppose. The little princess made some valid points." I look back at Sama. "But I can't discuss them with her if I can't find her."

"Oh. Right," Sama mumbles. "I think she's by the waterfall with Nyco."

I let my eyes lift toward the waterfall not too far away, preparing to wisp.

"Jess," Sama says, drawing my attention. "When you leave with Cadewynn, may I go with you?"

"Well, I suppose it could be useful to have a Syphon along, though, when our little mission is done, do you intend on returning to the Valley or Callenia?"

Sama avoids my eyes. "I'm not entirely sure."

"Great," I mutter with a sigh. "My brother is stealing my most trusted citizens."

"It's not just Ehren," Sama says quickly. Too quickly.

"Who else is there?" I ask, narrowing my eyes. "Wait, you haven't fallen for one of his Guard? Nyco, perhaps?"

Her cheeks redden. "I . . . he's quite nice, but I'm not sure how I feel about him alone." She raises her eyes to mine. "Ehren and his court are all very kind. They are like a family and never hesitated to make me feel a part of that."

"And you didn't feel like you had family here?"

"I . . ."

"Don't worry about it," I cut her off with a sharp wave.

"Honestly, Sama, you should go where you feel the most comfortable. I'll not hold it against you if you choose Ehren and Callenia."

Her surprise shows in her every feature as she says, "Truly?"

I nod. "Of course. I appreciate everything you've done for me here, but if you feel called elsewhere, I wish you the best. For now, however, we have a common goal so, if you don't mind, I'm going to find Cadewynn and make the necessary arrangements."

Sama gives me a parting nod before I wisp away. As promised, I find Cadewynn and Nyco behind the waterfall. Cadewynn is grinning, looking up at the water, completely unaware or not caring about the droplets of water soaking her hair and clothes.

"Never seen a waterfall before?" I yell above the roar of the falls.

Cadewynn turns to me, eyes shining. "No, I have only ever seen them in pictures or read about them in books."

Gods. She's so blissfully innocent. This war is likely to destroy her, and I almost feel bad about that.

"Well," I yell, "the waterfall may be fascinating, but it's hard to discuss things here. Shall we go elsewhere?"

Cadewynn nods, a bit of her previous joy diminishing slightly as reality slams back in. I take a step toward her, extending my hands to her and Nyco. They accept without hesitation. I wisp us to my office rather than a meeting room. I want the upper hand.

"Okay, here are my terms," I say, jumping right in. "I will help you with your quest to recruit the additional provinces, though I fear your expectations may be a bit high. Kaeya and Brock have gathered a decent army, large enough we may divide them into two groups. Brock will take them and head to Koshima to await orders and potential allies. If we take too long on whatever it is that you have planned, one small army will travel out earlier, heading directly to your brother, while the other will stay behind in Koshima waiting for us."

Cadewynn nods, eyes bright. "Thank you."

I hold up a palm, shaking my head. "Don't thank me quite yet. My armies are small, most likely insignificant against the forces assaulting your kingdom. And, while you may truly believe that I have some sort of great influence in the other provinces, I fear you'll be very disappointed."

"Even if that turns out to be true, it's still more support than we had before," Cadewynn says, her voice firm. "I am very grateful for that."

I wave her off. "Save your gratitude for if we actually accomplish something."

She nods once. "Very well, but I have faith in you. When do we leave?"

"First thing in the morning we'll head to the province of Jakuma. It's a little ways to the Southeast near the border. The leader there owes me a favor. I was saving it for something more personal but . . ." I end with a shrug, as if using my favor for a war is a minor inconvenience.

Cadewynn nods eagerly, her eyes unfocused a touch. I'm sure her mind is already racing with all the things she needs to prepare. She seems like a planner.

"Well, I suppose that's all we need to discuss," I say. "You can go prepare as needed."

Cadewynn nods, her mind still turning as she exits the room. Nyco follows along behind her, but pauses in the doorway, turning back to me.

"You're making the right decision," he says.

I narrow my eyes at him. "I don't recall asking for your opinion or approval."

"Don't care," he replies with a half-shrug. "You have it anyway."

I'm still marveling at his words long after he's gone. I may put on a hard mask, but the truth is that I crave the support of my people. I want to know I'm doing right by them. I finally manage to clear his words from my mind enough to settle back at my desk to write some letters. Traveling to all the provinces will take far too long given our timeline, so pleas via letter to some of the more amicable provinces will hopefully do the job. I'm nearly done when I'm interrupted by a sharp knock. I raise my eyes to the door with a scowl. Anyone I want to see wouldn't bother to knock. My scowl deepens when the door opens and Deven Leghari strolls in, a sloppy, knowing smile on his lips.

"I'm busy," I mumble, turning my attention back to the letter in front of me.

"Oh, but I think you'll want to hear my proposition," he says, shutting the door.

"I doubt it, but go ahead and bore me," I reply, not bothering to look up.

"I hear you've agreed to go on some sort of little mission with our visiting princess," he says.

"And?"

"And I thought you might want me to be in charge while you're gone."

My eyes snap to his face. "Why the hell would I want that?"

"Because," he says, drawing the word out as he takes a seat on the corner of my desk, leering down at me, "you need someone to be in charge who knows what they're doing.

Before your mother waltzed back in here, throwing you into her family's previous position of power, your title was going to be mine."

"But, alas, I did take your position, so you get no say," I reply sharply, turning back to my letters. "Brock will lead in my place well enough."

"You'll need him for your armies."

"I have Kaeya."

"So, just the one army then?"

I growl and look up at him. "I have other people who can lead an army. Now, get off my desk. It's not a chair."

"People you trust?" he asks, sliding from the corner to stand.

"Are you suggesting I trust *you*?" I laugh.

He frowns. "Why wouldn't you trust me? I'm more than qualified." He pauses, his eyebrows arching as realization strikes. "Ah, I see. You're afraid that I won't relinquish my position should you return. Well, I promise you, *if* you want your position back, I'll give it to you."

"If? I rather think I'll want it back," I snap.

He shrugs, picking a speck of dirt off his pants and flicking it away. "Perhaps, but then again, maybe your brother will welcome you back to be part of his court. That's what you really want, isn't it, Jessalynn? To be wanted by your family and have a piece of the inheritance you deserve?"

My eyes flash as I stand, meeting his eyes. He has the good sense to stumble back a step.

"The Hundan Valley is my birthright just as much as Callenia, more so really. It would do you well to remember that. Now, get out of my sight. I have work to do."

Deven flashes me a smile, but it lacks his previous fire.

"So be it, but when you change your mind, you know where to find me."

He exits, leaving the door wide open. Once he's gone, I sink back into my chair with a heavy sigh, not bothering to shut the door. I almost don't notice Kaeya enter the room, closing the door behind her.

"He's right, you know," she says, crossing her arms as she looks down at me.

I arch an eyebrow. "You were spying on me?"

She huffs. "It is my job."

"To spy on me?"

"To take care of you, *Jaanu*."

I take a deep breath and release it slowly. "I know. I know he's right, but I can't trust him."

"No, you cannot," Kaeya agrees with a nod, "but you may have to take that risk."

"Brock will be fine—"

"No, he is not prepared for such a task," Kaeya cuts me off. "He is loyal and would never deny your request to stay behind, but Deven is much more qualified to lead in your absence."

"Brock has led when I've gone away before," I argue.

"Short trips. This will be a lengthy excursion, and you know it. Besides, Brock is far more qualified to help lead the armies. It works well."

I sigh and slam my forehead down on my desk.

"I hate this," I grumble, my words muffled by the desk.

"I know, *Jaanu*," Kaeya says, stepping around the desk to rub soothing circles on my back. "But you are not alone."

I raise my head and twist in my seat to look up at her. "Am I making the right decision?"

Kaeya nods without hesitation. "Yes, I believe you are."

"Fine. Make the necessary preparations. Let Deven know he can rule in my absence, but make it clear that any resistance when I return will be handled as treason."

Kaeya's eyes turn almost feral as she grins. "I will make sure he understands the consequences of a rebellion."

I match her grin. "Now, my dear," I purr, "leave him intact enough to run the Valley."

She laughs, her eyes shining. "Of course. I know my boundaries."

"Though, perhaps pushing those boundaries may not be the worst idea. Either way, make sure everything is in place. I'll finish my letters to the other provinces and have them send their replies to Koshima. We will assess our next move when we arrive."

Kaeya nods. "That is a good plan." She leans down and brushes a quick kiss across my lips. "Finish your letters and I will make sure everything else is ready. Do not worry. Everything will work out."

I sigh and look down at the half-finished letter before me. "I hope to the gods you're right. Otherwise, we're all fucked."

CHAPTER TEN
ALAK

Bram and I barely speak our first day of travel. We both fix our eyes on the road in front of us, focusing on the task at hand. Ehren provided us with a pretty detailed map of the path we should follow, and Bram is determined to stick to that general path while staying off the main roads and avoiding villages and towns to limit interactions with other people as long as possible. He claims that the fewer people who know our location, the more secure our mission will be and the more likely we are to succeed. Given he's the Captain of the Guard and all, I'm inclined to let him make the call.

Felixe spends most of his time curled up in my lap sleeping, but he occasionally hops down to bound along beside our horses. I create a basic illusion to protect us from any prying eyes. Since Astra and I completed our bond, my magic has been stronger. At first, I thought my magic was only strong near her, when I could draw from her power. While my magic is undeniably strongest when she's by my side, my magic is stronger than before we completed our bond, even when we're apart.

When we stop for lunch, I try to goad him into conversation, but he's excellent at his one-word answers that stop every attempt short. When we get back on the road, I try a different method—aggravation. I sing every single pub song and ballad I know in an attempt to at least get him to yell at me, but even then I fail. When we stop and make camp for the night, I've had enough.

"Are you going to ignore me the entire trip?" I snap as Bram makes a fire.

He raises his eyes to mine. "That was the plan. Was it not obvious?"

I sigh and run a hand through my hair. "I really thought we were past this. I thought—"

"I am trying," Bram says through gritted teeth, standing straight. "I spent six years hating you. I cannot undo that in one day. I am trying to come to terms with the truth but it is not easy."

I swallow, nodding. "I guess I can understand that, but I don't think closing yourself off is quite the way to do it, mate."

Bram sighs and glances away. "I don't know how to make friends, let alone mend fences."

I laugh. "I'm shocked. And here I was thinking you were the friendliest person on Ehren's Guard."

A smile twitches at the corner of Bram's lips. "I know. I surprise a lot of people with that fact."

I laugh harder. "At least you have a sense of humor."

Bram smiles, shaking his head.

I sit down on the ground next to the fire and riffle through a bag. "Why don't we have a bit of dinner and chat?

We can pretend we've only just met and start over. How does that sound?"

Bram eyes me for a moment before nodding, taking a seat across from me. "I can do that."

I release a sigh of relief, pulling a small loaf of bread from my pack. Felixe settles next to me, eyeing the bread hungrily. I break off a chunk and offer it to him. He grabs it in his teeth with a little growl.

"So, where are you from?" I ask. Bram narrows his eyes and I shrug. "We're starting over, remember?"

Bram rolls his eyes and sighs, pulling out his own portion of bread. "Fine. I am from Hounddale, a farming village."

I nod, chewing on my dinner before replying. "Interesting. Any family?"

Bram stands, shaking his head. "Forget this. I am going to set up the tents."

"Wait!" I yell, jumping to my feet. "I'm sorry. I guess there's no way to start over completely, but let's at least try to get to know each other."

Bram sighs, turning to face me. "What do you suggest?"

"I don't know. Maybe . . . I know! Tell me about when you met Astra."

Bram arches his eyebrows. "Are you sure?"

I nod. "Yes. I want to know. I really do."

"I thought you already knew the story."

I shrug. "I know some of it but no details. Besides, I'm interested in your perspective."

Bram considers me for a moment before he nods. "Fine."

"Good. Let's sit and eat while we chat," I reply, sinking down to the ground.

Bram sighs but sits back down. "I am not sure where to start, really."

"Why were you in Timberborn? I know you and Ehren were looking for the twins, but what exactly led you there?"

"Well," Bram says slowly, tearing a piece of bread, "Winnie had fallen down a rabbit hole of information following the stories of the twins. When she discovered they were born near her birthday, she was especially entranced. She shared a few things here and there with Ehren and, when he realized that they were potentially dangerous, he became invested in finding and helping them."

"He wanted to help? Not destroy or eliminate?"

"Ehren's first instinct is always to aid before he does any harm. You have experienced that firsthand yourself," Bram replies, shooting me a knowing look as he takes a bite of food. "Despite the warnings that the twins could destroy the world, he was determined to find a way to save them. He assisted Winnie with her research, and they eventually came to the conclusion that the twins would receive their powers when they turned eighteen. Time was running out, but he used census records to narrow down the village where they were and we headed out. I went a little ahead of the group to scout and find the twins before Ehren arrived."

"And that's how you found Astra? You were looking for her?" I press.

Bram's lips twitch as he resists a smile. "Yes and no. Yes, I was looking for her, but when I first ran into her I had no idea who she was."

"How did you find her?"

Bram gives way to the smile. "She ran into me. Knocked me clean off my feet into the dirt. At first I was annoyed, but then I looked up at her and . . . I know it may be ridiculous, but I felt something for her right away. She was so embarrassed and flustered, but there was something about her that just . . ." He sighs. "She made me feel."

I smile softly. I know exactly what he means.

"So she knocked you off your feet and stole your heart?"

Bram nods, tearing off more bread. "Yes. I knew I had a mission to find the twins, but I was unable to stop thinking about her. I spent a couple hours asking around about the twins, but most people shrugged me off as a nuisance, gave me useless gossip, or ignored me entirely. I could have tried harder but I couldn't really focus on my mission. I sought her out at the festival later that night. I told myself I would simply pursue a friendship to find out what she knew about the twins. After all, she was around the right age, so it was possible they were friends. But the second I saw her in the crowd, I forgot my mission again. I was caught up in her laugh, smile, her eyes, everything about her. She enchanted me."

I smile, once again recognizing the feeling. "When did you realize she was who you were looking for?"

Bram shrugs. "I suspected it slightly when I met Kato. They were very close in age, but they looked nothing alike." He pauses for a moment before meeting my eyes. "That was the first time I saw you in six years."

My stomach twists and I nearly drop the bread in my hands. "You saw me?"

Bram nods. "Yes. You were performing magic tricks."

"I didn't see you."

"I suspected as much."

I scowl at Bram. "Why didn't you confront me?"

"At first, I was too startled by your presence. I thought for sure you were in another country, so finding you in Callenia was a shock in and of itself. I didn't know what to do. Once I regained my senses, I, of course, wanted to run you through then and there."

I pale and swallow. "But you didn't. Why?"

The corner of Bram's lips turns up as he raises his eyebrows. "Why? Did you want me to kill you in the middle of a crowd of revelers?"

I laugh, shaking my head. "No, I suppose not."

Bram laughs softly, shifting. "I knew that the time wasn't right. Despite having only known Astra for a such a short time, I was already foolishly smitten. I figured slaughtering a cheerful performer in front of her was likely *not* the way to win her over. I also needed to keep a low profile until Ehren arrived."

"Well, I appreciate your restraint," I say, lifting my last bite of bread to Bram in a "cheers" motion.

Bram snorts, shaking his head. "You got lucky. When I went back later that night after the festivities ended to confront you, you were already gone."

"I tended to move on quickly back then. Good thing for my neck. Anyway, after you contemplated my murder, how did you and Astra meet again?"

"I actively watched for her the next morning. While we were eating breakfast, she revealed that she was one of the twins."

"What did you think about that?"

Bram smiles, meeting my eyes. "I was relieved. It meant that I had done my job and all the time I spent focusing on her wasn't wasted." His face darkens. "Of course, once she discovered my true reasons for being in Timberborn she wasn't happy. She felt betrayed, and her betrayal hurt more than it should have. Ehren encouraged me to seek her out to mend our relationship and save her life. In the end, she came around and we moved forward."

I nod. "I more or less know the story from here. She trusted you and Ehren, and you saved her life when she came into her powers."

Bram studies me for a long moment before he says, "Did you know Astra was being forced into an arranged marriage?"

My eyes widen, betraying my surprise. "What?"

Bram nods. "Her father had paired her up with one of his associates to fulfill a debt."

Anger roils through me, awakening my darkest magic. "You can't be serious."

"I wish I wasn't, but it is true, nonetheless."

"What happened to him?"

Bram meets my eyes and his mouth turns upward into a hard grin. "She killed him."

The air around me thins and it's difficult to catch a breath as I process his words, what this means.

"She what?"

"She slit his throat with a dagger I gave her."

I still, my eyes locked on Bram. Without warning I'm in the past, the broken shard of glass cutting my hand. The coppery scent of sticky, hot blood flooding my nostrils. I clench my fists in my lap, my breathing uneven.

"Of course," Bram continues, completely unaware of the thoughts rolling through my mind, "she was provoked. He pulled her away from the festival into a dark alley. He was hitting and kicking her. Gods know what else he had in mind."

My fists tighten. "He struck her?"

"Yes. She called out to Kato, but by the time we found

her, she had already taken action. I used my sword to finish him off, but he was already as good as dead. It was in that moment I knew I would do anything for her."

Astra slit a man's throat in self-defense, just like I did. We're not so different. We're not . . . Another thought strikes me and I struggle to keep my emotions in check as my magic ebbs within me. I long to unleash it, but somehow manage to keep it reined.

"Where were you?" I ask, my voice hard, my accent thick. "What were ya doing when she was attacked? Why weren't ya there?"

Fear and regret flash across Bram's face. "I was nearby, but I let my guard down."

"You seem to do that a lot," I snap, instantly regretting my words.

Bram meets my eyes, his fury evident. "You think I don't know that? You think I don't realize how badly I failed Astra? You think those moments don't replay in my mind over and over? Because they do. I failed her and I know." He drops his gaze to the flames between us, his shoulders dropping. "That is why you are better for her."

His words steal my breath, my anger snuffing out. "What?"

He raises his eyes back to mine and I see how broken he is. "You have always been there for her, even before you were bonded. Even when she was mine. You were there, expecting nothing in return. I hated you for that."

"I . . ."

Bram waves me off. "I am grateful, of course, but it did not make it much easier when she chose you."

I smile softly and nod. "I can imagine. But, surely, there

are other girls out there you could love just as much as, if not more than, Astra?"

Bram shrugs, glancing away. "Perhaps, but if they exist I have not met them. To be honest, I have not had much opportunity to find anyone." I laugh, shaking my head and Bram glares at me. "What?"

"You're the Captain of Ehren's Guard, mate. You'd have a line of girls if you'd just relax."

Bram shakes his head. "I don't want a girl I have to play a part for. I want a girl I can be myself around. I cannot explain it, but Astra was immediately that girl for me."

I nod, mulling over his words. "I suppose I understand that, but most girls will be chased away by your scowl before you even have a chance to show them your charming personality. Why don't we practice? Pretend I'm a pretty girl and flirt with me."

Bram stands, shaking his head. "I am going to set up the tents."

"Come on, Bram. Let's try."

Bram ignores me. "Do you need help setting up your own tent?"

"We could share a tent and stay up all night talking," I offer with a wink as I stand.

Bram glares at me. "That is not happening. Do you need help or not?"

I shake my head. "Naw, I've got it."

"Good."

We fall back into our pattern of silence as we set up our tents. I'm about to enter mine when Bram calls out to me.

"Alak."

I look up, meeting his eyes. His face is hard and stoic, his shoulders straight and tense. He's every bit the deadly soldier.

"Yes?"

He hesitates, as if he's rethinking what he wanted to say.

"Promise me you will never hurt her."

My heart stills as his words sink in. I smile weakly.

"Never. I would rather die than hurt her."

Bram nods once. "I figured as much, but I had to say it. Goodnight, Alak."

He disappears into his tent, but I stand there a moment, staring toward where he stood moments before. I almost feel guilty. Bram's a good man. In the end, however, it was Astra's choice and she chose me. I smile and duck into my tent. She chose me and I chose her. We are more than our soul bond. I don't deserve this happiness, but I'll take it. I'll savor every moment, even as I wait with bated breath for her to change her mind, for our happiness to be ripped away.

I settle down on my bedroll and feel Astra's absence keenly. The bond is still here, but it's weak. It makes my heart hurt. Not too much longer and I will be able to go back to her. I take a deep breath and close my eyes. I can do this. I have to.

BRAM DRAGS me from my tent the next morning before the sun has even fully risen. At first we travel in silence, but eventually the silence gets to me and I start singing more drinking songs. Bram sighs and I expect him to tell me to shut up.

"Do you know anything besides those ridiculous songs?" he says, his voice even and controlled.

I shrug. "I know a few other songs." I shoot him a wide grin. "Any requests?"

He's quiet for a moment before he replies. "I know a few war ballads."

My eyes widen. "Are you offering to sing with me?"

He scowls, focusing on the road ahead. "If you intend to continue being ridiculous for our entire trip, you might as well sing songs I can remotely enjoy."

My grin grows. "Anything you say, mate. Teach me your bloody ballads."

Bram releases a long sigh. "Forget it."

"No, you can't go back on this! Come on. Teach me one ballad."

"All right. One."

"Whatever you say, mate."

Bram relinquishes and teaches me a war ballad. As expected, it's bloody and dark. I kind of love it. In return, I teach him a ballad from Athiedor about the gods descending to earth. Despite agreeing to only one, Bram and I go back and forth for a few hours sharing songs and singing together. By the time we stop for lunch, the air is noticeably lighter between us. Shortly after lunch, however, a cold, dreary rain drives us to silence. We end up stopping early and setting up camp to get out of the rain. I take the moments of silence to begin a letter to Astra. Felixe curls up next to me, sleeping soundly as I write. I'm only a few lines in when I hear a noise outside my tent. Curious, I set down the letter and step outside.

"Bram, wha—"

My words are cut off as a hand slams over my mouth, a second hand holding a dagger to my throat.

"My boots are new, so I'd rather not get blood on them,"

a low voice says in my ear. "Let us take what we need and we'll be on our way."

I swallow, my heart racing. I manage a nod and the man holding me shoves me to the ground, mud splattering across my face. He presses his foot on my back to keep me down.

"Good. Stay down, keeping your forehead and palms to the ground."

I grit my teeth but follow his orders even after his foot is gone. I gather my magic, weighing my next move. I can attack, but I don't know how many of them there are. If I attack and miss some of them, I could be dead within seconds, especially if they also have magic. Where the hell is Bram? It seems it's not only Astra he abandons in a time of need.

"Doesn't look like they have much," a second gruff voice mutters.

"Nothing much in this tent," a female voice says from my left where Bram's tent stands.

No new voices join theirs. So three intruders? I can handle three. Probably. Maybe.

"I found basic supplies and a letter," the man who threatened me says, stepping out from my tent.

I clench my teeth and dig my fingers into the mud. I take a deep breath and leap to my feet, magic swirling around my fingertips. Three pairs of frightened eyes blink back at me, clearly startled that I didn't obey orders.

"I'd like my letter back," I say, extending my hand toward the young man who holds my things.

His eyes widen and, gods, he's young—fifteen, maybe sixteen. He looks genuinely terrified as he takes me in. The man standing to his left steps forward, putting himself between me and the boy. A quick glance between the two has me guessing he's the boy's older brother, but he's still likely younger than me by a couple years.

"These things are ours now," the older brother says, pointing a blade toward me.

I raise my chin. "I don't think so."

I strike with my magic, swift and direct. It's a basic blow, just meant to knock them back a step. I don't really have much attack magic without Astra near, but I hope it's enough.

"You have magic," the girl whispers in awe.

I look at her for the first time. She's probably the oldest of the three. She's possibly related to the boys—their sister if I had to guess—but where they have dark hair and eyes, she has long blond hair and bright eyes.

"Aye," I reply, not backing down. "I do have magic, and while I have no intent to hurt you, I will use it to my advantage."

The girl and older boy exchange a quick glance. Before they can respond, Bram leaps from the shadows, blade gleaming. He points the tip of his sword at the younger boy, who gulps and stumbles back, dropping my things.

"We don't want any trouble," the older boy says, stepping back to place his arm protectively in front of his brother.

"You should have thought about that before you broke into our camp," I snap.

"Please," the girl says, taking a step toward me. "We really don't mean any harm. We're just desperate."

"How so?" Bram asks, not taking his eyes off the boys.

"Our village was destroyed by the Dragkonians," the girl explains quickly. "My brothers and I were lucky. We managed to get away, but most of our village wasn't so fortunate. We fled so quickly we weren't able to take any supplies with us."

"So," I say, meeting her eyes, "you thought stealing was better than simply asking us for help?"

The girl drops her gaze to the ground. "We've been on the run for nearly a week now. We've tried asking for help, but most travelers are unwilling."

"We're trying to find the refugees," the youngest cuts in.

"The refugees?" Bram asks, still not lowering his sword.

The boy nods. "Yes. We heard they were gathering near here. We heard they can help us and train us."

I exchange a quick look with Bram.

"Train you how?" I ask slowly.

"With magic *and* swords," the older boy replies.

"You have magic?"

The older boy nods toward his brother and sister. "They do but have no idea how to use it."

Bram and I exchange another look.

"And you're seeking someone to train you in magic amongst the refugees?" Bram asks, glancing between the three siblings as he lowers his sword.

Without Bram's sword pointed at them, the boys relax.

"There's a camp of refugees that accepts both magic and non-magic out this way according to the rumors we heard in the last village we visited. We don't want to split up, so we're looking for them. If we can find someone to really train us, that's a bonus," the girl replies.

"We're actually looking for the refugees as well," I volunteer.

The siblings exchange a look, scowling.

"Why?" the younger brother asks. "You don't look like refugees."

I meet Bram's eyes and he shakes his head almost imperceptibly. Great. So the truth is off the table.

"We might not look like refugees," I answer with a shrug, "but we've been displaced as well."

"Why don't you three stay here tonight," Bram suggests. "We will share some of our food rations and you can take one of the tents for the night. We can continue our journey together."

"We don't even know you," the girl says sharply, placing her hands on her hips. "For all we know, you could be murderers."

Bram shrugs, sheathing his sword. "Trust us or not, the offer stands."

"Come on, Priss," the youngest says, his voice almost a whine. "I'm hungry and cold."

The older boy meets his sister's eyes and shrugs. "I wouldn't mind some food and shelter."

"Fine," the girl sighs. "We'll stay tonight and talk it over."

Bram nods. "That works for me. Alak, get them some food."

"What?" I cry. "Why me? *You* get them some food."

Bram arches an eyebrow. "Do you have problem with giving them food?"

"I . . . No, but why can't you do it? Why are you ordering me around?"

"They're either siblings or lovers," the younger brother whispers.

I say "We're not brothers" at the same time Bram snaps "We are not lovers."

The girl giggles. "Whatever you say."

I start to smile but when Bram shoots me a look that could kill I bury it quickly. Together, we make sure our guests have a decent dinner before getting them set up in my tent. I don't trust them, so I take everything I have into the tent with me and Bram. It's a small tent, no more than nine or so feet wide. With both of us plus all our things it's a little crowded. When Felixe decides to reappear, it feels even smaller. In order to put aside any thoughts of us being lovers, Bram stacks everything between our bedrolls, pushing us up against opposite sides of the tent.

"You know," I say, grinning over at Bram as I adjust my bedroll and lie down. "You could have a worse lover than me. I'd take good care of all your needs. I have experience, you know."

"I still have my sword, Alak."

I grin, propping my head up on my hand. "Is sword code for—"

"For the love of all the gods, shut up," Bram mumbles.

I laugh and settle down beneath my blanket. "Goodnight, lover."

Bram only grumbles as he lies down, making himself comfortable. I can't see his face, but I'm pretty sure he's smiling.

CHAPTER ELEVEN

ALAK

When we wake the next morning, the siblings are gone.

"Well, I guess that is a firm no on traveling together." Bram sighs, staring off in the distance as if his eagle eyes can spot them.

"At least they left our tent and horses," I muse with a shrug.

"I suppose that is something," Bram mumbles. "Let's not dawdle. I think we must be on the right trail. If I am correct, we should run across a town by the end of the day."

I raise my eyebrows. "Do we want to visit a town? I thought we were trying to avoid people and keep a low profile."

"We are, but we can't completely stick to the shadows if we want to find out information. If people are fleeing towns in search of these refugee camps, that means gossip is circulating as to possible whereabouts. Our unexpected guests did mention rumors from a nearby village. If we don't narrow our search soon, we could end up wandering aimlessly for longer than necessary."

I nod. "I guess that's logical enough, but I thought Ehren narrowed it down pretty well already? At least that's the way you made it seem."

"He did, but even he is not sure the location is as precise as it could be. It is a lot of conjunctures based on secondhand information. Ehren also has a theory the camp may be moving to avoid detection. Either way, we need more information. I still think we should keep visits to towns and villages to a minimum, but I would like to confirm we are going in the correct direction before we end up too far off course."

"You're the boss, Captain," I say with an exaggerated salute.

Bram groans and rolls his eyes. "I don't know why I thought traveling with you would be much different than Ehren, but it is apparent I misjudged."

I grin. "Did you just compare me to your best friend? I knew you liked me."

"I was comparing your reckless immaturity to his. There is a difference."

I shake my head, clapping a hand to Bram's shoulder. "You can't take it back now."

Bram sighs and shakes me off. "Pack quickly so we can get on the road. If you are not ready in five minutes, I am leaving without you."

Grinning, I pack up my things, realizing with a pang of guilt I never finished my letter to Astra. I carefully fold the mud-crusted paper and carefully pack it, determined to finish it when we stop for the night.

The ground is muddy and yesterday's rain clouds hang

over us, making the day gray and dull. Thankfully, the rain holds off. We pause only briefly for a quick lunch, eager to make it to the next town. A little before sunset, we finally arrive, but it's not a welcome sight. The village is a remnant of what it once was. At least half of the shops and dwellings are destroyed—some by fire, others by sheer force. Rubble decorates the streets and the people that wander about duck immediately indoors when they spot us. When we stop and tie our horses outside a tavern called The Speckled Pig, things look even worse. Felixe hops onto my shoulder with a whimper.

"What are you here for?" a man barks the moment we enter.

My eyes fall on a stout bartender, glaring at us as he wipes a mug. Felixe whines and disappears before the man can notice him.

"We're just traveling through," I reply, trying to make my voice sound as carefree and light as possible.

The man still has his guard up, not swayed the slightest by my words.

"No one is just traveling through these days. If you're looking for handouts, I've got nothing. This is business, not a—"

"Please, Sir," Bram says, holding up his hand. "We are patrons. We expect nothing for free."

The man arches an eyebrow and looks from me to Bram. "You'll pay, huh? Because my prices have gone up due to supply issues."

I grit my teeth but force a smile. "We understand times are hard."

The man nods, still looking wary. "Fine then. Take a seat

and I'll bring you ale and food if you want it, though all I got is stew."

"Stew will be fine," Bram says with a smile as he walks toward an empty table.

I follow him, eyes of the other patrons following us as we choose a booth at the back corner.

"I get the feeling we aren't welcome here," I mutter to Bram once we're seated. "I doubt we'll find anything useful."

Bram nods, letting his eyes scan the room. "Things are far worse than I expected, though we have to try."

"Fine," I grumble, easing back into my seat. "But if they drag us out of our beds and murder us in the middle of the night, I'm telling Astra it was your fault."

Bram sighs but doesn't reply. When the bartender brings us our food, Bram inquires about a room. They go back and forth and agree on a sum that is far too much for one room. Once that negotiation is done, Bram goes for information.

"We were also wondering what you know about the refugee camp open to magic and non-magic alike," Bram asks, his voice casual.

The man rears back like he's been slapped. "What do you need to know about that for? You're not refugees."

I scowl up at the man. "How could you possibly know that?"

"You're fed and have coins," a sharp voice says from behind the bartender.

I jerk around in my seat to see a young woman a few years older than me approaching, her eyes hard and cold.

"Refugees are people fleeing their homes, and you look too well-kept to be fleeing," she continues. "You look like hunters."

Whispers reverberate around the tavern. I exchange a look with Bram, but he shrugs and shakes his head. Whatever the woman is talking about baffles him as much as it does me.

"Hunters?" I repeat. "I don't even know what a hunter is."

"Some people call 'em scouts," another man volunteers, rising from his seat to join the woman. "They go around gathering people up for coin."

"We really have no clue what you are talking about," Bram says. "The truth is that our city was attacked and we managed to escape. We regrouped before setting out again, but we mean no harm. We want to help."

"How can you help?" the woman demands, crossing her arms across her chest.

Bram looks over at me and I shake my head. These people are crazy and there's no way I want them to know who we really are. Now is *not* the time to come clean. Bram, however, decides to live dangerously.

"My name is Captain Bramfield. I am Captain of Prince Ehren's Guard."

I kick Bram under the table as hard as I can. He shoots me a sharp glare but continues.

"We are aware that the kingdom is in disarray, and Prince Ehren is seeking a way to move forward. He cannot do so, however, until we know the full extent of damage."

Those already standing exchange a look that appears very much to me like they've just openly agreed to murder both Bram and I and cover it up. I wonder if Astra would hate me terribly if I up and left Bram and his stupid, big mouth behind. The few patrons that were seated until this point all stand and gather behind the woman, mumbling amongst themselves. Bram straightens. He doesn't seem intimidated by the growing mob, but I can tell by his shift in posture he has his hand on the hilt of his sword. I wonder how many people he can take on his own.

"Prince Ehren ran away," one the newcomers spits. "He saw trouble and he hightailed it to safety. He don't care about us or any refugees."

"That's right!" someone else yells. "He's probably gathering the scraps of those his father and the Dragkonians left behind. He just needs bodies for his war."

I stand to my feet before I even realize what I'm doing, my hands clenched at my sides.

"You're wrong," I hiss.

Great. I'm as bloody insane as Bram.

"Alak," Bram whispers. "Sit down. I can handle this."

I shake my head. I've gone this far so I might as well go in all the way. "No, these people need the truth."

"The truth?" the woman scoffs. "We already know the truth."

"Clearly, ya don't," I reply, my accent sharp. "When Ehren saw that Embervein was under attack he didn't run from battle. He ran *into* it, even though he knew he couldn't stand against the Dragkonians. He risked his life for his kingdom."

"Well, where's he now?" the bartender demands, glancing around like he expects Ehren to pop out if we're speaking the truth.

"He is gathering allies and reinforcements," Bram answers calmly as he stands. "He sent us to find the refugees and gather them together. Those that wish to fight for his cause to take back the kingdom and instill peace are welcome to join him. Those that wish to remain behind will also have his full support. He wants to build his kingdom back up from the ashes and return Callenia to a level of greatness only dreamed of."

Bram's voice resonates off the walls of the tavern and I'm reminded of how he manages to stay in a position of authority despite his prickly personality and permanent scowl. He isn't just the best friend of the prince. He's a trained soldier who can command an army. All eyes are on him, weighing his words, but he doesn't shy away. He meets their eyes with confidence befitting his position. I smile in pride.

"And who are you?" the woman demands, nodding to me. "He's the Captain of the Guard, but who are you?"

Answers swirl through my brain as my smile falters. My guess is that "I'm the lover of the Court Sorceress" is probably not going to get us the support we need. I straighten my shoulders, trying to mimic Bram's confidence.

"I'm a good friend of the prince who is well versed in magic. I'm using my magic to help find the refugees, and I plan on helping train those with magic who don't know what to do with their new powers," I answer as honestly as I can.

"What say you, Elias?" the woman says, turning her head slightly to speak to a young boy behind her, no more than thirteen or fourteen years old.

The boy steps forward, brushing his shaggy brown hair out of his face as he studies Bram and then me.

"They aren't lying," he says slowly, narrowing his eyes, "but it isn't the whole truth."

"Well, what aren't you saying?" the woman snaps.

I ignore her and focus on the boy, offering him a smile as my Syphon powers reach out toward him, tasting his magic. "You have magic that detects lies, don't you?"

Elias hesitates, eyes wide, before giving me one sharp nod.

"I have illusion magic," I reply. "Would you like to see it? I won't hurt you."

"Be careful of tricks," the woman hisses, placing a hand on the boy's shoulder.

Elias tilts his head, studying me, but there's no fear in his eyes. "It's safe. I'd like to see it."

I grin. "As you wish."

I raise my hands palms up and close my eyes. I envision a forest glade and call the memory forward, pushing it into the air around us. I hear gasps and open my eyes. My illusion works in full force, surrounding us in a forest teeming with life. The boy's eyes are bright as he looks around, and even the more disagreeable of patrons seem almost delighted by my presentation. Even Bram looks impressed.

"Now, Elias, you can tell if I'm lying, right?" He meets my eyes and nods. "Good. Then listen to me when I promise that we mean no harm and this world"—I motion to the bright forest around us—"is what we want to bring to all of Callenia. We want to restore peace and harmony. We want to make Callenia great where magic and non-magic people are equal in every way. Yes, we have our secrets because we're protecting those we love, but we aren't lying about our intentions. We want to save you, not harm you."

Elias holds my gaze for a moment before he breaks into a grin and looks up at the woman. "He really wants to help."

The woman releases a long breath as I allow my illusion to fade. She studies me for a moment before she shakes her head.

"Fine. I'll tell you what we know while you eat your food, but then you're on your own."

Bram smiles, taking a seat. "Those terms are acceptable."

The woman slides in next to me and I scoot over to give her ample room. Elias slides in next to Bram.

"Well, to start with, my name is Alis. I've lived here in Greenhollow my whole life. We never had any trouble. We're a small merchant town and nothing more. When magic returned, we were baffled. It started showing up in little things. The healer's assistant suddenly had actual healing magic. Elias could tell when people were lying. A lot of people had magic far less incredible, but we were sure it was magic all the same. We were only getting used to it when the king's men showed up. They dragged people from their homes. Anyone accused of magic, whether it had any real claim or not, was taken. Those that went willingly were locked up and taken away for gods know what."

"And those that didn't go willingly?" I ask quietly, even though I fear I already know the answer.

Alis meets my eyes with a harsh glare and I shrink back. "Those that fought even the slightest were slaughtered in the street to make an example."

I swear under my breath as Bram straightens.

"Prince Ehren had nothing to do with that, I can assure you. He fought his father on every order and decree."

Alis nods. "We heard rumors confirming as much, and it gave us hope until we heard the prince fled Embervein. We lost even more hope when news reached us that he had fled the country seeking asylum with allies."

I shake my head. "It wasn't that simple. Yes, Ehren fled, but it wasn't for his own preservation. He had a plan. He went to those allies to secure funds and soldiers to fight against his father. Even after Kato turned on him, he continued gathering resources. He's still gathering resources and armies. He hasn't given up or abandoned anyone."

"He is right," Bram says with a firm nod. "While I can't tell you where he is right now for security purposes, I can confirm that he is currently putting himself at potential risk to secure more forces for his kingdom. He would never abandon Callenia, even if it meant his own safety."

Alis glares at Bram but Elias nods. "He's telling the truth."

"Truth or not, it doesn't help us now, does it? This Kato you speak of is worse than the king. His Dragkonians attacked our village, stealing what little we had. They whisked away many of the magical citizens that remained, gathering others for slaves and breeding. They also slaughtered us without a care, destroying our buildings with force and fire. There exists no weapon that can stand against them. Even if your prince can gather an army and find a way to fund them, they can't fight the Dragkonians."

Bram inhales sharply, hesitating as he chooses his next words carefully. "We have a way to defeat them, but it is something that takes time."

Alis narrows her eyes at Bram before glancing to Elias, who looks up at Bram, his face set in a scowl.

"He's not lying," Elias says slowly. "I think there's something he's not telling us, though."

Alis crosses her arms in a challenge. "Well?"

Bram smiles. "Of course I am not telling you everything. I cannot go around sharing classified information. If Kato and his minions were to return they could torture you for information."

"Fine," Alis huffs.

"Now," Bram says, leaning forward and meeting Alis's

eyes. "Where can I find those refugees?"

"Do you have a map?"

I grin and grab my bag from the floor, withdrawing a copy of Ehren's map. "We do."

I scoot our mugs of ale and bowls of stew out of the way and spread the map across the table. Alis scrutinizes the map before pointing toward the area Ehren already circled.

"It seems you already know where to go."

Bram looks from the map to Alis. "You're sure?"

Alis crosses her arms again and glares at Bram. "You doubt me?"

"Yes."

Alis stiffens. "Then why bother asking?"

"Because even slightly inaccurate information is better than none at all," Bram answers with a shrug. "And while I don't doubt that the marked area is correct, it is a wide area. I think you can perhaps narrow down our search for us."

Alis releases a long breath through her nose. "Fine. They say that you need to reach this forest." She taps a grouping of trees near the circled area. "There are supposed to be clues once you arrive that will guide you the rest of the way."

"Clues?" I ask. "What sort of clues?"

Alis shrugs. "Don't know. I haven't done it, have I? Some say magical clues, others say clues trackers will pick up on. I suspect it's a bit of both. If you two are who you claim to be, you shouldn't have any trouble."

Bram considers her words with a nod. "Thank you. Is there anything else you can share?"

Alis shakes her head almost too quickly. "No. Just get out of our town and do something to actually help us."

"I give you my word—we will do everything we can and more."

Alis gives a stiff nod and stands, Elias rising with her. They return to their table without another word. I quickly roll up the map and return it to my bag. Bram and I eat in silence before retreating upstairs to our room. It's a small room with two beds, a bedside table between them with a washbowl and candle.

"Do you think she really told the truth?" I ask after the door is shut and barred.

Bram nods with a sigh. "I believe so. I suppose our only choice is to keep following the trail already laid out for us."

"How long will it be before we reach the forest?"

"Two days is my most likely estimate."

I nod and settle down on one of the beds. I riffle through my bag and withdraw my letter. Felixe appears next to me and licks my hand. I smile and scratch his head.

"You are writing Astra?" Bram asks, nodding to the letter in my hand.

I look up at him. "I thought it best. I was writing last night when we got interrupted, but I guess it's better I waited. There's more to write now." Bram nods, glancing away. "Anything you want me to add?"

Bram snaps his gaze back to me. "No. Why?"

I shake my head with a shrug. "No reason, mate," I mumble. "I was just asking."

Bram relaxes and sinks down on the other bed with a sigh. "No, nothing I need you to add."

"All right. If you think of anything, just let me know."

Bram nods and lies down on the bed, staring up at the ceiling. I make quick work of my letter and double check with Bram before sending it off. Once Felixe disappears, I settle down into my own bed. It's not long before sleep claims me.

CHAPTER TWELVE

EHREN

I t's good to be back on Dauntless. He feels like a piece of the old me—the me that was happy, or at least happier. Our first day of travel is easy and smooth. Without any magic users, we have to rely on a basic camouflage spell and our senses as soldiers. When night falls, we keep our camp simple, setting up one of our two tents. Lorrell and I take the first watch while Cal and Pascal sleep, switching midway through the night.

The second day is also filled with fairly easy travel. We make good time and reach the nearby mountain range around midday. We naturally slow due to the incline and rocky path. Once night falls, we're forced to stop. There's no ground level enough for the tent, so we make camp against the side of the mountain, our campfire keeping us warm enough. Tonight, I take first watch with Pascal while Cal and Lorrell sleep. A couple hours into my shift, I drift off and Pascal doesn't bother to wake me.

"You needed sleep and, well, you're the prince," Pascal mumbles when I confront him the next morning.

"Exactly," I say, my voice cold and hard. "I'm the prince, so if I say I'm taking first watch, I'm taking first watch. You defied a direct order."

Pascal shrinks back from me, exchanging a wary glance with his brother. I sigh and turn away, shaking my head. I wish I had a bed I could crawl into so I could disappear. We're not that far from the Summer Palace. We could turn around, but that would just be more proof that I can't do this, more proof I'm truly a failure.

"Just respect my wishes next time," I say, not bothering to look at Pascal.

"Yes, of course," he mumbles, tacking on a quick "Your Majesty."

A cloud of darkness swarms my thoughts as I pack up my bag. I was a fool for believing I could do this. Even my own Guard don't respect me. I'm a farce of a prince. Can I hold it together once we get to Ascaria? My hand trembles as I attempt to attach my bag to Dauntless.

"Let me," Cal says, his voice soft as he catches my hand.

I look up at him, meeting his eyes. He holds my gaze for a moment before looking down at the bag, his fingers lingering against mine as he takes over adjusting my pack. I jerk my hands back, dropping them to my sides.

"Thanks," I mumble, staring down at my feet.

"Pascal," Cal calls over his shoulder. "You and Lorrell go on ahead and make sure the path is safe. Ehren and I won't be far behind."

I look up at Cal, my brow furrowed in confusion. He meets my eyes and smiles, but doesn't say anything—not until Lorrell and Pascal are gone.

"Are you okay?"

"Is that why you sent them on ahead? So you could ask if I'm okay?" I snap.

Why am I snapping at Cal? I swallow and turn away from him.

"That's exactly why I sent them on ahead," Cal answers, his voice lighter than I expect. He places his hand on my shoulder. "Now, are you okay?"

Tears sting my eyes as I nod, jaw clenched. His grip tightens on my shoulder and he turns me around, his eyes searching my face.

"Ehren, are you okay?" He emphasizes each word, his eyes locked with mine.

"I . . ." I swallow, shaking my head. "I don't know."

"Because you don't have to be okay. You can fall apart if you need to. You just need to get back up."

"But what happens if I can't get back up?" I whisper, my voice trembling.

Cal reaches out and takes my hand in his. "You can get back up, because I'll always be here for you, to help you stand."

I link my fingers with Cal's and tighten my grip on his hand. Cal's eyes go wide and drop to our hands, like he didn't even realize what he had done. The corner of my lips turn up slightly as I release his hand.

"Sorry. Instinct."

Cal meets my eyes and his lips part. "It's okay."

We stand, frozen, lost in each other's eyes for a moment before Cal pulls his gaze away.

"We should catch up with Lorrell and Pascal. We don't want them to get too far ahead."

I nod and mount Dauntless. Cal and I ride side-by-side in silence, catching up with the other two quickly. We spend the day shrouded in awkward, tense silence. Shortly before nightfall, we find a flat clearing complete with a small mountain lake.

"We should stop here for the night," I say, looking around. "It's not likely we'll find a better spot, so we might as well take advantage."

The others nod their agreement as they dismount.

"Set up both tents. I'll place some wards around us so we won't have to worry about shifts tonight."

"Are you sure?" Lorrell asks with a scowl.

I offer him a forced smile. "I'm positive."

Lorrell relaxes and he and Pascal start setting up the tents and gathering wood for a fire. I take my water skein to the lake to refill. Cal follows with his.

"I don't like the look of this water," Cal mumbles as I squat down at the water's edge.

I glance up at him. He's staring off toward the center of the lake. I follow his gaze and scowl.

"Why? It looks normal to me."

Cal scowls at the water like it's a puzzle he needs to decipher. "It's too murky."

I chuckle, shaking my head. "Lots of water is murky. That doesn't make it bad. Hand me your skein."

I reach up toward him and he places his water skein in my hand. I quickly fill it and stand, giving it back.

"Thanks," he says. "You didn't have to fill mine. I could have done it."

"No, I needed you to keep an eye on that water," I tease, bumping my shoulder against his.

He smiles. "You seem to be feeling a little better."

I nod and take a deep breath. "Yeah, I feel okay right now. I think the fresh air is helping."

"I'm glad, Ehren. I'm really glad."

I smile. "Me too. Let's see how long it sticks."

We rejoin Lorrell and Pascal, who have the camp mostly set up. We debate briefly over whether to use some of our rations or fish for our dinner. In the end, we decide to try our hand at fishing. We only have one net to fish with, so Lorrell and Pascal go first. In typical brotherly fashion, they end up arguing more than successfully catching anything, but they do manage to wrangle one fish into their net while Cal and I sit watching from the campsite.

"Just put the net deeper into the water," Pascal says, jerking the net away from Lorrell.

"I know what I'm doing!" Lorrell argues, yanking it back.

"We are never going to have enough fish for dinner if we don't help them," Cal whispers, leaning toward me.

I chuckle, glancing over at Cal. "I think you're right. Should we take over?"

Cal meets my eyes and grins. "I think we'd better if we want to eat."

I push up from the ground and offer Cal my hand. He grins up at me as he accepts and I pull him to his feet.

"Pretty sure I'm supposed to be the one helping you up. You are the prince after all."

I shake my head. "As if that has ever mattered."

I lead the way down to the water and tell Lorrell and Pascal to go ahead and gut the fish they caught and get it over the fire. I roll up my pant legs and wade into the water, Cal not far behind me with the net. We work together and manage to catch five more fish. Cal takes the fish up to Lorrell and Pascal while I use the net to try to catch one or two more before the sun finishes setting. I feel a flurry of motion around my ankles and look down. I'm puzzled at the large number of creatures and fish scurrying past me. They don't seem threatened by me at all. By the time it registers why they might be reacting this way, it's too late. I hear someone scream my name behind me, but I don't look back. I look up.

Charging toward me is the most terrifying creature I've ever seen. It's ten times the size of a horse, covered in green slimy scales that shimmer in the evening light as water slides from its back. It has a snout at least three yards long, lined with rows of jagged teeth. Its long tail whips through the water as it claws its way directly toward me.

I reach instinctively for my sword, only to realize that I've left it near the tents. I dodge to my left, stumbling in the muck of the lake. I splash headfirst into the shallow water, twisting onto my back. The creature lunges toward me, its mouth wide, eager to consume me. I squeeze my eyes shut, waiting for my impending death, but it doesn't come. There's a loud splash followed by an earth-shaking roar. I open my eyes to find Cal standing over me, his sword buried to the hilt in the creature's neck. I scramble to my feet as he jerks his blade, tearing open the creature's throat, blood and guts spilling over us. I'm frozen in place, blinking in disbelief, my heart pounding in my ears, as Cal jerks his sword from the creature, shoving the body away with his foot. He turns to me, eyes wide.

"Are you okay?" he asks, his voice quivering as his eyes search me frantically for any sign of injury.

I nod, swallowing hard. "I—I think so." I glance over at the creature's corpse, half-hidden in the bloody water. "What is that thing?"

"I have no idea, but we should get out of the water in case there are more."

As we stumble from the lake, Lorrell turns his head to puke while Pascal places a hand on his brother's back, staring at me and Cal, face pale. I'm suddenly very aware of the blood and gore in my hair and on my clothes.

"Why don't you two go change?" Pascal suggests, his voice thin. He looks like he might copy his brother at any moment. "We'll keep an eye out for any more creatures."

I nod and duck into the nearest tent, Cal following me. Our bags are already in the corner. I dig through mine and find a change of clothes and discard my shirt, throwing it as far from me as I can.

"I, uh, I can leave you to change first."

I turn and look at Cal. He's avoiding looking at me, his eyes focused on the ground.

"I don't mind if you change at the same time—unless it makes you uncomfortable."

Cal raises his eyes to mine and nods. He hesitantly lifts his shirt over his head, revealing a muscular torso that steals my breath. Cal is always so reserved. I've rarely seen him so . . . casual. And believe you me, I remember every moment. It's impossible not to take a second to drink in and appreciate his beauty. Cal stills under my gaze and I realize I'm staring. I clear my throat and turn away, a blush coloring my cheeks. I go to remove my pants when I realize how much of the creature is on my skin.

"We should really wash this off," I say my back still to Cal.

"You can't be serious. We cannot go back in that water."

I turn back around and face Cal, trying very hard to focus on his face. "We're covered in blood and guts. Changing is only going to remove one layer. Lorrell and Pascal can watch from the shore as we—"

146

"No," Cal says, cutting me off. I arch an eyebrow and he glances away again. "I wouldn't be comfortable with that."

I take a tentative step toward him. "Are you comfortable with me? We can watch out for each other. Would that work?"

Cal glances at me briefly, the tips of his ears flushed red, and nods. "As long as you'd be comfortable, I wouldn't mind."

The corner of my mouth turns up into a smile. "I'm quite comfortable with that."

Cal's eyes shoot up to meet mine and I laugh. Cal shakes his head and a smile plays at the corner of his lips.

"Grab your clean clothes," I say, grabbing my own from my bag. "That way, we can change down by the water."

Cal nods, fiddling with the filthy shirt in his hands, debating if he wants to slide it back on.

"I can have Lorrell and Pascal go off and do something before we head back to the water, so we can walk down without having to put our clothes back on."

"No, it's fine," Cal says, forcing a smile as he slips the shirt over his head. "We should probably rinse out our clothes, anyway."

"Fair point," I reply, plucking up my own discarded shirt, but I don't put it back on. "Let's go, then. We don't have much daylight left."

Cal follows me out of the tent and down to the water. We go around a slight crook in the mountain for a little privacy out of the direct line of sight of Pascal and Lorrell and away from the bloody water. We quickly shed the rest of our clothes, taking them with us into the water to wash away some of the gore. I wade in first, turning my back so Cal can enter the water without my eyes on him. Even without looking his way, I'm very aware of his every movement as we wash quickly in the icy water. Cal slinks from the lake first, and I follow once he's had a chance to begin dressing. He averts his eyes as I quickly pull on a clean pair of pants. I go to put on my shirt, but Cal stops me.

"You still have a bit of something in your hair," he says, brushing his hand through my wet locks and removing a small green scale and tossing it away.

My heart stills under his touch, my breath catching in my throat. My eyes meet his as he drops his hand. He's so close.

I tilt my head, grinning. "Do you need to check for more? I probably missed a lot, considering how quickly I washed."

Cal flushes as his eyes flick to my hair. "I don't see any more."

His gaze drops to my bare chest before he jerks his eyes away, stepping back quickly. I frown.

"Do I make you uncomfortable?" I ask slowly. "I don't mean to, if I do."

Cal pulls his shirt over his head as he turns to me, forcing a smile. "You're the person I'm the most comfortable around."

"Really?" I challenge, arching an eyebrow. "Because if this is you being comfortable around someone, I would hate to see you uncomfortable."

Cal glances toward the water, avoiding my eyes as he answers. "It's not you. I promise. I feel generally uncomfortable in situations like this. I always have. It's something I'm working on, working through. It's difficult to . . ."

He trails off and I nod, slipping on my shirt.

"If I ever make you feel uncomfortable in the slightest, please, let me know."

Cal nods and meets my eyes. "I will."

I take a step toward him. "I really want you to be comfortable around me. As comfortable as you were with—"

I drop off, unable to complete the sentence. A shadow flickers across Cal's face and guilt stabs my chest. I squeeze my eyes shut, clenching my hands by my sides.

"I'm sorry," I mutter, turning my back to Cal. If I look away, I don't have to see his pain. "I didn't mean—"

I startle as Cal's hand falls on my shoulder. I turn my head just enough to look at Cal.

"It's fine," Cal says, his voice barely above a whisper. "Talking about Makin makes me miss him, yes, but it also makes him seem alive again, in some ways."

I turn to face him and his hand falls from my shoulder.

"Are you sure?"

Cal nods, a sad smile on his lips. "Yes. And I want to be as comfortable around you as I was around Makin. I really do." He pauses, glancing away for a moment before he adds, "Maybe even more so."

I open my mouth to ask he what he means, but he pulls away before I can get any words out.

"The fish we caught smell delicious and I'm starving," he says, striding around the corner toward the camp. "Don't forget your wet clothes. We can dry them by the fire."

I smile and follow, my own stomach grumbling in anticipation of dinner.

After dinner, I add more wards around our campsite— wards that will protect us from detection and from any other creatures that may consider us tasty snacks. Pascal and Lorrell take one tent while Cal and I settle into the other. Cal lies down on his bedroll, his back toward me as he pulls the blanket up around him.

"Cal?" I whisper, as I snuggle beneath my own blanket.

Cal shifts to face me. It's dark, but his eyes manage to catch what little moonlight shines through the tent flap, a light against the darkness. My breath catches and, for a moment, I forget what I want to say.

"Yes?"

I swallow and force myself to focus. "I wanted to say thanks. I don't think I said it earlier."

Cal smiles softly, his eyes twinkling. "You don't have to thank me. It's my job. I'm starting to have a whole new appreciation for everything you've put Bram through over the years."

I grin, propping my head up on my palm. "Yeah, I know, but hopefully that's not the only reason you jumped in and killed that beast."

Cal swallows, locking his eyes on mine. His lips part and he shifts almost imperceptibly closer. My heart races so fast I feel like it might burst free at any moment.

"No," he says, his voice low as he shifts even closer, "I reacted on instinct."

I'm very aware that we are mere inches apart. It's everything I can do to keep my voice steady as I close the distance a bit more and whisper, "Instinct?"

"Yes."

"Instinct, like Guard instinct? A soldier's instinct?"

He doesn't speak for a moment, and my mind races with what he might say next.

"Yes, but also . . . I don't know. I saw you in danger and I . . . I couldn't let anything happen to you. Not just because you're the prince, but because I—"

"Do you guys have an extra blanket in here?" Lorrell says, pushing aside the tent flap and poking his head in.

Cal jerks away, sitting up. "Yeah, we have one over here." He reaches to his right and grabs a blanket, tossing it to Lorrell.

"Thanks!" Lorrell grins. "Somehow, we only ended up with one, and Pascal isn't good at sharing."

"Well, you have it now, so you can go," I say, my voice tense, my irritation barely masked.

Lorrell doesn't seem to notice my aggravation at his interruption and leaves with a smile and a parting nod. Cal lies down, his back to me again. I sigh and settle back on my own bedroll. I close my eyes, trying to will sleep, when a soft voice drifts across the darkness.

"Goodnight, Ehren. Sleep well."

My mouth stretches into a grin. "Goodnight, Cal. I'll always sleep well with you nearby."

The tent falls silent but I still hear the whispered, "Me too."

For the first time in weeks, my dreams are happy and bright.

CHAPTER THIRTEEN
EHREN

The morning after the lake monster attack, we wake up and debate whether or not we want to try to cut up the creature for food.

"What would it even taste like?" Pascal muses with a scowl.

"Probably like fish," Lorrell says. "It does live in the water."

Pascal rolls his eyes at his brother. "Just because it lives in water doesn't make it a fish. It has legs, you idiot."

"It could still taste like fish," Lorrell mumbles with a frown.

"But it pro—"

"Let's just leave it," Cal cuts them off with a wave of his hand, exchanging a look with me conveying his irritation at their bickering.

I duck my head to hide my smile. "Cal's right. We don't know anything about it. It could be poisonous. Astra would never let me live it down if I ate a poisonous lake creature and died."

"If you're dead, she couldn't berate you too much," Cal counters, grinning.

I shake my head and chuckle. "She'd find a way to raise me from the dead just to yell at me for being so stupid. I can promise you that."

Cal laughs. "You're probably right."

Our morning may start out lighthearted, but it quickly turns into a frustrating battle up the mountain. The pathway is narrow and steep, littered with uneven rocks jutting out at odd angles. The wind whips around the edges of the mountain, cold and bitter. I clutch my cloak around me, my fingers nearly numb by the time we stop for the night. The ledge is relatively narrow, but there's enough space to erect the two tents with the horses secured between them. I set up more wards and make sure Lorrell and Pascal each have their own blankets before I settle in for the night. When I duck inside my tent, Cal already looks asleep, so I don't bother him.

I slip in and out of sleep for a couple hours, unable to get comfortable. I try to keep my thoughts focused, but they start wandering to memories of blood-soaked castle walls. I squeeze my eyes shut and decide to use the dream walking spell. Quietly, I rise and gather the necessary supplies. I whisper the enchantment over my feather and slip it under my pillow. I take a deep breath and lie down, whispering the incantation. Almost immediately, the tent fades around me and a snowy field appears. No, not just any snowy field—a battlefield, soaked with blood and lined with fallen soldiers.

"I'm sorry," Astra sobs. "I'm so sorry."

I spin around and race toward where she stands, the hand of an older woman on her arm.

"My son," the woman says. "You killed my son."

"I . . ."

"Astra!" I cry out.

She turns and faces me, tears on her cheeks. I halt a couple feet away and her eyes search my face, trying to make sense of my presence. After a moment, her eyes widen in realization.

"This is a dream," she says, her voice filled with awe as the she looks around. "It's just another dream."

As the reality settles, the blood and bodies fade, leaving us standing in a field of only snow. She turns her eyes back to me and smiles softly.

"I thought these dreams had stopped," I say, frowning.

"They had, more or less. I think it was the soul bond. Having Alak so close helped to calm my nightmares," she answers.

Guilt washes over me. "And I sent Alak away. And then I left, too."

Astra reaches out and places a hand on my arm. I can't quite feel it in the dreamworld, but the memory of her touch is enough to make it feel real.

"Ehren, I'm okay. It's all temporary. I'll be fine until one of you returns. Maybe I'll check with Healer Heora and see if she has something that can help me in the meantime."

I force a smile and rake a hand through my hair. "Yes, that might be good."

"Now," says says, smiling, "I assume you had a specific reason to enter my dream besides discussing my nightmares? If I recall correctly, this spell doesn't last long."

I nod. "I mostly wanted to check in and see how everything is going on your end."

"Nothing exciting here," she confesses with a shrug. "Just more of the same, really. Kai and Ronan keep me company."

"You mean Lord McDullun? It still throws me when you refer to him so casually."

Her cheeks redden slightly. "He's not that much older than we are. It feels silly calling him Lord McDullun, especially since he's told me to call him Ronan."

"I wasn't suggesting it was incorrect," I say quickly, trying to hide my smile.

She straightens her shoulders. "Well, get used to it."

My smile breaks free. "Yes, Ma'am."

She grins. "Anything happening on your end?"

I shake my head. "No, just lots of boring travel. I think we're nearing the peak. At least, I hope so. It's getting steep. Oh! I did almost get eaten by a lake monster."

Her eyes go wide and she hits my arm. "That is not nothing, Ehren Andrewe Daniel Montavillier!"

My grin fills my whole face as I say, "Hey! You finally learned my whole name!"

She rolls her eyes but doesn't hide her smile. "That is beyond the point. What even happened?"

I wave my hand. "It was nothing. I wasn't paying proper attention, and the next thing I know there's this monster charging toward me."

"Did you kill it?"

"Cal did."

Astra sighs dramatically. "Let me guess—Cal had to kill it because you didn't have your sword?"

I glance away sheepishly, and she hits me again. "Ehren! For gods' sake! We should have known better than to let you go off without me or Bram."

"Cal was there. He's responsible."

"Thank the gods for Cal." She pauses and then narrows

her eyes at me. "You didn't eat it, did you? This strange creature?"

I shake my head. "No, though there was some debate over that fact."

"Well, at least you had that much common sense."

I laugh and Astra meets my eyes, smiling.

"You seem to be doing okay."

I nod. "I am. At least, I think I am. I still have my dark moments, but . . ."

Cal's face flashes in my head and I smile, my cheeks warming at the memory. Astra cocks her head curiously at me.

"What aren't you telling me?"

I shake my head, laughing. "Nothing."

I feel the dream flicker and I glance around. I'm not ready to leave yet. I look back at Astra.

"I miss you, Ash."

She reaches out and wraps me in a hug. Gods, I wish I could feel her warmth. I return her embrace, even though I'm sure she can't feel it either.

"I miss you, too," she whispers. She draws back and looks up into my eyes. "Come back to me safely. Okay?"

I nod, kissing her forehead. "I promise."

The dreamworld fades and the cold of the mountain rushes back in. The tent is dark, and for a moment, I feel alone and lost. Cal shifts in his sleep, drawing my attention. I twist and look at him. He's little more than a shape in the dark, but just having him there is enough. I smile softly and drift to sleep.

WE RISE and get on the road early the next morning, the desire to be off this mountain our driving force. The day starts off much like the previous one, but quickly gets worse. A slow, half-frozen drizzle begins midday. When we stumble across a shallow cave a couple hours before nightfall, we make camp. After a bit of searching, we manage to scrape together enough wood for a decent fire. Its warmth floods the cave, and soon I'm able to feel my fingers and face. Cal brews a pot of tea that warms me up inside.

Even though we mostly agree that no one would bother us, I set up some basic wards around the mouth of the cave before we settle down for the night. When I'm done with the wards, I go to grab my bedroll, but find it already laid out next to where Cal is stretched out. I meet his eyes and raise my eyebrows in question as I lower myself into a seated position. Cal blushes and glances away.

"I figured I should keep an eye on you so you don't get eaten by a cave monster or something."

I throw back my head and laugh. Lorrell and Pascal shoot me half-curious, half-concerned looks from across the cave. Cal looks back up at me and grins, tucking a hand behind his head.

"Thanks, Cal." I grin as I straighten out my blanket and slide beneath its warmth. "I think, though, it's probably my turn to save you. We should keep this even."

Cal's smile softens. "You've already saved me."

I furrow my brows. "How? When?"

"It doesn't matter," he mutters, turning his head to stare up at the cave roof.

I decide not to press the issue. "Goodnight, Cal. Sweet dreams."

Cal opens his eyes and turns toward me. I meet his eyes and my heart skips a beat.

"What other dreams would I have with you sleeping nearby?" he whispers, so quietly I know there's no way Lorrell or Pascal heard. I'm not even sure *I* heard him correctly. My breath catches as my brain scrambles to find a reply.

"You dream of me?" I ask, breathless.

He smiles and closes his eyes. "Goodnight, Ehren. Sleep well."

It takes several minutes for my heart to stop racing enough for me to fall asleep, but I do have very good dreams.

Our sixth day of traveling starts out even drearier than the previous day. The annoying drizzle continues all morning, turning into swirling snow. Ice coats my eyelashes and my cloak is so soaked it's almost useless against the cold. The only good thing about our travel is that sometime mid-afternoon, we start downhill.

When we stop for the night, it's too damp and wet for a fire and there's no shelter beyond our tents and small overhanging bit of rock that we use to shelter the horses. We erect the tents as quickly as possible. I duck inside mine, lighting a lantern with trembling hands. Its warmth is slight, but it's better than nothing. Cal is helping Lorrell cover the horses with blankets and making sure they have food, so I'm alone. My clothes are soaked through and I can't stop shaking. I fumble with my shirt, eagerly ripping the frozen fabric away from my skin, and am kicking my pants off when Cal ducks into the tent. When he sees me standing mostly naked in the center of the tent, shaking so hard my teeth are chattering, his eyes go wide and he quickly crosses to me. He grabs a blanket up off the ground and wraps it around me, gathering me against his chest. I melt into his warmth.

"What the hell are you doing?"

"M-my cl-clothes were s-soaked." I shiver. "I-I n-need—"

"You need common sense," Cal sighs. "Stay wrapped up and I'll grab your clothes."

I nod as Cal releases me. He digs through my bags and produces a fresh shirt and pants. I drop the blanket and dress as quickly as I can before wrapping the blanket back around me.

"You should change, as well," I say, eying Cal, who's also shivering.

He swallows and nods. He has enough common sense not to strip entirely, removing one article of clothing at a time and replacing it immediately. I give him a semblance of privacy, focusing on laying out our bedrolls side-by-side. I sit on top of mine and stretch my frozen fingers toward the flickering flame of the candle in the lantern. Cal wraps a blanket around his shoulders and sinks down next to me.

"Is that lantern offering any warmth at all?"

I shake my head. "I don't think so." I pause and glance around the small tent. "We probably can't start a real fire in here, can we?"

Cal looks over at me, the corner of his mouth quirking up into a smile. "That would probably not be the best idea. This tent isn't made for that. Someone insisted we leave the larger tents behind to travel faster."

"That person was an idiot."

Cal chuckles. "He has his moments, for sure. For example, a few minutes ago he was stripped completely naked, nearly freezing to death."

I grin and shake my head. "My logic was sound. I had to get out of the frozen clothes. My execution was just flawed."

"To say the least." Cal laughs.

I glance toward the tent exit. "Will the horses be okay in this weather?"

Cal nods, stretching his fingers toward the lantern. "I think so. We made sure they were safely stored out of the wind and elements. Their blankets are thicker than ours, too. I think they'll be okay."

I pull my blanket tighter around me. "Yeah, these blankets don't seem as thick as I first thought."

"They're not too bad, but I wish I had an extra I could use tonight."

"You know, technically," I say, staring very intently at the lantern, "we do have two blankets in the tent."

Cal's eyes snap to my face, and I turn toward him slowly.

"What do you mean?" he asks, his voice oddly controlled and even.

"Well, we each have a blanket, and they're fairly large. We can both fit underneath one easily enough, so we could, in theory, share both blankets, doubling our protection from the cold. Plus, we could share our body heat. Keep each other warm." I jerk my gaze away, my cheeks flushing a deep red. "Never mind. It's a stupid idea." I wiggle my fingers above the lantern, eager for a change of subject. "I think I can almost feel my fingers again."

Cal reaches over and wraps his hands around mine. I inhale sharply and look over at him. He slowly lifts my hands to his lips and blows a warm breath over them, never taking his eyes from mine. My stomach flips and my heart races as he repeats the process, my fingers tingling with the heat.

"We can share the blankets," he says, his voice low as he releases my hands. "It makes sense. It's a good plan."

"Well, you know me," I say, trying to keep my voice light but failing miserably. "I'm good at the plans."

Cal grins. "That you are. That's why you'll make a great king." My face falls and Cal frowns. "What did I say?"

I shake my head and pull the blanket tighter around my shoulders, fixing my gaze on the lantern.

"Ehren, what's wrong?" Cal presses, his voice gentle.

"I don't think I'll make a good king."

"What? Of course you will! How can you doubt that?"

I raise my eyes back to his, fighting back tears. "Because I'm broken, Cal. How can I fix a broken kingdom if I can't even fix myself?"

"You're not broken, Ehren," Cal insists, his expression looking as shattered as I feel. "You're just struggling right now and, given everything you've been through, that's normal."

"Even if it's normal, it makes it difficult to be everything I need to be in order to lead a kingdom."

I feel a hot tear on my frozen cheek as the darkness and shadows I've been keeping at bay come creeping back to drown me. My chest feels tight and I can't breathe. I squeeze my eyes shut, shaking my head. Cal clasps both my shoulders.

"Hey, look at me."

I open my eyes and stare into the swirls of brown in Cal's. I take a deep breath and release it slowly.

"You are the strongest person I know. The fact that you're dealing with all of this and still managing to function at all is an amazing feat. You're an incredible person, Ehren, and you will make a wonderful king. I've known this for years. It's okay if you don't have faith in yourself right now, because I have enough faith for both of us."

"Do you really think I can do it?"

Cal smiles and nods. "With every ounce of my being, I believe in you, my prince and my king."

"Will you stay by my side?"

"Of course," Cal says without a breath of hesitation. "There is nothing that can keep me from my duty."

I look down at my hands clasping the blanket. "Ah, yes," I mumble with a nod. "Your duty. Your oath."

"Ehren, you will always be more than an oath to me, and I think you know that." I jerk my eyes back to his as he continues. "I don't feel obligated to stay by your side. I *want* to be here. There's no place I'd rather be, and nothing can keep me from being here for you in whatever capacity you will allow."

Gods, I want to kiss him. More than anything I want to kiss him. But what would he do? Would he kiss me back? Or would it ruin everything? I hesitate a moment too long, and he breaks our gaze, glancing toward our packs.

"So do you want cheese, bits of dried meat, or dried fruit for dinner?"

I swallow and exhale slowly, trying to slow my racing heart. "Surprise me."

We settle on bits of cheese and fruit, falling into easy, more casual conversation as we eat. By the time we're done, the tent feels warmer, but we adjust our bedrolls so they touch. We extinguish the lantern and slide beneath both blankets.

My heart thrums inside my chest as I stare up at the tent roof, my hands folded across my chest. I feel Cal shift next to me and realize his hand is at his side, mere inches away. I release a shaky breath and let my hand slide down my chest to the ground, brushing his beneath the blanket. His breathing hitches and his hand shifts to push firmly against mine, which does nothing to calm my heart. I inhale and exhale slowly, debating my next move. Slowly, deliberately, I fold my fingers into his. I half-expect him to pull his hand back, but instead he tightens his grip. I smile.

I suspect we'll both have sweet dreams tonight. I know I will.

CHAPTER FOURTEEN

ASTRA

I still smell the blood when I jerk awake. My heart races and I'm soaked in sweat. Alak hasn't even been gone a full day and my nightmares have already returned in full force. I thought they might. On our journey to the Summer Palace, there were a few nights when Alak was on watch and not sleeping next to me. On those nights, my nightmares would return to an extent, but his presence nearby was enough to calm them some. Now, he's gods know where and I'm alone.

I'm still exhausted, but I can't make myself close my eyes, not ready for more blood-soaked battlefields. With a sigh, I rise from my bed and wrap myself in a robe. I slink down the dark corridors and out into the garden. It's cold, but I don't care. I need to see the stars.

"Shouldn't you be in bed?"

I glance over my shoulder as Kai steps out of the shadows.

"I couldn't sleep."

Kai gives me a knowing nod. "You're not used to sleeping alone."

I sigh and look back up at the stars, pulling my robe tighter around me. "I've never slept alone. Not really. Even when I didn't share a bed, I still shared a room. But it's more than simple loneliness."

"Nightmares?" Kai asks, stepping to my side and following my gaze to the night sky.

I nod. "Yes."

"I know I'm not Alak, and I don't have Ehren's spell skills, but if you want, I can keep you company."

I pull my eyes from the sky and meet Kai's eyes, smirking. "So, Alak and I share a bed and you automatically opt to sleep on our floor, but he goes away and you decide to ask permission?"

The corner of Kai's lips twitch as he fights a smile. "I am watching out for you." His expression sobers as he adds, "Sometimes I need to see you with my own eyes to know that you're okay, that you're alive and breathing. It puts my mind at ease."

I smile and loop my arm with his. "I know, and I appreciate it. But I also appreciate alone time with Alak." I lift my eyes back to the stars. "Just a few more moments of fresh air and then, if you're done with whatever you were doing, I wouldn't mind the company."

Kai nods and shifts closer. We stand for several more minutes in silence, staring at the stars winking down at us. When we finally resign to my room, I curl up against Kai, praying the nightmares stay away. I drift into sleep, and what I find might as well be a nightmare.

"It's been awhile."

"What are you doing here, Aoibhinn?" I snap, my voice sharp.

"Your hostility is uncalled for," she replies with a scowl.

"You withheld information from me that could have changed everything. I think my hostility is very well placed," I reply, crossing my arms. "You knew Kato was under the influence of Caedios and didn't think to warn me until it was too late."

She shakes her head. "You know that's not exactly true. I only had a vague awareness of what was happening, and I did give you the information when I could."

I shake my head, turning away. "You could have done more."

"Let me make up for it now."

I spin and face her, my eyes flashing. "How?"

"I know how to defeat Caedios. I'm the only one who has ever done it."

I stumble back, my eyes widening. "I don't want to kill Kato. I—I can't kill him. He's my twin. He's—"

"He's lost," Aoibhinn cuts me short, her eyes filled with knowing sadness. "I know exactly how you feel, Astra. I've been there myself."

"No," I snap, shaking my head. "You know nothing about what I am going through. Killing your lover"—Aoibhinn flinches—"and killing your brother are two very different things. I will not kill Kato unless I am sure there is no other way."

"Very well. And while you wait, the rest of the world can just go to hell."

All color leeches from my face. "That's not fair."

"No it's not," Aoibhinn says, her voice hard. "That's how life works. There's nothing fair about this situation. There was nothing fair about when I had to kill Caedios the first time. Whether or not it's fair changes nothing."

"I will not kill my brother on your word alone simply because you failed to properly dispose of the demon haunting his mind. Your failure will not dictate my actions."

Aoibhinn rears back as if I slapped her. "You have no idea what you're up against."

"Maybe not, but I'm looking for more answers."

Aoibhinn sighs, shaking her head. "I would wish you luck, but I'm afraid the time for luck has passed. When you're ready to listen, I'll be here."

Without another word, she disappears and I'm left alone. I should be relieved, but somehow I know the worst is yet to come.

Kai is up, staring out a window when I wake. He glances toward me with a smile as I ease into a sitting position.

"Did you sleep okay?"

I nod, rubbing the sleep form my eyes. "I slept well enough. You?"

Kai nods, looking back out the window. "As well as any other night."

"Have you been awake long?"

Kai shrugs. "A few minutes. I didn't want you to wake up alone."

I smile at him affectionately. "Thanks, Kai. I know you have rounds to make, so I won't keep you."

Kai nods and walks toward the door, pausing halfway to look back at me.

"What are your plans today?"

"I don't know. I feel a little lost right now, to be honest. My instincts tell me to go to the library. Knowledge is one of the greatest resources and books hold their own arsenal."

A smile plays at the corners of Kai's lips as he nods. "You're not wrong, but may I propose a different option than immediately locking yourself away?"

"Of course."

"Come with me and check the borders of our wards. Shift and run with me. It's been a while since you've shifted, and I think it would be good for you."

I smile, the idea of shifting warming my soul. I nod, pushing back the covers and rising from the bed.

"All right. Give me a few minutes to get ready for the day. I'll meet you down by the kitchen."

Kai leaves without another word and I dress quickly. The castle feels still today, almost too quiet. Only a few people are missing, but their absence is felt in every corner. Things are finally moving forward and we all bear the weight of what that means. War is already here, but now we march to battle. Or, at least, we will in the very near future.

The kitchen feels alive compared to the rest of the castle. Kai leans against the wall outside the main door, a steaming mug in his hands.

"I thought you might need this," he says, handing me the mug as I step to his side.

I accept it from him and breathe deeply. "Coffee. You do love me."

He rolls his eyes and pushes away from the wall. "I figure if we're going to spend the next hour or so together it would be best to have you in a good mood."

I narrow my eyes at Kai. "I can be in a good mood without coffee."

He arches an eyebrow as I take a long sip, sighing in contentment.

"Though," I add, "coffee does help."

Kai shakes his head, the corners of his lips turning upward into what could almost be called a smile.

"Drink that and we'll get going. When we come back, you can have a proper breakfast."

"Coffee is br—"

"It is not."

"Fine. As long as I get coffee, I don't even care."

It only takes a few minutes for me to drain my mug. As I drink, I listen to the casual chatter coming from the kitchen. Two young men talk about a pretty girl. Cook scolds a kitchen maid for spilling milk. Moments like this make things almost feel normal.

When I finish my coffee, Kai takes my mug to be washed and we head outside. Once in the courtyard, Kai shifts and I follow suit, taking the form of a silver wolf. Kai meets my eyes and I sense his excitement. He races off and I chase after him. A few of the guards and servants dive out of our way, watching with wide, concerned eyes, but I don't care. After weeks of being trapped inside, I feel free.

Kai winds around to the farthest edge of the wards. I follow. Even in my wolf form I can sense the magic. It's mostly constructed by Alak and I weaving our magic together, but it's also reinforced by spellwork. Now that Alak is gone, it's my responsibility to make sure that the wards remain intact. When Alak was here, maintaining the spell was as easy as breathing for both of us. Now that he's gone, I can feel the drain on my magic. It's not enough to exhaust me, but it's enough that I notice. I haven't told anybody yet, but I really need to figure out another way to maintain the wards while Alak is gone.

It takes roughly half an hour to check all the wards. At

the final corner, I shift back into my human form. Kai looks disappointed but shifts back as well.

"Feel better?" he asks as I sink down to the ground. "Or was it too much?"

I reach out and touch the ward, the magic tingling against my fingers.

"Not too much but I am a little tired." I scowl at the invisible ward, twirling my fingers in the magic.

"What is it? Is the ward weak now that Alak is gone?"

I shake my head, standing up and brushing loose bits of grass and dirt from my dress. "It's not weaker, but it's harder to maintain on my own." I raise my eyes to meet Kai's as I grin. "I know you wanted to keep me from the library, but I think I need to go search my books for a new spell or two that can maintain this magic with less help from me."

Kai chuckles. "I didn't necessarily want to keep you out of the library all day. I merely wanted to remind you to live and breathe. You are doing good work here, Astra. When we win this war, it will largely be due to you. But you need to remember to take time for yourself, too. You can't bear the burdens of everyone without breaking."

I smile softly. "I know. You're right." I place my hand on his arm. "Thankfully, I have you here to remind me."

"I'll always be here for you," he replies. "Let's go in and get you a proper breakfast and then you can hole up in your library as long as you need. Sound good?"

"Can I eat my breakfast in the library?" I ask as we start walking.

Kai sighs and shakes his head. "I suppose."

I go straight to the library, Kai arriving a few minutes later with a plate of sausages, toast, and fruit. Kai doesn't stick around long and leaves me to my work. The books left behind at this palace aren't terribly helpful. From what Cadewynn told me when we first arrived, this castle was built when her grandfather was king. While that means many things are nicer and less worn, the library is stocked with more recent books and texts, not the ones I actually need right now. There's very little here on magic, and what magical texts are available are more history and less practical instructions. With a sigh I close yet another book, leaning back in my chair.

"Do you need help with the big words?" Ronan teases from the doorway, a tray of sandwiches balanced in his free hand.

I grin. "Not yet, but I'll keep you posted if I find any really tough words."

He laughs and takes a seat across from me, setting the tray on the table between us.

"I was looking for you and was told you'd likely be in here. I wasn't sure if I would be disturbing you or not, so I brought food. I've discovered in my vast life experience that people are much less likely to hate your presence if you arrive with the offer of food."

I laugh and reach for a sandwich. "You're not wrong. I don't mind a little company either way."

"What exactly are you researching?" Ronan asks, opening the nearest book and scanning the pages while I nibble my sandwich. "Magical histories?"

I nod, swallowing. "I need a spell to reinforce the wards. I was hoping to find something in these books, but so far they've been pretty useless. Ehren might know a spell, but he took most of his spell books with him."

"Hmm," Ronan muses, tapping a finger to his chin. "I might be able to help, if you'll allow it."

"Really? I'd be open to any and all help."

"Good," Ronan grins. "You see, I'm a bit of a bookworm myself. My favorite place in my home is the library. It's my sanctuary. When magic resurfaced, I gathered every text on magic I could, including spell books. I brought a few with me."

My eyes light up. "Really? I would love to look through them."

"Of course. I'll go fetch them right away. Though, I may be able to help you more directly."

I tilt my head. "How?"

Ronan's grin fills his face. "Well, my particular magical skillset so happens to be wards and shielding of all sorts. The magical ward you created with Alak is far beyond what I can typically do, but if we work together, I believe we can make a decent shield around the palace that will be more than sufficient. I think even have some books containing a spell or two to make the wards self-sustaining so they don't drain our magic constantly."

"That would be amazing! Can we go get the books now?"

Ronan laughs. "We can, but it would be a pity to leave these sandwiches sitting here. It would make them sad not to fulfill their life purpose of being eaten."

I throw back my head and laugh. "I wouldn't want that. Let's eat and then we can get those books."

We make quick work of the sandwiches. I have a feeling Ronan could have downed the entire tray without my help, but I do my part. Ronan leads me up to his room, and I'm pleasantly surprised he's been given a room only a couple doors down from my own. He opens the door and sweeps into the room, and I follow behind. Everything is neat and organized, and if it weren't for the many books and papers scattered across the desk in the far corner, I would doubt this room was in use. There are seven books stacked on top of the desk with a few more piled on the floor next to a bag that looks to be filled with scrolls and other loose texts.

"Feel free to look at any of these," Ronan says, walking toward the desk and nodding to the books.

"Are there any you would recommend as a good starting point?" I ask, picking up a smaller green book with silver etching.

"Well, not that book." He chuckles, easing onto the edge of his bed. "I'm afraid that one is mostly a work of fiction I enjoyed as a boy."

I turn the book over in my hands, eying it curiously. "Faerie stories?"

"Aye. They were written long ago, back when magic was still alive. While the stories are mostly fiction, I believe some may be based in truth. I've enjoyed looking at my favorite childhood tales in a new light now that I understand a little bit about magic."

I open the book, taking a seat next to Ronan as I flip through the pages. Each short story is accompanied by a few sketches. I smile as some of the stories and tales I read as a child flood back into my mind. I stop short, however, when a familiar face stares up from an illustration. Aoibhinn. The sketch is rough, clearly drawn from another picture of her, but it's Aoibhinn all the same, the very face that haunts my dreams. In this illustration, she looks calm and beautiful, leaning down to hand a flower to a young girl.

"Ah, the story of Aoibhinn," Ronan muses glancing over my shoulder. "Have you heard of her? You know, in some ways, you remind me of her."

I snap the book shut, standing abruptly. "I've heard that before." I force a smile as I place the book down and reach for another. "Let's dive in, shall we? After all, we need more than faerie stories and legends."

Ronan nods. "Aye, love. Right you are. I suggest we start with these," he replies, lifting his cane to point at the stack of books atop the desk.

I take a seat at the desk and start searching a couple of the texts while Ronan relocates to spread out across a couch near a window. Every few minutes one of us finds a possible spell, but after closer inspection, none are quite what we are looking for. Some require ingredients I doubt we have access to. Others are simply too weak or would drain too much magic to make it feasible for more than a day or two. We do find one spell that might work, but it requires its magic to be refreshed every four hours. I'm starting to wonder if we'll find anything when Ronan jumps up from his couch, rushing toward me.

"This one should work!" He drops the book down in front of me, leaning forward to tap the words. "See, it's a basic warding spell, but it's made stronger by certain types of magic. Since I have warding magic and you have raw magic, we can make it nearly as strong as the warding spell you and Alak currently have in place. We can use these symbols to put the spell into rocks."

I nod, leaning forward to scan the text. "And it looks like it lasts twelve to fifteen hours in the stones." I lift my eyes to meet Ronan's. "You're right—this one should work."

Ronan stands straight, placing both hands on the head of his cane and grinning down at me. "You can always trust me, love."

I laugh, shaking my head. "Well, the ingredients for

the initial spell to prepare the rocks to absorb the warding magic seems simple enough. I'll go down to the kitchen and check our supplies if you don't mind finding the stones. I'm sure the gardens will have a good supply we can use."

"I'll get right on that. Judging by the text, we'll need at least six for the wards to cover the entire palace and grounds. I'll meet you in the courtyard when I've found a few."

"Good," I reply, standing, warm hope blossoming in my chest. "See you there."

Cook has nearly everything I need and the Healers have the rest, so I'm able to make the potion quickly. When I get to the courtyard with my concoction, Ronan is already waiting with several smooth stones the size of my palm. As per the instructions, we place each stone in the potion, reading the required text from the page. After we carefully lift each stone, Ronan uses a knife to carve the appropriate symbol in each. After we're done preparing the stones, we place them evenly spaced around the barrier of the warded area. We repeat the spell each time, sealing the warding between each stone. Ronan takes the lead, his magic naturally flowing into the warding. Once he's started the spell, I reach out with my magic and support his. My magic doesn't combine with his as easily or willingly as it does with Alak's but, with a bit of effort, we make it work. After we've placed the last stone, I step back, letting my magic feel out the wards. The wards Alak and I put up are still humming with life against the new ones. It almost feels like a betrayal as I pull down the old wards, letting the new ones stand on their own.

"Did it work?" Ronan asks, watching me carefully.

I force a smile and nod. "Yes. The new wards are

working well. We'll have to make sure to renew the spell every twelve hours, though."

Ronan grins, pride twinkling in his eyes as he turns to face the invisible ward. I wonder if he can feel the hum of magic like I can.

"Magic is beautiful, isn't it?" he asks, his voice full of awe. "It's hard to believe how quickly we've adapted to it. Magic returned less than a year ago, and we're already using it in everyday life."

"Yes, it's both wonderful and terrifying at the same time."

Ronan glances down at me, his face somber. "No one in the world quite knows the trials you face because of magic, Astra, but most of us will help however we can. I know you're used to relying on Ehren and Alak, but now that they're gone, I hope you see me as not only an ally but also a friend."

"Of course." I smile. "Friendships, not allies, are what will truly win this war. Allies work together for a common cause, but friends fight together for a greater purpose. They don't just care about the outcome. They care about the people. It's more than just wars and battles. It's souls."

Ronan nods thoughtfully. "You might be young, but you have insight few men my age and older possess."

I glance down, my smile fading. "I suppose."

"Hey," Ronan says, placing a finger under my chin and tilting my gaze to meet his. "We're friends now, so don't hold back. I'm here for you whenever you need me."

When my smile returns it's almost sincere as I say, "Likewise."

Ronan drops his hand and stares off toward the invisible

ward. "I have a feeling our friendship may be something that changes everything. At least I hope so."

I laugh. "Wouldn't that be something?" I pause and glance back toward the palace. "Well, friend, why don't we head inside for a bit of tea? This air is chilly and I need to warm up."

"Sounds like an excellent idea." Ronan offers me his arm. "Shall we?"

With a smile, I accept and we head inside.

CHAPTER FIFTEEN
ASTRA

My sleep is restless for the second night in a row. It switches between bloodied battlefields to dreams of horrific things happening to Alak and Bram. I wake covered in sweat, immediately reaching for the bond to make sure Alak is alive. Kai sleeps next to me, but he remains in his wolf form for "propriety reasons." As if anyone would care or enter my room to see us sharing a bed.

Shortly after I wake I head to the kitchens. It's still early, but servants already bustle about in preparation for the day. The second I step into the kitchen, Cook motions for me to take my usual seat and immediately starts scooping freshly scrambled eggs onto a plate next to strips of bacon.

"Any news from the village?" I ask, talking a bite of bacon as Cook fills a mug with coffee.

"Yes, and I'm afraid it's not good news," Cook sighs.

My heart sinks. "More attacks?"

Cook nods. "It would appear so. There were a few newcomers to Oxwatch yesterday from a village a little to the east. The Dragkonians destroyed their town, killing, torturing, or kidnapping most of the residents."

"These refugees, they have family in Oxwatch?"

"Most of them. There was one main family of five that sought refuge, but they brought with them a couple others who had no place to go. One of them was an orphaned child."

My stomach twists, my appetite disappearing. "A child? How old?"

Cook shrugs. "Don't know for sure. Eight or nine, perhaps. Too many orphans are being made from this war, and the battles have yet to truly begin."

My chest tightens as I stare down at the plate in front of me, my hunger completely dissipated. How many more will die? And how many of those lives will be lost at my own hand?

"Hey, now!" Cook yells, snapping my attention back to her, but she's not talking to me. A couple of younger servants, one boy and a girl, are trying to sneak bacon while she's distracted. Cook narrows her eyes and points at them shaking her head. "You think you can just sneak in here and take all my food?"

"Sorry, Ma'am," the girl says as the boy looks down at his shoes.

Cook sighs, shaking her head. "Well, get yourselves each another piece and be on with you." The servants lift their shocked faces to Cook. "Well? Go on. I have work to do."

Without another moment of hesitation, they each grab a couple more pieces of bacon before scurrying off. Cook leans against the counter, watching them go.

"You know, I once minded the little mice in my kitchen, but when you lose one of those little mice, you realize how much you enjoyed their presence," she whispers, a hint of a tear in her eye.

I smile softly, knowing exactly which little mouse she's referring to. I snuck him cheese once. The memory pierces like a sharp needle to my heart. When Cook turns back to me, her face shifts into her normal mask.

"So, what are you up to today? Any more spells? Or are you going to hide away in your library?"

I shrug, forcing myself to take another bite of bacon. "Ronan and I need to refresh the warding spell, but after that I suspect I will end up in the library."

Cook nods. "Do you need any more spell ingredients? I'm sending Jeremy into Oxwatch to grab a few things for me and I can have him get anything you need."

I shake my head, pushing my plate back. "I think I have everything I need. You might want to check with the Healers to see if they have any shortages in their supplies."

"I checked with Healer Heora last night," Cook replies. "She gave me a short list."

"Good," I reply, standing and turning toward the door. "Well, I suppose I should get my day started."

"Would you mind taking a tray of breakfast breads to the come-and-go room?" Cook asks, shuffling across the kitchen to scoop up a tray of assorted breakfast goodies.

"Of course I will," I respond with a smile as I accept the tray.

"Thank you." Cook pauses and places a hand on my arm. "Remember, my girl, I'm here for more than just cooking and fetching ingredients. If you need anything at all, I'm available."

My smile threatens to falter, but I hold it in place. "I appreciate it."

She drops her hand, offering me one last smile and nod before she turns back to her work. I scurry away, tray in hand, to the come-and-go room. It's a simple room in the corner of the castle that serves as a place for those coming and going to gather. With all the guards and servants and guests having different, constantly changing schedules, it gives everyone a place to grab bites to eat and socialize. Cook keeps the room supplied with food and pots of tea and coffee. I'm often too busy to visit even in passing, so several pairs of surprised eyes turn my way when I enter. Guards and a few servants make up the majority of those gathered, but Ronan also leans in the back corner, a cup in his hand. I force a grin as I step into the room, my mind racing to remember the names of the others in the room.

"Not only do you grace us with your presence, but you bring food?" a Guard named Max teases, plucking a sweet bun from the tray before I've even had a chance to set it down.

"Gods, Max," chides another Guard, whose name I'm not sure of. "Let her set the tray down first."

I chuckle as I slide the tray on the table in the center of the room. "I don't mind."

Ronan pushes away from the wall, draining what remains in his cup. I meet his eyes and my smile turns more genuine.

"Are you ready to check the wards?"

"Aye, love," Ronan grins, setting his cup down and crossing to me. "I was thinking you'd never ask."

I roll my eyes but can't hide my smile. He offers me his arm and I accept it as we leave the room. We exit the castle through a side door, a cold wind greeting us. I shiver, shifting closer to Ronan.

"Do we need to fetch your cloak?" Ronan chuckles, glancing down at me.

I shake my head, even though I really would rather grab my cloak. "Let's just be quick. I can survive a few minutes outside."

"All right, if you're sure," Ronan replies, eyeing me skeptically.

When I shiver again, he throws his arm around my shoulders and pulls me closer. I start to protest, but I do feel warmer and his body blocks the worst of the wind. We work quickly to reinforce the wards before hurrying back inside. Once we're indoors, I sigh with relief, heading to the library. Ronan follows along.

"Do you need any help today?" Ronan asks.

I glance up at him as we walk. "I suppose. I need to get back to researching a way to contact the Fae. So far, I haven't had much luck. If you don't mind sharing your texts again, they might come in handy."

Ronan gives me a thoughtful nod. "Aye, you're more than welcome to use any of my books, though I'm not sure how helpful they'll be. Why don't you head on to the library and I'll grab my books and meet you there?"

I nod. "That sounds good."

We part ways and I enter the library, heading straight to the fireplace at the far end to start a roaring fire. Once the flames are flickering steadily, I turn and stare at the shelves of books, recalling the layout in my head. I'm still pulling books from the shelves when Ronan enters, a bag slung over his shoulder and a tray of tea and biscuits balanced carefully in his free hand.

"Tea?" I ask, arching an eyebrow.

Ronan grins. "Tea and food in general help one think more clearly, don't you think?"

I laugh. "I suppose."

"Of course," Ronan adds, ambling toward the small table nearest the fireplace, "I also think a good mead can help one think, but it's a bit early for that."

"Yes, it is." I lean down and scoop a few books off the floor and carefully balance the stack of books as I cross the room toward Ronan, who has set the tray down and is now unloading the books he brought.

I settle into a chair near the fire, placing my books on the floor. Ronan fills a cup with tea and hands it to me. I balance it carefully on the arm of the chair while opening a book in my lap.

"What exactly are you looking for in regards to the Fae? You mentioned contacting them," Ronan says, settling into the chair across from me with his own cup of tea, his cane resting against his knee.

"I need to find a way to essentially summon them or find a bridge between our realms," I reply, scanning the pages of text in my lap.

"Any particular reason?" he asks. "Or is it top secret? I'll admit, as a boy I used to fantasize about stumbling across a handsome Fae warrior in the woods near my house and winning his heart."

I grin and look up at Ronan. "Well, as amazing as that would be, that's not quite the reason. It's not a secret, per se, but not necessarily open knowledge. The Fae have a way to kill the Dragkonians."

Ronan's eyes widen as he gasps. "They what? How do you know this?"

"Alak, Bram, and I ended up in their realm for a few days

recovering after an attack. Apparently, the Fae have a berry that's deadly to the Dragkonians, but it only grows in their realm. When we were there, the berries were far from ripe."

I pause, reaching into my pocket and pulling out a small handkerchief holding a few of the berries. I lean forward, passing them to Ronan. He accepts, still wide-eyed as he stares down at them in awe.

"These can kill one of those beasts?" he whispers.

I nod. "According to the Fae, at least. It takes a fully ripened berry to have full affect, but even these can potentially harm or weaken them."

"So," Ronan says, passing the berries back to me, "you need to contact the Fae to check on the supply?"

I nod, slipping the berries back into my pocket. "Yes. Time works differently between our realms, so it's possible the berries are ready to be harvested and used. The Fae promised they would find a way to contact us when the time came, but it makes me uneasy having no way to communicate in the meantime. I'm hoping to find references in old texts that shed light on how to contact or cross into their realm."

"And I'm guessing these books are less than helpful?"

I sigh, leaning back in the chair. "I've found a couple references to the Fae in historical documentation but nothing about actually reaching out to them. I have a feeling I need a much larger library to find what I need."

"You know," Ronan drawls, tapping a finger on the head of his cane as he thinks. "There are several well-stocked libraries in Athiedor. If anywhere had the references you need, Athiedor might be the place to look."

My heart falls slightly and I stare intently at the book in my lap. "Does that mean you'll be leaving?"

"I don't have to," Ronan says softly. "I can send letters to those I know with the best libraries and ask them to send resources. It would be more efficient that way."

I look up and meet his eyes. He smiles gently.

"How soon do you think we could have an answer?"

Ronan stares into the fire, calculating. "It shouldn't take long. Athiedor itself isn't much more than a day's ride so a messenger could be there by morning if we send him now. A few more days for all the letters to reach their destinations . . . Perhaps two weeks at most to hear from everyone, less for those closest." He looks back at me. "Is that acceptable?"

I nod, a smile curling on my lips as hope blooms in my chest. "Better than nothing, I suppose."

Ronan nods, rising from his seat. "I'll start the letters right away, then. Where might I find some parchment and ink?"

I nod toward the desk. "Everything you need should be there."

Ronan gives me a quick nod of thanks and strides to the desk. He settles down to write as I flip through the books I selected from the shelves, switching to Ronan's texts after a few frustrating minutes. Ronan finishes up his letters and summons a servant to send them off. He helps me research for a while before going off in search of lunch. He returns with sandwiches and mead.

"So, I suppose noon is when you find it acceptable to switch from tea to mead," I tease.

"Well, naturally." Ronan grins, his eyes twinkling. "Of course, if you find it objectionable, I will drink it all and spare you."

"Well, I don't really want to imbibe too much this early in the day, but I wouldn't mind one glass."

Ronan grins, pouring a soft red liquid into a glass. "That's my girl."

I accept the mead and take a sip, my eyes widening. "This is delicious." I take another small sip. "Incredibly delicious."

"I'm glad you think so. This cherry mead is from my private collection, made in my little corner of Athiedor."

"I'm honored you're sharing it."

Ronan's rich laughter fills the library. "Well," he says, his eyes shining, "in my opinion, mead always tastes better when you share it with friends. But don't drink without eating. It is quite strong."

I nod, remembering that dreadful night in an Athiedor pub—well, rather the morning after—and reach for one of the sandwiches.

Ronan and I fall into easy conversation as we eat. I do accept a second glass of mead but turn down future offers. After eating, we dive back into our research, but we get nowhere. We end up pushing the books aside in favor of a card game, losing complete track of time until Kai shows up to see why we aren't at dinner. With Kai as an escort, we head to the dining hall.

The dining hall buzzes with activity. Here, at the Summer Palace, everyone eats together. No one is divided by class or station. It's friendly and welcoming. We take three seats at the nearest table and no one blinks an eye at our late arrival. I ladle soup into bowls from a pot in the center of the table while Kai distributes the bread. I sit and eat quietly, listening to all the conversations swirling around. Sometimes when I'm in here, I can almost forget that war is pressing outside our doors. I can forget that my brother betrayed me and my friend was slaughtered for his cause. I can pretend to be happy and not have all this pressure on me. I can act as if I'm a normal girl no Seer ever cared about.

My mouth suddenly feels very dry and I struggle to swallow my piece of bread. I take a gulp of water from a nearby goblet, but it does little to help. I try to push my darker thoughts aside, but my pounding head brings them back to the front of my mind. I sigh and push up from the table. Kai shoots me a concerned look and Ronan looks up at me, curious.

"I need some fresh air," I say with a forced smile. "We need to refresh the wards soon, too, and I probably should take my cloak this time."

Kai's scowl deepens, clearly not believing me.

"All right. I'll meet you out in the front courtyard in a few minutes," Ronan says, his voice tinged with worry.

I nod and hurry from the dining hall. I head to my room and grab my cloak, truly eager to be outside. I take a side door and wander along the outside of the castle, eager to be alone. When a dark figure steps from the shadows, I nearly jump out of my skin.

"Kai," I mutter, pressing a hand to my fluttering heart. "You startled me."

"If I scared you, perhaps you shouldn't be out here walking alone after dark," Kai replies, stepping to my side.

I wave him off. "I'm fine. These wards are doing their job. I was just caught up in my thoughts and didn't see you stalking me."

Kai scoffs. "I wasn't stalking you."

"Oh, you most definitely were," I counter, the corners of

my mouth turning up into a slight smile as I link my arm with his. "I don't mind it though."

He sighs and looks up at the sky. "No stars tonight."

I follow his gaze, disappointed to see he's right. Dark, ominous clouds roll above, blocking out the stars and moon. With no more seemingly left to say, we walk in silence to the front courtyard, where we find Ronan waiting. He grins as we approach.

"Ready?" His eyes drift to Kai. "Are you joining us?"

Kai huffs and shakes his head, turning to me as I slide my arm from his. "I'll be in your room when you're done."

I give Kai a grateful smile before he slinks off into the darkness. Ronan arches an eyebrow but doesn't say a word.

"Let's go reinforce the wards," I say with forced cheer.

It doesn't take long before the wards are ready and we're heading back inside. Ronan walks me to my door, promising to meet me in the library first thing in the morning. With a parting nod, I slip into my room. Kai sits on the floor, leaning against the foot of the bed, his legs stretched out in front of him with a book propped up in his lap.

"I didn't know you could read," I tease as I hang my cloak up in my wardrobe.

Kai chuckles, shaking his head. "I actually can't read Callenian, but this book is written in my native tongue."

I start. Sometimes I forget Kai is from Gleador since he's become such a key part of our group. It doesn't help he speaks fluent Callenian with hardly any accent.

He closes the book with a snap and stands, stretching. I grab nightclothes and slip behind the changing screen. I'm almost dressed when Felixe appears at my feet, blinking up at me with his crystal blue eyes.

"Hey, boy," I murmur, leaning down to scratch him

behind his ears. He lifts his head, offering me a folded slip of paper covered in bits of mud. "What do you have here?"

"Are you talking to me?" Kai asks.

"No," I say, stepping out from behind the screen, Felixe popping up onto my shoulder. "Felixe is here."

Kai nods as he takes a seat on the edge of the bed. I settle beside him, unfolding the note as Felixe hops from my shoulder, prancing to curl up on my pillow.

My Most Beloved Astra,

Well, let's start with the good news: Bram hasn't tried to kill me yet. I must say I am very proud of the restraint he shows on a daily basis. As much as I hate to admit it, I can see what you saw in the man. (Please don't leave me.)

~~There's not much to report so far, except dreadful weather.~~

We ran into a few siblings who spoke of the refugees. They came from a destroyed village themselves, and they confirmed that the rumors shared in the reports are indeed spreading. When we rolled into a small village earlier today, we were able to confirm more details. It took some convincing because everyone is very guarded and cautious, but we think we know where the camp is set up. Bram thinks we can find it in just a couple days, assuming the information we received is correct.

It's so discouraging, though, seeing these towns torn apart and all these broken families. ~~I know what it's like to have everything ripped away and~~ Sorry, you don't want my melancholy, I'm sure, but sometimes it is hard to be happy with you so far away. I think of you often. I miss you so much it hurts. I can't wait to be done with this bloody business and be back by your side.

Yours until the stars fade,
Alak

Kai starts to read over my shoulder, but he eventually glances to the side, blushing. I grin, reading it over a couple times before tucking it away safely. I convince Kai to stay in his human form as I tuck myself underneath the covers, but he refuses to share the blanket. I fall into a restless sleep, familiar nightmares creeping up on me. Kai wakes me twice, holding me tightly and singing a soft lullaby in Gleador until I fall back asleep. When I wake in the morning, Kai is already gone.

The day is almost an exact repeat of the previous day. As promised, Ronan meets me to refresh the wards before we head to the library for a day of frustrated reading. We give in much earlier to the card games and meads, putting me far behind my research. After a quick lunch of sandwiches, I pull out my journal, scanning my previous research until time for dinner. I opt to skip the more festive dining hall and take a small tray alone in the library. After dinner, Ronan and I secure the wards.

Everything is familiar and routine; it's comforting. Without question, Kai shows up in my room again, this time dressed in more casual nightclothes, bearing his own blanket. I smile softly and climb into the bed. I slip into sleep, the nightmares swarming me almost immediately.

I'm in a snow-covered battlefield soaked in blood and littered with broken bodies. The air is thick with the coppery scent. I stumble back, wanting to run as far as I can, but an older woman with stringy gray hair stands in my way. I gasp, stepping back from her, but she reaches out and grabs my arm.

"My son. You killed my son."

I look down into her brown eyes, unable to find words. I can feel her pain. Tears break free, sliding down my cheeks.

"I . . ."

"Astra!"

I jerk my gaze upward and see Ehren standing not far away, rushing toward me. The world around me feels hazy. Ehren stops a few feet away, and I struggle to make sense of his presence. Then, awareness rushes over me, and relief floods me. A dream. It's all dream and Ehren is here. I'm not alone. I never have to be alone.

CHAPTER SIXTEEN

JESSALYNN

The little princess and her crew are ready to go at dawn. I, however, need food before I can lead their little expedition. I eat a quick breakfast before we leave. Nila makes her presence known as we're loading the horses, and Cadewynn seems fascinated by the tiny creature, though Nila seems perfectly content to ignore her in true cat fashion.

We take a side path cutting through the mountain to head east. It's not as quick or efficient as the caves leading to the west, but they work and allow us to bring horses. It takes us three days to travel the mountains. I keep watching Cadewynn, expecting her to show her true colors and weakness, but she only seems to get stronger every minute of every day. It pisses me off, which amuses Kaeya. The first time Cadewynn actually shows any sign of being anything short of perfect is the day we leave the mountains.

"So, how much longer will it be before we reach the first province?" she asks, her eyes scanning the terrain around us, likely looking for some sparkling city.

"Technically, we're already in the Jakuma Province," I say, holding back a grin at her confused scowl. "But, like most of the larger provinces, there's a main capital city. We won't reach the city of Forduna until tomorrow."

Cadewynn frowns, shaking her head. I grin, tilting my head. "Disappointed?"

Cadewynn looks up at me, her eyes filled with a fierce fire. "I'm glad you find amusement in my kingdom's suffering."

Her reaction feels like a smack in my face. I recoil back with a sneer. "I said nothing of the sort."

"Perhaps not directly, but your quick dismissal of my frustration is enough," Cadewynn says, her voice sharp. "My people are literally dying and more will die every day until we can stop Kato. I need these armies. Every day we spend traveling is another day they suffer."

Kaeya catches my eye before I can snap back. She raises an eyebrow, barely holding back her smile. Damn. She agrees with the little princess. I inhale slowly, releasing the breath in a huff.

"I'm sorry if it seemed that way, but I can't do a thing to change it. Unless, of course, you or someone in your current party can wisp us all to Forduna?" Cadewynn frowns and shakes her head. "So, then, be content we're as close as we are."

Cadewynn falls silent, but I can tell she's not pleased with my answer, although she keeps her shoulders straight. When we finally stop for the night and set up camp, I can't stop watching her. I keep looking for something, though I'm not sure what. It's almost as if I'm torn between wanting to see her fail and celebrating her success.

"Just talk to her," Kaeya whispers in my ear, making me jump.

I jerk away with a scowl. "Why should I?"

"Because you are not the cold-hearted bitch you pretend to be."

I spin to face Kaeya, my teeth clenched. Kaeya only grins in her obnoxious knowing way, crossing her arms.

"Do what you want," Kaeya says before I can speak my mind, "but unless you at least attempt to resolve your issues with the princess, you will need another place to sleep."

"Are you kicking me out of our tent?" I demand, taking a step back.

"Your angst is keeping me up and I need my rest," Kaeya replies with a shrug. "Choose wisely."

Kaeya turns and ducks into the tent that's supposed to belong to both of us while I stand like a fool, blinking after her. With a huff I turn and look toward Cadewynn. She's chatting easily with Sama by the fire Nyco built while they eat their night's rations. I sigh and storm across the camp, dropping down on Cadewynn's free side. Sama freezes, her eyes darting to me.

"You don't mind if I sit here, do you?" I ask, staring into the fire.

"I mind if you have only come to remind me how foolish I am and berate my choices further," Cadewynn says, her voice sharp.

I inhale sharply, but before I can snap back, Sama leaps to her feet.

"Nyco, there's something I forgot to show you," Sama says, nodding toward her tent. "Come with me?"

For a moment Nyco blinks up at her in confusion, red tinging his cheeks before it clicks. He clears his throat and

THE STARDUST IN THE ASHES

leaps to his feet, glancing away awkwardly in such a way I wonder what exactly is happening between the two of them.

"Oh, of course," Nyco mumbles, crossing over to Sama. "The, uh, the thing we were discussing before."

He follows her into a tent before I can study their odd relationship further. Once we're alone, I glance over at Cadewynn.

"Look, we got off on the wrong foot, and I take full responsibility. You have no idea what it feels like to be the discarded and unwanted princess."

Cadewynn glares at me, her jaw set, and I fight every instinct I have that screams for me to shrink away from her. I will not let her intimidate me.

"Perhaps rather like being the broken princess hidden away in the library," Cadewynn responds, her voice like ice.

I frown, gritting my teeth. "What are you talking about? Why even bother pretending you're not the pride and joy of the kingdom?"

Something close to hurt flashes across Cadewynn's face as she turns her attention back to the flames.

"It's probably easier for you to think that. It makes it easier to hate me, but it's not true. Not really. Yes, I'm the pretty little princess, pulled from her corner for balls and dinners, but most of the time nobody cares."

"Ehren seems to care."

A whisper of a smile plays on Cadewynn's lips as she nods, but her eyes remain sad. "True, in recent years Ehren and I have grown closer, but there is a significant age gap between us. I was always what my nursemaid considered a sickly child. I got very sick when I was six and was bedridden for months. What little childhood joys I had before were taken away. My only escape was through books.

Thankfully, my governess was quick to supply as many books and texts as I desired. I loved my books, but I expected life to return to normal once I was better. It didn't. Everyone kept treating me like a doll that would easily break. I resigned to my fate and found my home in the library."

I cock my head, studying the girl. "I always thought you preferred the library. At least, any reports I've received always painted you that way."

Cadewynn shrugs, still not looking my way. "I don't mind it. Not really. It was my place and I was content there. I had a friend once a few years older than me named Isabella. She was Bram's sister and I loved spending time with her in the library."

"What happened to her?"

Cadewynn finally looks up at me, meeting my eyes. "I'm not sure. I was told she died in her sleep, but I've always felt there was more to that story. She was healthy and strong, but I have no real proof what I was told is false."

I scowl. Young girls dying mysteriously in their sleep is suspicious at best. What is happening in the Callenian court? Maybe it's a good thing I was kicked out at a young age.

"Well, you and your brother seem closer now."

Cadewynn shrugs again and looks back into the fire. "Perhaps, but now I feel more useless than ever. When I found the prophecies about the twins, I finally had a way to help someone beyond my library walls. Ehren cared, too, and worked closely with me. And then Astra came and spent time with me in the library. Everything was falling into place, but now I'm back to being the useless princess."

She looks up at me and I see her former fierceness and determination shining in her eyes. I bite back a smile.

"I told you before I can't wield a sword or physically fight a war, but I can build an army. I'm sure you think I'm foolish, but it's all I can do. I have a task and I will not fail. I *will* save my kingdom."

Heavy silence falls between us, filled only by the crackling of the fire. I play out a dozen different replies in my head, but none feel right. I'm guarded for a reason, but now seems like a time for honestly, a time to lower the mask. I sigh, shaking my head.

"Look, I can't pretend to understand exactly what you went through, but I get why you're doing this. I . . . I admire you, damn it."

Cadewynn's eyes widen as her lips part. "What?"

"I admire you. I keep expecting you to break, but you keep pushing forward. Not many would put themselves out there like you do, and I admire that. I've been there myself, at the point where it's probably better, smarter, to give up, but you keep pushing forward, knowing that there's got to be something greater you can achieve."

Cadewynn smiles softly. "Exactly." She pauses, taking a deep breath. "Jessalynn, I know you hate me for what I represent, but I have always dreamed of having my sister back."

I startle. "What do you mean back? We—you and I . . ."

"I know you left when I was still a toddler, but I knew you existed. Ehren and my governess would tell me stories. I asked to meet you once when I was around four or five. Oh, did I make my mother furious."

She chuckles and I can't help but smile. "Yeah, I can imagine that didn't go over well."

Cadewynn's eyes meet mine. "I mean it, though."

I swallow and glance away. "I'll think on it." I stand,

glancing toward my tent. "Well, I'm heading in. Be ready first thing in the morning and we may reach Forduna by noon."

Cadewynn nods in reply but makes no move to rise. Whatever suits her. I march into my tent and duck inside. Kaeya is sprawled out on her bedroll. Mine is set up next to hers, the edges touching. Nila has seen fit to curl up in the middle of mine.

"I see you prepared my bed even though you had no plans to allow me to sleep in here," I say, my voice low as I lift Nila, passing her to Kaeya.

Kaeya smiles up at me, taking Nila who immediately struggles in her grasp and leaps away the second she's released. "I knew you would make the right choice. You usually do."

I shake my head, turning my head to hide my smile as I settle into my bed.

"You always think the best of me," I reply, wrapping her in my arms and making myself comfortable.

She leans into my touch and I kiss her cheek.

"Of course I do. People usually assume the best of those they love."

I agree with another kiss, pulling her closer so she's more on my bedroll than her own. Nila sniffs me indignantly before curling up with me and Kaeya, purring softly.

"Goodnight, *Januu*," Kaeya whispers. "Sleep well."

Cadewynn is up and ready to go before I wake. Her eagerness is expected, but I still find it annoying. Thankfully, the weather cooperates and Forduna comes into view after a few hours. Cadewynn's shoulders sag with relief, but her gaze is sharp. I can only imagine the nerves she's feeling, and I'm suddenly overwhelmed with the urge the make sure she succeeds. Shit. The little princess is winning me over, too.

Forduna is perfectly situated in the corner of Gleador to be an optimal trade city. The streets are flooded with vendors crowding every available space. Weaving through the streets on our horses is nearly impossible, and we discard them quickly to elbow our way through the crowd. Nila vanishes entirely and even Sama's Shadow Hawk takes to the skies.

Cadewynn is tense and obviously overwhelmed by the flurry of activity. Her eyes dart around wildly and every time someone bumps into her, she inhales sharply. I want to help her in some way, but I'm not really sure how to go about doing it. She might not accept my help anyway. I don't have to debate long before Nyco and Sama take up positions on either side of her, lacing their fingers with hers to help guide her through the crowd. Good. It's more their job than mine to take care of the princess.

We halt in front of a large, ostentatious building covered in bright banners and flags. I take a deep breath and march up the white marbled stone steps. I throw back the red silk curtain that serves as a door and choke on the smoke filling the air. Cadewynn trips in behind me, waving smoke out of her face.

"What is this place?" she coughs, squinting through the smoke toward the crowded floor littered with tables, people, and alcohol galore. "Is this a tavern?"

Kaeya chuckles. "Not quite. More like a gambling hall. And a bit of a brothel."

"A what?" Cadewynn stutters, her eyes wide with something akin to horror. "Why are we here?"

Before either of us can answer, a young woman in a dress that accentuates every curve leaving little to the imagination slides toward us.

"May I help you?" she asks, her white teeth shining in the dim light.

I lean forward, grinning wickedly. "Let's not play. You know as well as I do that Sobek is expecting us, so why don't you just let us through?"

"I'm sorry, but Mr. Sobek is busy and not able to entertain today. Perhaps try scheduling a meeting and—"

I push forward and the woman grabs my arm, her painted red nails digging into my flesh. I hiss and spin to face her, my hand going to the dagger strapped to my thigh.

"I wouldn't test me," I snap.

"And I said you have to come back."

I grit my teeth, ready to pull the dagger from its sheath, but Kaeya is one step ahead, her dagger already under the woman's chin. I grin as the woman narrows her eyes at me.

"Come, let's not get blood all over the floor. It's so difficult to clean," a cheerful voice cuts through the tension as a charming figure steps forward.

I relax as Kaeya's dagger drops. At first glance the newcomer looks young, maybe twenty-five, but I know for a fact they're pushing forty.

"I take by your presence, Gen, that Sobek is ready to meet?"

Gen smiles, crossing their arms. "You really don't think Sobek has more important things to do than deal with your attitude, Jess?"

I tilt my head, smirking. "Good thing I brought guests."

I nod to Cadewynn over my shoulder and Gen follows the movement with a scowl, their arms dropping back to their side.

"Who are your guests? We don't let just any—"

"I'm sure Sobek knows," I cut them off sharply with a wave. "Now, will you take us back or do we need to fight our way through?"

Gen sighs, motioning for us to follow them. We wind through the masses toward the back hall, separated from the main room by a door of dangling beads. It's quieter in the back, but the hum of the business up front still sounds around us.

Gen leads us to the room at the very back corner and holds back another curtain of beads for us to enter. Sobek sits in the corner of the room on a mountain of plush, silk pillows smoking a pipe. He's shirtless but wearing a lavish blue and gold robe with several chains of gold and jewels draped around his neck. Dozens of rings glitter on his fingers. I have no doubt he added extra jewels and silks to make an impression. A quick glance at Cadewynn proves she's more disgusted by his tacky display than impressed, and I have to bite back a smile.

"Ah! Jessalynn!" Sobek says, spreading his arms wide in greeting. "What have I done to deserve the honor of your presence?" His eyes flit behind me and he adds, "Who are your traveling companions?"

I take a deep breath and motion for Cadewynn to step forward. "May I introduce Princess Cadewynn Montavillier of Callenia."

Cadewynn inclines her head as Sobek takes her in, drawing a long drag from his pipe.

"Pleasure to meet you, Princess. I take it you didn't come here to gamble or for other . . . pleasures?"

A smile curls on Cadewynn's lips as she steps forward, assessing the man in front of her. I smirk, folding my arms, as Sobek scowls.

"You seem like an assertive man," Cadewynn answers slowly in flawless Gleador. "I assume you knew exactly who I was before I stepped foot in your building, and you know precisely why I am here. Let's not play games, even if they are your specialty."

Sobek blinks rapidly before nodding. "Fine." He stands, handing his pipe off to Gen who rushes forward to grab it. "You want to jump straight in, let's. I assume you're here to ask for money or men to fight. I know your brother came through begging King Naimon for help months ago and he was denied armies."

"He wasn't denied armies outright," Cadewynn cuts in. "Provinces have the option to provide them."

"And that's why you're here. You want my army, but I'm afraid I have to deny your request." Sobek folds his hands behind his back as he takes another step forward. "I have businesses to run. Trade flourishes here in Jakuma, and I have to protect my investments. I only have so many trained soldiers."

"Trained soldiers and mercenaries," Cadewynn replies calmly.

Sobek staggers back a step, his confidence wavering. Even I can't hide my shock.

"My merca—but how . . . ?" Sobek stutters.

"Oh, I'm sorry. Did you mistake me for a foolish princess?" Cadewynn says with a smile that chills even my bones. "I know you rely heavily on mercenaries in addition to the army that has been provided by the king. You have men to spare."

Sobek straightens, regaining his composure. "Even then, I think I will still deny your request."

Cadewynn nods once. "So be it."

She turns in one smooth motion toward the door behind us. I blink, sure that the princess who got down on her knees and begged me for help isn't really just giving up so fast. Even Sobek seems baffled, calling after her.

"That's it? You come all this way to walk out after barely a minute of discussion?"

He sounds furious and I kind of love it. Cadewynn turns back to him slowly.

"Did you expect me to grovel?"

Sobek scowls. "I . . ."

"I assume you made your decision after careful deliberation. Why should I waste my words? Clearly, you have already decided that the risk isn't worth it."

"What risk?"

Cadewynn arches an eyebrow. "What risk? There are Dragkonians loose in the world again, and while they may be in Callenia now, they will not stay there. They are greedy beasts who will come for you sooner or later. Sooner, if we fail to get the aid we need to hold them back. But I assume you have already considered this and are preparing for the day they come to take your city and wealth from you."

Sobek shakes his head, but he looks a good shade or two paler than normal. "You're wrong. Even if you lose the war, they won't come for me."

Cadewynn laughs, shaking her head. "Oh, come now. I know you're not foolish enough to believe that. Good luck when the war comes to Jakuma and it's just you and your mercenaries against a hoard of evil."

Cadewynn turns again, but Sobek lunges forward, grabbing her elbow. My reflexes kick in and Sobek finds my dagger against his chest. He releases Cadewynn with a jerk, putting his hands in the air.

"What difference will my armies make if you plan to lose anyway?" he demands, dropping his hands as I lower my dagger.

Cadewynn sighs but doesn't bother to turn around.

"You seem like a gambling man, so let me put it this way." She turns and meets his eyes. "Let's say you're playing a game of cards and you need three very specific cards to win the game. You're given the choice of drawing three cards or ten. Which would give the better chance of getting the hand you need to win?"

Sobek scoffs. "The ten cards, of course."

Cadewynn nods. "Exactly. Right now, we are going against the Dragkonians with a hand of three cards. While we might have the draw we need, our armies may fall short. The more cards or armies we have, the more likely we are to win. If we remain divided, we are all more likely to lose, one right after the other, but if we band together now, we just may come out with the winning hand."

Sobek studies Cadewynn, chewing on his lip. "I understand what you're saying, but I'm still not sure what I can commit."

"You have one hour," Cadewynn says, spinning and marching toward the door. She pauses as Nyco parts the curtain of beads, glancing over her shoulder. "I eagerly await your reply."

Cadewynn disappears, Nyco tripping after her. I nod to

Kaeya and she and Sama follow them. Once they're gone, Sobek glares at me, his face red in frustration.

"What is the meaning of this, Jessalynn?" he spits.

I shrug, fighting back a grin. "I thought the princess made it quite obvious."

"I heard she was a bookworm not suited for war. That girl," he sputters, thrusting a finger to where Cadewynn stood moments before, "is no simple bookworm."

My smile slips free as I fold my arms across my chest. "No, she is not. So, what are you going to do?"

"What choice do I have?" he cries throwing his hands in the air. "I'll assemble some soldiers for her army, but an hour? That's not enough time to decide the numbers I can afford to extend!"

"It is if you have Gen help," I reply, nodding to where they stand against the wall watching. "After all, we both know they're the real brains behind your operation, and you wouldn't be worth a thing without them."

Gen grins, pushing away from the wall while Sobek fumes.

"I can help if you'd like," Gen says.

Sobek sighs, dragging a hand down his face. "Fine. We will get the numbers for the princess within the hour, but you owe me, Jess."

I throw back my head and laugh. "You just try and call in that bargain."

Sobek glares at me as I turn and stride from the room. When I reach the main room, the crowd between me and the exit practically parts on its own. I blink as I step back out into the sun, my eyes focusing on the rest of my group waiting for me at the base of the stairs. For the first time since arriving, Cadewynn looks nervous.

"Did he . . . ? Will he . . . ?"

I grin and nod, clapping a hand to her shoulder. "He's figuring out the exact number now."

Cadewynn sighs, relaxing. "Good. Then we can be back on the road soon."

My eyes widen as I drop my hand. "Define soon."

"Well," Cadewynn replies, squinting at the sun. "It's still early in the day, so I figured we could be back on the road within an hour or two. The sooner we get to the next province the better."

I shake my head. "We need to rest."

Cadewynn meets my eyes, her hard, determined look returning. "There's no point in wasting daylight. Besides, the sooner we finish, the sooner you can escape my company."

I sigh, shaking my head again. "Fine. But I'm drinking and eating until it's time to leave."

If Cadewynn has any objections to my plans, she doesn't voice them. She merely nods once and turns to Sama and Nyco, allowing them to lead her away into the city. With a sigh, I watch them disappear into the crowd.

This princess will be the death of me, but I think I can tolerate her. Maybe. All I know is that I definitely don't want to end up on her bad side.

CHAPTER SEVENTEEN

EHREN

I wake in a pocket of warmth, only vaguely aware of where I am. I feel something shift beneath me and realize with a start that I'm snuggled up against Cal. I'm debating what my next move should be when he shifts again, his eyes fluttering open. He blinks at me in groggy surprise as I draw away to lie beside him.

"Morning," I mumble with a smile. "It seems like sharing the blanket worked well enough to keep us from freezing to death in our sleep."

Cal returns my smile. "It would appear so."

I sit up and the cold air swoops in around me. I immediately lie back down, snuggling against Cal as I pull the blanket closer around us.

"Nope, it is far too cold to leave our blankets," I mumble into his chest as he chuckles, slipping his arm around me.

"We have to get up and get on the road," Cal says, though he makes no move to do so. "Besides, I think I smell coffee."

"You do not . . . Wait." I lift my head and sniff the air. "There *is* coffee."

Cal laughs. "Come on. Let's go grab some."

Reluctantly, I allow Cal to pull back the blankets and we rise. We grab our cloaks, still a bit damp from the previous day but dry enough to work, and head outside. Lorrell squats over a small fire, examining a brewing pot of coffee.

"Good morning!" he greets us as we approach. "The coffee is almost ready."

"I'll pack our things while it heats up," Cal offers. "That way we can get on the road as soon as possible."

Lorrell nods. "Pascal is packing up our things."

Cal disappears into our tent, emerging a few minutes later with our packed bags. We secure them to our horses and then I help him break down the tents. By the time we finish, the coffee is nice and warm. We decide that coffee is more than substantial enough to call breakfast, and we're soon on our way.

The wind is sharp and biting, but the rain and snow have ceased, making our day of traveling down the mountain easier than the previous day. Shortly before nightfall, we find a level spot surrounded by trees. We make a fire and eat strips of dried meat and what remains of our cheese. After dinner, I check my supplies by the light of the campfire for the warding spell ingredients and find them lower than anticipated.

"What's wrong?" Cal asks, noting my scowl as I stare down into my bag.

"The warding spell. I only have enough for a few more nights." I raise my eyes to his. "We should probably save them for further into Ascaria in case we run into any problems and need the extra protection."

THE STARDUST IN THE ASHES

Cal nods. "So, we should split up on Guard duty tonight, then?"

"That would probably be best."

"Good," Pascal cuts in. "Cal and I can take first shift. That will give me a break from Lorrell. He talks in his sleep."

"I do not!" Lorrell cries.

"You do too," Pascal counters.

"How would you even be able to hear me talking over your snoring?" Lorrell snaps.

"Fine," I cut in a little too sharply. "Pascal and Cal can take first shift and Lorrell and I will take second. Since we're taking shifts, there's no need to set up both tents. One will do."

Lorrell and Pascal nod in agreement, going back to eating the last few bites of their dinner. Cal and I rise and erect the tent. We play a couple hands of cards until our fingers are too numb from the cold to hold them properly. Lorrell and I settle in the tent as Cal and Pascal start their patrol. Lorrell falls asleep quickly, and I discover that Pascal was not wrong about Lorrell talking in his sleep. Thankfully, it's a low enough mumble it doesn't bother me. I'm awakened a few hours later by Pascal and Lorrell arguing.

"It can't be time for my shift yet," Lorrell grumbles.

"It is. Now, get out there and let me sleep."

I sit up and roll my neck. "So I guess it's time for my shift as well?"

Pascal nods, looking a bit sheepish. "Yes, though I didn't mean to wake you."

I shrug, standing. "It's fine. Is Cal still outside?"

Pascal nods. I thank him and slip out, the night air cold and bracing. Cal sits next the fire, staring into the flames. As I approach, he lifts his eyes to me.

"I was going to let you sleep a bit longer," he confesses as I sink down next to him. "You need your rest."

"You need sleep too, you know," I counter. "Besides, didn't we cover this a couple days ago? I don't want any special privileges because I'm the prince."

Cal smiles softly. "I wasn't letting you sleep simply because you're the prince. I was letting you sleep because I want you at your peak the next time we meet a lake monster."

I chuckle. "Ah, I see. Well, I'm up now, so you can get some shut eye."

Cal's eyes lock on mine and I realize how close we're sitting. My heartbeat heightens. My eyes fall to his mouth, and as if he can read my thoughts, his lips part. I shift closer, placing my hand over his. Cal takes an unsteady breath as he shifts closer.

"I'm up. I'm up," Lorrell grumbles from behind us, exiting the tent.

Cal jerks to his feet and I swear under my breath. Lorrell looks at me curiously but doesn't say anything.

"Goodnight," Cal mumbles quickly, turning and striding to the tent.

My frustration at Lorrell fades as he pulls out his deck of cards. He's horrible at every game we try, but we have fun. In between each round, we take turns walking around the barriers of the camp. Everything stays calm without a hint of trouble. When the sun begins peeking around the rocky ridge, Lorrell starts a pot of coffee. I fill two cups and head inside the tent. Cal is awake, sitting on his bedroll, but Pascal is still dead sleep, his arm slung over his face.

"I see you didn't share a blanket with Pascal last night," I whisper, handing Cal his coffee as I sink down by his side, our legs brushing.

Cal's eyes shine as he takes a sip. "I heard he's a blanket hog."

"I heard that, too." I pause before hesitantly adding, "Did you sleep well?"

Cal's shining eyes meet mine as the corners of his lips turn up into a slight smile. "Not as well as the past couple of nights, but well enough."

A smile twitches on my own lips as I glance away, sipping my own coffee. "Oh? Why is that?"

"If I have to say it, then perhaps I'm the only one who's been sleeping better than usual."

I look back over Cal and my heart flutters. "You're not the only one."

Cal smiles into his coffee. "Good."

Pascal stirs, his arm flopping from his face, but he doesn't wake up all the way. Cal and I exchange a look, grinning.

"Give him a few more minutes, but then we should be on the road."

Cal nods, taking another sip of coffee. "I've got everything packed, I think, but I'll make sure he's up in time."

I nod and head back outside with Lorrell. Within the hour, we're on the road. After only a couple hours of travel, we come around a bend that looks down off the mountainside. We're almost off the mountain. In fact, we should be leaving the mountains by the end of the day. Our moods lighter, we travel downward quickly, making up for any lost time due to the weather the previous days. It's a couple hours from nightfall as we finally leave the mountain behind us, traveling across mostly open land made of rolling hills.

We're on Ascarian soil, but we don't feel any of the risk until roughly an hour before dark falls. A line of horses appears in the distance, riding hard toward us. We all exchange wary glances but continue forward. The closer the riders get, the better we can see them. They're Ascarian soldiers, but not soldiers alone. In the center of the soldiers ride two royals.

"What do we do?" Pascal asks as they approach.

"Stay calm," I order, sitting straighter in my saddle. "We're here on a peaceful mission. Let's not give them any reason to think otherwise."

Pascal nods, licking his lips, every muscle tense. I ride on ahead just slightly, inclining my head when I'm within speaking distance.

"I am Prince Ehren of Callenia and I come in peace," I say, my voice ringing around us.

"We know who you are," the princess says, her voice clipped and harsh.

"We've been expecting you," the prince says, his tone warm and friendly. "I am Prince Luc and this is my sister, Princesse Nicolette."

I raise my eyes and look from the prince to the princess, my confusion evident.

"Do you have a problem?" the princess snaps, sitting straighter on her horse. "Because it is rather rude to stare."

I bow my head. "I do apologize. I must have remembered incorrectly, but I was under the assumption that Ascaria had two princesses and no living prince."

Princesse Nicolette bristles, but Prince Luc gives me an easy smile.

"Once," he says, "that was true. However, in recent years, I have embraced my true identity as a prince, instead of the identity placed on me when I was born. I hope this will not be a problem with our negotiations."

I shake my head and smile. "Any negotiations will not be affected in the slightest. I can't imagine why they would be."

Princesse Nicolette relaxes slightly on her horse and whispers something in rapid Ascarian to her brother I can't quite catch. Prince Luc responds with a nod and a tight smile before turning his attention back to us.

"We were hoping you would arrive a bit earlier in the day so we could make it back to Château des Chamans before nightfall but, alas, it is nearly a full day of travel. We are situated in a camp not more than an hour away and we invite you to follow us and rest among our company. Tomorrow, we can travel together to Château des Chamans, if it so suits you," Prince Luc offers, inclining his head.

"Of course," I reply. "It would be rude to disregard such hospitality."

"Very well, then."

Prince Luc turns his horse, the rest of his company following suit. He gestures for me to ride between him and his sister, and I oblige. Cal, Lorrell, and Pascal trail behind me with Prince Luc's guards. I sit straight and regal on Dauntless, reacting instinctively as I have been trained my whole life. In some ways, it feels natural to converse lightly with Prince Luc and Princesse Nicolette, switching between Callenian and my rusty Ascarian, but it also feels off. It's a very different change of pace from the past few months.

We arrive at our destination a little after nightfall to find a full camp bathed in silver moonlight. There are at least a dozen more soldiers and a handful of servants scurrying around. Prince Luc dismounts and I follow his lead, most of the soldiers and my own Guard doing the same. A man rushes up to the prince, speaking in rapid Ascarian. I struggle to follow the conversation, catching only a couple of words.

Prince Luc nods, turning to me. "This is Marcel. He will happily take your horses and care for them, giving them food and whatever else they need."

I hand Dauntless's reigns to Marcel, doing my best to put my Ascarian to good use. "Thank you, Marcel. This is Dauntless."

His eyes light up at my use of Ascarian. "I will take good care of him," he replies, slowly enough I can process his words.

Cal steps forward behind me, handing off his horse as well.

"Thank you. This is Galant."

His Callenian accent is heavy, but he otherwise speaks the little bit of Ascarian flawlessly. I watch Cal, eyes bright as he steps to the side. I can tell he feels my eyes on him by the way he's purposefully avoiding my gaze, a smile playing on his lips.

Once Marcel has taken all four of our horses as well as the horses of the prince and princesse, Luc leads us toward one of the many campfires. Logs have been set up around this particular fire, giving us convenient places to sit. Luc and Nicolette sit side-by-side on one log and I take up the one opposite. Pascal and Lorrell seat themselves on the log to my right. I expect Cal to take a seat next to me, but he opts for the remaining unoccupied log. I try to hide my dismay, focusing on the servant who is making her way from person to person with roasted meat kabobs on a tray.

"Thank you," I say, plucking up two.

"Has your journey been easy thus far?" Prince Luc asks.

"More or less," I reply before taking a bite of my dinner. My eyes widen with delight as a citrusy, smoky flavor fills my mouth. "This is quite delicious."

"But of course," Nicolette says with a wave of her hand. "We brought with us one of our cooks." She lets her eyes drift over Cal, Pascal, and Makin. "Did you, perhaps, bring a cook of your own?"

I smile and shake my head. "We brought only what was necessary—basic supplies, two tents, food rations . . ."

"You only brought two tents?" Nicolette says with a scowl. She exchanges a look with her brother, slipping into Ascarian. "You were correct. They are worse off than we suspected."

I shift uncomfortably on my log, forcing a smile, but it's Cal who speaks.

"We had plenty of tents and fineries to choose from, of course, but opted to trade comforts for speed."

I shoot Cal a grateful look before looking back to Luc and Nicolette. "Cal is correct. The more supplies and people that accompany us, the more time and exposure we risk."

Prince Luc studies me, nodding. "I can understand that very well. Nicolette doesn't like to go anywhere without every bit of finery accessible."

Nicolette frowns at her brother. "I am a princesse after all. Why shouldn't I have nice things?"

"Either way," Luc says, waving his sister off, "we did erect a spare tent worthy of a visiting prince if you would like to stay there tonight."

"Thank you for your kind offer, but I have no problem sharing a tent with my Guard like I have done most nights during our journey."

Nicolette's eyes go wide, something akin to disgust on

her face. "You mean to say that not only have you been sleeping in a regular tent, but also you have been sharing it with a common soldier?"

I bristle, sitting straighter. "No, I have not been sharing my tent with a common soldier, but a good friend."

"A friend?" Nicolette eyes me for a moment before her lips turn up into a smile. "Ah, a *close* friend perhaps?"

I notice the tips of Cal's ears redden slightly as I fight my own blush.

"Nicolette!" Luc hisses, shooting his sister a lethal glare before reprimanding her in Ascarian. "Your manners are unacceptable." He turns his attention back to me, switching to Callenian. "I apologize for my sister's words and actions. She often forgets that other countries and people have different customs and arrangements. Regardless, a tent is ready for you should you desire it."

"Thank you," I murmur. "I do appreciate it."

We fall silent for several minutes, finishing our dinner, before Luc rises.

"It is early yet, but I will show you to where we have your tent and show your Guards where they may set up theirs. If you choose to retire after days of travel, that is fine, but you are also welcome around any campfire."

I nod my thanks and stand, following him to the tent. It's very similar to the one King Naimon of Gleador gave me when we left Koshima. Inside is a low bed, adorned with blankets and pillows. A washbowl sits in one corner next to a lantern. Cal, Pascal, and Lorrell leave with Luc to set up additional tents. I sit down on the edge of the bed and look around. It's so much space compared to the last few nights. Space filled with void. I don't like being alone. The tent flap opens and I startle, looking up to see Cal entering. I smile and rise, but Cal doesn't return my smile.

"I think you have my blanket in your pack," he says, looking past me to where my bag sits.

"Stay here with me," I say, making no move to get the blanket.

Cal shakes his head. "I don't think that would be appropriate tonight."

"Cal . . ." I reach my hand toward him, but he steps out of my reach, still refusing to meet my eyes.

"We need Ascaria as an ally and appearances are half the battle," he says, his voice flat and lifeless.

I want to argue. I want to tell him I don't care, but decades of training keep me silent. I nod and glance away, motioning to my pack.

"Take all the blankets you need. I have others."

Cal nods and quickly crosses to grab the blanket. Seconds later he's gone and the emptiness of the tent sinks in around me. I should probably leave and find Luc. I need to make connections and win them over. I need to seem as much a friend as an ally. Any energy I possessed earlier, however, has faded away. I can't bring myself to leave my tent. The air feels heavy, crushing. I can barely breathe let alone put thoughts into words. Luc said he would understand. I can start relations tomorrow.

I sink down onto the bed, into almost familiar comforts. I pull the blankets around me, shutting out the cold, but I still don't feel warm. I toss and turn, time meaningless. I know it has to be late at night by now, but I can't sleep, although I'm exhausted. I sit up, throwing back the covers. I lean forward, placing my head in my hands, and tears break free. I can't even place why I'm crying. Everything just feels like too much. After a few minutes, I manage to pull myself together. I stand and peek out of my tent. The camp has settled into quiet, most people gone off to bed. A few soldiers patrol between the tents and around the edges, but it's otherwise still. I step outside, looking around, wondering where Luc had the others set up their tents. I should have followed. I should have—

"Ehren? What are you doing out here?"

I spin as Cal steps from the shadows next to my tent. My mouth drops open as I meet his eyes.

His forehead furrows with concern as he closes the distance between us, his eyes darting over my face. "What's wrong?"

"I was . . . I came to find you," I confess.

"Why?"

My face falls as my shoulders drop. "Do you have to ask?"

Cal glances around before he says, "Let's discuss this inside."

I nod and follow him into my tent. I light the lantern to chase away the darkness before I turn to face him, taking his hands in mine.

"I want you in here with me. I don't want to be alone, Cal. I need you."

Cal shakes his head, pulling his hands away as he takes a step back. "You heard Nicolette. You know what people will assume. You can't—"

"So let them assume!" I cut him off, my voice louder than I mean. I sigh and rake a hand through my hair. "What I mean is that I don't care what they think. It's not as if their assumptions are entirely wrong."

Cal takes a step toward me, locking his eyes with mine. "You should care, though, and you know it."

"Tell me why I should care." I lift a hand, brushing my fingers across his cheek. "Because right now I'm struggling to find a reason to let their opinions matter."

Cal's shoulders fall as he turns away, moving away from my touch. "Because we both know that one of the best ways to seal an alliance is through marriage. If they think you're ineligible, everything could fall apart." He glances over his shoulder, his face shrouded in sadness. "Tell me I'm wrong. Tell me that if Nicolette agreed to marry you tomorrow to seal a treaty that you wouldn't do it."

I feel deflated looking into his eyes. I can't find the words or sort through the emotions flooding my thoughts. My brain wars between years of training and duty and my true desires and the happiness I find in Cal's presence. Cal takes my silence as admission and nods, stepping toward the exit.

"I thought so."

I reach out and grab his wrist, pulling him back to face me. "That doesn't have to change anything."

"I know you, Ehren," Cal whispers, gently twisting his hand from my grasp. "You're good and loyal. You'll do what's best for your kingdom, and I love that about you. I know you've sworn to be devoted to your future bride, and I respect you for that. I'm happy to stay in the shadows, watching you prosper. It's where I've been my entire life. I made my peace with it long ago."

I swallow hard. "What if I don't want you in the shadows anymore?" My voice is a hoarse whisper, barely audible, even in the silence of the tent.

Cal licks his lips, everything about his expression pained and it kills me. "Do you really think that's an option?

Because I'm not sure it is. I know what your kingdom and duty mean to you. I won't get in the way of that."

"That doesn't have to change anything about tonight," I argue, my voice breaking.

"Yes it does! It changes everything, Ehren!" Cal yells, startling me with the voracity of his tone.

I long to reach out and take him in my arms, prove him wrong. He takes another step back, fighting back the tears brimming in his eyes as he rubs the back of his neck, struggling to compose himself.

"Gods, I can't do this," he mumbles, moving back another half-step. "I thought I could . . . The past few days and nights have been a dream, but it's time for me to wake up."

Tears sting my eyes as I whisper, "Please, don't leave me alone with my thoughts. Even if you don't share my bed, please, don't leave. My world is too dark without you." Realization strikes and I add, "Why were you outside my tent, anyway? Didn't Prince Luc give you a tent of your own, or at least a place to set up a tent?"

Cal swallows, glancing to the side. "I wasn't going to leave you unguarded in a camp run by another kingdom."

"Good. That's good," I say, taking a step toward Cal. "Tell them that if anyone bothers to ask why you're here." I take his hand and feel a brief flutter of hope when he doesn't try to pull it away. "Stay with me. Please."

Cal forces his eyes to mine and I can read the conflict there.

"Please, Cal. I—I need you."

"Fine," he says with a heavy sigh. My shoulders sag with relief. "But I'm sleeping on the floor. Give me a moment to gather my things."

"Thank you, Cal. I mean it."

He offers me a tight smile that doesn't reach his eyes. "You don't have to thank me, Ehren. I'll do anything for you. I only wish things could be different."

He slowly pulls his hand from mine and leaves me, thoughts spinning and heart beating wildly. Without him, the tent feels even emptier than before, but at least this time I know he'll be back. It isn't quite what I wanted, but it's better than being alone with my thoughts. Everything is better with Cal near, and I'll take every moment I can.

CHAPTER EIGHTEEN

ALAK

We get on the road as early as we can, eager to reach our destination within the estimated two days. The weather, however, decides to work against us. By noon, my clothes are soaked through and even my magic isn't helping to keep me dry.

"We should really stop," I suggest through chattering teeth.

The rain between us is so thick I can barely see Bram shake his head. "No. I am not wasting daylight."

"What bloody daylight?" I yell back at him, gesturing dramatically at the sky. "Even the sun doesn't want to be out in this downpour."

"We are not stopping, Alak."

I grit my teeth, my hands tightening on the reigns. I summon more magic, attempting a shield from the rain, but it does little to no good. I decide Bram is officially my least favorite person alive at this moment, and I glare daggers into the back of his head. When he finally agrees we can set up camp for the night, I hate him a little less, but he's still near the top of my hate list. I use magic to erect my tent quickly and dash inside, stripping down and using more magic to dry off before slipping into fresh clothes. I light a lantern and am about to use more magic to dry my wet clothes when Bram ducks into my tent, eying me in my dry clothes.

"What the hell do you want?" I ask, my voice sharp.

Bram narrows his eyes. "I was going to ask if you wanted to eat together, but I take that as a firm negative."

He turns to leave and I sigh, raking a hand through my hair. "Wait. I'm sorry. Yes, you can eat in here."

Bram turns back toward me, his lips in a tight almost-smile. He sloshes toward me and I sigh again.

"Would you like me to use magic to dry you off?"

Bram pauses. "I wouldn't want you to strain yourself."

I roll my eyes and extend my hand, sending a wave of magic toward Bram as I mumble, "I'm not *that* weak. Gods."

Once Bram is dry, he holds out his arms, examining his clothes like he's looking for mistakes. I mutter swears under my breath as I sit down on the floor, pulling my pack into my lap. Bram finally sits crossed-legged across from me as I withdraw food from my pack. I'm not entirely sure why Bram invaded my solitude because he doesn't say a word the entire time we eat. When he's finished the portion of food he brought, he stands to leave.

"Wait," I say, jumping up.

Bram arches an eyebrow. "What?"

"What the hell was this?" I ask, motioning wildly.

"What was what?" Bram asks, eyeing me like I'm the insane one.

I sigh and shake my head. "Never mind." Bram continues staring at me. "Look, I just thought that maybe you wanted to talk or play cards or . . . something."

Bram nods glancing away. "I guess we could play cards, if you want."

"Look, mate, if you want to play cards, fine, but I just . . . you're acting odd."

"I am not acting odd," Bram says defensively, crossing his arms with a frown. "You are the one acting odd."

"Me? How the hell am *I* being odd?" I demand, hitting my chest with my palm for emphasis.

"You just are. If you didn't want me to eat with you, you could have said no."

I sigh and drag a hand down my face. "What the he—"

"I am trying, okay?" Bram cuts me off.

I furrow my brow at him and he meets my eyes.

"I am trying," he repeats through gritted teeth. "I don't make friends easily. I never have. Ehren was a fluke and the Guard are mostly my friends from obligation. I am not even sure how many of them consider me a friend, to be honest. I am not truly close to any of them in that way. So, I am trying, but I feel a little lost. You and I have nothing in common, save for Astra. I don't know what to say or do around you."

I relax my shoulders and offer Bram a smile. "We were friends years ago, mate. All we have to do is resume that relationship."

Bram shakes his head. "We are not the same people we were then."

I release a long breath and nod. "You're not wrong. Let's start with playing cards. Maybe I'll even teach you a magic trick."

Bram's frown returns in full force. "A magic trick?"

I grin. "Aye. A magic trick." I wiggle my fingers. "A bit of illusion."

I resume my seat and motion for Bram to do the same. He hesitates, but slowly sinks to the ground.

"Did you bring cards?" I ask. Bram nods and I extend my hand. "Here, let me see them. I'll teach you a basic card trick."

Bram scowls as he pulls a deck of cards from his pocket and places them in my hand. "I don't know how well I will be at magic."

I grin, shuffling the cards with flare. "I'll start with a basic sleight of hand." I lift my eyes to his. "Don't worry; even children can do this one."

He huffs and crosses his arms, regret flashing across his face, but he's too proud to back out now. I grin and hold the deck out to him.

"Pick up the top card and look at it, but don't show it to me." Bram complies, eyeing me warily before glancing at the card. "Now, memorize it. Got it?"

Bram rolls his eyes. "This is stupid."

"Work with me," I insist. "Now, if you've got it memorized, place it back on top of the deck."

With a long sigh, Bram follows my instructions. I quickly shuffle the cards before holding up a card.

"Is this your card?" Bram's eyes go wide and I grin. "It is, isn't it?"

"How did you . . . Did you use real magic?"

I throw my head back and laugh. "No. Not at all. This is one of the oldest tricks. Let me show you how it works."

I pass the cards to him and order him to shuffle them. Once he's done, I draw the top card, show it to him, and place it back on top. I then demonstrate how to palm the card, only pretending to shuffle it back into the deck before revealing it again.

"That's deceitful," Bram mumbles after we've tried the trick a few times successfully.

I chuckle, shuffling the cards. "Most magic is. Or, at least it was before real magic returned. Want to learn another one?"

Bram considers my offer for a moment before nodding. The rain patters against the tent roof but we barely notice, spending the next couple hours switching between sleight of hand and playing card games. Though, after seeing me at work and learning my secrets, Bram is wary every time I win a hand, even when I swear I'm not using any magic, real or otherwise. I have no idea what time Bram decides to head to his own tent, but my eyes are tired when he finally leaves. I blow out my lantern and snuggle beneath my blankets.

Sometime during the night, the rain stops, leaving behind mud-soaked terrain. We eat breakfast quickly before loading up our tents and supplies and getting on our way. Despite the mud, we actually make good time, opting to ride through lunch, though my stomach grumbles in protest. It's early evening when the forest we're seeking comes into view. Even though the sun is starting to set as we approach the tree line, we head on into the trees.

"Keep your eyes open for the clues," Bram says. "Let me know if you sense anything magical."

I snort, shaking my head. "Mate, I can sense every little magical insect in this forest."

"Well, see if there is anything you sense that is, I don't know . . . distinct."

I sigh and nod. There's no point in arguing with him. We wander aimlessly for a bit, less light leaking through the trees every minute. And then, I sense it. It's a faint trail of magic, but it's purposeful. It's meant to attract someone like me. I look over at Bram to call his attention, but he's spotted something as well. I grin and give him a thumbs up. He can follow his path and I'll follow mine. Hopefully, we'll end up in the same spot. I dismount Fawn so I can follow the trail better since it's clearest closer to the ground. Bram disappears in the trees to my left as I continue straight, the magic trail growing stronger. When I hear someone in the brush to my left, I assume it's Bram until they speak.

"What are you doing here?" a sharp, female voice demands.

I turn, a sloppy grin fading from my face when I see the young woman standing a few feet away, a bow in her hand with an arrow pointed directly at me. I raise my hands slowly.

"Look here, love," I say, swallowing hard. "I mean no harm. Chances are you and I are on the same side."

"Well, if you have nothing to hide, tell me your name and your purpose in these woods."

I meet and hold her bright hazel eyes. "I'm looking for the refugee camp for those with magic. I heard there was one such camp in these woods."

Her eyes narrow at me, her shoulders relaxing, but she doesn't lower the arrow. "Why? How can I trust you?"

I offer her a weak smile. "I have magic, you see. I can show you if—"

"No! Just hold still." I notice a movement behind her and Bram emerges from the shadows. I breathe a sigh of relief as the girl continues eying me. "I need to think a moment."

"I take it you aren't the usual guard for the camp," I say, eager to keep her attention on me until Bram can get into a better position.

The girl glares at me, setting her jaw. "Are you saying

you don't think I can shoot you with this arrow? Because I can."

I take a tentative step back. Rule number one of survival is not to piss off the people with the weapons. "Not what I'm saying at all, love."

Bram steps behind the girl, unsheathing his sword without a sound. I marvel at his stealth as he lifts the sword point to the back of the girl's neck, her eyes going wide.

"I suggest you—" Bram starts.

"Oh!" the girl cries out, releasing her hold on the bow, the arrow flying free.

I jump out of the way, barely avoiding the arrow. She lifts her hands in the air, looking terrified.

"You could have killed me," I snap, glaring more at Bram than at the girl.

"I'm sorry, I just—" she turns her head and glances at Bram and her eyes widen even more but her fear vanishes. "Wait! I know you!"

Bram lowers his sword slightly as he studies her face.

"Mara?" he asks, dropping the sword to his side, his confusion evident.

The girl grins and claps her hands. "Yes! I do know you! You're Bram, right?"

Bram nods, still trying to put together the pieces of the puzzle while I stand to the side, completely lost. Mara looks behind him eagerly.

"Is Astra with you?"

At Astra's name, Bram stiffens, shaking his head. I, however, take a step closer to the girl.

"You know Astra?"

Mara turns to me with a scowl, crossing her arms as she scans me from top to bottom.

"Of course I know her. She's been my best friend since, well, forever. Who are *you?*"

I grin, extending my hand. "Name's Alak, Alak Dunne."

Mara's eyes light up as she crosses to me, shaking my hand enthusiastically. "Yes! Astra mentioned you. You're a performer who is teaching her how to control her magic."

My face falls into a frown as Bram snorts a laugh.

"It's not funny," I snap at Bram.

He grins at me. "Oh, I disagree. It is hilarious."

Mara looks from me to Bram and back again. "What did I miss?" She looks back at Bram. "Are you still engaged?"

Bram's grin fades. "Unfortunately, no."

"Oh dear. That's such sad news," Mara says, her face looking like she's sincerely disappointed.

"Don't worry," I cut in, my grin resurfacing. "Astra found someone better."

"Who? Wait, did she end up falling in love with Prince Ehren?" she asks, her eyes bright. "A royal wedding would be lovely."

Bram snorts again as I shake my head. "Um, not exactly."

"Well, who could be better than the prince or his captain?"

"Yes, Alak," Bram presses, his grin fighting to return. "Tell us, who is better than the Captain of the Guard?"

I sigh and rake a hand through my hair. "I don't think I want to say now."

Mara scowls. "Why not?"

"Because it's me," I yell without meaning to, throwing my hands in the air.

"You?" Mara cocks her head, assessing me as Bram chuckles behind her. "Well, I suppose she must see something in you."

"Gods," I mutter.

Mara's face breaks into a grin. "I'm only teasing. Of course I can see why Astra would be attracted to you. Even with those scars, you're quite handsome."

My hand absentmindedly traces the jagged scars snaking across my face. Sometimes I forget about them. All amusement vanishes from Bram's face. He knows how I got these scars and what they represent.

"Well, Mara, it is almost dark. Is there a camp nearby?" Bram says.

I shoot him a grateful smile as Mara turns back to him.

"Oh, yes! I was just checking the barrier. Normally Paul does it, but he was busy. It's why I'm a bit jumpy. I'm not used to being so far from the camp itself. I never know what to do if I find someone. I'll take you there."

Bram nods and fetches Solomon from where he's hidden in the trees. Mara marches through the forest. I walk to Mara's left, leading Fawn, and Bram takes her right leading Solomon. As we walk, Mara rambles endlessly, explaining exactly how she and a few others from her village were forced to flee and how they banded together to form the refugee camp and army.

"So there is an army?" Bram muses.

Mara nods emphatically. "Yes. After you left, Pax discovered he had some basic magical abilities. He began trying to integrate his magic into his skills as a soldier, figuring a war was brewing. When we finally fled Timberborn, he began to send out signals for others to train with him. His army has gained a lot more traction and momentum than he ever expected. It seems word of mouth travels fast."

"How many soldiers?" Bram presses.

Mara shrugs. "I don't know the exact numbers, if I'm

honest. There got to be too many of us, so Pax had to take the army a little way to the west. There's a low pass that leads to a hidden valley in the nearby mountains that he says works well for sheltering the soldiers with enough open space for training. There's also no one living nearby so they don't have to worry as much about collateral damage."

"How far is the camp?" Bram asks.

"Just under a day," Mara replies. "Pax makes a trip back on the weekends to take back any new recruits, so he should be back sometime tomorrow afternoon. He can discuss all the details with you."

"And you're in charge of the other refugees?" I ask.

"I suppose, though I'm not the only one. I was just one of the first, so I guess everyone kind of looks to me. Ah, we're here."

Even as she says the words I feel the magic as we pass through a barrier. The warding isn't as complex as what Astra and I set up around the Summer Palace, but it's still exceptionally strong. Strong enough I'm blown away by the sheer number of people it was concealing. Stretching out before us is a camp with at least a hundred people. Makeshift tents are scattered all around, with bonfires in between. People sit around, casually chatting while children run around playing. It's a little city, tucked away in the woods.

Mara wends through the crowd, nodding and greeting multiple people until we come to what I assume is her tent.

"You can tie your horses up wherever you feel best and then join me in my tent for some tea or food or whatever you'd like. Afterward, we can find a place for you to set up for the night."

Bram nods. "Thank you."

Mara gives him a quick nod before ducking into the tent.

Bram and I secure our horses, making sure they have grass to nibble, before we join Mara in her tent. She offers us each a cup of tea, each cup chipped, but we eat food from our own rations. Mara chats idly about various aspects of how the camp works.

"So," Mara says, folding her hands in her lap as she grins, glancing from me to Bram. "How is Astra? She's well?"

I nearly choke on my food at the abrupt shift in conversation but manage a nod. "I suppose so. As well as anyone else right now."

"And you're together?"

Gods. I feel like her eyes are boring into my soul.

"Aye. We are. We're uh . . . well . . ."

"They are soul-bonded," Bram cuts in, his voice hard.

"Oh! That sounds interesting. What does is it mean exactly?"

"It means they can't keep their hands to themselves when they are together," Bram answers.

This time I do choke on my food. After sputtering for a moment I manage, "That is *not* true and you know it."

Bram shrugs and takes a sip of his tea. "Then what is it, Alak? Do share."

His overall expression is somber, but I don't miss the twinkle of amusement in his eyes.

"It's complicated, but essentially, we're compatible in every way, especially with magic. We complete one another." I smile softly as Astra's face appears in my mind. "We're one."

Mara sighs, a dreamy expression on her face. "You're in love."

I duck my head, heat rising in my cheeks as I nod. "Very

much." A thought strikes me and I jerk my head up. "I can see if she can come here tonight."

Mara's eyes widen. "Is that possible?"

I grin, nodding emphatically. "Yes. It's part of our connection. We can always find each other."

Mara clasps her hands over her heart. "That's so romantic."

I grin but Bram mutters, "It isn't all that amazing. Just fancy, over-rated wisping."

My grin grows. "Once we finish up here I'll send for her."

Mara nods. "Yes, please. It's been so long since I've seen her. I wonder how she's changed."

"Anyhow," Bram says, bringing our attention to him, "while we finish our dinner, why don't you tell us more about how the camp is organized?"

Mara nods, diving back into her explanations. I only half listen, my thoughts focused on seeing Astra, but Bram absorbs Mara's every word. When we've finally finished, Mara guides us to a corner near her own tent where we can set up our camp. After our tents are erect, Mara leads Bram off to introduce him to the other refugees. With a smile, I write a quick note and summon Felixe. I've felt him nearby the entire time, even if he was keeping himself invisible.

"You know, you don't have to hide," I say to him as he shimmers into view. He gives me an argumentative bark and I laugh. "Fine. Have it your way. Can you take this to Astra?"

Felixe cocks his head, blinking up at me. He yips and takes the note from my extended hand. He spins a few times before disappearing. Now I just have to wait, and I'm strangely nervous.

CHAPTER NINETEEN
ASTRA

The day starts off in the normal pattern of monotony. I wake next to Kai, the dream with Ehren at the back of my mind. After I dress, I swing by the kitchen and chat with Cook as I enjoy my breakfast before meeting up with Ronan in the come-and-go room. The morning air is brisk and biting as we make our rounds refreshing the wards.

"I see you remembered your cloak this morning," Ronan observes as we approach the third ward stone.

I nod, pulling the cloak tighter around me in an attempt to block out the wind. "I learned my lesson yesterday."

Ronan nods, studying me carefully. "You seem distracted."

I shake my head as I lean down, placing my hand on the third stone. "I'm trying to figure out the next steps."

Ronan squats down next to me, placing his hand next to mine. We quickly reinforce the spell and stand, walking toward the next stone.

"What steps are you wanting to figure out? Maybe I can help."

I sigh and shake my head. "That's the problem. I'm not even sure. I know I need to find a way to contact the Fae, but beyond that, I don't know. I feel so useless."

Ronan furrows his brow. "I don't think you're useless, if it's any consolation. Sometimes I think we put too much weight on being useful."

I scowl and glance up at Ronan. "What do you mean?"

"Well," Ronan replies, knocking a stone out of our path with his cane. "I think people feel that in order to be useful they have to do these big, grand things—take down armies, win wars, make treaties—but those things aren't all that's important. Sometimes it's the little things, the movements behind the scenes, that hold everything together. Small sacrifices and hidden moments can have just as much impact as the grand gestures that everyone sees."

I nod, but I can tell Ronan isn't entirely convinced I've accepted his words.

"Take Cook for example."

"What about Cook?"

"Can you imagine running everything without her?"

I shake my head. "No, I can't."

Ronan's head bobs in agreement. "And how many times have you seen her outside her kitchen?"

I frown, thinking hard, but shrug after a moment. "I don't know. Not often if at all."

Ronan grins and I understand his point. I smile and shake my head at him.

"Just because you're the holding down the fort here doesn't mean you can't still be incredibly useful. You're the glue holding all this together, you know."

I'm prepared to argue, but I set it aside as we reach the fourth stone. Once the magic is secure we resume our walk, but Ronan immediately switches the conversation to talking about his home. I know he does it to keep my mind distracted, and I appreciate it.

Once we've finished our rounds, I head directly to the library. Ronan fetches more books from his collection and joins me. Ronan's texts have much more information regarding magic than the books in the palace library, but so far we still haven't found anything about how to contact the Fae. When Kai brings lunch, it's a welcome break.

After lunch, I encourage Ronan to go with Kai and join the hunting party going out to restock our meat supply. I can tell he's feeling a little restless in the library and he practically lights up at the promise of fresh air. As much as I've enjoyed his company the past few days, I do enjoy the quiet of the library. Plus, I don't have to worry about him judging me when I throw a book in frustration when it refuses to yield any information.

I opt to once again hide away from the dining hall in favor of a quiet dinner in the library. Kai joins me, procuring us plates of food, but Ronan seems to have integrated into the dining hall crowd already. Kai and I are in the middle of dinner when Felixe appears.

"Hey, boy!" I greet him, scratching his ears as he drops a note onto the table.

Kai scowls down at the paper. "Is it good that he's writing again so soon?"

I shrug, lifting the paper from the table. "It did seem as if they might be close last time to finding the camp, so maybe they found it after all."

236

Kai nods but, despite my words, my stomach still swirls with nerves.

My Most Beloved Astra,

I have news, but I must share it in person. No exceptions.

Forever Yours,

Alak

P.S. You'll probably be gone all night so let your guard wolf know.

I frown, reading the note twice before passing it to Kai.

"I am not a guard wolf," he growls.

I laugh. "You are a bit, you know."

Kai passes the note back to me. "Do you really think he has something to say that absolutely can't be said in a note?"

"I don't know why he would lie."

Actually, the truth is I don't even care. I'm happy for the excuse to see him.

"Should I come with you in case it's a trap?"

I shake my head. "No, I need you to stay here."

Kai sighs and shakes his head. "Please, be careful."

I place a hand on Kai's arm. "I will." A thought occurs me to and I add, "Can you have Ronan meet me by the wards? We need to make sure they're reinforced before I leave."

Kai nods, standing. "Sure."

Once Kai is gone I jot a quick note to Alak to let him know I'm coming shortly before I head outside. My stomach twists in nervous, excited circles, and by the time Ronan arrives I feel like I'm glowing.

"So, you're off to a secret rendezvous?" Ronan teases, waggling his eyebrows.

"How secret can it be if you know?" I laugh.

Ronan shrugs, a wide grin on his face. "Not everyone knows. I'm one of the privileged few."

I laugh again, my heart feeling light for the first time in days. "I'm sure. Don't worry, though, I'll be back in time to strengthen the wards tomorrow morning."

"Don't feel like you have to rush. Warding magic is my specialty and, while your magic does help strengthen the barrier, I can pour a little extra into the wards if needed."

I smile. "Thank you. I appreciate it, but I really will try not to leave you hanging any more than necessary."

I'm not entirely sure if it's the cold night air or the anticipation of seeing Alak, but we seem to walk much quicker than normal. Ronan brushes a quick kiss on my cheek before he heads inside, wishing me luck. I take a deep breath and call for Felixe. I know I can follow the bond on my own, but Felixe makes it a little easier. I close my eyes and follow the bond, diving into the wisp. When I open my eyes I'm in a dark tent, lit only by a flickering lantern. I barely have time to register Alak before I'm swept into his arms, his lips pressing against mine.

"Gods, love," he whispers, pulling back as he runs his fingers though my hair, his other hand pressing against my back. "I missed you so much."

I lean into another eager kiss, all thoughts beyond being with Alak flee my mind. After a moment he draws back, one arm dropping to his side as he rakes his other hand through his hair, glancing toward the tent opening.

"As much as I want to continue this, there is a real reason I wanted you here."

I frown. "Is there trouble?"

His eyes meet mine as he smiles, making my heart skip a beat. "Not at all, love."

I step up against him, brushing his lips quickly with mine. "Can it wait?"

Alak groans and shakes his head. "Probably not." I sigh and step back, but Alak grins. "But, whatever you have in mind we can definitely follow up on later."

I laugh. "I plan to."

"Well, love, let me show you the refugee camp," Alak says, offering me his arm.

My eyes widen as I accept his arm. "So you did find it?"

"Aye, love, but there's more. Just wait."

Alak leads me outside and I stare around in awe. I was expecting a small camp but this as large as a town. Tents and bonfires are scattered all around.

"This is—"

I drop off as a familiar voice cuts across the night air. I follow the sound to where Bram sits talking with a girl. His eyes are bright and he's smiling as the girl chatters. My breath catches in my throat as I stumble forward.

"Mara?"

The girl turns, her eyes going wide as soon as she sees me. She jumps to her feet, her eyes bright. I stare in disbelief, trying to make sense of the picture in front of me. This girl is a ghost of the Mara I've known my entire life. She's far too thin, her simple dress too large for her frame. Her hair has lost its full luster. But somehow she's still the same. Even her current circumstances haven't taken away the life from her eyes. I run toward her, and her toward me, clashing midway in a crushing hug.

"You're really here!" Mara marvels, drawing back, her

eyes searching my face. "When he said he could bring you, I wasn't sure I believed him, but here you are."

"Here I am," I grin. "But what are you doing here?"

"Mara is running the refugee camp," Bram answers from where he's still seated on the ground next to the bonfire.

I look back at Mara in awe but she shakes her head, waving Bram off.

"I'm not really in charge. I just help to organize things," Mara says dismissively. "I'll tell you all about it. Would you rather stay here next to the fire, or I can show you my tent? I have tea."

I glance toward Alak, feeling a little guilty. It's the first time I've seen him in days and I don't really relish being away from him. He smiles gently and offers an encouraging nod.

"Go on, love. It's why I told you to come." He pauses, his eyes twinkling mischievously. "We'll have the rest of the night."

I blush slightly, shaking my head at him, but I can't hide my smile.

"Bram wasn't kidding, was he?" Mara laughs. I shoot her a curious look but she only grins, linking her arm with mine. "Never mind that. Let's have tea."

Mara's tent is small but cozy and so very Mara. Somehow, she's managed to make a little home in the middle the forest. I settle on a pillow as she lights a lantern and fetches a cup of tea in a little cracked teacup.

"So," Mara says, taking a sip of her tea, "tell me what you've been up to since your last letter."

Guilt swarms me again and I stare down into my teacup. "I suppose I really should have written you again."

"You know, I really don't expect my friends who are on

the run for their lives to keep up correspondence," Mara teases with a gentle smile.

I force a smile and take a sip of tea. "Well, I'm not sure where to start. So much has happened. Why don't you tell me how you ended up here."

"Well, I suppose that's interesting enough. As I mentioned in my letter, soldiers came to Timberborn not too long after you left. They sowed seeds of dissension, and it didn't take long for everything to start falling apart. Pretty much anyone with magic was hiding it. Pax and his sister both ended up showing signs of magic."

"Pax?"

Mara nods, taking a sip of tea. "Yep. And plenty of others. Not me, though, but I wanted to help. We started by getting those with obvious magic out of Timberborn, but news spread and we found ourselves helping people from other villages escape their pursuers. Pretty soon, it got to be too much for us to do publicly, so we set up camp here. One of the refugees we met was able to make magical trails that could help others with magic find us. The more people that showed up, the more Pax realized the potential for an army with both magical and non-magical soldiers, so he began recruiting."

"So, Pax is the one building the army?"

"One of the people, anyway," Mara confirms. "Once the king and Embervein fell, we started having more and more refugees without magic so we had to leave additional clues. As the camp grew, Pax moved the soldiers to a nearby pass. I help to organize everyone here and Pax returns every weekend for the soldiers."

I study Mara for a moment before asking, "So, are you and Pax . . . ?"

Mara blushes, staring intently into her tea. "No. We've only ever been just good friends. I don't think he's ever quite gotten over Kato."

My eyes widen. "Pax and Kato? What do you mean?"

Mara tilts her head, eyeing me curiously. "You never . . . You mean to tell me you had no idea that Pax and Kato were together at one point?"

I shake my head, trying to wrap my head around her words. "When?"

Mara chuckles. "When we were sixteen, I think it was. They were all over each other for nearly three months. You really didn't know?"

I pause, pulling up memories. In retrospect it suddenly seems quite obvious. The way Kato was always laughing and sneaking away. The extra bounce he had in his step. The looks he and Pax would exchange. The way they practically glowed in each other's presence.

"I know they seemed closer but I never guessed it was more than friendship," I mumble, shaking my head.

"I guess they hid it better than I thought."

A smile twitches at the corner of my mouth before fading away, my heart clenching. What I wouldn't give to get that carefree Kato back.

Mara senses the shift in my mood and clears her throat. "I suspect you don't really want to dwell on your brother's romantic activities." She offers me a tight grin. "Enough about the past. What are you up to now? I know you're no longer engaged. What happened there?"

Red rises in my cheeks as I grin. "Alak happened."

"Bram said you're soul-bonded?"

I nod. "Yes. It's a bit complicated, but it's so much more than the the soul bond."

"But he makes you happy?" Mara asks, a gentle smile on her lips. "Because in the end that's all that matters."

"Happiness doesn't even begin to describe how he makes me feel."

Mara grins. "I'm glad. Now, tell me everything else that has happened. Spare no details."

I grin and dive into my own story. I start with fleeing Embervein and work my way up to the present. Mara mostly listens without interruption, nodding and smiling. When I talk about Kato leaving, she wraps an arm around my shoulders as I cry. When I finish Mara places her hand on mine.

"I know everything is all over the place for you," she says, meeting my eyes with a soft smile. "But you're really incredible."

I shake my head and glance away. "I don't know about that. I know I have this raw magic and power, but it seems like everything still falls apart. My magic can only take me so far."

"You've always been one of the strongest people I know, and I'm confident you'll make it through this."

"I'm so tired of being strong," I confess.

Her gaze softens and she pulls me into a hug. "I know," she whispers against my hair. "But you don't have to be strong alone." She draws back. "You'll always have me, even if I'm not right by your side. And from everything you've told me, it seems like you have more support in Bram, Alak, Prince Ehren, Kai, Ronan, and dozens of others."

I look back up at her and smile, tears brimming my eyes. "Thank you, Mara. You're right. Gods, I didn't realize how much I've missed you. Do you think you would consider coming back with me to the Summer Palace?"

Mara smiles but shakes her head. "No, not right now.

Maybe once things start to settle, but right now, my place is here."

I nod. "I understand. You've really done something amazing here, you know?" She opens her mouth but I wave my hand, silencing her. "I know you said you have help, but you're at the front of this, Mara. Without you, many of these people wouldn't have a place. You gave them a home."

Mara's eyes are as bright as her smile as she leans over and hugs me. "Thank you, Astra. It's been so good to see you and catch up, but I know you have someone else longing for your attention tonight."

I smile and duck my head, red rising in my cheeks. Mara laughs, standing, and I stand with her.

"Come. I'll show you where they set up camp."

I nod and follow her outside. I can sense the trail to Alak, but I let Mara lead me anyway. The camp is mostly quiet now, many of the bonfires dying to embers. When we stop outside the tent, Mara gives me one last parting hug before heading back to her own tent. I take a fortifying breath and duck inside. Alak is stretched out on a bedroll, playing with a deck of cards by lantern light. He looks up at me and grins.

"Hello, love."

His low voice sends shivers down my spine as I sink down next to him. I waste no time and immediately lean in and press my lips against his. He tosses the cards to the side and wraps me in his arms, his lips sliding to my neck. A moan escapes and he shifts closer.

"Hold on," I whisper, pulling back and waving my hand to set up a silencing spell.

Alak arches an eyebrow. "I'd ask where you learned that but I feel I know."

I shrug with a grin. "Ronan did one once and I copied it."

"You really are brilliant, love." Alak chuckles. "And to think, I used to believe I could teach you magic."

I smile, tracing my finger along one of the scars on his face. "You taught me much more than you realize."

He smiles and reaches up, taking my hand in his and moving my fingers down to his lips for a tender kiss.

"Well, either way, I suppose that's a good spell to know," he says, flipping me over so that he hovers above me. "Now we can be as loud as we want."

I look up into his emerald eyes, basking in the warm desire pulsing down the bond.

"That almost sounds like a challenge."

Alak laughs, his eyes shining with mischief. "Oh, absolutely."

After that, he doesn't need words. Our bodies speak all on their own in a language we ourselves created. We don't stop until exhaustion pulls us under, mere hours away from dawn.

CHAPTER TWENTY

JESSALYNN

Per Cadewynn's demands, we are on the road again by early afternoon. Even Kaeya seems a bit disgruntled with the princess, but she doesn't openly voice her frustration. We have a good day of travel, and don't bother making camp until a couple hours after night has fallen. Cadewynn is once again up and ready before I am the following morning, eager to be on our way. We ride fast and hard all day, making good time, traveling a little into the night. The hints of Hyati, the main city of the Luma Province, appear on the horizon a couple hours after the sun has set.

"Don't get too excited, Princess," I say, slowing my horse. "We won't make it tonight. We really should stop and make camp now."

"But it's right there," Cadewynn protests, gesturing to the gentle lights in the distance.

"They likely closed the city gates at dark," Sama says, giving Cadewynn an apologetic smile.

Cadewynn looks from Sama to me, desperation lining

her face. "Can we at least try?"

I shake my head with a sigh. "Even if we got inside the city, it's not like Tola would be ready to receive us."

"If we're in the city we can meet with her first thing in the morning, though. Please, Jessalynn?"

For the first time since our journey began, I see a glimpse of the petulant, spoiled child I always expected Cadewynn to be. I'm about to deny her request out of pure spite, but I notice something else in her eyes. To her, every second counts and a missed second could mean the death of someone in her kingdom. She's put this unbearable weight on her shoulders, and while it's largely her own doing, I can't help but respect her for it.

"Fine," I relent, several shocked pairs of eyes darting to me. "Let's be quick, though. You have no idea what prowls in the darkness."

"Thank y—"

I wave my hand, cutting Cadewynn off as I spur my horse forward. "Save your thanks. You'll owe me one."

Cadewynn falls silents with a nod as Kaeya shoots me a curious look. I ignore Kaeya and take up the lead. Sama looks about ready to topple from her horse by the time we reach the gates of Hyati, which, as expected, are locked. Lucky for us, they have guards on duty.

"Hey!" I call out, knocking on the door of the gate. "We require entrance."

"We don't often open our gates after nightfall," a voice calls through the gate. "What business have you in Hyati?"

"My name is Jessalynn, Head of the Hundan Valley, accompanying Princess Cadewynn of Callenia. Our business is our own," I respond, my voice echoing as much authority as I can manage.

Whispers come from the other side of the wall as the guards weigh my words.

"Fine," a second voice responds as the gate creaks open, "but if there's any trouble—"

"It won't be from us," I promise as we push through the gate.

The streets are deserted, candles glowing in the occasional window. We set about finding a stable for our horses. The owner seems largely disgruntled to have his sleep disturbed and demands double the pay. With a sigh, I oblige and lead the way to the closest inn. It's not until we stumble inside the dimly lit room I notice how exhausted Cadewynn looks. I half expect her to fall over at any moment.

"Can I help you?" a man asks, stepping from behind a curtained room in the corner.

"We're looking to find a place to sleep tonight," Kaeya speaks up. "Do you have any rooms?"

The man eyes us suspiciously for a moment before nodding. "I have a few. How many do you need?"

"Three," I answer.

The man nods slowly, disappearing behind the curtain. When he returns he's holding three keys.

"Right up those stairs you'll find your rooms," the man says, nodding to a winding staircase behind us.

"Thank you," Kaeya says, taking the keys.

The man lets his eyes drift over us before nodding and disappearing again. Kaya hands one key to Sama for her and Cadewynn and a second key to Nyco.

"So, this is the inn?" Cadewynn says, looking around with a tired scowl. "No tavern?"

I snort. "Sorry, but no, princess. You won't find much alcohol in this province, I'm afraid. They tend to be a bit more religiously inclined and don't encourage the consumption of alcohol. They believe it muddles communication with the gods. You'll find pockets like this all around Gleador. So, if you're looking for a drink—"

"No, that's not what I meant," Cadewynn says, shaking her head. "I just . . ."

She trails off into a yawn and I laugh. "You're tired. Go on up and rest. You have another Province leader to bring to your side tomorrow."

Cadewynn nods and follows Nyco and Sama up the stairs. Kaeya starts to follow them but pauses when she realizes I haven't moved.

"Coming?"

I shake my head and glance toward the exit. "Not yet. I have something I want to do first."

Kaeya nods. "I figured you might sneak off. Don't be long."

I grin up at her. "Yes, mother."

Kaeya rolls her eyes but a smile tugs at the corners of her lips. Once she's gone, I slink back into the night. It's probably pushing midnight, but I enjoy the quiet of the night, my mind drifting back to my first visit to Hyati. It was shortly after my mother and I had been ejected from Callenia. My mother hadn't known what sort of reception she would receive in the Valley, so we came to Hyati first. I can remember being so terrified of everyone and everything and finding comfort in Tola.

I'm smiling softly when I knock on the old, familiar door. No one answers and I knock again. I'm greeted again by silence. I turn with a sigh. It is late after all. I take a step away when I hear shuffling inside.

"Who's there?" a groggy voice calls out, cracking the

door open.

I turn around and grin. The door flies open, revealing a middle-aged woman with long black hair clutching a robe around her.

"Jess?"

"The one and only," I reply. "I'm sorry to come so late. If I'm disturbing you . . ."

"Nonsense. You know you're always welcome no matter the time of day or night," Tola replies, motioning me inside. "Now get in here before you catch cold."

I trot inside her house. She closes the door behind me before heading to stoke the dying fire.

"Now, while I make us some tea, why don't you tell me why you're on my doorstep instead of in bed."

I plop down in the nearest chair with a sigh. "I'm not entirely sure, to be honest."

"I don't suppose it has anything to do with your sister?" Tola says, pulling a kettle from its resting place next to the fire. "Ah, good. The water is still warm."

I rear back like I've been slapped. "She's not my sister."

"Oh?" Tola says, arching an eyebrow as she pulls two teacups from a cupboard, dropping in tea leaves and pouring water over them. "Is there a new term for a girl who shares the same father besides 'sister'?"

I shake my head. "We might be sisters in blood but that's all. And it doesn't even count because our father disowned me. She's not my sister."

"Ah, well then, forgive me," Tola says, easing into the chair across from me, offering one of the cups of tea. "It appears I was indeed mistaken. Your reason for being here, though, does it have to do with this not-sister?"

I shrug, glancing away from Tola's prying gaze, clutching

my teacup. "It's why I'm in Luma. She's asked me to help her recruit people to fight to win Callenia back from the Dragkonians."

"News of the Fire King and his creatures has reached my ears. I was wondering how long it would be before someone came asking for help, but you know I don't really have any soldiers for an army."

"I know."

"So, my child, why are you here? Specifically, why are you here at this time of night, all alone?"

I raise my eyes to meet Tola's and find no judgment, only calm understanding. I've forced up walls around me. It's how I stay safe, protected. It's how I have survived and become a leader strong enough for the Valley. Under Tola's gentle gaze, however, all those walls fall, and I'm that young, unsure child again.

"I need to know if I'm doing the right thing," I admit, my voice barely above a whisper.

Tola takes a long sip of tea as she considers my words. "What parts do you doubt?"

I shrug, staring down into my tea. "I was discarded like trash by my father, and yet, here I am helping his precious legitimate children to build an army. Part of me wants to let their kingdom fall, even though I know Gleador is likely next."

"And the other part of you?"

I raise my eyes to meet hers. "And part of me still thinks of Callenia as *my* kingdom. I was born there and spent over a third of my life there. While I was never treated quite the same as Ehren, I have many fond memories of my time there." I sigh and take a sip of tea before continuing, Tola watching me closely. "I thought I was over that. I had pushed everything to the side, but then Ehren showed up and all those feelings flooded back."

"And now your sister—his sister—has shown up as well and you're further conflicted," Tola assess softly with a nod. "That's understandable. You said yourself if you don't help, Gleador could be next. That means the destruction of two places you've considered home. It's a heavy price."

I nod. "Yes, but it's more than that. I—" I shake my head and look away. "Never mind. It's foolish."

"Come child," Tola says gently. "The only truly foolish things are the things that we keep hidden away when speaking them aloud can help us move forward."

"I wonder if I can be accepted back into Callenia if I help them win this war." I look back up at Tola and find her smiling at me. "It's not that I don't love the Valley, but . . . I don't know."

"Callenia will always be your true home, and that's okay," Tola says. "You don't just want to help Callenia because of obligation but because you love it. You're a good person, Jess."

I huff a laugh. "You're the only person who thinks that, I'm sure."

"You know I'm not."

I shake my head. "It's more than just loyalty or whatever you want to call it. I respect Cadewynn for what she's doing. She was put in an impossible situation and instead of shrinking away like most princesses in her position might do, she rose to the challenge. She's fighting fiercely for her kingdom, and I can't help but respect her."

"Something else you two have in common."

I jerk my eyes to Tola's. "What?"

"Jess, you are one of the most determined people I know.

It's what makes you a good leader. You're resilient and it takes a lot to bring you down. You respect Cadewynn for those qualities because you know firsthand how difficult it is to maintain them. You can deny she's your sister all you want, but you are far more similar than you want to believe."

I shake my head firmly. "No, I don't . . ." Tola gives me a knowing look and I sigh. "I suppose it's possible, but I don't think that's entirely true."

"Either way," Tola says with a shrug, "you've agreed to accompany her on her mission. You've chosen to help her, but you're not really wondering if you made the right choice, even if that's what you claim. You're really wondering what your mother would think of your decision."

I nod, taking a gulp of my tea.

"Well, I don't know all the details, but from what I can tell, you're on the right path. You aren't one to be duped, so if you find her cause worthy, I have no doubt it is. I think your mother would understand."

"And will you also support Cadewynn's cause?" I say, trying to act as if I don't care, but I'm sure Tola can see right through my mask.

Tola chuckles. "I thought Princess Cadewynn was the one going to meet with me and request aid." I eye her steadily as she continues. "I already told you I don't have soldiers, but if you find her cause worthy then I will do what I can to find a way to help."

"Thank you, Tola," I whisper, a smile creeping onto my lips.

"Now," Tola says, rising from her seat. "You should really get back and get some sleep."

I nod as I stand, setting my teacup down on a nearby side table. "You're right. Thank you for your time."

Tola leads me to the door, holding it open as I step into the night. I'm only a few feet away when she calls out to me.

"Jess?"

I turn back to her. "Yes?"

Tola smiles softly, her face lit by the moonlight. "Your mother would be very proud of the woman and leader you've become."

She offers me one last smile before closing the door. It takes a few moments for me to recover from her words and get my feet moving again. By the time I make it back to the inn, I'm beyond exhausted. I slip into my room to find Kaeya already asleep, Nila curled up on her pillow. I creep across the room and snuggle up against Kaeya. She shifts slightly in her sleep but doesn't wake. I wrap my arms around her and drift off, feeling a little lighter.

By some miracle, I'm already up and ready for the day when Cadewynn knocks on my door the next morning. Kaeya opens the door and Cadewynn steps in hesitantly.

"I don't suppose you're ready to go meet with the Head of Luma?" she asks quietly.

"I'm more or less ready," I sigh. "I suppose there's no need to wait around."

I motion for Cadewynn to follow as I sweep past her. Kaeya follows. Downstairs, Nyco leans against the wall next to the door looking half asleep while Sama stands next to him chattering away, her Shadow Hawk on her shoulder.

"Everyone ready for a day of adventure and fun?" I say as Nyco pushes away from the wall.

Sama shakes her head at me as Kaeya rolls her eyes.

"Fine. I'll be the only one having fun," I say with a shrug, pushing through the door.

The streets are much more alive today, yet it still feels calm compared to Forduna. I take up the lead, Kaeya walking barely a half-step behind me. I guide our little group of misfits to Tola's place of business, a small stone building in the center of the city. A young woman ushers us inside the moment we arrive, guiding us to a wide-open room with a low table set for tea. Instead of chairs, round cushions mark the places. Tola sits at the head, a colorful headscarf hiding her hair.

"Welcome to Hyati," Tola greets with a wide smile. "Please, take a seat. The tea has already been poured, but only just, so it's still quite warm."

Her voice sounds odd and it takes me a moment to realize she's speaking Callenian. Cadewynn notices as well, her surprise registering on her face. After a moment she quickly picks a cushion and sinks down, Sama and Nyco on either side. Kaeya and I take the remaining cushions.

"Thank you for your hospitality," Cadewynn says, taking a sip of her tea.

She's in her element here and I can tell she's already at ease.

"Of course," Tola replies, inclining her head. "It is always my pleasure to meet anyone, whether royals from a neighboring country or my own kinfolk. Perhaps one day when things are less volatile, you can return for a more casual chat."

Jealously sears inside me at Tola's words. I don't want to share her, although she's far from mine.

"Thank you," Cadewynn replies with a sweet smile I have an urge to smack from her face.

255

I clench my hands in my lap and glare at Cadewynn, though she seems blissfully ignorant of my renewed hate. I jump when Kaeya places a hand over my mine. My eyes meet hers and something about her own calm seeps through to me and I take a deep breath.

"As lovely as tea is," I cut in, "I'm sure Princess Cadewynn is eager to get straight to business."

"Yes," Cadewynn says, setting down her teacup with a soft clink. "Though I don't wish to rush the proceedings, time is precious."

"Whatever suits you, my dear, works well enough for me," Tola agrees with a smile. "Why don't you start at the beginning and tell me everything?"

Cadewynn's bright blue eyes widen. "Everything?"

"Yes, dear." Tola's smile is kind. "Start with how this all began and what you need from me."

Cadewynn takes a deep breath, sorting through her thoughts before leaping into the story. She starts with how she discovered the prophecies of the twins and everything she and Ehren did to find and help them. She continues, sharing her relationship with them and how they become friends. I've heard much of the story before, but there are so many details I didn't know. I'm left feeling more respect for my brother and his companions. When she gets to the attack on Embervein, I find myself hanging on her every word.

"I was in the library," Cadewynn says, "but I couldn't just hide. I went out and gathered as many people as I could and took them to a room hidden beneath the library. No one knew of it, so we were safe, but trapped until Astra showed up and wisped us away. Once in the forest, I did what I could—bandaging the wounded and helping the Healers however they needed—but I always felt like I could do more.

Before my brother sent me to Gleador I had already decided I would gather his armies for him."

I stare at my sis—the princess in awe. I had no idea she thought so well on her feet or that she put herself at risk like that.

"That's why you're here, then," Tola says, drawing me from my thoughts. "To ask for an army."

Cadewynn nods meekly, sipping what remains of her tea.

"Well, I'm afraid I don't have much of an army. We are a peaceful province that grows spices, herbs, and other food. We don't require the soldiers many other provinces do."

Cadewynn's face falls, but she remains firm. "Every sword counts."

Tola nods, mulling something over, although I know she's already made her decision. "Indeed. I could maybe gather a dozen or two swords for you, but I have a counteroffer. I can offer resources. I will send those dozen soldiers with food and goods to feed and care for the armies. Many of our spices and herbs are medicinal and your Healers will find them useful, I'm sure. Would this be acceptable?"

Cadewynn's head bobs up and down as she smiles, her shoulders sagging with relief. "Yes, thank you."

"Good," Tola says, standing. Cadewynn follows suit. Nyco trips up after her, the rest of us rising more gracefully. "Then, I suppose we will call this meeting to an end. I encourage you to enjoy the city a bit. We have many excellent delicacies that are sure to delight your tongue."

Cadewynn shakes her head. "I would love to enjoy your city, but I have many more provinces to visit."

Tola smiles as if she knows a secret, and I scowl, exchanging a curious look with Kaeya.

"I think you may be in luck," Tola says. "You see, we have a portal that leads directly to Heldonia."

"What?" I gasp, taken completely by surprise.

Tola nods, grinning. "Yes. It's a special kind of portal that occurs naturally. It's been dead for centuries, along with magic, but it's reactivated now."

"And it's safe?" Cadewynn asks.

"Yes. We have tried it many times and every trip has been a success."

"But there's another province between here and Heldonia," Cadewynn says slowly, her brow furrowed.

"I would be happy to write a letter to Fascha in Muldainah encouraging her to aid as much as possible. If Jessalynn adds her voice, I'm sure she will send as much help as she can. This will allow you to move on to Heldonia, which I would assume is a priority for you since they make magical weapons that would be most useful in your war."

Cadewynn gnaws on the inside of her bottom lip as she considers Tola's offer. Finally, she nods.

"Okay. I think that will work." Her face breaks into a cautious grin. "I think it will work very well."

Tola claps her hands together once. "Excellent. I will write my letter immediately." She turns to me. "If you'll get me your letter, I'll have them sent out together."

I nod. "Of course. I may have to borrow some parchment and ink."

"I have plenty to spare," Tola replies. "I can lend them to you now."

I fight to hide my grin as I turn to Cadewynn. "Why don't you head on back to the inn? I know you couldn't have gotten much sleep last night. Rest a bit, enjoy Hyati, and I'll make all the necessary arrangements."

Cadewynn inclines her head. "Thank you, Jessalynn."

"Do you wish for me to stay here with you?" Kaeya asks as Cadewynn turns to leave, flanked closely by Sama and Nyco.

I shake my head. "No, I'll catch up with you later."

Kenya nods, pressing a kiss to my cheek before leaving with the others. Once they're gone, I follow Tola to a small back room that serves as her office. I sit across from her at a desk as we compose our letters. When I finish, I look up to find her staring at me, a smile curving on her lips.

"What is it?" I ask, a little more guarded than I normally am around Tola.

She shakes her head, her smile growing. "You and that princess are much more alike than you want to believe. I could see it almost immediately."

I scoff as I fold up my letter to seal it, pressing the creases much more firmly than necessary. "I don't know what you mean."

Tola chuckles. "Ah, but you do, and it scares you." I raise my eyes to meet hers. "It's okay, my child, to trust someone without understanding why. You two need each other more now than ever before."

"What? Are you a Seer now?"

Tola's eyes sparkle but she doesn't deny my words, leaving me to wonder. "Place a little trust in the girl. I don't think you'll regret it."

I swallow, considering her words. "I don't trust easily."

Tola places a hand over mine. "I know, but things are changing."

I take a deep breath. She's right. Everything is about to change and it terrifies and excites me at the same time. I only hope I can live with whom I may become.

CHAPTER TWENTY-ONE

ASTRA

Morning sneaks up on us. I long to stay wrapped in Alak's arms all day, but obligation calls to me and I force myself to dress for the day. Alak props himself up on his elbows, watching me.

"You sure you have to rush back, love? Can't you stay a bit longer?"

I try to smile but I can't quite manage it. "I want to . . ."

Alak leaps up and wraps his arms around me, drawing me close to press a kiss to my forehead. I sigh and lean against his bare chest.

"Then stay," he mutters, his fingers trailing up and down my back. "Stay with me."

"You know I can't," I whisper. "I have to go back."

"I know," he replies with a heavy sigh, kissing the top of my head. "I know and I hate it."

I draw back and look up into his eyes, seeing my own sad desperation reflected. My chest feels tight as tears sting my eyes. I don't want to leave Alak, and the more I consider it, the more impossible it seems.

"There now, love," Alak says, brushing a lock of hair from my face to tuck it behind my ear. "No need for tears. I shouldn't have even suggested it. I know we both have jobs to do. The sooner we get them done the sooner the war will be over and the sooner we can hide away in a secret home in the mountains far from anyone who would demand a single thing of us."

A smile twitches on my lips. "That's your dream? To whisk me away to a secret mountain home?"

Alak grins. "Well, a mountain near Athiedor, I suppose. I need to stay close to my roots. But really, I'll be happy anywhere you are." His smile falters as his expression sombers. "We'll have forever together soon enough, love. We just have to finish this bit first."

"It doesn't make it any easier to say goodbye."

Alak's smile returns but I can feel his sadness through the bond. "Aye, I know, love. Let's go have some breakfast before you rush off. You can manage time for that at least?"

I nod, managing a small smile of my own. "I think so."

"Good. I'll meet you out there after I've dressed," Alak says, releasing me from his hold.

I nod and leave the tent, though the bond begs me to stay. I wind through the camp until I find Bram and Mara in the center of the tent village. I pause a few feet away, watching. Bram seems so relaxed as he chats with Mara, an easy grin on his face. Mara looks up at Bram, practically glowing. I smile, my heart warming at the sight of the two of them. I'm so caught up in observing them, I don't realize Alak has arrived until he loops his arm around my waist, pressing a kiss to my cheek.

"Stalking people is often frowned upon, love," Alak whispers in my ear.

I laugh and Mara turns, her eyes finding me. She breaks into a wide grin and crosses to me, Bram on her heels.

"Good morning! Did you sleep well?"

"Oh, were we supposed to be sleeping?" Alak asks, feigning innocence. He leans closer and whispers in a voice loud enough the other two can clearly hear him. "I think we did it wrong, then, love."

Heat rises in my cheeks as I elbow Alak, shaking my head at him. He laughs as Mara grins and Bram rolls his eyes, glancing away.

"Are you staying until Pax arrives?" Mara asks. "He should be here early afternoon."

I shake my head. "Unfortunately, I really need to get back. I have to help Ronan reinforce the wards around the castle and be ready to receive any information from allies."

"I understand. You have time to eat a bit of breakfast first, right? We have coffee, which, if I recall correctly, is something you rather enjoy."

"I still love coffee," I reply with a smile.

Mara's face lights up. "We don't have much to offer food-wise, as you can imagine, but we do all right."

Mara guides us through the camp to one of the bonfires surrounded by people. She offers us each a cup filled with coffee and another refugee steps up offering us toast with jam. We take seats around the fire, enjoying our light breakfast, when I hear a soft gasp behind me.

"It *is* the butterfly girl!"

I turn and discover a young girl standing behind me, staring at me wide-eyed. A broad-shouldered man stands next to her, holding her hand. Recognition sparks and I leap to my feet.

"Eissa!" I say, the little girl's face lighting up at her name.

Her head bobs up and down enthusiastically. "Yes! You remember me?"

I laugh. "Of course I remember you. You had marvelous magic that allowed you to grow things. How could I forget?"

Her father beams down at her with pride as Eissa grins.

"Eissa is very helpful here," Mara offers, stepping up behind me. "She uses her magic to provide a lot of the food we eat. Without her, our resources would be very limited."

Red tinges Eissa's cheeks as she glances down, her small hands fidgeting with the fabric of her dress. "I don't do much, really. It's very simple magic. I wish I could do more and actually fight in the war and save people."

I kneel down in front of Eissa, meeting her eyes. "You know, I recently had a friend remind me that sometimes it's the smallest things that hold everything together. Without you, this camp might very well fall apart. You're helping much more than you realize."

Eissa's eyes widen. "Do you really think so?"

I smile, nodding. "I know so."

"She's right," Mara agrees with a nod. "You're very important, Eissa."

Eissa beams, bouncing on the balls of her feet. "Are you going to stay with us in the camp?"

I shake my head as I stand straight. "Unfortunately, I can't. I was only here for a short visit."

"Are you still helping the prince?"

"Now, Eissa," her father cuts in, placing a hand on her shoulder. "Don't pry."

I smile. "It's okay. Yes, I am still helping Prince Ehren. He's actually become a very good friend."

"I understand," Eissa states matter-of-factly with a nod. "You are a very important person."

Her words take me back a bit, and I tilt my head looking down at her.

"We all have our jobs," Bram says, stepping forward. "And every job is important."

I shoot Bram a grateful look. He meets my eyes with a smile.

"And we need to let her get back to her job," Eissa's father says, squeezing her shoulder.

"It was nice to see you again," I say with a nod as Eissa and her father turn. "Hopefully we will meet again in better circumstances."

Once they're gone, I focus on Alak, my chest tight. Alak meets my eyes and his smile fades.

"You should go," he says quietly, stepping closer and taking my hands in his.

Mara clears her throat, linking her arm with Bram's. "Why don't I start the tour of the camp? Alak can catch up with us later." Mara glances over her shoulder as she leads Bram. "It was lovely to see you again, Astra."

I offer Mara a smile, but it's weak. "I wish I could stay longer. Give Pax my love."

Mara nods. "Of course."

She pulls Bram far enough away to give us some privacy without wandering too far, chattering away about the function of the camp as I turn my attention to Alak. I look up into his emerald eyes and am immediately lost.

"I don't want you to go," Alak confesses, tracing his thumb over the top of my hand. "I thought seeing you would help, and when it came to it, I could let you go. It's not that easy, though."

"I don't want to go, either," I admit, fighting back tears. "But I have to."

Alak squeezes his eyes shut for a moment as he nods. I reach up and brush my lips against his.

"Don't worry. We will be back together soon," I whisper as I draw back.

Alak looks down at me and I feel his passion swarm the bond. Without warning, he gathers me in his arms and presses his lips to mine. The world stops around us and everything else ceases to exist. I wind my fingers in his hair, bringing him closer. Our magic hums around us, the world bowing to us. When he pulls back, I'm left breathless.

"You need to go now or I'll never be able to let you go," Alak says, his voice cracking.

I nod, taking a step back. "I love you, Alak."

He smiles softly. "I know. I love you, too, with all my soul."

Before I can change my mind, I wisp away, my heart shattering in my chest. I land just outside the wards surrounding the Summer Palace, struggling to breathe. I long to go back, but I know I can't. I take a fortifying breath and step through the warding. It's strong and I can't sense any of my own magic, so Ronan has already reinforced it at least once in my absence. I stride to the palace, entering in through a back door near the kitchen. It only makes sense to swing by and check in.

"Astra, dear," Cook greets me as I step into the flurry of activity. "I wasn't expecting you this morning. I heard you were out. I can have a bit of breakfast ready for you in a minute if you'd like."

"I've already eaten, but thank you. I was mostly wondering if you had any news."

Cook shakes her head. "Nothing new. Just more of the same rumors we've been hearing. Nothing specific to add."

I sigh, nodding as I glance off down the hall. "I don't suppose you might know where Kai or Ronan may be?"

"Lord McDullun requested tea in the library, so I would imagine he's still there. Not sure where the shifter is," Cook replies.

I thank her and make my way to the library. Sure enough, Ronan is leaning back in an easy chair next to the fire, his nose in a book. At the sound of my footsteps, he glances up, a smirk twitching on his lips.

"You're back. I expected you to take a little longer to return, if I'm to be honest," Ronan says as I cross the library, taking a seat in the chair next to him.

"I wanted to stay longer, but I'm needed here. Though, it seems you already reinforced the wards?"

Ronan nods. "Aye, I did. It took more out of me than I expected, but I managed." He pauses, studying me for a moment before he continues. "How was your trip? You seem . . . I'm not sure. Not as happy as I expected, but also not terribly disappointed."

I offer him a weak smile. "It was actually quite a nice night. It's just difficult to say goodbye. It's hard on the bond."

The door to the library creaks open as Kai enters. I sit up straighter, my smile growing into something more sincere. Kai furrows his brows as he takes me in.

"Well, you came back in one piece," he muses.

I laugh. "What did you expect? Did you really think Alak would lead me into a trap?"

Kai shakes his head. "You can never be sure. What did happen?"

"Well, he and Bram found the refugees."

Ronan inhales sharply. "So the prince was right about the army?"

I nod. "Yes. While I didn't get a chance to see it for myself, I did get a glimpse at the camp. But that wasn't all. The camp is being run by two of my dearest friends from my hometown of Timberborn."

Kai settles into a nearby chair as I launch into quick explanation of everything I learned. Ronan and Kai listen with rapt attention, not interrupting. When I finish, they both sit quietly, absorbing all the information.

"So," Kai drawls, "when will the army be ready? Or do we not know yet?"

"I think Bram has plans to talk things over with Pax today when he arrives. I'm sure once they have a stable plan, Alak will pass on the information."

Kai sighs, easing back into his chair. "Well, at least that's something."

"And you got to meet up with a dear friend," Ronan adds with a smile. "That is rather lucky for you."

I nod, my smile returning. "It really was. I'm hoping all this will be over soon and we can get back to life as it was, or at least life as normal as it can be."

Kai and Ronan nod in agreement, but neither speak. What will life look like after the war?

"Anyway," I say, turning back to Ronan, "any news on the books from Athiedor?"

Ronan shakes his head. "I'm afraid not, though, if my estimates are correct, it's possible some may arrive tomorrow."

"I guess I'll have to continue combing through what I already have. Maybe I'll get lucky and stumble across something."

"Or," Ronan says, grabbing his cane and pushing up from his seat. "We go into Oxwatch and spend the day not stressing over all the little things we can't control."

Kai nods as he stands. "That's not a bad idea. I can go with you."

I look up at the two men towering over me. "Are you sure that's a good idea?"

Ronan grins down at me as he offers me his hand. "If I didn't, I wouldn't have suggested it."

I place my hand in Ronan's and he pulls me to my feet.

"I'll let a few people know where we've gone so they can find us if necessary," Kai says, walking toward the library door. "I'll meet you by the front gate in a few minutes."

Before I can protest further, Ronan has linked his arm with mine and is ushering me from the library and outside. Kai joins us a few minutes later and we stroll into town. I clutch my cloak around me to block out the sharp wind. Kai notices and positions himself next to me to block the brunt of it. I smile up at him and bump my arm against his.

When we first came through Oxwatch weeks ago, I barely paid any attention to the village. I was too focused on getting to the castle safely. Now, I wonder what has changed in these few weeks. At first glance, it seems like any normal village I've witnessed during my recent travels—people bustle about, talking and conducting business—but at a second glance everything seems stiff. There's fear in the air, like something could go wrong at any moment. Too many villagers talk in low whispers, their eyes darting around. My chest feels heavy as we walk through the town. Cook shares all she knows every morning, so I more or less know what to expect, but seeing everything firsthand is disheartening.

A few people watch me curiously when we first start

going from vendor to vendor, but word soon spreads and people act less surprised the longer we wander through town. It's easy to confirm what I know. Vendors share trials of short supplies, and I meet a few of the refugees who have fled to Oxwatch. No one blames me, but I can't help but feel the burden of their troubles.

It's nearing noon when we pause outside the tavern, debating whether we want to eat lunch in the village or head back to castle and see what Cook has prepared. While Ronan and Kai debate the options, my gaze drifts toward a group of children playing nearby. The oldest can't be more than ten with the youngest around four. All of the children, nine in total, are giggling as they run around, kicking a ball. Their laughter rises above the clamor of daily life. Their clothes are worn and their faces and hands are covered in dirt, but they don't care. They're happy and carefree. A smile sneaks onto my lips as I watch.

"See, love," Ronan says softly, leaning toward me, "there's still joy. No matter how bad things get, you can't get rid of all happiness. And with happiness, dwells hope."

I nod, tears rising in my eyes.

"Things may seem hopeless now, but hope will never be truly gone," Ronan continues, his eyes watching the squealing children. "Even if we fail, others will rise up."

"I don't want to fail," I whisper, shaking my head. "I don't want this burden to pass to anyone else."

Kai slips his hand into mine, and I look up at him, my brow furrowed. He smiles down at me.

"It's not your burden alone, you know."

"He's right," Ronan says, taking my other hand. "You have us, Ehren and his Guard, Alak, and hundreds of other people, I'm sure. We'll all make it out somehow, even if you can't see how yet."

I smile, squeezing their hands. "I hope you're right."

"Of course I'm right, love," Ronan says with a wink. "I'm seldom wrong. Now, let's go inside and eat."

I nod as Ronan and Kai release my hands, shuffling into the tavern. It's busy, but not full, so we easily find a place to sit. We order stew and mead and lose ourselves in mindless chatter. The casual atmosphere takes me back to the days when I was a new outlaw, on the run from a king with no idea where my future would lead. How things have changed in the past months. I barely hold back a chuckle at the thought that those early days seemed almost easy compared to my life now.

Once we've finished eating, Ronan starts up a card game with a few other patrons. Kai watches the game with a scowl, standing behind Ronan with his arms crossed. The other players constantly glance up at Kai's foreboding presence, and I attempt to hide my grin somewhat unsuccessfully. After a few rounds of cards, we head back to the castle. Ronan and Kai keep me from the library for a while, but I still manage to get in a couple pointless hours of study before dinner.

I'm in the middle of going over my notes after dinner when I remember my dream conversation with Ehren. Last night I didn't have any trouble sleeping because I was with Alak, but tonight, my nightmares might return. I carefully pack up notes and head to the Healers quarters. Healer Heora sits next to a low fire, mixing medicines. When I enter, she smiles up at me.

"Evening, dear," she says, setting her mixing bowl aside.

"Evening," I reply, matching her smile.

Healer Heora eases up from her chair, meeting my eyes. "What I can do for you at this late hour?"

"Well, I've had some trouble sleeping," I confess. "I had found ways to manage, but recently . . ."

I let my voice trail off and Healer Heora nods.

"I do have a few things that would work to aid your sleep." She shuffles to nearby shelves, scanning the contents. "Ah, here it is." She pulls a small vial from the shelf and holds it out to me. "A drop or two of this on your tongue when you're ready to sleep will help ease you into peaceful dreams."

I take the vial and look down at it in my palm. "Will it interfere with any spells such as a sleepwalking spell?"

Healer Heora shakes her head. "No, it should not."

"Good," I say, raising my eyes to Healer Heora's. "Thank you."

Another thought pushes forward and I stand still for a moment, considering whether to ask or not. Healer Heora cocks her head, studying me.

"Well, child, out with it."

"I . . ." I stop, shaking my head as I glance away. "It's nothing. I just . . ." I sigh and look back up at the Healer. "It's my monthly cycles. I haven't . . ."

"Ah," Healer Heora says with a knowing nod. "Have you been taking the preventative tonic I provided?"

Red rises in my cheeks as I nod. "Yes."

"Well, the tonic is not without its flaws, but if you're not having any other symptoms, I believe your concerns may come from magic."

I frown. "Magic?"

Healer Heora nods. "Yes, in what I've read regarding magic and how it affects the body, it is not uncommon for things such as a young woman's cycle to be disturbed or even stopped completely if she is suddenly presented with a large, overwhelming amount of magic. Have you had your cycle since obtaining the full force of your magic?"

I pause, thinking as I play through the last few hectic months. My stomach twists as I shake my head.

"Then I think magic is surely the cause."

"Will my cycle ever return?"

Healer Heora shrugs, but there's sympathy in her eyes. "I cannot be sure."

"But if it does not return, does that mean that I will never . . ."

I stop, unable to complete the thought, the words catching in my throat. Healer Heora, however, reads the concern left unspoken, her eyes meeting mine with a hint of sadness.

"It is unlikely you will bear children," she says, her voice low, almost inaudible. "Very few women of your power ever conceived. According to the legends, it is the gods' way to ensure that powerful magic isn't passed on, growing stronger with each generation."

I stagger back, clutching the vial of sleeping tonic against my chest. I never put much thought into my future as a mother, especially in recent months, but being presented with the harsh truth makes it hard to breathe. I jump when Healer Heora places a hand on mine.

"I could be wrong. Despite my years, my knowledge of magic and how it affects us is still very new. And much of the information I have is speculation."

Her words are meant to comfort, but they're only a reminder of how little control I have over anything. I manage a nod and a weak smile.

"Thank you for the sleeping tonic," I mumble, eager to leave.

When I get upstairs to my room, I don't even bother undressing before I take the tonic and slip beneath the covers, my tears soaking my pillow as I drift off.

CHAPTER TWENTY-TWO

ASTRA

When I wake the next morning, my eyes are sore from crying. I know Kai is lying next to me, but I don't move. I don't want him to know I'm awake. I'm not ready to face the world. I want to stay here in bed. I want to hide from the world as long as possible.

Kai shifts, wrapping his arms around me, pulling me closer. I squeeze my eyes shut as the tears threaten to begin again.

"What's wrong?" Kai asks, leaning his forehead against me.

"What makes you think anything is wrong?" I manage, trying to keep my voice as level as possible.

"Please," Kai replies, his voice breaking. "If there's anything I can help with, let me. You were crying in your sleep when I came in last night and I—I could barely handle it. Please, Astra, let me help."

I turn to face Kai, a tear sliding down my cheek. "There's nothing you can do. There's nothing anyone can do."

Kai blinks back his own tears. "Are you sure?"

I nod. "Unfortunately."

"Do you at least want to share your burden?"

I hesitate, wiping away my tears with the back of my hand. "I'm still . . . processing." Kai nods patiently. "I can't, it seems, have children." Kai's expression falls and he opens his mouth to speak, but I hurry on before he can. "I want today to be normal. I need something to stay the same. I'm tired of everything going wrong and me being helpless to change anything. I just want one little thing that I can hold on to."

My voice breaks as tears fall free, and Kai pulls me tightly against his body. I bury my face in his chest and sob uncontrollably for several minutes. Kai says nothing. He just holds me, and that's enough. When I finally pull back, he brushes a stray lock of hair from my face.

"Feel a little better?"

I nod, forcing a smile. "A bit."

"Good," Kai says, though he doesn't look convinced. "Why don't you take a bath and take your time getting ready. I'll have breakfast sent up."

I nod, not having the energy to fight him. He leans forward, kissing the top of my head before rising from the bed to head to his own room to get ready. I force myself to move across my room into the washroom. I run a bath of hot water and sink into it. For several minutes, I sit just staring at the wall. The water is lukewarm by the time I find the motivation to wash and cold by the time I'm done.

I just need to make it to the next breath. That's all. I just need to take it one breath at a time. I can do it. I've done it before, and I can do it again.

I leave the washroom and discover a tray of assorted breakfast items sitting on a small table. I didn't even hear anyone enter. It must have been Kai. He's the only person in the entire castle with that level of stealth. I try to eat, but I can only manage a couple bites of a pastry. Even the coffee isn't tempting me. With a sigh, I dress and head downstairs to find Ronan. He's in his usual spot in the corner room, chatting with the guards and servants. When I enter, his face falls and he rushes to my side.

"You all right, love?" he whispers.

I manage a nod, forcing a smile. "Of course. We need to go reinforce the wards."

Ronan studies me for a moment. "All right, love. It's dreary and rainy out today, so let's grab you a thicker cloak."

I shake my head. "I'll use my magic to shield us."

"You sure?"

I nod. "Yes. I'll be fine."

Ronan doesn't argue as I turn and march toward the door leading outside. As soon as I step out into the light drizzle, I throw up a shield around me and Ronan. Silently, we go from stone to stone reinstating the wards. I just want to be done so I can get back inside and hide from the world. We're about to enter the castle through the one of the gardens when Ronan stops me, a firm hand on my arm.

"Stop, love," he says, his voice firm but gentle.

I turn toward him and nearly break down at the look of concern in his eyes.

"Yesterday, you came back from seeing the love of your life and your dearest childhood friend. You were happy, or something very close to it, but today, you're covered in a dark shadow. What happened?"

I swallow and glance away from Ronan, shaking my head. "Nothing."

"That's a lie, love, and I won't allow it. I won't let my friends go on suffering if I can help it," Ronan says softly.

"That's just it!" I yell, my emotions rushing forward as the rain patters around us. "You can't help it. No one can. It's yet another thing beyond my control. One more thing I never expected, never considered, never even knew if I wanted, and now it's just gone." A small sob escapes. "Why can't I have one normal thing? Is that too much to ask? Just one thing."

"What thing, love? Please, just tell me. I hate seeing you in pain like this."

I take a deep breath and turn my back to Ronan. "It doesn't matter. It's foolish."

Ronan grasps my shoulder and turns me back to him. "Anything that has you this upset matters."

I shake my head, looking up at the gray sky. "I just— the magic changed me, changed my body. I can't . . . I never really imagined myself as a mother but now . . ."

"Oh," Ronan says, his voice barely audible over the increasing rain. "So, that's it, love. You're unable to have a child?"

I nod, tears breaking free. Before I can speak, Ronan gathers me in his arms. I tuck my head under his chin and he tightens his hold on me.

"That's not nothing, love," he whispers against my hair. "That's a very big something, even if you've never given it thought before. You have every right to be upset. You don't have to be okay. "

I crumble against him, clutching his cloak in my fists and as I struggle to gain control over the tears. "I hate feeling helpless."

"I know, love," Ronan whispers, pressing a kiss to the top of my head. "We all hate that feeling. We all long for control, and right now, we're all a little lost. We're all pain in one way or another."

"But how can I move past this?" I sniff, pulling back enough to look up in Ronan's eyes.

"I don't know that you can ever truly move past something like this," Ronan says, shaking his head. "I'm likely not the best person to ask as this is something I will never have to deal with. However, I have struggled my entire life balancing things I can't control, things I feel have been stolen from me. Personally, I've found the best way to move forward is to find something else to focus on, something you can control."

"Like what?"

"Well," Ronan says, glancing off, "like what you want to have for lunch or getting out of this rain. Start small and then move on to bigger issues. You may not be able to have children, but after the war, there will be more children than usual without parents. You can start planning a way to help them, if that's something that appeals to you. I won't pretend it will be at all the same, but perhaps it's something?"

I nod, shivering. At some point during my breakdown, I let the shield fall. Ronan and I are now soaked, but he's not complaining.

"You're right. Let's go on inside, and I'll focus on other things."

I draw back, but Ronan keeps his free arm looped around me as we stroll inside. He doesn't drop his arm until we reach the library. Someone had the forethought to light the fire, so it's cozy and warm. I quickly discard my soaked cloak, drying myself and Ronan with a wave of magic, and sink to the ground directly in front of the fire, craving its warmth. Ronan rings for tea before settling into the chair behind me, his green book in hand.

"Why don't we take a break for a while from pointless scouring of texts and I'll read to you," Ronan suggests.

I shoot him a curious look over my shoulder. "What?"

"I'll read you some of my favorite fairy stories," Ronan grins, flipping through the book. "It will help to relax your mind."

He begins reading, his voice warm and comforting as it fills the library. I lean back against his chair, resting my head on his leg. He only pauses slightly when the servant arrives with tea before starting up again. I'm not sure how long we stay wrapped up in the world of stories, but when a messenger arrives with a delivery from Athiedor, it's too soon.

"We don't have to dive directly into the next project," Ronan says, noting the hesitation on my face as we stand, waiting for the servants to bring whatever has arrived.

"No, as much as I have enjoyed listening to you read, it's time to jump back in. This is one of the things I can control."

Ronan nods, giving me a knowing smile. "All right, love."

My eyes widen as the servants bring in several stacks of books and scrolls, spreading them across the tables

"This is far more than I expected," I marvel, picking up an old scroll that looks like an official court document of some kind.

Ronan grins. "I knew I reached out to the right people. Let's just hope it's written in a language we can read."

I grimace, realizing that a good bit of the books are written in Yallik, and not even commonly spoken dialects. We divide the texts according to their languages, and then divide them according to what kind of text they are. Ronan dives into the Yallik texts, starting with more official documents. I grab some written in Callenian, or at least an older dialect I can still read, beginning with journal entries.

Kai comes by around noon to check on us, bringing lunch with him. He offers to help, but he seems relieved when I tell him we're fine on our own. The hours tick by as I scan record after record. Every so often I find something that could be useful and I scribble it down in my notebook, but most of what I find isn't helpful in the slightest. When it's time for dinner, my eyes are tired and ready for a break.

I spend a little longer than usual in the dining hall before excusing myself to go look back over the texts. I lay my head down for just a moment to clear my head and accidentally drift off to sleep. I only realize I've fallen asleep when I'm woken by Ronan gently shaking my shoulder.

"Sorry to wake you, love," he says softly as I blink up at him. "We need to reinforce the wards."

I nod, stretching as I stand. "Let me grab my cloak."

"I already got it," Ronan says, handing me my cloak with a grin.

I slip it on and follow him outside. The rain stopped hours ago, but the air is still damp and dreary. I feel like I'm sleepwalking but manage to stay upright. When we're done, I try to head back to the library but Ronan stops me with a chuckle.

"Sorry, love, but I'm going to insist you go straight to bed."

"I still have work to do," I argue, but my words are are lost to a yawn. Ronan laughs and I give him a conceding smile. "I should at least clean up my mess in the library."

"I'll take care of it," Ronan insists. "Go on to bed."

Part of me wants to argue, but the other part of me is too exhausted. I stumble up to my room and dress for bed. I take a couple drops of the sleeping tonic and snuggle beneath the covers. At some point in the night I'm vaguely aware of Kai joining me in wolf form, but I never completely wake.

When I do wake the next morning, Kai is gone. I dress quickly and almost run into Kai as I go to leave. He stumbles back, nearly spilling a cup of coffee.

"You're awake," he mutters. "I was bringing you this."

I accept the coffee with a smile. "Thank you."

Kai studies me as I sip the coffee. "Are you feeling better today?"

I nod and manage a somewhat genuine smile. "I am."

"Good. I—I don't like seeing you upset."

I reach out and place a hand on Kai's arm. "I know."

Kai clears his throat and avoids my eyes. "What's on the agenda toady? More books?"

I laugh. "Yes, more books."

Kai smiles down at me, offering me his arm. "Well, then, let me escort you to the library."

I grin and accept. When we get to the library, I find Ronan already sorting through the piles of texts. Without a moment of pause, I dive right in. Even though I'm still not finding anything dealing with the Fae, I am finding more information on magic in general. I'm not sure what may be helpful later, so I take careful notes, jotting down anything that seems important.

Kai brings us lunch again, sticking around for a while after to help as much as he can. Since he can't read Yallik or Callenian, he can't do much as far as research, but he keeps our stacks and piles organized as we work.

It's nearing dinner when a wide-eyed servant enters the library looking for me.

"What is it?" I ask, straightening in my chair.

"A small caravan from Paravlia has arrived."

I jump from my seat. "A messenger from Paravlia?"

Th servant shakes his head, looking around nervously. "Not exactly. Not a messenger. The queen herself came."

I feel the air rush from my lungs. "What? The queen? Queen Khristiana?"

The servant nods. "Yes. She's in the Meeting Hall waiting for you now."

I nod, my head spinning. "Make sure rooms are prepared for her and whatever guests she brought with her. She receives the finest we have to offer."

The servant nods and leaves with a bow. I smooth my hands over my dress as I draw a shaky breath. I wasn't prepared for this. I've never had to meet with a royal without preparation or Ehren by my side.

"Would you like for me to accompany you?" Ronan asks, studying me.

I look up, meeting his eyes. "Yes. Please." I turn to Kai. "And you'll come as well, won't you?"

Kai scowls but nods. "If you want me, of course, I will come."

I nod. "Good. Good. Well, we shouldn't keep her waiting."

My heart flutters nervously the entire walk to the Meeting Hall. I pause outside the door and take a fortifying breath before I stride inside, my head held high. I march forward with far more confidence than I feel and struggle not to fall prostrate at the glory of the queen before me.

Queen Khristiana sits at the head of the table, a thing of true beauty and power. Her dark skin is highlighted by a necklace of gold and rich, colorful robes. Her steady brown eyes meet mine as I incline my head, feeling terribly inferior.

"Your Majesty, I hope your journey was smooth," I fumble, hoping I seem composed and relatively competent.

"It went well enough." Her voice is cold and sharp. I'm not sure if it's due largely to her thick accent or her disdain for meeting with me instead of Ehren.

"I do apologize for my lack of Paravlian. I'm afraid it's a language I never had the opportunity to learn."

Queen Khristiana waves her hand. "It is no issue as I can speak your language well enough." She pauses, her eyes drifting to Ronan and Kai behind me. "What of your guests? Are they from Callenia as well?"

Red rises in my cheeks. "Allow me to introduce Lord McDullun. He is our current ambassador to the region of Athiedor."

Ronan steps forward, oozing charm as he bows from the waist. "It is an honor, Your Majesty."

Queen Khristiana eyes him before nodding once and looking to Kai.

"And this is Kai," I offer as Kai steps forward with a stiff bow. "He's originally from the Hundan Valley in Gleador but has been aiding our cause here in Callenia."

"Your shifter," Queen Khristiana says with a sharp nod.

My eyes widen. "How did you—"

"I know many things. Time is too valuable to discuss them all. Please, sit and we shall begin our negotiations."

I nod, sinking into a nearby chair, Kai on my right and Ronan on my left. "I hope you don't mind if my companions join us?"

Queen Khristiana shakes her head. "If you trust them, who am I to doubt their loyalty? After all, what I have to discuss involves your shifter."

"Oh? How so?" I ask with a frown as Kai tenses in the seat next to me.

"First, tell me how much you know about how my kingdom is run," the queen demands, folding her hands on the table in front of her.

"Well," I say, trying to bring forward every memory I have about Paravlia from my years of study. "Paravlia is made up of seven states, each run by a governor. Every ten years those governors elect the next king or queen, often selecting the current leader or a member of their family."

Queen Khristiana nods. "You are correct. And the votes the governors cast are based on information passed on from the heads of each individual city or tribe within their states. Before I became queen, my uncle ruled for thirty years. I obtained the throne with no struggle and have maintained a peaceful reign full of prosperity. My next ten years were secure until magic returned. Now, I have less than a year before the governors meet again and, thanks to my kingdom being unsettled by magic, I risk losing the throne. That is why I need your help."

I frown, studying the queen. "I'm afraid Callenia is in no position to send any aid right now."

The queen straightens. "I am aware. I also know better than most the terrors the Dragkonians can unleash. My kingdom is the closest to the Isle of Atroxmorte. We witnessed their flight, felt their evil roll over our land. When your call for aid came, it was immediately my desire to send my armies. However, there is a rebellion rising in my own kingdom, threatening everything. What do you know about shifters?"

I startle, blinking back at the queen. "Shifters?" I

exchange a quick look with Kai. "I'm not sure I know much about their histories, if that's what you mean."

Queen Khristiana nods as if she expected my answer, turning her gaze to Kai. "And you? What do you know of your own history?"

Kai clears his throat. "Most shifters originated in Paravlia. When magic reigned before, the majority of magic from Paravlia was shifter magic. Not just wolves like myself—though wolves were quite prevalent—but shifters of every species."

Queen Khristiana nods with a hint of smile. "Yes. You are correct. And now that magic has returned, so have the shifters. Among them is a wolf named Hammon. Before magic, Hammon was always a problem. His brother is a governor and he held too much influence. Now that magic has given him the ability to shift, he has created a large pack of rebel shifters. At first, it was a normal pack of shifter wolves, but it has evolved. He has become the leader of dozens of packs of wolves and has gained power over shifters of other species. He threatens to take my throne.

"If Hammon is not stopped, my kingdom will fall. As it stands, all my loyal soldiers are fighting back his rebellion and I have none to spare for your war. If he can be stopped, however, I will send you every spare soldier I can. I simply require your assistance."

I shake my head. "I'm sorry, but I don't see how we can help."

Queen Khristiana meets Kai's eyes. "He knows."

I glance over at Kai. He's sitting far too straight, his jaw set.

"What ... ?"

"In a wolf pack, the leader can be challenged by another

wolf. If the challenger can take the leader out, they gain control of the pack," Kai explains slowly. "At least in theory that's how it works. In reality, it can be much more complex. Loyalties are not always so easily shifted."

"Indeed," the queen says. "In the case of Hammon's uprising, we believe that there are certain magics at play that make taking control of his shifters a straight-forward process."

"You want Kai to take control of the shifters?" I ask in disbelief.

Queen Khristiana nods. "Yes. From what I've heard, he's more than capable."

My thoughts swim and I feel like I need to throw up. I can't send Kai away into a situation like this. I can't send him to a possible death. I need him here.

"I'll go," Kai says, jerking me from my thoughts.

"Kai," I gasp, fixing my eyes on his.

"If it will help us win the war, I will go."

Queen Khristiana smiles, nodding. "Good. Time is of the essence. Can you be ready to leave in the morning?"

Kai nods once. "Yes."

"Excellent." Queen Khristiana rises from her chair in one smooth motion. "Is there a place I can rest?"

I stumble to my feet. "Yes, I have had the servants prepare the best rooms."

"I can lead Her Majesty to the rooms," Ronan offers, stepping forward.

I manage a nod.

"If you'll follow me, Your Majesty," he says with a low bow, offering the queen a charming smile.

Queen Khristiana crosses the room. Before she follows the servant out, she turns back to me, meeting my eyes. "I think you are on the right side of this. Together, we can most certainly win."

I'm still staring after her several moments after she's disappeared, my hands trembling by my side.

"Astra," Kai says softly, taking my hands in his. "Are you okay with me doing this?"

I spin to face him. "Do I have a choice?"

His face falls. "I want to protect you and make sure you are safe. Helping to secure these additional allies is the best way to do that. I've felt helpless here by your side. I can't even comfort you. This is a way I can be useful again."

A sob catches in my throat. "But what if you don't come back?"

Kai pulls me into his arms and I crash against him.

"I will always come back for you, do you understand?" he whispers.

He releases me and I step back, looking up at him. "As long as you come back, you can go."

He forces a smile before pressing a kiss to my forehead. "Always."

I long for the evening to last, but it passes more quickly than usual. I spend every moment I can with Kai, but it's not enough. All too soon it's morning and I'm watching someone else I love ride away from me. I feel like the world is crashing down on me again as he disappears with the small caravan of Paravlian soldiers and their queen.

"He'll come back," Ronan says, draping his arm across my shoulders. "If anyone can fight the odds and win over a pack of insane shifters, it's that man."

I manage a weak smile as I lean into Ronan. "I know you're right, but it doesn't make it much easier."

"I know, love," Ronan says. "Let's go distract ourselves with books. Books do make the best distractions after all."

I nod, turning toward the door inside. "All right. Let's focus on the things we can control."

I offer Ronan a smile, which he returns.

"That's the spirit, love."

Together we hide away in the library, eating lunch and dinner by the fire. We make some headway, but not enough. I still find my thoughts floating back to Kai. I find myself worrying about Alak and Bram and all the soldiers. I wonder if Ehren is alive or dead.

When it comes time for bed, I stand in the doorway, staring at the bed. I don't want to sleep alone. The thought hurts. I debate for several minutes before I grab my tonic and the dream walking feather from beneath my pillow and pad down the hall to Ronan's room. I knock softly, my heart pounding as I wait for him to reply. When he opens the door he blinks down at me in confusion. He's clearly dressed for bed and, for the first time, he's without his cane. He hesitates only a moment before throwing the door open wide, gesturing me in.

"My bed is plenty big enough for both of us," he says with a gentle smile as he walks toward his bed, his limp much more pronounced.

"How did you know?"

He chuckles, shaking his head as he eases down onto the edge of his bed. "Because I don't like sleeping alone either."

I nod, suddenly feeling awkward. Ronan laughs again.

"Don't worry, love. You're safe with me."

I shake my head, red rising in my cheeks. "I know. It's just new."

"Not all new things are bad. Some of them can be rather delightful," Ronan grins.

I smile and nod. "I suppose so."

I take a seat on the opposite side of his bed, placing the feather under my pillow before taking the tonic. I snuggle under the covers as Ronan douses the candles before settling in beside me. Soon, I'm happily wrapped in the arms of sleep, and I'm happy to discover I'm not alone. Ehren comes, and everything feels right, even if the world is falling apart.

CHAPTER TWENTY-THREE

EHREN

When I wake the morning after arriving at the Ascarian camp, Cal is already up and gone. I try not to dwell on or read into his early disappearance as I rise and prepare for the day. The camp is bustling with activity, everyone prepping to leave, so it doesn't take me long to find Prince Luc and Princesse Nicolette. I'm not surprised to find them next to a tray of breakfast croissants with assorted jams and coffee.

"Good morning," Prince Luc greets me with a gentle smile. "Did you sleep well?"

I nod, plucking up a croissant. "Well enough."

"That is good to hear," Luc smiles as I fill a cup with coffee.

"You said the Château des Chamans is a day from here?"

"A little less, but yes. We should be there in plenty of time for dinner. I have already sent a runner ahead of us so rooms will be ready for you and your guests."

"Since you seem particularly attached to your Guard,

you will share a suite of rooms with them," Nicolette says with a grin that makes me uneasy.

I force a smile that I hope makes her equally uneasy. "Thank you. I appreciate it."

I quickly finish up my croissant and coffee and go off to find Cal. He's with the horses, making sure everything, including my bag, is packed. When he sees me approaching, he meets my gaze with a weak smile.

"Everything ready to go?"

He nods. "Yes. I was talking to some of the Ascarians and they said the journey should be easy and quick today."

"Where did you learn to speak Ascarian? You're quite adept."

Cal blushes and glances away at the compliment. "Noah's mother was Ascarian, so he speaks it fluently. I loved the language and asked him to teach me. We used to speak it often to hide our conversations from the other soldiers."

Jealousy rises in my chest but I force it away. "Ah. I had forgotten the two of you were close at one time. You used to be practically inseparable."

Cal smiles, tightening a strap on the saddle. "I never expected to use Ascarian outside our conversations, but it's coming in handy after all. Though, I'm a bit rusty. Noah and I haven't really used it much in recent years."

I glance away. "I'm sure with as early as you rose, you had plenty of time to chat and sharpen your language skills. You'll be fluent again in no time."

I regret my harsh words almost as soon as I've said them, but I don't try to take them back. Cal's expression hardens as he sets his jaw, his eyes full of shadows.

"Ehren, you know why I—"

"There you are!" Pascal says, striding toward us with Lorrell not far behind.

Cal forces a tight smile. "Just packing everything up. The prince and princesse seem eager to be on the road."

"This whole camp is like an anthill," Lorrell agrees with a nod. "Everyone is busy to get moving."

"Good, then let's not dawdle. Gods forbid we not live up to their expectations of us," I mutter.

Cal shoots me a glare as I turn and slide back toward camp to find out exactly when we are leaving. I want Cal to chase after me, but I know he won't. Maybe it's better that way. Maybe it's time to move on and stop pretending I have choices in this world. This war is bound to take everything from me, and the sooner I accept that fact, the better.

As promised, it takes less than a day to reach Château des Chamans. We arrive early evening while there's still daylight, so we see the castle in its full glory. I've been to the main castle in the capital of Beaurac, but never this smaller castle, though it is no less grand. Seven white stone turrets stretch into the sky, each adorned with the deep purple Ascarian flag bearing a silver lion crest.

We are barely inside the castle before servants rush forward to assist us. Our horses are taken off to the stables as we are ushered inside, servants carrying our bags. As promised, we are given a suite of four rooms that share a large sitting room but have separate washrooms and dressing rooms. Pascal and Lorrell seem almost giddy with the arrangement, but things are still too tense between me and Cal for me to fully relax. When a servant comes to fetch us for dinner, it's a welcome distraction.

The dining hall is similar to the one in Embervein. Royals and nobles are seated at the head of the room on a raised platform with more tables arranged in order of rank scattered throughout the hall. As a royal and official diplomatic guest of Prince Luc and Princesse Nicolette, I am given a seat on Luc's left. As we eat, I'm introduced to various nobles whose names I am unlikely to remember. I nod politely and curse the fact that I have allowed my Ascarian to grow so rusty and unused. It doesn't help my concentration that I can't seem to keep my eyes from constantly wandering to where Cal sits among other guards and soldiers. He's smiling and seems caught up in conversation, likely doing better with the language than I am.

"You are rather close to your Guard, no?" Prince Luc asks, his eyes shining.

I force a cordial smile, though my gut twists with equal parts guilt, longing, and maybe a bit of shame for wanting something I don't deserve. I look down at my plate, poking at a pile of steamed vegetables with my fork.

"We've trained together since we were children. We're friends."

Luc nods, watching me closely. "It is all right by me if there is more to it than that."

I raise my head and cock an eyebrow. "What do you mean?"

"I mean," Prince Luc replies, a sad smile playing on his lips, "that I have had many people judge me for things beyond my control, and I will not do that to anyone else." He glances sideways at his sister who is caught up in vibrant conversation with a noble to her right. "My sister may act harshly, but I can promise you that she would also be accepting when it came down to it."

"It's not that simple," I counter, shaking my head, wishing with everything I possess it could be that simple.

"For us royals, it seldom is." Prince Luc sighs. "Still, I believe we often overthink things, pushing ourselves into corners, setting ourselves up for failure. Tell me, my friend, what sort of marriage or attachment would best suit your country: one where you have a loving partner who supports and encourages you, or one that has political gain and respect but no real love or support? Which would make you a stronger king?"

I hesitate, playing his words over in my head. "The former, assuming it did not heap more problems on me."

Luc smiles and nods. "I agree. I assure you, you would receive no additional problems from Ascaria. In fact, I believe many of my people would respect you for your honesty."

A noble approaches with a bow, bringing our conversation to an end, but I continue to mull over Prince Luc's words. Even after we've settled in our rooms for the night, I can't get his words out of my head. Astra has told me essentially the same before. Astra. I rise from my bed and quickly prepare the dream walking spell. Moments after my head hits the pillow, I'm whisked away to a quiet forest glade. Astra sits by the edge of the water, staring down.

"Ash?" I call out and her eyes lift to mine.

She studies me for amount before her face breaks into a smile as she rises. "I'm dreaming?"

My eyes dance as she approaches me. "Do I only ever appear in your dreams?"

She laughs, shaking her head. "I wouldn't have to dream about you if you were here. How are things going? Are you in Ascaria? Have you managed to avoid any more near-death experiences?"

I laugh. "I've managed to avoid death very nicely, thank

you and, yes, we have arrived in Ascaria. Prince Luc and Princesse Nicolette met at us at the base of the mountains and escorted us to the Château des Chamans, which is their closest castle to Callenia."

Astra scowls, studying me. "Is that good? That they were waiting for you?"

I nod thoughtfully. "I think so. They seem very willing to work with us. At least, Prince Luc does. I'm meeting with them and their advisors tomorrow morning to go over specifics."

"Where's the king?"

I shrug. "I don't know. He's not here. I'm assuming that's one of the details I'll find out tomorrow."

"Okay, then what else is wrong?"

I furrow my brow and tilt my head. "Who said anything was wrong?"

Astra sighs and rolls her eyes. "I know you well enough to know everything isn't okay. What's wrong?"

I shake my head and glance away. "Nothing I can't figure out on my own."

"Ehren, I'm here for you, if you need to talk."

"No, there's only a little time left on this spell, and you haven't even told me what's happening on your end. Have you talked to Alak?"

Astra nods. "Yes, and there's more news on that front than I think I have time to share. Let's suffice it to say that you were correct. There is an army forming of magic and non-magic training side-by-side. Alak and Bram are working with them. Do you remember my friend Mara from Timberborn?"

I nod. "Yes, she was the lovely young lady that accompanied you to that disastrous dinner."

Astra laughs, her eyes shining. "Yes, exactly. Well, it seems that she and Pax, another friend from Timberborn, are largely to thank for organizing the army and refugees."

"That's amazing!"

"I know. I was surprised in some ways, but it's something that they would do. Also, we heard from Paravlia."

"We did?"

Astra nods but doesn't immediately elaborate. My heart sinks, any hope I felt vanishing like a wisp of smoke. "They turned down aid, didn't they?"

"Not exactly. Queen Khristiana came herself with a proposal."

I frown. "What kind of proposal?"

Astra waves her hand. "It's complicated, but essentially they've had a minor uprising led by a shifter. Kai went to help her settle the uprising, and she promised she'll send aid if he succeeds."

My stomach drops. "So, you're alone now?"

She smiles softly and shakes her head. "Ronan is still here and I still have constant contact with Alak. I'm fine."

"I'm sorry, Ash. I know you say you're fine, but I'm sorry all the same. Is there anything I can do?"

"Just make it back safely. That's all I need," she says with a sad smile.

I feel the dreamworld flicker and I glance around. "The spell is fading."

"Then tell me quickly what's bothering you."

I hesitate, but finally relent with a sigh. "Do you remember when I told you I would never let myself fall in love because I would likely have to marry for diplomacy?" She nods. "Did you mean it when you said you thought love would make me stronger?"

"Yes, Ehren." She places her hand on my arm, and I wish I could feel it. "Love is always worth it. If your heart is telling you to love someone, trust it. Your instincts are sharp and worth trusting."

I nod but the dream fades before I can reply. I wake alone in my room, my thoughts swirling. I've spent years building up a wall, a barrier, and now, I'm not sure if I can take it down. But I sure as hell want to, and I'm damn well going to try.

I WAKE the next morning still feeling exhausted. Even after weighing Luc and Astra's words all night, I'm still not sure what I should do. I wash and dress quickly, putting on the one decent, princely tunic I brought with me. I manage to tame my hair into something that looks semi-respectable, and I trim up my beard. When I enter the shared sitting room, I find my Guard all dressed in their sharpest uniforms. My eyes fall on Cal and my heart skips a beat. We stare awkwardly at each other over a tray of breakfast pastries and coffee until a servant comes to fetch me for my meeting with Prince Luc and Princesse Nicolette.

"Your soldiers may accompany you down to the meeting, but they may not attend," the servant says in a very clipped voice, looking toward my Guard with disdain. "It is old protocol that shall not be broken."

Irritation swarms over me and I clench my fists by my sides. But I don't allow my frustration to show. I inhale slowly and nod. "Of course."

The servant leads us through the halls at a quick pace. My stomach swirls with nerves. I wish I knew what to expect from this meeting. If Astra were here, I would feel better. She seems to know how to do this whole winning people over thing.

We stop abruptly outside a pair of ornate doors, and the servant sniffs dismissively toward my Guard. I turn and glance over my shoulder, meeting Cal's eyes. He holds my gaze for a moment and smiles, nodding his head just enough that I know, despite our recent disagreements, he's still on my side. He still supports me. No matter how this meeting goes, he'll be waiting for me when it's over. It's all I need. I raise my chin and stride into the room, exuding more confidence than I feel.

Prince Luc and Princesse Nicolette sit side-by-side in matching thrones, for lack of a better word, at the end of a long, regal table. Eight men are divided around the table with an empty throne-like chair at the end nearest me. Of the men assembled, the youngest looks a few years older than me, and the oldest is gray and wrinkled, easily in his eighties. Luc meets my eyes and nods to the ornate chair. I stride to it and take my seat.

"Well, shall we begin?" Luc says, with a smile that looks genuine but nervous.

"I'm ready if you are, though, may I ask where the king is?"

Nicolette and Luc exchange a quick glance before Nicolette replies, "It is not hidden that our father is well advanced in his years. His health is fading and, while he is still sound of mind, he has chosen to pass the leadership of the kingdom on to Luc and I so he may live out his remaining years in peace."

I arch my eyebrows. "Both of you?"

Luc nods. "Yes. My sister and I rule Ascaria as equals. I

am unlikely to produce an heir, so she helps to secure the royal bloodline. Besides that, we have never had to be alone, so it only makes sense that we share this responsibility for the good of the kingdom."

"Tell me," Nicolette says, leaning forward, "what do you know of the history of our family?"

I shake my head. "Not much, I'm afraid. Only what little was taught to me by my tutors. I know your father became king at a young age, himself, and has married three times."

Nicolette nods sharply, looking pleased with my answer. "You are correct. His first wife provided two heirs. One died as a child and one as an adult in a border skirmish with Deknia. His second produced three heirs. Two died in childhood but the middle child lived to adulthood, marrying and producing the first of his three heirs before my brother and I were even born. It was assumed that the line would continue through him, so my brother and I were treated like the useless spares we were.

"We had the occasional diplomatic meeting here and there, but mostly our mother raised us as she saw fit. While our older siblings were taught that Ascaria was undoubtedly made of warriors and victors of war, we saw a different side. We got to know the people of our kingdom as friends, not subjects. It changed the way we would lead."

Luc nods, taking up the story. "When our brother, the heir to the throne, and his family died in a tragic fire two years ago, our futures shifted drastically. We were forced into a mold where we did not fit. It has been a struggle combining the world we grew up in with the world we are meant to lead. At first, we were heavily influenced by what we thought was expected of us but, as time has gone on, we have found our own pace. Callenia and Ascaria have a tentative peace, but we wish to strengthen that."

I sit straighter, barely daring to breathe lest I wake and find this all a dream. "You do?"

Nicolette nods. "Yes. We were dealing with our own unrest with the return of magic when news of the disasters in your kingdom reached our ears. The instinct of our council was to destroy you." Her eyes drift to some of the men around the table who shift uncomfortably under her gaze. "However, Luc and I had a better idea. We sent you a letter that was purposefully obscure to see if you would have the initiative to actively seek aid."

"And here you are," Luc says with a smile.

"You were testing me? My country was in the hands of a madman and a demon race, and you wanted to test me?" I say through clenched teeth, my wrath and frustration barely controlled.

"We understand that it may seem . . . cruel, but we did what we thought best," Luc answers.

I scowl. "So, are you volunteering to send aid?"

"I'm afraid we do not yet have enough information," one of the middle-aged men around the edge of the table says.

Another man nods. "Indeed. We wish to hear the exact story from your own lips."

"If you please," Nicolette adds with a smile that is both charming and threatening.

I take a deep breath and look around the table at the ten pairs of eyes boring into me. I start at the beginning, with my quest to find Astra and Kato. I don't leave out a single detail as I describe how we fled my father, only to be chased down by his men. I pour emotion and fervor into every word, leading up to the moment my kingdom and crown were stolen. My voice grows hoarse, threatening to break, but I don't pause even for a second. When I finish, the room sinks into a deathly silence for several minutes as they all weigh my words.

"If what you say is true," Nicolette says at length, "then this Kato and his Dragkonians will eventually come for Ascaria as well."

"I have no doubt. And you will need magic to fight against him. I know that Ascaria has a rocky history with magic, but we all need it to win this war."

Luc smiles. "Ah, yes. Our history books are bathed in the blood of sorcerers and, had we been taught as other heirs, it is likely we would believe the kings of the past were right in their passions against magic. However, we are not so biased, for we know the truth of how magic was good and thrived in much of Ascaria. Do you know what 'Château des Chamans' means?"

I shake my head. "No, I'm afraid I do not."

"It means 'Castle of the Shamans,'" Nicolette replies. "This castle was once a home to a sacred magical order within Ascaria. We thought it would be more than appropriate to gather here for this meeting, not only because of the location but because of the meaning."

"So," I say, shifting my eyes between Nicolette and Luc. "You are willing to aid my country in its magical cause?"

"Perhaps," one of the older men speaks up, drawing a sharp look from Luc.

"We're leaning toward that, yes," Luc amends. "If you would not mind giving us a couple days to get to know you and see who you really are, what kind of leader you will be, it will help us decide."

"How long? Because my people are dying right now. I don't have time to waste."

"The Festival of Visc starts in two days. We will celebrate with a ball the first night with other grand festivities in the following three days, ending with a feast," Nicolette answers. "Give us until the end of the festivities—five days in total—to get to know you. Is that acceptable?"

I nod, pushing my frown back. "I can make that work."

"Good," Nicolette smiles, rising from her seat with a flourish. "Then we shall adjourn this meeting for now."

The men around the table shift and stand, some eyeing me warily and others giving me nods of encouragement as they leave. Nicolette follows behind them as they exit, turning in the doorway to look at her brother.

"Coming, Luc?" she asks in Ascarian.

Luc smiles, replying the same. "I will be along in a moment."

She gives him a nod and leaves, the door closing behind her.

"I thought there was perhaps one other matter you and I might discuss," Luc says, switching back to Callenian.

My stomach swirls with nerves as my mind races with the many things that he could say that make everything fall apart. I bury my concern beneath a smile.

"Oh, and what is that?"

"Marriage."

I blink at him. "Marriage?"

"Yes," he says, folding his hands in front of him on the table. "You came here knowing that my sister and I were of marrying age, and given our brief conversation last night, I imagine the idea of sealing an alliance through marriage has crossed your mind more than once. Of course, arriving to find me a prince and not a princesse may have changed your plans."

He offers me an easy smile, but I catch the tension and concern beneath it. I arch an eyebrow and grin.

"Honestly, your being a prince is not a deal breaker for me," I say with a wink. Prince Luc's smile turns more genuine as I continue. "If marriage is how you prefer to seal an alliance, I am not entirely opposed, whether it be with your sister, you, or another member of your court."

My chest tightens at the offer and I pray to the gods Luc can't hear the strain in my voice.

"That is good to know," Luc replies. "However, I do not believe it is an option, and I wanted to speak with you more to take it off the table than to present it as a possibility. I have been compelled to accept many things, and forcing myself to marry someone I do not love is not an option for me. I also will not require it of my sister. There may be several willing people in my court should you desire to pursue such an alliance, but I truly believe that the strength of a country can be made greater by a marriage made of love and true companionship, rather than politics. What good is an alliance with a country weakened by a political marriage?"

"So, you're saying you *don't* want to marry me?" I ask, my eyes sparkling with mischief even as my heart feels suddenly lighter.

Prince Luc laughs. "Correct, though, please do not be insulted."

I wave my hand. "I'm not."

And I mean my words. In fact, hearing that a marriage alliance isn't being considered is a relief—a relief I didn't know I needed. I feel like I can breathe.

"Good. Very good. Because I do enjoy your presence,

Prince Ehren. I think you and I can become good friends, if we allow, and I look forward to the future we can build between our two kingdoms."

"I agree, Prince Luc." I pause before adding, "You and your sister are not quite what I expected, but I am glad you are who you are."

Luc smiles, rising from his seat. "And you, as well, were different than what I remembered, but you live up to the grand stories that follow you."

I startle at his words as I stand. "Stories? What stories?"

"Perhaps that is a tale for another time, but let me assure you that your love for your kingdom precedes you."

Prince Luc strides toward the door, pausing before he exits to look at me. "I expect over the next few days you will have meetings with nobles and councilmen and any others who feel the need to suss you out. Between that and the upcoming festivities, you may need new garments. Please, do not hesitate to use the resources available here. They may not be as vast as in Beaurac, but they will more than do. Your Guard is welcome to use them as well."

I incline my head in gratitude. "I appreciate your hospitality."

Prince Luc smiles. "I am glad to give it."

CHAPTER
TWENTY-FOUR
ALAK

The moment Astra fades from sight I feel like a hole has been ripped in my chest. I gasp and stagger backward, dropping to my knees.

"Are you all right?"

I take a shaky breath and look up at Bram, managing a weak smile. "Doing great." I rise with a groan. "Half my soul just left but, you know, otherwise I'm good."

Bram scowls, glancing off. "I'm sorry."

He almost sounds sincere.

"It is what it is," I reply with a shrug. I glance past Bram to where Mara watches with genuine concern. "Perhaps we should get this camp tour done so we can start forming whatever plan we need before this Pax fellow shows up."

Bram nods. "Not a bad idea."

I follow him back over to Mara who energetically agrees. The camp is larger than I first suspected, and it takes most of the morning to view all the ins and outs of how it works. To put it simply, I'm impressed. I'm pretty sure Bram is equally impressed. Then again, his eyes keep fixating on Mara rather than the surroundings, so perhaps it's less the camp he's impressed with and more the young woman. For my own entertainment, I start calculating how long Bram goes without scowling or frowning when he's talking to Mara. I'm almost stunned when he goes nearly fifteen full minutes not only without frowning but also wearing an expression very close to a smile. It all resets, however, when he notices me watching him with a wild grin.

"What the hell are you up to, Alak?" Bram demands in a low whisper as Mara steps away to discuss something with one of the other refugees.

"I have no idea what you're talking about, mate."

"I swear to the gods, if you are up to some sort of mischief . . ."

"Everything okay?" Mara asks, looking from me to Bram curiously as she approaches.

Bram forces a smile. "No problems here."

Mara's gaze falls on me and I nod in agreement. "Everything is peachy. Cross my heart."

Bram sighs through his nose as he rolls his eyes.

"Well, I think I've pretty much shown you everything," Mara drawls, still eyeing us suspiciously. "There are a few duties I need to take care of, if you'll excuse me. Feel free to continue looking around. Rations are passed out around the fires at noon."

"Oh, we couldn't take any more of your food," Bram protests, shaking his head.

"Nonsense," Mara chides, placing a hand on her hip. "You're risking your lives to help Prince Ehren take back his kingdom. A bit of food is hardly even enough to show our gratitude."

Bram inclines his head. "Well, if you insist."

"I do." Mara grins triumphantly. "If you need me, I'll be around. Otherwise, relax and enjoy yourselves until Pax arrives."

Once she's gone, Bram turns his attention back to me. "I still think you are up to something."

"What could I possibly be up to? You've been two feet away from me the entire morning." Bram narrows his eyes as I look away. "I was maybe noticing how much Mara makes you less grumpy."

"What?" Bram spits. "What does that even mean?"

I quirk an eyebrow. "If I have to explain what 'less grumpy' means . . ."

Bram sighs, shaking his head as he turns away. "I don't know what you are thinking, but you are wrong."

"How can I be wrong about nothing? Look, I'm merely saying that Mara seems like a nice girl and you should maybe go for it."

Bram spins to face me, his eyes flashing. I stumble back, reflexively throwing my hands up in defense.

"It isn't like that."

"Okay! Fine! It doesn't have to be like that," I rush. Bram sighs, raking a hand through his hair as I lower my hands. "But if it were something like that, you know that's okay."

Bram scowls at me, and I'm pretty sure he wants to stab me with his sword. And we were making such good progress.

"There wouldn't be any point," Bram says at length. "We are likely leaving with Pax, but Mara will stay here. I cannot maintain a proper relationship with her like she deserves. And while she is a nice enough girl, she isn't . . ." Bram's voice trails off as he turns away shaking his head. "Never mind. It just would not work."

I swallow, my brain filling in the rest of his sentence. *She isn't Astra.* I release a long breath.

"Well, it's your choice, mate. Either way, let's chat with the locals, grab some lunch, and do our thing."

Without another word, Bram nods and we make our way back around camp. This time, many of the people know our names. A couple times we spot Mara and she offers us—mostly Bram—a gentle smile. We're about halfway through our lunch when Mara joins us. She begins chattering away and I quickly find an excuse to leave the two of them alone. Bram shoots me a deathly glare, which I meet with a grin and a wink. I wander around for a while until I find myself where we left the horses.

"Hey, Fawn," I whisper, rubbing her neck. "How are you holding up? You good?"

Fawn snorts and nods her head. I chuckle. I startle when Felixe appears on Fawn's back, licking his paw.

"Gang's all here," I mutter, but my smile falters when I realize there's one very important person missing.

I hang out with Fawn and Felixe until Pax arrives. The camp goes into an excited frenzy, so all I have to do is follow the energy to its source. Mara is introducing Bram to a young man with dark skin and a bright smile surrounded by a vague aura of magic I can't quite identify.

"Ah, there's the magical one," Mara says, motioning me over.

"So, I've been reduced to 'the magical one.' I see how it is," I sigh with a grin. I offer my hand to the young man. "Alak Dunne."

The young man grins, his eyes shining as he grips my hand firmly. "Pax Hilling. Pleased to meet you."

He releases my hand and looks from me to Bram. "So, both of you are going to help me train the army?"

"Well," Bram jumps in quickly, "I will take the lead, but Alak can enhance the training with his knowledge of magic."

Pax nods, crossing his arms. "We'll take any assistance we can get. To be honest, we've been mostly winging it, but I think we figured out a good bit."

"All magic is different," I say. "Even magic that seems the same can differ from wielder to wielder. A lot of it comes down to instinct and listening to the magic itself. Practice always helps, of course, but you can't force it into a mold it doesn't fit."

"Figured that out the hard way." Pax grins. "Tried a bit a magic that was far beyond me and passed out for nearly two days from overexertion."

I wince. "Yeah, mate, you gotta be careful. What kind of magic do you have?"

"Oh," Pax mumbles, glancing away. "It's nothing much."

"That's not true!" Mara cuts in. "It's actually fascinating, but I don't know really how to describe it."

"I have learned lately that any magic can be a game changer," Bram says with a nod.

"Well," Pax drawls, his eyes wandering around the group. "I can, uh, whisper and send it over miles to a desired recipient."

My eyes widen. "You're a Whisperer?"

"Uh, maybe?" Pax replies, lifting a shoulder in a partial shrug. "I wasn't aware it has any specific name."

Bram furrows his brow, looking down at me. "Is that a significant bit of magic?"

I nod eagerly. "Yes. Even when magic was alive, Whisperers were supposed to be rare. Even rarer than Syphons."

AMBER D. LEWIS

"It's really not that big of a deal," Pax mumbles. "And it's rather useless in battle. I've managed to perform some basic shielding, but most attack magic is beyond me. That's what knocked me out."

"It is possible that if you start small you'll be able to build up your magic for some basic attacks, but we can also find ways to use your magic in battle. I don't suppose you happen to have a list of the different types of magic the soldiers in your care possess?"

Pax nods. "I have a list in my bag but it's not complete. Some of the soldiers are still a little apprehensive about sharing their magical skills, and we add more people practically every day. It's a bit of challenge to keep track for an accurate catalog."

I lick my lips, nodding. "If you don't mind me looking it over, I can assess what magic might be the most useful in battle and start planning." Bram clears his throat and I roll my eyes. "I'll double check everything over with our illustrious Captain of the Guard, of course, to make sure it's plausible."

Pax's eyes shine as he bites back a grin. "Of course." He shuffles through the bag slung over his shoulder, pulling out a few sheets of paper. He hands them to me before turning his attention to Mara. "You said you have a few new recruits?"

Mara steps forward, nodding. "Yes, eleven."

Pax starts to follow Mara but pauses, glancing back at Bram. "Would you like to come with me, Captain?"

Bram nods. "If you don't mind me tagging along." Bram looks over at me. "Are you fine on your own?"

I blink at Bram. "I've been on my own for the last hour or two at least. I think I'll manage without you for a few more minutes."

Pax cocks his head, studying us. "Are you two . . . together? Because I thought—"

"No," Bram shouts, his eyes wide with horror, while I double over laughing. "Why do people keeping asking that?"

"You have this energy," Mara explains with a smile.

Bram's face turns bright red as he clenches his hands by his side. "Well, there is nothing more than friendship, I can assure you. We barely even have that."

"If you say so," Pax replies with a shrug. "Doesn't matter either way to me. Anyway, let's go see those recruits."

Bram seems too eager to turn his back to me so I can't resist calling after him. "Don't take too long, Sweetheart. I'll be in our tent."

Bram straightens, the tips of his ears crimson now, but he refuses to even acknowledge me as they walk away. With a chuckle, I head to my tent and start looking over the list Pax gave me. Felixe appears a few minutes later, curling up in my lap. I start by attempting to divide the magic wielders into basic groups, but it's difficult. At least half of the names only have "Unknown" written next to their names or, at best, a very general term like "earth magic" or "Attack." Without seeing them in action, there's not much I can plan.

I eventually give up and head back out into the camp and find Bram, Pax, and Mara around one of the bonfires. Bram is leaning back on his palms, his right arm positioned slightly behind Mara. I don't even bother hiding my grin as I settle down on Pax's free side.

"So, mates, what are we talking about?" I ask as Pax offers me a portion of bread and a bowl of vegetable soup.

"Bram was filling me in on everything that's happened,"

Pax explains. "I'm a little impressed you managed to steal Astra's heart."

"Well, mate, I haven't always had these scars," I say, attempting a smile, but everything falls flat, far too heavy to make humorous. Pax eyes me steadily and I shake it off. "Believe you me, I know I'm a lucky man."

Pax nods, fixing his gaze on the fire in front of us. "I also can't believe that Kato has done all this. He was my best friend, more at times. We were . . . We were close. We grew up together, and he was always kind and gentle. He was a good man."

Pax's voice is lined with pain. I've only just met the man, but I can tell he has a good heart.

"Well, I don't know what consolation it is, but it's not entirely Kato's fault," I offer, taking a bite of my soup.

Pax lifts his eyes to mine, searching my face, "What do you mean?"

Bram catches my eye and shakes his head slightly. I sigh and glance down for a moment before looking back up at Pax.

"I can't really give you any details, but Kato's magic affected him. He didn't just change overnight on his own."

"Is all magic dangerous?" Mara asks, her voice quiet.

I shake my head. "No. Most magic is neutral—neither good nor evil. Kato is an exception."

Both Pax and Mara relax a little.

"Is there any way to undo its dark effects?" Pax asks.

"I don't know. Astra thinks there may be some hope, but we really don't have a firm answer."

"If anyone can find a solution, it's Astra," Mara says with conviction. "As long as she has hope, I have hope."

Pax nods, smiling softly. "Me too."

We sink into a heavy silence for a few minutes while we finish eating. When we're done, we stack our bowls in a neat pile next to the fire. Pax is the first to stand, stretching and rolling his neck.

"We have eleven recruits ready to go and not enough horses, so our pace will be slow. I still want to make it to the pass tomorrow, though. We will start out early in the morning, so I suggest you get some sleep while you can." He turns to me and Bram and gives us a parting nod. "Goodnight."

Mara rises a moment later with me and Bram.

"I'm not sure if I'll see you in the morning before you leave, but good luck," Mara says, her eyes lingering on Bram a moment longer than me.

"Thanks, love," I say with a sincere smile.

I walk off, Bram staying a minute longer, speaking to Mara. I don't know what he says, but if he doesn't at least try to kiss her, he's missing out on a grand opportunity. I'm well tucked into my bed when I hear Bram enter his tent next to mine. I'm tempted to ask if anything more happened with Mara, but I decide to leave it be. I rather like my head where it is.

PAX IS A BLOODY LIAR. This is not morning. Morning isn't even whispering on that horizon, and yet, I'm already out of bed. I'm lucky I have magic to pack up my tent and other things, because there's no way I would be able to pack everything up with my brain still half asleep without magic.

Bram, however, seems perfectly in his element. I'm almost convinced he's not human. Humans need sleep and show emotion. Bram seems above all that. It explains a lot, really.

My rambling thoughts are still spinning as I join the group ready to be on the road. I start when I realize that one of the recruits is ten, maybe eleven years old. Two women are also included among those ready to leave.

"What has you looking so baffled?" Bram asks, stepping up behind me with Solomon.

"How old is that boy?" I ask, nodding at the youngest.

Bram shrugs. "I think Pax said he was ten. Why?"

I blink up at Bram. "Why? Because this is war. Children shouldn't be fighting in a war."

Bram meets my gaze steadily. "I agree. I will do my best to keep him from the front lines, but a soldier is a soldier. Don't forget most villages start training their soldiers quite young. He's volunteering, so I won't turn him away."

Ten. I know what it's like to kill at that age. I know how it affects you, changes you. But I'm not in charge here. Instead of arguing I turn my gaze to the women.

"What about them?"

Bram arches an eyebrow. "You are debating whether women can fight after what you have seen Astra accomplish?"

Heat rises in my cheeks as I shake my head. "No, I don't doubt that a woman can be a highly skilled soldier. What I meant to ask is whether some villages train girls from a young age as well."

"Some of the smaller villages do, though it's uncommon. Many girls learn from the male members of their families like Astra did," Bram replies, mounting Solomon. "Now, stop doubting the recruits and get on Fawn. We have a long journey."

I sigh but know there's no point in discussing it further. I climb on Fawn and wait for Pax to lead us to the mountain pass.

We're on the road a couple hours before we see the first hints of sunrise. The cold remains after the sun rises, but it's more bearable. Despite the majority of our group walking, we keep a good pace. We break only a few minutes for lunch before we get back on the road. I keep my eye on the young boy, but he's as determined as the rest of the recruits, showing no signs of weakness. I'm impressed.

Night is falling as we approach the mountains, no sign of the pass in sight. Pax, however, keeps us moving. The mountain terrain is rough to navigate in the dimming light, but Pax knows the way well. I'm about to ask if we're close when I feel the magic. It comes all at once, stealing my breath. A few feet later warm magic washes over me as we pass through another barrier. My eyes widen at the sight I find.

We're in a pass in the mountains that's as wide as it is long. Tents and semi-permanent structures are arranged in neat clusters around low-burning fires. I haven't seen many soldier camps in my life, but I have no doubt this one is as well organized as any. Several people call out and greet Pax and the recruits as we make our way through the camp. We're nearing the center when two men rush up to Pax grinning.

"Who do we have here?" the taller of the two asks as Pax dismounts his horse.

"More men and women for the cause," Pax grins. "Can you help these new recruits find a place to stay the night?"

The man nods. "Absolutely." He turns to the weary travelers and motions for them to follow him.

As the others are led away, Bram and I dismount.

"This is my Lieutenant for all intents and purposes," Pax says, introducing the broad-shouldered man who remains. "Lieutenant Miller, meet Captain Bramfield of Prince Ehren's Guard and Alak Dunne, bond-mate of the Court Sorceress."

Lieutenant Miller eyes us for a moment before inclining his head. "Pleasure."

Another man of few words. He and Bram will get along just fine.

"They will be assisting us with our training and helping to guide us in combat using magic and non-magic skills," Pax explains.

"How long will you be here?" Lieutenant Miller asks, practically glaring at Bram.

Bram offers the man an easy smile. "As long as necessary to assess the troops and find the first round of soldiers to take back to our prince. I am hoping we can get the job done in a week, but I won't know for sure until I have seen everyone in action."

The man grunts and nods. I guess that's soldier speak for, "Excellent plan. I like that idea." But since I'm not a soldier it could mean, "I hope you both die." I'm really hoping it's the former.

"I'll take you to where we keep the horses and then I'll show you where you can set up for the night," Pax says, turning his attention back to us.

I nod my thanks, happy to leave the grumpy Lieutenant behind. As we approach the makeshift stable a young boy around seven years old rushes out to meet us. Pax grins down at the boy, giving him an affectionate pat on the head.

"This is Frederick," Pax says. "He's excellent at caring for the horses."

The boy doesn't speak, but blinks up at us with wide, shining amber eyes. I don't know exactly where the thought comes from, but I get the feeling this boy is an orphan of the current circumstances. I kneel in front of him.

"This is Fawn," I say, nodding toward my horse. "She likes just about anybody but I have a feeling she'll get along with you a bit better than most. She can tell when someone really loves horses."

The boy's eyes light up even more as his head bobs enthusiastically. I grin and stand. I glance over at Bram and find him watching me with an odd smile.

"What?"

Bram shakes his head and steps forward, introducing Solomon to the boy. Once our horses are safely stored for the night, Pax guides us to a corner of the camp where we can set up our tents before heading off to wherever he needs to be. I get my tent set up and am about to slip inside when Bram calls my name.

I turn and grin at him. "No, I'm not sharing my tent. I don't care if people do think we're lovers."

Bram rolls his eyes. "Never mind."

"No, no. I'm sorry. What did you want to say?"

Bram glances off, running a hand through his hair. "Just . . . You are a good man." He finally meets my eyes. "Astra is lucky she ended up with you."

I stare at Bram in bafflement, my mouth gaping.

"Come again?" I ask, my mind reeling.

Bram takes a deep breath and exhales slowly. "If she wasn't meant to end up with me, I am glad she has someone like you."

I'm still blinking at him, waiting for the insult to drop when he smiles and ducks into his tent. Even after Bram is in his tent, it takes me a few moments to collect my thoughts and go into mine. A day doesn't go by when I wonder if I'm good enough for Astra, but if Bram thinks I'm worth something...

I laugh, shaking my head. I guess miracles may be real. And if miracles are real, so is hope. Thank the gods, because right now, hope is all we have.

CHAPTER TWENTY-FIVE

EHREN

The meeting was quick enough we have most of the morning free. I half-expect my time to be spent leisurely, getting to know the castle and the surrounding village, but I instead find myself invited to tea with a nobleman and his brother following a fitting for new tunics. Cal, Lorrell, and Pascal come along as my Guard, hanging back around the edges of the room while I suffer through tea. While my rusty Ascarian had gotten me though negations and charmed enough people so far, it becomes quickly evident that it's severely lacking. I start by switching the word for "Count" for the one for "story" when I address them and end a flustered mess, accidentally referring to the late queen as a "reindeer" instead of their queen. When I finally escape to the refuge of my my room, I have never been so happy for a tea to come to an end.

"Lorrell, Pascal," I say, calling them to my side as soon as the door to our room closes behind us. "Go throughout the castle and see what you can gather about the prince and princesse. I know you don't know the language, but see if you can't build some good relations among the soldiers and servants."

Lorrell and Pascal nod, eager to explore, drink, and gamble. Once they're gone, I spin to face Cal.

"You *have* to help me with my Ascarian."

Cal's eyes twinkle and his lips turn up at the corners. "Are you sure? Because you seem to be doing very well on your own. The late reindeer herself would agree."

I laugh, shaking my head as I sink onto a couch. "That tea was a royal disaster! I have to win these people over, and I have a feeling that will not be the last tea I have to attend."

Cal crosses his arms across his chest as he stands above me, studying me, his eyes shining. "What makes you think my Ascarian is any better?"

"We both know it is. Your accent may be thicker than mine, but you understand it better." I stop and he just stands there grinning. "Are you going to make me beg?"

Something flashes in his eyes as he says, his voice low, "I would like to make you beg, but I won't make you beg for this."

Heat rises in my cheeks at the implications behind his words, and I realize that I might very much like him making me beg. I push the thought aside and focus on the task at hand.

"So you'll help me?"

Cal laughs. "Of course I'll help you." His eyes soften. "I'll always be here for you, you know that."

He settles on the opposite end of the couch, and I turn to face him, draping my arm carelessly over the couch back. We go back and forth, starting with basic phrases before moving on to less common words that are still likely to come up.

After a couple hours, my Ascarian is sharper, and I feel much more confident.

"Should we dig up a late lunch?" Cal asks, still using Ascarian as he stands.

I nod, stretching as I rise from the couch. "Yes," I say, slipping back into Callenian. "I'm starving. We can ring a servant to bring us some food."

Cal glances away. "Perhaps, but maybe you should venture out into the castle, see what additional relations you can build instead of spending the day hidden away with me."

I place my hand on his arm and he raises his eyes to mine. "There is nothing I would enjoy more than spending the day hidden away with you."

"Are you sure?" he asks, his voice so quiet I barely catch his words.

I tighten my grasp on his arm. "More than anything. Cal, I know things are very undecided right now, and I hate that. There are very few things about which I am sure, but one thing I know with more surety than anything else is that I *need* you by my side. I need you, Cal. If I lose you in all of this, I come away with nothing of value, even if I manage to save my kingdom."

"You can't mean that," Cal whispers, shaking his head.

I hold his gaze. "I mean every word."

I barely breathe as I stare into the swirls of brown in Cal's eyes, my heart racing. After a moment he slowly nods.

"Even then, you must remain cautious. *We* must remain cautious. Callenia needs this alliance and many more. I don't want to be the reason it falls apart. I can't have you come to hate and regret my presence." He pulls away from me.

I open my mouth to argue, to tell him I could never regret him, but he cuts me off before I can get a word out.

"I will find us some lunch," he says, walking toward the door.

I long to spend more time with Cal, but I find myself pushed into a flurry of activity before we've even had time to finish our lunch. Before dinner, I meet with three separate nobles who have arrived for the upcoming festivities. After dinner, I'm roped into drinks with even more nobles and people of significance. Thanks to my lessons with Cal, my Ascarian is much more fluid, and I feel like maybe I don't do too badly charming those I need on my side.

The next day is equally busy, and I end up having more tea than any one person ever needs. Everywhere I go, Cal accompanies me as my Guard, but he sticks to the shadows. He's there but not there at the same time.

When the morning of the ball dawns, we awake to find the castle covered in decorations celebrating Visc, the god of spirits and guardian of the afterlife. Some of them are eerie in design, almost macabre. Others are bright, almost too cheerful given their content but, regardless of appearance, everything holds a certain reverence. The holiday may begin with a fine ball tonight, celebrating life, but the focus tomorrow will be a somber day of honoring the dead.

I spend most of my morning and early afternoon meeting and conversing lightly with more nobles and people of standing. I've gotten so used to Ascarian, it takes little thought or effort now. I enjoy a nice lunch with Duc Dubois and his daughter Gabrielle. It takes all of five minutes before the conversation turns toward marriage.

"Yes," Duc Dubois says, leaning back in his chair, his eyes studying me. "We have considered many matches for my Gabrielle, but none have been quite what we desire."

My stomach twists as I look toward Gabrielle. She's

beautiful—there's no denying that. A few months ago I would have jumped at the opportunity to pursue someone like her. Part of me is still very much tempted. She eyes me like a slice of a decadent dessert, and I force a weak smile, my eyes sliding past her to where Cal stands guard a couple yards away. Unfortunately for Gabrielle, my heart is taken.

"I can imagine that you have a line of suitors," I manage, struggling to keep my voice even as I lift a piece of cheese to my mouth.

"I do," she says, looking at me through long, dark lashes, "but my standards are quite high. I will not settle for just anybody."

Duc Dubois smiles affectionately at his daughter. "And what kind of father would I be if I didn't support my daughter?" He turns his penetrating gaze back to me. "Gabrielle is my only child, so she will inherit my title and my wealth. She would make an excellent wife for any man, but especially one seeking to secure positive relations in the Ascarian court."

I swallow and nod, quickly taking another bite of food to avoid answering. I can't help but look past Duc Dubois at Cal, who has pointedly fixed his gaze far from me. I wash my food down with a sip of rich wine as I wonder how much of the conversation he can hear.

"I can understand how those connections would be beneficial to the right person," I concede. "Perhaps she will find someone who needs such connections who is also interested in her hand in marriage." I scoot my chair back and push up from the table. "I'm terribly sorry to cut this luncheon short, but I do have a few things I need to take care of before the ball tonight."

Duc Dubois looks confused and affronted as I stand.

Gabrielle looks less surprised and more angry. Duc Dubois recovers quickly, standing to his own feet and inclining his head.

"Ah, I see. Perhaps we shall see each other tonight?"

I nod once, a bit sharply. "I expect that will be the case." I bow from the waist. "If you'll excuse me."

I turn to leave, eager to escape, but Gabrielle calls after me. "I will save a dance for you."

I look over my shoulder at her, offering her a tight smile. "I would be honored."

She smiles like she's secured a prize as I quickly leave the luncheon room and rush back to our suite, Cal following behind. Once the door closes behind us, Cal turns to me, shaking his head.

"You were a bit rude."

I rake my hand through my hair. "I don't care, Cal."

"Gabrielle Dubois comes from a prominent family. Her father has sway and her uncle is a general in the Ascarian army," Cal presses as I pace the room.

"I'm well aware of his connections."

"Then why would—"

"Because!" I yell, spinning to look at Cal. "I have given up *everything* for my kingdom. My father, my castle, my dignity, my crown—everything. I can't— I can't give up any more." Tears well in my eyes, unbidden. "I simply can't give up anything else. It might be selfish, but I can't marry someone who I have only just met. Not anymore."

Cal stands very straight and tense, his face betraying nothing.

"Perhaps you will feel differently after the dance," he says slowly, refusing to meet my eyes. "There will be many eligible young women in attendance, all more than suitable for a prince. You can dance with them in a less-pressured environment and get to know them a little better. After the dance, if you still feel you have not found someone you think you could make your queen, then, perhaps, the answer is not here in Ascaria. Now, I must go pick up your tunic from the tailor. Take the time between now and the dance to think about what you really want and what you're willing to risk."

Cal is gone before I can respond. For several minutes, I stand staring at the door, considering chasing him down. I even go as far as walking to the door and placing my palm on it, leaning my forehead against the cool wood. In the end, I decide it would be pointless. I collapse onto a settee with a sigh. I wish more than anything Astra was here, but I left her behind, all alone. Gods. I'm an idiot. I can't seem to make any decisions that work. Everything is on the verge of falling apart. I can't hold back the tears any longer. Everything—the weight of every decision, every choice I've made and have yet to make—crashes in on me. It all feels so heavy, and I can barely breathe.

I struggle alone for several minutes, struggling to make sense of my purpose. Astra would be fine without me. She was born for court life. She's secured strong allies. The allies we have are largely due to her influence. I'm nothing. Would anyone even care if I were out of the picture? Who would actually miss me?

I'm sure Astra would miss me at first. I suppose it would be unfair to add to her burden, but she's so strong, much stronger than I am. She would adjust. She would move on and be much more successful than I could be at fixing everything.

Cal's face flashes in my mind, but even he's rejected me. He can live without me. He'd find a way to move on. If I were out of the picture, his life would probably be easier. Then again, he's already lost Makin, and that loss devastated him and nearly destroyed him. I couldn't make him go through that again. Even if I have to marry for a political alliance and force myself into the mold created for me, I could be here for Cal. I could still be near him. Hear his laugh. See his smile. I may be broken and falling apart, but he's someone worth living for.

Eventually I manage to pull myself from my gloom, forcing away my darkest thoughts. I go into my washroom and take a long bath. Cal returns barely long enough to drop off my tunic before he disappears again. I don't see him again until he, Lorrell, and Pascal escort me to the dance.

CHAPTER TWENTY-SIX

EHREN

The ballroom is all glittering splendor. A massive chandelier hangs from a domed ceiling painted with dancing revelers. It's still early in the evening but the dance floor is already filled with women in sweeping dresses and men in sharp tunics. Prince Luc sits on a throne on a raised platform at one end of the room, watching, while Princesse Nicolette immerses herself in the festivities, dancing in the arms of a handsome Comte. Lorrell and Pascal quickly acclimate, finding dance partners almost immediately. Cal, however, seems content to watch from the edges of the dance. I find myself no shortage of willing women. As promised, I dance with Gabrielle, along with several other daughters of nobles. As I shift from partner to partner, I feel Prince Luc watching my every move and decision, taking note of the mask I wear to look the part of a diplomatic prince, eager to please.

I lose count of how many tunes I dance to, my chest growing heavier with each new partner. To hell with this. I'm tired of playing the perfect prince, putting on a false face of cheer. I hate this disguise I'm forced to wear. I want to feel genuinely happy. I want to truly enjoy myself and do what I want, as selfish as that may be. I don't want to dance with an endless line of beautiful women with fortunes and connections. I can't make myself pretend to care anymore. I just can't. I know what it feels like to lose nearly everything, and I won't allow anyone or anything else to slip through my fingers.

I scan the ballroom avoiding the eager gazes of multiple women, their eyelashes fluttering in the hopes they can draw my attention. But I don't care about them. I look past them all, my eyes drifting along the outer edges of the room until I find him. My heart leaps and beats a steady staccato rhythm the second my eyes land on Cal. He's leaning against the wall, arms crossed. His head is turned and his eyes stare absentmindedly toward the dancers, but he's not really watching them. He's staring at empty space. My heart flips as I take him in. Damn, he looks good in that green tunic.

My boots click against the marble floor as I stride to him in focused determination, weaving in and out of the ever-moving crowd. Even as I near him, he doesn't look at me, but I can tell by the slight shift in his posture he senses my approach. I stop a couple feet away, heart pounding in my ears, barely daring to breathe. He pushes from the wall and finally turns to me with a sad smile.

"Why aren't you dancing?" he asks casually, his brown eyes flicking over my face.

My voice catches in my throat for a moment under his gaze and I swallow. Words. I need to say words.

"No one out there holds any interest for me," I manage, my voice quiet and rough.

Cal's lips part slightly as his eyes lock with mine. I draw

an uneven breath and press my palms against my thighs to steady them. My heart is thrumming so wildly inside my chest I'm afraid it's going to burst free.

"You can't find a single person you want to dance with?" Cal asks softly, cocking an eyebrow as he takes a half-step toward me. He looks past me and nods to one of the groups of young women I passed on my way over. "They all seem very eager."

I don't even turn to look. I don't need to see them to know they're not who I want to dance with. Instead, I keep my eyes locked on Cal as I take a half-step toward him. We're inches apart now. Cal brings his eyes back to mine.

"I didn't say there weren't people who wanted to dance with me," I clarify, my voice oddly hoarse, a smile twisting on my lips. I take one last step and close the space between us. I reach a shaky hand to Cal's face and stroke his cheek gently with my thumb. He inhales sharply and instinctively leans into my touch. I press my forehead to his and close my eyes, letting my hand drop from his face and slide tenderly down his arm. He shudders slightly beneath my touch and presses closer.

"You're the only one I want to dance with," I whisper. "And I think you're well aware of that fact."

Cal pulls back, putting a breath of distance between us. I open my eyes and look at him. His eyes meet mine. They're swimming with so much emotion I can't quite sort through what he's thinking, feeling. I swallow and take a step back.

"Will you honor me with a dance?" I ask, bowing at the waist and offering my hand.

Cal chews on his lip, his eyebrows furrowed in concern as his eyes flick to the crowd behind me. "What will everyone think?"

I give a short laugh and shake my head. "Quite frankly, I don't give a damn what anyone thinks. I'm tired of caring. I want to dance with the man who's stolen my heart, and I don't care who sees or what they think."

I swallow nervously, my breath caught in my throat, my eyes scanning his face, struggling to interpret his reaction.

"So," I press, stepping toward him and gently taking his hand, tracing my thumb over his knuckles, "will you honor me with a dance?"

My heart thrums in my chest as Cal considers my offer. I'm afraid he'll decline but his eyes soften as a smile flutters on his lips.

"I would love nothing more," he says, his voice barely audible over the clamor of the ball.

I release a long breath of relief and Cal's eyes sparkle. Fresh music strikes up, a new dance beginning. I lead him onto the dance floor without a moment of hesitation. It's a fast dance, and soon we're spinning and dancing in time, caught up in the flow of dancers. I don't know if anyone is watching us, though I'm sure they must be. My eyes are locked on the man in my arms. He's all I care about in this moment. The glow of his face, the shades of brown swirling in his eyes, the sensual curve of his lips. Gods, I wonder how those lips taste. I press my palm against the small of his back and draw him closer. He doesn't fight it but moves eagerly into my embrace. He's not paying attention to anyone else, either. We might as well be the only two in the room.

When the song ends, it's all too soon. I'm about to ask Cal if he'll dance with me again when a shadow crosses his face and he pulls his gaze from mine, stumbling back.

"I—I need air," he stutters, spinning away from me and rushing toward the nearest balcony exit.

I hesitate, frozen in the middle of the dance floor, confusion swelling in me. Should I let him go? Should I leave him alone? What did I do wrong? How did I screw this up so quickly?

The dance floor is filling with new couples preparing for the next dance, and their bustling shakes me from my thoughts. They're eying me curiously as I stand there, alone, arms empty. I shake my head and make my way off the dance floor.

I notice a cluster of young women like Cal pointed out earlier. They're huddled together, whispering, their eyes locked on me. Maybe Cal noticed. Maybe he didn't like the attention. Did I push him too far? I'm used to everyone watching me, judging me. But Cal isn't. He's always been more comfortable on the sidelines. Come to think of it, I've rarely seen him dance, and it's always only ever been with a woman and usually one we're close friends with like Astra or Winnie. Did I shove him outside his comfort zone?

My heart plumets in my chest. I screwed up. I have to make this right. Without another moment of hesitation I walk over and step outside, the cold night air hitting me in full force. Cal stands at the far end of the balcony, his back to me as he leans against the railing, looking down into the courtyard below. I slowly approach him but freeze less than a foot away when I realize he's crying softly.

"Cal?" I whisper, my voice breaking.

I reach toward him but stop, my fingertips a breath from his shoulder. I curl my fingers back into a fist and drop my hand to my side. This is my fault, and I don't want to make it worse.

"Are you okay?"

Cal lifts his head and looks up at the sky but doesn't turn

to face me.

"Do you think the dead watch us from the heavens?" he asks softly.

My world crashes in around me with crushing force. I stagger back a half-step and squeeze my eyes shut for a moment. Makin. Of course. He's thinking of Makin. How many times had I noticed the two of them disappearing together at dances? I knew they were close but I thought . . . Damn. I should have known. I should have been more considerate. I should have . . . I don't even know.

"I think so," I manage, surprised I can find the words. I feel like I'm suffocating slowly.

Cal turns his head toward me slightly and the trail his tears left on his cheek reflects silver in the moonlight. My heart shatters, and I can't just stand here and watch him suffer. Even if I'm not the one he wants. Even if I'm to blame for his pain. I cross to him and place my hand over his on the railing.

"I'm sorry if I tread on your memories of Makin," I whisper, dropping my gaze to our hands, unable to meet his eyes. "I didn't mean to cause you pain. It seems all I can do lately is ruin one good thing after another. I really—"

"Ehren," Cal interrupts quietly but firmly. I lift my eyes to his. "You didn't do anything wrong."

He forces a weak smile and something shifts in his eyes. Hope blooms in my chest and it aches a little less or, at least, a little differently.

"I've always dreamed that one day the handsome young prince would ask me to dance with him," Cal confesses, weaving his fingers with mine. "Tonight was quite literally a dream come true."

I can finally breathe again.

"Really?" I manage, my voice raw with emotion. Cal nods, his eyes sparkling. "Then why . . . ?"

He takes a deep breath and looks away. "I loved Makin, but he didn't love me. Not like I loved him, anyway." He brings his eyes back to mine. "Every time there was a dance of any kind, he always danced with me at least once. Just rarely on the dance floor." I find myself scowling unintentionally and Cal quickly shakes his head. "My choice, not his."

He squeezes my hand tenderly and shifts closer to me, his other hand dropping to his side as he angles his body away from the balustrade and toward mine. "It wouldn't have been fair to him or me to dance together on the dance floor when we both knew there was no future beyond friendship. It would have felt like a lie. In the shadows, somehow, I could accept it for what it was—two friends enjoying a dance."

I reach out and take his other hand and for a moment we just stand there, drowning in each other's eyes until I finally find my voice, though it's weak.

"But you didn't mind dancing with me publicly tonight?"

Cal smiles and shakes his head. "Not in the slightest. You make me feel comfortable and safe in a way no one else ever can." He pauses and furrows his brow. "Did you mind the stares?"

I grin. "What stares? I couldn't take my eyes off of you."

Cal's lips part like he wants to say something but he doesn't. He swallows and bites his lip, glancing away. My heart swells inside me.

"Cal," I say, my voice rough, "I'd really like to kiss you, if that's okay."

Cal's eyes snap back to my face, searching my expression wildly, like he's looking for a reason to say no.

"We don't have—"

Cal cuts my words short, his mouth crashing against mine. His lips are surprisingly soft and warm despite the brisk night air. They taste like rich wine and sweet honey cakes. I barely have the time to register more than that before he's drawing back.

"I'm sorry," he mumbles, starting to turn away. "I—"

Now it's my turn to cut him off. I grab the fabric of his tunic in my fists and pull him back, my lips crashing against his. I release his shirt to wrap my arms around him, drawing him flush against my chest. This kiss lasts longer, our lips moving frantically as he presses his body against mine. I reach my hand up and cradle the back of his head tracing my fingers along his neck. One of his hands presses against my back as if he can't stand any space or distance between us while the other twists into my hair.

The night isn't cold anymore. Heat swarms around us. His tongue flicks tentatively against my lips, and I release a soft moan, parting my lips. His tongue is in my mouth and I oblige him by following suit. He groans and I feel him press against my leg. I feel all of him. Gods. I want him. I want him more than I've ever wanted anyone before. Years of longing and desire have my hands playing at the hem of his shirt so I can slide my hand up onto his back, skin on skin. Cal starts and draws back from the kiss, cheeks flushed.

"I'm sorry," I mumble, my hand pausing in its caress, but I don't remove it. Not yet. "Am I moving too fast?"

Cal swallows and slowly shakes his head, his eyes fixed on mine. "No. Yes. I don't know." He sighs and nestles his forehead in the crook of my neck. I'm sure he can feel every rapid pulse from my racing heart. "I've never really done this before. I know what I want, but—"

He stops short with a sharp gasp as I trace my fingers up his spine, his breath hot on my neck as he arches into my touch.

"I can stop," I whisper, my lips brushing his ear.

"Don't you dare."

His response sends shivers of pleasure coursing through me. I nip his ear and he releases a soft moan, his lips moving down my neck to graze along my collarbone in short, precise kisses. My eyes shutter closed. If we don't stop soon, I'm not going to be able to hold back. I already ache for more.

"We should go back inside and rejoin the festivities soon," I mumble, my voice rough.

I nip the tip of his ear and he shudders, raising his lips to mine in a quick kiss. "In a minute." He rests his head on my shoulder and wraps his arms around my waist. "I—I need a moment. Can we stay like this for just a bit longer?"

I nod, lowering my hand and wrapping my arms around him, holding him tightly. I need a moment or two myself before I can rejoin the ball.

"We can do whatever you want." I kiss his temple and he sighs in contentment, relaxing into the embrace.

I'm not sure how long we stand on the balcony wrapped in each other's arms. Time doesn't exist beyond us. I would happily stay like this for eternity. Eventually, reality seeps back in and Cal pulls away, dropping his arms to his side as his eyes meet mine. I keep my arms around him, my hands clasped firmly behind him.

"I'm sure you're missed," he says quietly, leaning back against my arms.

I shrug. "Probably, but I don't really care."

Cal tilts his head and gives me an admonishing look, but his eyes hold too much joy for it to be successful. I sigh anyway and drop my arms, sliding my hand into Cal's, intertwining our fingers with a gentle squeeze. My heart skips a beat when he glances to our hands and back up into my eyes, his own eyes shining.

"Fine, we can go back in, but I'm not dancing with anyone besides you."

Cal laughs as we walk hand-in-hand back toward the ballroom.

"You have to dance with other people," he insists. "You're on an ally-building mission, remember? You have to get everyone to like you."

"Are you saying I'm not a likable person?" I tease. "I'll have you know I'm downright charming."

Cal's laugh is rich and warms my entire being. Maybe I'm not ready to go back inside after all.

"That's not what I'm saying and you know it. I, of all people, know exactly how charming you are."

I pause at the door and look into his dancing eyes. "Fine, but I'm pretending they're all you."

Cal laughs again and I grin. I can't resist pulling him in for one last kiss. My lips linger on his for a second or two longer than I intend, but when he returns the kiss I'm not about to end it quickly. I finally back away, unable to hide my smile. I give his hand a squeeze and we stride back inside together. I feel the heat of gazes drifting toward us, some judging, some simply weighing what our presence together means. I avoid them and instead meet the eyes of Prince Luc. He offers me a smile and an approving nod. My smile grows and I glance over to Cal and find he's looking at me too. I laugh.

"You can't look at me like that and not dance with me," I murmur, guiding him onto the dance floor as another dance starts.

Cal laughs, shaking his head, but doesn't fight it. We dance the next two dances together before I finally let Cal drag me from the dance floor. Even then, I don't release his hand from mine as we make our way over to the food table. Eventually, I do dance with a few others, but now that I've danced so many times with Cal, my pursuers are far less adamant to catch my attention. And I couldn't be happier.

It's into the wee hours of the morning when Prince Luc finally descends from his throne, taking the hand of his sister, who has danced without pause the entire night. When their dance ends, Prince Luc thanks everyone for their attendance and leaves with a flourish. People trickle from the ballroom, heading back to their quarters. I scan the crowd for Lorrell and Pascal, but they're nowhere to be found. If I had to guess, they're off with lovers of some sort who are more than happy to settle for a Guard of the prince if the prince himself is unattainable.

I slip my hand into Cal's as we join the exiting crowd. At first, he doesn't seem to mind, lacing his fingers with mine, but the farther we get from the ballroom, the more self-aware he becomes. I feel him tense and straighten, the glamour of the dance fading. As we turn the corner to our room, he slides his hand from mine. I frown, but I don't push it. I don't want him to feel uncomfortable or pressured.

Our suite is quiet, bathed in silver moonlight. There are no signs of Pascal or Lorrell. If Bram were here, he would have their heads but I, for one, am glad they're absent. I walk toward my room, but Cal remains standing by the door, watching me. I turn back to him, extending my hand.

337

"Come with me?"

He looks at my hand, slowly raising his eyes to mine. I can read the unsurety there, the questions, the fear.

"Is that a good idea?" he asks, his voice barely above a whisper. "What if someone found out?"

I laugh, dropping my hand. "Cal, we just danced a dozen times in front of the whole Ascarian court! I think I've made my intentions quite clear."

He nods, licking his lips as he glances away toward Lorrell and Pascal's rooms. "Things are different here, though."

"You're worried about Pascal and Lorrell?" I ask, arching an eyebrow. "If I had to bet money on it, they're not returning tonight. Even if they were, I wouldn't care."

Cal avoids my eyes, glancing to the side. "You should care at least a little."

"Do *you* care?"

Cal hesitates and my stomach twists, terrified of his answer. Every second the air grows thinner, making it increasingly harder to breathe. Finally, he looks up, meeting my eyes.

"I don't care as long as it's what you really want. I don't know how to navigate this, and I don't want to be the reason this alliance fails. No matter what you choose, I can't just be one night, Ehren. I don't necessarily need the promise of forever, but I need to be more than one night that's discarded in the morning."

My heart stills as my breath catches my throat. Is that how he sees me? Does he really think that one night is all I could have of him?

"I could never toss you aside so easily," I manage, the tremble in my voice betraying the ache in my chest. "If you can't tell that much by now I'm doing a dreadful job of showing you how I feel." I take a step toward Cal. "Please, Cal. Just sleep next to me. That's all I ask. We can talk more in the morning when the exhaustion and wine aren't clouding our thoughts. All I know is that, tonight, I need you next to me. Gods, if I'm being honest, I want you next to me every night and have for a while. I'll swear to all the gods that it's the honest truth. If you need more discussion, if you need to go over all the ramifications of everything, we can do that tomorrow. But, please, don't leave me alone tonight." My voice breaks on one last "Please?"

Slowly, he nods. "Just sleep." He glances away, a smile curling on his lips as the tips of his ears redden. "Together."

I release a sigh of relief and extend my hand to him again. "Together."

This time, he accepts my offer. I lead Cal into my bedroom and shut the door, locking it behind me. I watch Cal's reaction carefully as I remove my shirt. He hesitates for a moment before doing the same. It takes every ounce of willpower I have not to cross the room and pull him into another heated kiss that will surely lead to something more. Taking a deep breath of resolve, I climb onto the bed, slipping beneath the covers. Cal joins me, lying on his back and staring up at the ceiling, his hands by his side. I move my hand closer to his, my pinky brushing his. I half expect him to draw away and, for a moment, I think he considers it. When he laces his fingers with mine, my heart races. He shifts, moving closer so his arm touches mine, his head resting against my shoulder.

"Goodnight, Cal," I whisper, squeezing his hand as I kiss his head. "Dream of me."

Cal laughs, tightening his grip on my hand. "Always."

CHAPTER TWENTY-SEVEN

JESSALYNN

We meet outside the side gate of Hyati a little after dawn. I'm still half asleep, but I manage to rally enough to look like the competent leader I'm supposed to be. Cadewynn is fidgety and for some reason that really irritates me. I try to focus on everything except her, but I'm failing. Relief washes over me when Tola arrives.

"I do apologize for my tardiness," she apologizes with a wide smile. "I had a couple things to deal with before I was able to leave."

"It's fine," I reply, stepping forward. "We understand."

"Now," Tola says, rubbing her palms together as she looks around at our little group. "If you'll follow me, I'll take you to the portal."

Having never noticed any sort of portal before, I expect to have walk some ways out of the city, but it's quite close. Within ten minutes we reach a small garden with pebbled paths. In the center is a simple arch of carved white stone.

Nila immediately shimmers into view on Kaeya's shoulder and leaps down to investigate.

"This is it?" I ask, staring up at the arch.

It doesn't look like much. It's worn and faded by the sun with cracks and wear. It's practically a ruin. Even Nila seems to agree, making a low sound somewhere between a mewl and growl.

"Don't judge things so quickly by their appearance, Jess," Tola scolds gently. "Some of the most rundown and broken things have the greatest power and potential. This arch was erected hundreds of years ago over a naturally occurring portal. It has aged well considering all it has been through."

"Well, I suppose you would know better than I," I mumble, still having my doubts.

"How does it work?" Cadewynn asks, stepping forward.

Tola smiles and steps toward the arch, placing her hand on the side. She whispers a few words I can't quite make out.

"Shit," I mumble, jumping back as the arch starts to glow, a silvery liquid light trapped within the archway.

Tola steps back. "Now, all you must do is walk through. You will automatically be transported to the corresponding arch in Heldonia."

Cadewynn licks her lips and strides toward the arch. For reasons beyond anything that makes sense, I lunge forward and grab her arm. She spins to face me, her eyes like daggers.

"Sorry," I rush, releasing her arm with a jerk. "Just, maybe I should go first? Make sure it's safe."

Cadewynn raises an eyebrow. "What dangers could await us in Heldonia?"

Kaeya chokes on a laugh and Cadewynn scowls at her.

"Heldonia likes to make power plays," I explain.

"There's no telling what will be waiting for us, so I'll go first, okay?"

Cadewynn sighs and nods her consent, motioning for me to step forward. Despite my bravado a few seconds before, I feel very unsure as I approach the swirling magic of the portal, leading my horse. I take a deep breath and step forward, the magic washing over me. I feel weightless, spinning. My stomach lurches and I'm thankful that it only lasts for a few moments before a new scene unfolds. I blink rapidly, taking in the literal army in front of me. At least two dozen soldiers dressed in silver armor stand feet away, weapons in hand.

"You should probably move away from the entryway," says a young woman only a few years older than me as she grins.

I frown, clenching my teeth to bite back my response as I step to the side.

"Hello, Kiera," I say, attempting to keep my voice cordial but there's a bit of an edge.

Kiera laughs, tossing her long braid over her shoulder. "Welcome to Heldonia, Jess. It's been far too long."

Before I have a chance to respond, the magic in the arch flickers beside me and Cadewynn steps through with her horse. Cadewynn blinks, her eyes scanning our greeting party before they find me. As she steps to my side, Kiera grins, tilting her head.

"Ah, the sisters."

I tense, gritting my teeth, but I hold back. I know Kiera is only trying to get a rise out of me. I force a smile.

"Yes, allow me to introduce Princess Cadewynn of Callenia," I say, placing a hand on Cadewynn's shoulder. "Cadewynn, meet Kiera Lonia, Head of Heldonia."

Cadewynn dips her head. "A pleasure to meet you. I've heard many wonderful things about your province, and I have been looking forward to meeting you."

Keira's eyebrows shoot up. "You have?"

Cadewynn nods eagerly. "Oh, yes. I have studied the history of Heldonia with great interest. Your silver mines are well known."

I sigh and roll my eyes. She would bring up their damn silver mines. Kiera's grin spreads across her face.

"Well, at least one of you understands the importance of our mines."

"I understand the importance. I just think—"

My words are cut short as the portal swirls again, this time Nyco stepping through with his horse. He looks like a lost puppy as he eyes the soldiers. He stumbles over to us. I turn my eyes back to the portal as it flares up again, Sama stepping through, Ares perched on her shoulder.

"Kaeya will be through in a moment," Sama says with a soft smile as she moves out of the way.

"Good, then maybe we can get down to business," I mumble.

The seconds drag as I watch the portal waiting for Kaeya. When she finally steps through, my shoulders almost sag with relief. It's only by the grace of the gods that I manage to keep my composure dignified.

"Is that all?" Kiera asks, running her eyes over our small party.

Kaeya nods. "Everyone is here."

"Excellent." Kiera turns and nods to one of the soldiers standing nearby. "Miran, if you will."

The soldier nods, stepping forward and placing his palms on the arch. He mumbles a few words and the light within the archway dims to nothing. Kiera turns her attention back to me and flashes me a smile that looks as vicious as it is welcoming.

"Well, without further ado, let's jump right in, shall we?" Keira says, turning on her heels. "Follow me."

My nerves rise in agitation at being commanded like a dog, but I grin and bear it. Soldiers fall in on either side of our party, forcing us to walk in single file like a line of criminals. It's a power play and it's annoying as hell. Kiera guides us from the garden that held the Heldonian arch while our horses and packs are taken to wherever we'll be staying, but we don't go near a building. Instead, she leads us directly to the mine. At the entrance, most of the soldiers drop back, taking up stations along the outside wall.

I can't say I've researched much about how most mines work, but the sight that greets me is far different than I expect. We're several yards up on a thin pathway carved along the top of the mine, eventually curving so that it spirals down into the mine below. The mine is lit by torches and glowing magic as dozens of workers scurry around, most using magic. Keira pauses, looking down at the miners below.

"This is the silver mine of Heldonia," Kiera proclaims like it's not fucking obvious. "Very few get the privilege to see the mining in action."

"It's amazing," Cadewynn breathes, peering down in awe.

"It is, isn't it?" Kiera crows and I roll my eyes. "But the mine is only one thing Heldonia is known for."

Cadewynn nods. "Weapons and armor that are imbued with magic directly from the gods."

Kiera nods. "Yes. And I'm assuming that's why you're

here. You want to have some of our weapons to use in your war."

Cadewynn meets Kiera's eyes and stares her down. I barely dare to breathe as Cadewynn assesses the woman in front of her, Kiera returning the favor.

"What is the cost?"

Kiera grins. "Straight to the point. I like it. Unfortunately, it's not a straight answer. You see, some weapons can only be wielded by certain people, whereas others can be wielded by anyone."

Cadewynn scowls. "What do you mean?"

"Well," Kiera says with a shrug, "the gods ordain some weapons for certain warriors. If you search your histories, you'll see evidence of these weapons. Since these weapons are chosen by the gods, the cost isn't monetary. The cost is devotion to the weapon."

Cadewynn nods like what Kiera just said wasn't complete nonsense. I cross my arms and glare at Kiera.

"So, can you provide weapons or not?" I demand.

Kiera sighs and returns my glare. "We can. In fact, we already have an arsenal ready to go and can have more ready within the month. Enough for multiple armies. Those weapons can be wielded by anyone, though they are quite costly. Magical silver is not easy to mine and crafting weapons from it is even more difficult."

"You're milking us for every coin and gem we have, is that it?" I snap.

Kiera shakes her head and chuckles. "Not quite, but our services don't come cheap." She looks over and Cadewynn and adds, "However, we are willing to negotiate."

Cadewynn smiles and inclines her head. "Of course."

"Now that you've seen the mine, let's head to the

weapons factory. You can see what we have available, and we can finalize everything."

"Already?" I cut in. "You're just handing everything over this easily?"

Kiera arches her eyebrows. "This is a basic transaction. Surely, you are familiar with the process? Why should I drag it out when we're only going to end up in the same place? I don't like wasting my time."

Without another word she turns and brushes past us, striding toward the exit. "Come along."

Cadewynn falls into place behind her, Nyco and Sama following her without hesitation. I sigh and follow, shaking my head. Kaeya huffs next to me and I glare at her as we walk.

"What is it?"

Kaeya's sparkling eyes meet mine. "Nothing, *Jaanu*. I just rather enjoy seeing you go head to head with one as strong-willed as you are. Gives you a taste of your own medicine."

I snarl and step ahead of her while she chuckles to herself. I am nothing like Kiera and her self-decided importance.

Once outside, a few of the soldiers follow us, but most leave for stations elsewhere. We wind around the mine toward the actual city. Kiera pauses outside a large building and grins back at me.

"This should go without saying, but don't touch anything without permission."

I grit my teeth and force a smile. "Naturally."

She sweeps inside and we follow, this time the soldiers coming in with us. We wind through the hallways until we come to large room. In the center of the room is a long table lined with weapons. My heart leaps with excitement and I have to fight to urge to charge forward and grab one from the table to examine closely. Kiera shoots me a knowing look as she saunters to the far end of the table.

"These," she says motioning to the swords, arrows, and bows in front of her, "are basic swords crafted from our silver. They don't require magic to wield, but instead are imbued with magic. They will enhance any soldier's skill, holding up against magical attacks and weapons. The arrows will always find their target and the swords will strike true."

Cadewynn nods, licking her lips as she steps closer, her eyes trailing over the swords slowly as if she's committing every detail to memory. Even I have to admit they're far beyond any sword I've held. Kiera moves on further down the table to a pair of shields.

"These shields are crafted from our silver and work in much the same way as the swords. They require no magic to wield, and have magic all their own. They shield against even the most violent magical attack."

"Even the Dragkonians?" Cadewynn cuts in, her eyes meeting Kiera's.

For a flash of second, Kiera looks unsure, but she quickly masks it with a confident smile. "Everything in our records indicates that they can. Though, I will admit, we don't have much conclusive evidence to how long they can hold out against a Dragkonian's magic. I can promise, however, that they will far outlast a normal shield."

Cadewynn nods, satisfied with the answer.

"Now, these," Kiera says, her eyes shining with pride as she moves down to a set of weapons that practically glow, "are not only crafted from magical silver, but also respond to magic. In the hands of a powerful mage, they are unstoppable." She raises her eyes to mine and grins. "Go on, Jess. I know you want to experience one."

I clench my teeth but step froward. I know she's baiting me but hell if I'm turning down an opportunity to hold a one-of-a-kind weapon. I study the options for a moment before selecting a bow. The magic hums in my hand and I feel at one with the bow.

"Amazing, isn't it?" Keira asks, grinning.

"It really is," I mutter, turning the bow over in my hand. It's the perfect weight and size. I glance back to table. "Where are the arrows?"

Kiera grins. "Well, we can of course supply you with arrows, but we figured you would want to use your wooden arrows since you can already control the wood with your earth magic."

I start and look up at Kiera, eyes wide. "What?"

Kiera's grin widens as she nods to the bow in my hand. "That bow was crafted just for you, Jess. It's linked to your magic and yours alone. Just by using the bow, your aim will be better than ever before. Combine that with your control over your arrow and you will be unstoppable."

My mouth drops open as I study the bow in my hand. Somehow, I know she's right. This bow is mine. It's already a part of me. Though it makes me uncomfortable that she knows about my ability to control earth substances like wood. I clear my throat and look back at the other weapons.

"What about these others? Do they have owners?"

Kiera laughs. "Some do, yes. This sword"—she lifts a thin blade with amethysts in the grip—"is for your captain."

Kaeya starts, stepping forward like she's waking from a dream. "Me?"

Kiera nods, offering Kaeya the sword. "Indeed. Would you like to try it out?"

Kaeya barely breathes as she accepts the weapon. Her eyes widen the moment her hands touch the hilt and I know she's feeling the same connection I feel with my bow.

"Now, this one," Kiera says, motioning to a broader sword with a thick hilt embossed with a silver snake with ruby eyes, "is for your lieutenant. A few of these others are meant for others with magic, while some can be used by any magic wielder."

Kiera grins as she approaches the very end of the table where weapons are covered with silk. She pauses, her hand on the corner of the fabric, but she doesn't lift it.

"What's that?" I inquire, my curiosity getting the better of me.

"These," Kiera says, her voice low with reverence, "are weapons directed by the gods themselves."

She flips back the silk, revealing a collection of three swords and two daggers. Immediately I feel a rush of power from them. I raise my eyes to Kiera's.

"Who do these belong to?" I ask, my voice barely above a whisper.

"I have no idea," Kiera confesses with a smile. "The gods didn't share that information with me, but I do know that they are to go to Callenia."

I shake my head. "You speak of the gods as if you communicate directly with them."

Kiera laughs, shaking her head. "I wish I could be so lucky, but that is not my magic."

She turns her head and motions for a girl standing in the corner of the room. The girl is small, but around my age. She eyes us nervously as she approaches the table.

"This is Maeyana," Kiera says, placing a gentle hand on the girl's shoulder. "She comes from a long line of Veil Hags and speaks with the gods."

"Well, not exactly," Maeyana counters, her voice quiet. "They speak to me through dreams, visions, and feelings, but they don't much care for what I have to say."

Kiera smiles at her tenderly. "Either way, they direct her hands to craft their perfect weapons."

The girl's cheeks tinge pink as she glances away. "I only do my part."

"Everyone is important," Cadewynn says, stepping forward. "It's all the little parts put together that will help us defeat the darkness."

The girl raises her eyes to Cadewynn's, a smile curling on her lips. "Thank you."

"So, Princess," Kiera cuts in crossing her arms. "Do any of these weapons call to you?"

Cadewynn tilts her head, taking a step toward the table. For a moment she studies them in silence. She reaches forward, allowing her hand to hover a dagger before she finally relents and picks it up. It fits perfectly in her hand.

"This one," she whispers reverently.

Keira nods and grins.

"How are we supposed to find the owners of these other weapons?" I ask, glowering at the table. "It's not like we can have every soldier stroll through manhandling each one in the hopes they find their weapons."

"While I cannot say for sure who is to receive each weapon, I have an idea," Maeyana replies. "These,"—she gestures to a pair of identical swords with a sapphire in the center of each hilt—"are meant for a pair who fight side-by-side on the battlefield and as of one heart. One of these has a great purpose and will end the war, though which one has yet to be decided." She moves down to another sword. "This sword belongs to someone who knows what it's like to be lost and alone. It can cut through more than physical objects, wielding a magic unique to itself."

She pauses, tilting her head as she looks down at a dagger with a pink hilt. "This dagger belongs to someone who doesn't even know she has a destiny. A young girl, who would never think to harm, only heal." Her eyes shift to the dagger next to the first, identical except for its obsidian hilt. "And this is for a young boy whose destiny is tied up in this war in ways he can't even see, though he Sees more than most."

"That sounds a bit ominous," Nyco mutters under his breath and I nod in agreement.

"Well, now that we've seen the goods," I cut in, clearing my throat, "shall we discuss price?"

Kiera's mouth curls into a delighted grin as her eyes shine. "Of course. Let's not do it here, though. I have a tea prepared in my meeting room. Let's go and relax and we shall discuss the terms. In addition to the weapons, I am also prepared to provide armor and soldiers."

Cadewynn lets out a delighted gasp and inclines her head. "Thank you."

"Don't thank me yet," Kiera laughs, her lips twisting into a wry grin. "Wait until we've discussed payment."

Without even meaning to, my hand tightens over the hilt of my dagger. I'll be damned if Kiera takes advantage of Cadewynn. Kaeya places her hand over mine and I jerk my eyes to her. She shakes her head slightly and I exhale, letting my hand drop.

Kiera ushers us from the weapons factory and toward a

large white stone building with silver accents. Once inside, we make ourselves comfortable around a large table set for a tea. We start with casual, cordial conversation, which irritates the hell out of me, before we switch to business. When Kiera announces the prices for the weapons and armor, my mouth drops.

"That's highway robbery!" I shout.

Kiera meets my eyes with a firm smile. "These are not normal weapons crafted from normal silver. That alone would make them worth more. Add in the fact they're more difficult to make and take a considerable amount of magic and, well, you can see how this works." She folds her hands on the table. "So, do we have a deal?"

Cadewynn narrows her eyes at Kiera, and I can sense the storm brewing beneath her perfect complexion. I bite back a grin and ease back in my seat, ready to watch the show.

"How many soldiers will this provide for?"

"One thousand," Kiera answers. "I have five hundred ready now and can deliver the other five hundred with my army in a few weeks at the latest."

Cadewynn shakes her head. "That's not enough."

Kiera scoffs. "Not enough? Do you know how long it takes to make these weapons? You're lucky to have that many."

Cadewynn sighs, glancing off. "That falls very short of what I hoped for. I do believe you mentioned providing for multiple armies. This barely provides for one. And that pricing, while overall understandable, is a bit much." Cadewynn sighs again, rising in one smooth motion. "It's a pity we couldn't make a deal. I would like to rest a bit before we move on. Is there a room where I can stay?"

Kiera blinks up at Cadewynn, her mask of confidence

completely gone. I resist the urge to bounce up and down in my seat in unfettered glee.

"What?" Kiera spits. "Just like that you're done? No negotiations?"

"Well," Cadewynn says slowly as she floats back into her seat, "I suppose we could negotiate some but, as you said earlier, you don't like to waste time."

Kiera takes a deep breath and exhales slowly. "Fine. What do you have in mind as far as payment?"

"Half your asking price," Cadewynn says evenly as Kiera's mouth gapes. "And we will pay up front for what you have ready, but we will not pay for the remaining five hundred soldiers' supplies until they are made."

"I can accept partial payment, but half?" Kiera stutters. "You're insane. No."

"In return, Callenia will also provide for any soldiers you send, making sure they have food and any additional shelter beyond what you provide." Kiera only scowls so Cadewynn adds, "You already have five hundred weapons ready for war. Who else do you expect to buy them?"

Kiera hesitates, mulling over Cadewynn's words. "Add a quarter back to the price and you have a deal."

Cadewynn tilts her head as she considers the offer. "Very well. I will arrange the payment."

Kiera grins, her shoulders relaxing. "Excellent. Where should we send your order?"

"Koshima," I cut in, leaning forward. "Troops are already gathering there, preparing to move into Callenia. Send your army and weapons there and we will make sure they are distributed."

Kiera clenches her jaw but nods once after a moment. "Very well." She turns her attention back to Cadewynn.

"Rooms have been prepared for you, if you would like to relax while we finalize the details. I will send for you when we're ready to sign and complete the transaction."

Cadewynn rises from her seat. "Thank you."

As the rest of us stand, one of the soldiers who has been accompanying us steps forward and offers to take us to our rooms. We're led through the city to a small inn reserved for diplomatic guests. Cadewynn and Sama have one room, Nyco his own, and Kaeya is with me. I watch Cadewynn disappear into her room and I shake my head.

"You're more impressed with her every day, aren't you?" Kaeya asks, leaning against our doorframe.

I try to hide my grin as I shrug. "She grows on you. Like an unwanted stray pup."

Kaeya chuckles. "That she does." Kaeya glances to our room behind her. "Shall we relax?"

I laugh and arch an eyebrow. "Actually, I think our success might require a little more celebratory activity."

Kaeya grins, shoving off the doorframe to wrap an arm around my waist. "I very much agree."

My lips meet hers as I push her into the room, closing the door behind us. It's nice to have something to celebrate, even if the victory isn't exactly mine. I'll still take the reward.

CHAPTER TWENTY-EIGHT

ALAK

I wake the first morning at the camp to the bustling of soldiers trained to get their days started far too early for any normal human. I dress and stumble from my tent. I'm not surprised in the least that Bram is up and gone. Bleary eyed, I traverse the camp and find him within a few minutes, sitting around a crackling fire with Pax and several other soldiers. As I approach, a lanky young man leaps to his feet to offer me a wooden bowl. With a smile, I accept, but the smile quickly fades as I look down at the lumpy gray substance that I assume is breakfast.

"Too good for porridge?" Bram grins.

I shake my head as I fill an empty spot a couple down from Bram. "Porridge I like. This," I say lifting the bowl to my nose to take a sniff that makes me cringe, "is a new experience."

The young man who offered me the bowl laughs and slaps my shoulder. "It ain't all that bad. It'll fill ya up real good and keep yer innards warm."

I force a smile. I'm not sure I want my innards warmed this way.

"Here," the man to my left says, offering me a steaming cup. "The coffee helps."

I glance at the bowl in my lap while I take the coffee. I take a sip and nearly gag on the unexpected bitterness.

"Strong," I choke out while a few of the soldiers chuckle.

"Keeps ya alive!" the first young man crows, beating on his chest.

My second sip is a little better. I take a tentative bite of the so-called "porridge" and am relieved to find it mostly tasteless. The conversation flutters around me as I force down my breakfast and soon we're all standing.

"We start our morning with basic drills," Pax explains, leading the way through the camp. "I have most of the recruits divided up according to skill-level, but some of the newer soldiers don't have a firm place yet."

Bram nods. "What happens after drills?"

"Well, we change it up a bit. We tend to focus on individual skills and strengths, but those with magic also try their hand at offense and defense. It's been a bit hit and miss." Pax glances over his shoulder at me as he walks. "Perhaps that would be a good time for you to work with those with magic while Captain Bramfield and I work with the other soldiers."

"That works for me," I agree with a shrug.

Pax nods and focuses on the path in front of him. "After training, we take a break for a couple hours to eat lunch and refresh. The afternoons are for mock battles or whatever training we feel is best for the day."

Bram asks about specifics that make no sense to me but I nod along, pretending I can be useful. When we reach the border of the camp, we stop at the edge of a large training field already filled with soldiers. Little by little, more join the ranks and they begin their drills. Bram walks around the edges, mentally taking notes. I try not to fall asleep.

When drills finally end, Pax sends me and all the magic wielders to the opposite end of the field. Hundreds of eyes watch me expectantly and I can't find the words to say. Who thought this was a good idea? I take a deep breath and summon my memories of teaching Astra and Kato.

"So," I begin, trying to feign competence. "I'm sure you all know there are many types of magic. Some are based in the elements, others are a little less obvious or direct. Everyone has a specific type of magic you can master to its greatest strengths, but everyone with magic can also perform basic, small magical feats. If you have a strong magical heritage, you may be able to excel in multiple forms of magic. I, myself, have both Syphon magic and Illusion."

A few people shift and low whispers rumble through the crowd. I swallow and dive back in.

"Let's start by dividing up according to your magic. Find others with similar magic—earth with earth, fire with fire, healing with healing, and so on. Focus on using and controlling your magic. Don't try to use it as attack magic unless that's what it naturally is. I'll walk around and observe so I can get a feel for what we're working with."

I can tell by their wary glances I haven't really instilled much faith in these trained soldiers. I manage to keep my head high as I walk around the groups. Some of the soldiers are actually quite skilled while others can barely summon their magic at all.

"Don't try to force your magic into a mold," I call out as I stroll among them. "Let it guide you. Tell your magic what you want and get it started on the path. If you fight it, you'll exhaust yourself faster."

I take a deep breath. I hope I can do this right.

"If anyone feels their magic draining, please, stop. The more you use your magic, the stronger you will grow, but in the beginning it can be very easy to exhaust yourself. It can take days to recover if you drain all your magic and can even be fatal if done too quickly."

A few of the soldiers look a little fearful now, but focused. After about an hour of practicing, I have a better idea of what I'm working with. I divide them up into pairs and we work on shielding and attacking.

"If you have a tangible type of magic like wind, earth, or light, use that element to craft your shield or form your attack. If you don't have magic like that, try to block and attack the best you can by manipulating your magic to your advantage," I instruct, my voice ringing crisp and clear.

I pause occasionally, instructing individuals on their form, but I mostly observe. By the time the second hour ends, we've made some progress. It might be subtle, but even those that seemed hesitant at first appear more confident. The soldiers are exhausted but satisfied as we meet up with the others for lunch.

I find Bram and Pax near one of the bonfires, eating lunch. I'm hesitant to accept my portion, but it's not bad. Some sort of beans and bread. We rest for a couple hours. I sit nearby, listening to Pax and Bram discuss the soldiers' training for a while before they finally turn to me.

"So, what magic are we working with?" Bram asks. "Anything battle-worthy?"

I nod. "There are some very talented magic wielders.

Some others I think have decent talent, but they need to find a little more confidence."

"I think I'll join you tomorrow when you work with the magic soldiers," Pax says.

"Well, you do have magic," I reply with a shrug. "It would make sense for you to work with us."

"It will also give you a chance to see how Alak instructs," Bram agrees with a nod. "Alak is an excellent teacher and you would do well to follow his lead after we move on."

My eyebrows shoot up as I look over at Bram in disbelief. I'm sure I misheard him. There should be an insult in there.

"I have respect for anyone who even remotely understands magic, as I find it quite baffling," Pax confesses, meeting my eyes. "I will learn all I can from you."

I manage a small smile. "I'll do what I can." I glance away, eager to take the focus off of me. "What are the plans for the rest of the afternoon?"

"Well," Pax says, stretching his legs out in front of him, "I was thinking we could run some drills incorporating magic next to normal fighting skills and then do a mock battle."

Bram nods. "That's a good plan. It will allow us to assess how well the soldiers can adapt between using magic and regular weapons in battle."

The conversation slips back into more technical terms I don't fully understand, and my mind wanders until it's time to get back at it. Bram and Pax divide the soldiers up into groups and have them work together, switching between weapons and magic. It's not an exact system, but we make it work. By the end of the day, we have a reasonable plan.

The following days fall into the same pattern. We start out with basic training. I try to sleep through this, but Bram drags me out to watch every day, insisting I might learn something. Sometimes he hands me a weapon. Pretty sure he does it just for the laugh, but since I'm focused on not killing myself with my own sword, I don't have the opportunity to take note of Bram's level of amusement.

After drills, we split, Pax sometimes joining me and sometimes joining Bram. I work with the magic wielders, encouraging them to strengthen their own skills so they have full control. I often pair them off and watch them work together, feeding off each other's skills and magic. We also work on basics like wisping. By the fourth day, almost the entire group can wisp from one end of the field to the other.

The evenings are spent sparring. Occasionally we do a full mock battle and other evenings we divide into small groups. It's encouraging to see the magic wielders using their newfound skills effectively against swords and other weapons. Even Bram seems impressed.

At the end of the fifth day, Bram pulls me into his tent. Somehow, he's managed to make the small space seem like home. My tent is pure chaos.

"I thought we could go over who we think is ready to take on to the fortress," Bram says, easing down onto the ground next to a neat stack of notes and books.

I nod, sitting across from him, pulling the crumpled list from my pocket. Bram glances at the list and arches an eyebrow.

"Look, mate, we can't all be hyper-organized," I mutter. "Some of us are normal."

Bram shakes his head but doesn't press the issue. "I think we should take at least 150 of the soldiers with us now and have Pax send more as he feels they're ready."

"That sounds logical enough to me. When are you wanting to leave?"

"I think two more full days of training, ending with a full mock battle on the last day. We can divide them up into groups and make a final decision based on their performance." He pauses, glancing down at the sad paper in my hands. "Do you have a list of those you think might be ready?"

"It's not a list, per se," I say, smoothing the paper out over my lap. "It's more general notes. I do know which are the strongest and most likely to survive in battle."

"Good," Bram says with a sharp nod. "Let's make a list of the top 100 that we feel are probably ready to go and another 100 that might make the cut. I'd like the army to be evenly split between magic and non-magic."

"All right. Who do you have in mind?"

We fall into a deep discussion, figuring out exactly who would work the best. The first fifty or so are easy enough, but after that, it gets tricky. It's well into the night by the time we finish.

"Have you written Astra recently?" Bram asks as I stand to leave.

Guilt washes over me. No, I haven't. In all honesty, I've been too busy to really think about her. Not that I don't miss her—gods, I miss her so much—but being busy has its advantages. If I don't think about Astra and the bond, it doesn't hurt as much to be apart.

"I wanted to have something important to say," I mumble, shaking my head. "I'll write her tonight. Anything you want me to add on your behalf?"

Bram shakes his head. "Write what you feel is best."

I nod and duck out of the tent, crossing to my own. Felixe is snuggled on my bedroll, barely acknowledging my presence as I settle down next to him, scratching his ears. He snuggles tighter into his little ball as I dig through my bags to find ink and parchment. I write a simple note, straight to the point.

"All right, Felixe," I say, scratching his head. "Can you take this to Astra?"

Felixe yawns, stretching his legs out in front of him as he stands. He blinks up at me as I offer him the letter. He takes it, giving me one last blink before he disappears. I settle down on my bedroll, drifting off. I'm woken a few moments later by a sharp yip. I open my eyes and find Felixe blinking back, a letter in his mouth. I sit up, rubbing my eyes. It's unusual for Astra to respond so quickly. My mind races with a million things that could be wrong, but I smile when I see the words.

> *My Dearest Alak,*
>
> *I love you so much and I miss you terribly. I'm glad things are going well, mostly because it means you will come back to me soon.*
>
> *Yours Forever,*
>
> *Astra*
>
> *P.S. I don't think Bram wants to murder you. Probably. Just stay on his good side.*

I grin, reading the letter over several times, tracing her curling penmanship. At some point, I fall asleep. I wake, her letter still in my hand.

CHAPTER TWENTY-NINE
EHREN

J udging by the brightness and warmth of the sunlight flooding my room, it must be nearly midday by the time I wake. Memories of the dance flicker through my mind and I smile, glancing to my left. Cal sleeps soundly, snuggled against me, his arm slung across my chest. I adjust my position, wrapping my arm around him, drawing him closer. He shifts, his eyes blink open, and he draws back a bit to take me in.

"I didn't mean to wake you," I mumble, pressing a gentle kiss to his forehead.

For a moment, he sorts through his own thoughts and memories. He sighs at length, smiling softly, settling back against me.

"Good morning." He turns his head, glancing at the door. "I wonder if Pascal and Lorrell are back yet."

I shrug. "No idea. I've only been awake a few minutes myself, and my full attention has been devoted to the man in my bed."

"We should probably get ready for the day," Cal mutters,

making no move to rise from the bed. In fact, he snuggles closer, resting his head above my heart.

"I suppose," I say with a grin. "At least, eventually."

"What do we have to do today? Any more teas or luncheons with lines of eligible young women?" He asks, attempting to keep his voice light but I catch the tension in his words.

I chuckle, shaking my head as I absentmindedly trace the muscles on his back. "I have a feeling that after the dance last night, there will be a significantly fewer number of young women trying to catch my eye."

He rises up onto his elbow, his face serious. "That's not necessarily a good thing."

I sigh and look up at the ceiling. "I probably should care, but I just can't make myself." I look back over at Cal and offer him a weak smile. "Let's get ready for the day, find some food, and then we can discuss this as much as you desire. Though, I can assure you, my mind is rather made up."

He nods, sitting up all the way. "That sounds good."

He rises from the bed and pulls on his shirt. He pauses at the door to look back at me.

"For the record, I want this to work, you and me. I want it more than anything, even though it terrifies me."

A wide grin spreads across my face. "Don't worry, Cal. We'll find a way. I swear it."

After Cal leaves, I push up from my bed, feeling lighter and freer than I have in months. I dress quickly and head out into the sitting room. Cal is still in his own room, but there is a tray of sandwiches, cheese, and fruit on a table in the center of the room next to a pot of tea. I'm nibbling a sandwich when the suite door flies open, a disheveled Lorrell stumbling into the room. His eyes find me and a blush rises in his cheeks.

"I . . . ," he starts.

I cut him off with a roguish wink. "Seems like someone got lucky last night."

Lorrell's blush deepens. "She was lovely."

"And here I was thinking you didn't know the language well."

Lorrell shoots me a sheepish grin. "There are some things that have their own language."

I throw my head back and laugh. "I suppose there are."

Lorrell glances toward his brother's room and I answer his unasked question. "As far as I know, Pascal was also out all night."

Lorrell nods, licking his lips. "Well, I'm going to go clean up."

I give him a nod, still grinning. "You do that."

He stumbles into his room as I chuckle. Cal emerges a couple minutes later, dressed in his Guard uniform. I pour a cup of tea and slide it to him as he takes the seat next to me.

"Did I hear Lorrell?" he asks, selecting a sandwich from the tray.

"Mm-hm," I reply, taking a sip of tea. "It seems he had an active night."

Cal shakes his head. "He's lucky Bram's not here."

"Thankfully, I had a Guard close all night so his absence wasn't an issue."

Cal ducks his head, attempting to hide his smile. "Happy to be of service, my prince."

His words send a shiver of thrill through me, and I shift in my seat. I'm about to speak when the door is thrown open again, this time Pascal, looking as disheveled as his brother.

Pascal, however, doesn't look the slightest bit abashed. He meets our eyes, grinning wickedly.

"Good night?" Cal asks casually, lifting his cup to his lips.

"The best. I met a pair of siblings . . ."

"Eh, we don't need the details," I cut him off, waving my hand. Cal chuckles.

"Are you sure? Because the details are quite delightful." Pascal grins.

"I'm positive." I laugh. "But I am glad you enjoyed yourself. Now, go clean up. We have services and such to attend shortly."

Pascal nods and strides across the room, an extra bounce in his step.

"Which services do we have today?" Cal asks once Pascal's door closes behind him.

"There are several spread throughout the day, but we really only need to attend one of those. The main service, La Prière aux Saints, is tonight. They light candles to honor the dead." I pause, my voice quiet. "They believe tomorrow the spirits of the dead are closest to the living. The candles and prayers help light the way so those that have passed on can find their way home."

Cal stares down into his teacup, his hand resting next to it on the table.

"I suppose we have a few candles to light," he says, his voice a hoarse whisper.

I reach out and place my hand over his, and he lifts his eyes to mine.

"More candles than I would like," I admit, my voice soft. "But we don't have to do it alone. We have each other."

He nods, shifting his hand to weave his fingers with mine.

"Ehren," he says, slowly. "Are you sure that you don't want to try and find a nobleman's daughter?"

I squeeze his hand and shake my head. "I don't have the slightest desire for that. I could go on pretending, but it's exhausting. It would all be a lie. The truth is, I've been falling in love with you for quite some time. I've been pushing it aside, refusing to acknowledge my feelings, but I'm not content to push it aside anymore. I'm not sure I could even if I wanted to. I want to embrace this, Cal. If I force this away, I will be living a lie. I can't be the prince—the king—I need to be if I can't even be honest with myself. You make me the best version of myself."

Cal's lips part. "You're sure?" he asks, breathless.

"There are a lot of things I'm unsure about right now, but this is one thing I know—I want to be with you, Cal, and no one else. Will you let me?"

Cal tightens his grip on my hand and nods slowly, tears in his eyes. I trace my thumb over the top of his hand.

"Cal," I say, somewhat hesitantly. "You know, you're the reason I keep fighting. You're what keeps me going."

The confession leaves me raw and exposed.

"Ehren." Cal's voice is barely above a whisper, but I can still hear every hint of pure emotion behind my name. It gives me the strength to continue.

"It's no secret I was drowning after the attack on Embervein. I couldn't handle everything. I couldn't handle the loss of my father and the rejection from my mother. I—I didn't know how to navigate my way back. You saved me."

Cal is silent for a moment before he slowly shakes his head. "That was all Astra."

"Astra may keep me from sinking, but you're the one that makes me want to keep my head above the water."

I blink back the tears suddenly burning in my eyes. I reach and stroke his cheek with a trembling hand. He leans into my touch.

"You make me want to live, Cal. You are that light that chases away my darkest thoughts, and I've woken up these past few mornings marveling that someone like you wants to be part of my life. I thought that something like what we have was completely unattainable for me, but now that I've experienced it—allowed my heart to love as it desires—I can't undo it. I can't go back. I only want to move forward. I can't imagine my life without you by my side and I don't want to."

A tear drops from Cal's eye, his lips parting as he takes me in. I can see the words forming before he finally finds the courage to say them out loud.

"Ehren, I love you."

Everything in me melts to nothing. I release a shaky breath.

"I love you, too, Cal. So much it hurts."

The next thing I know, his lips are on mine. His kisses are hungry. A moan escapes me and he draws back quickly, his face flushed.

"I'm sorry," he mumbles, straightening in his seat.

I arch an eyebrow. "Sorry? Sorry for what?"

He looks at me and I'm lost for a moment in his dark brown eyes before he breaks the gaze.

"I know you probably don't want . . ." He trails off with a sigh, glancing to Pascal and Lorrell's rooms.

"That I don't want what? You? Because I do. I want every part of you that you're willing to give."

His breath catches as he looks back at me, longing in his eyes.

"But Pascal and Lorrell . . ."

I lean forward and trace his lips with my thumb. He shivers under my touch.

"Let them hear. Let them find out. Let them tell the world. I don't care, Cal. Not anymore. I'm not going to change my mind, so they might as well spread the news that my heart is forever taken. I'm yours. You never need to apologize for kissing me or showing me any sort of affection."

He holds my gaze for a moment before leaning forward and resuming our kiss. He lifts his hands and cradles my face, his fingertips tracing my cheek bones. I give in to the kiss fully. When he draws back, eyes shining, I stand, offering him my hand.

"Why don't we go somewhere a little more private?" I smile, nodding toward my room. "After all, we do have a little time to fill before we're needed elsewhere."

I see the fear and uncertainly flash across his face. I reach out and cup his cheek.

"It's fine, Cal. Everything will be okay. I swear it. I'll always protect you."

The corner of Cal's mouth quirks up into a half-grin. "I thought it was literally in my job description for me to do the protecting."

I huff a laugh. "How about we protect each other?"

Cal smiles softly. "I'd like that."

"Good." I stand and offer him my hand. "Will you come with me?"

He nods, accepting my hand and rising from his chair. He follows me into my room, closing the door behind us. I draw him into another kiss, withholding nothing. After a moment, Cal pulls back and glances away.

"What's wrong?" I ask, trailing my fingers up and down his arm.

"I've never really had any sort of relationship before, let alone one with physical intimacy," he admits, his cheeks flushing crimson. "I'm not . . . I don't . . ."

I press my lips to his before answering. "That's okay, Cal. We will take everything at your pace. I only want to be alone with you for a while. You can take the lead on how far and fast we go. Is that okay?"

Cal meets my eyes and nods, something almost wild flickering in his eyes that sets a fire in me. "That is more than okay."

He draws me against him, and our kisses consume us. It quickly becomes evident Cal doesn't need experience to make him skilled in any area of physical intimacy, because he manages quite well. We don't leave my room for over an hour and, even then, it's very much against my will.

CHAPTER THIRTY

EHREN

The religious service we attend stretches on endlessly. It starts with several hymns, honoring the saints and the gods. A minster in black, somber robes steps up next, droning on and on about the promises of life after death, reading occasionally from a holy text. His voice is low and monotone, lulling me to sleep. I feel an elbow in my ribs and jerk upright. I glance at Cal out of the corner of my eye. He sits straight and tall at attention, his gaze fixed on the minister, but his eyes sparkle with glee and his mouth holds a small smile. I glance further down our row at Pascal and Lorrell. Lorrell's head is bobbing as he fights sleep as Pascal stares straight ahead, his eyes glazed over.

I sigh and lean slightly toward Cal.

"How much longer can this service be?" I whisper.

Cal raises a fist to his mouth pretending to cough in an attempt to hide his grin. "If you were following along, you would know he's on the last line of the passage now."

I shake my head. "That means nothing when he turns every word into a twenty minute speech."

Cal coughs to hide a laugh and I smile. I rather like making Cal laugh.

"It's almost over," Cal whispers.

I reach over and grab his hand, lacing my fingers with his. He tenses at first, not used to showing open affection, but relaxes after a moment, holding my hand more firmly as he shifts closer, his thigh pressing against mine. I lift my eyes back to the minster, forcing myself to focus, which is not an easy task with Cal sitting so closely.

"And it is because of the actions of Saint Vançoius that the forbidden dark arts allowed the spirits to rest. No longer do we use wickedness to call them forth, but instead, we bask in their memory, honoring them. This is the semblance of La Nuit des Saints and La Prière aux Saints. We ask the saints to come forward and protect our loved ones who have passed beyond."

His words catch my attention, but I'm not entirely sure why. I've known about this Ascarian festival and tradition nearly my entire life, but something about this particular text seems to have new information. I'm so caught up in my thoughts I miss the cue to stand for a hymn, stumbling to my feet moments after everyone else. Cal laughs silently and I bump my shoulder against his, our hands clasped between us.

When the service finally ends, everyone starts to file out. Cal drops my hand and steps away as people brush past. I catch Prince Luc's eye as he walks out with a Duc, and he pauses, waiting for me outside the door. Luc and I step to the side, Cal, Lorrell, and Pascal moving on ahead out of the way.

"Did you enjoy the service?" Luc asks.

"It was very enjoyable," I lie. I decide to add in a bit of

honesty lest the gods strike me down. "The last part of the message really caught my attention."

"Which bit?"

"The part where the minster mentioned the forbidden arts. I assume that was a reference to magic?"

Luc gives me a solemn nod. "Ah, yes. That was a reference to one of the more significant slaughters of magic, dating back hundreds of years."

"What magic was it referring to? I'm afraid I missed how it was connected to La Prière aux Saints."

"It was a crusade by King François to wipe out les nécromacromanciens," Luc says. "It was bloody and tragic."

"Les nécromacromanciens? Necromancers? People that can raise the dead?" I ask in disbelief.

Luc nods. "Yes. Though, from what I understand, most did not raise the dead, but only spoke to the dead, passing on messages from the realm of spirits. They were revered by many and often performed special ceremonies during the Festival of Visc when the veil between the worlds was the thinnest."

I absorb his words, my mind racing. "This was a common practice?"

"Yes, though, after the slaughter none of les nécromacromanciens remained, at least not that would openly admit to practicing such magic. Now that magic has returned, there may be more, but I would imagine their craft would not yet be mastered." Luc pauses, placing his hand on my arm. "I suspect you have many with whom you would wish to speak."

I nod, glancing over to where Cal stands, talking to Lorrell and Pascal. "Though, I don't wish it as much for me as I do others." I look back at Luc and I'm sure he can read the heaviness in my expression. "It's hard to move forward when you never got to say goodbye."

"It can be, yes. When my mother passed away, it was after a year of illness. We expected it and had our chances to say goodbye, but it did not truly ease the pain. I cannot imagine losing someone with no closure. Though, it seems you and your Guard have found a way to move on, together."

I smile and dip my head. "Yes. I thank the gods every day for Cal, but I don't feel I deserve him."

"Let us be grateful, then, that the gods don't always give us what we deserve," Luc says with a gentle smile.

He walks away from the chapel. I match his stride, my Guard following along behind.

"Are you and your men going to be participating in La Prière aux Saints tonight?"

I nod. "Yes, we plan to, though, we have not yet procured our candles for the lighting ceremony."

"There will be plenty to choose from tonight, or you can go into the village and buy some that may have more meaning. They say that the more personal the candle, the more likely the spirits will see them," Luc replies.

"I think I may go see what I can find. Thank you." I glance back and Cal meets my eyes with a smile. "If you'll excuse me, Prince Luc, I think I will go into the village now, before the selection has dwindled too much."

Prince Luc comes to halt and inclines his head. "I bid you luck, that you find ones that suit your needs. I will see you later."

He strides away and I turn to my Guard, quickly explaining what I want to do. They agree to the plan, wishing to purchase candles themselves. The village is filled with vendors selling candles of every color, many with specific meanings. We stay together for a while, but eventually split off into pairs, the act of buying candles for La Prière aux Saints a bit personal. As I search the available sections, Cal stays near but hangs back to give me a little privacy. As much as I crave his presence, I appreciate the space.

I find a small shop half-hidden behind a larger, flashy vendor. She has a wide variety of colorful candles, and I find myself drawn to one made of black and maroon wax that reminds me of my father. I sort through a few more, selecting a deep blue to honor Makin. I'm about to ask my total when a third candle catches my eye. It's different than the rest. It's a cream-colored wax with flecks of gold and black. Symbols I don't recognize are carved into the sides. I pick it up, turning to over in my hand.

"It's lovely, isn't it," the vendor says, nodding at the candle.

"It is," I reply. "What do these symbols mean?"

"Well, the symbols are meant to illuminate the candle's flame to attract multiple spirits. You see, that candle is special. It is one that is often burned in memory of mass death, popular during times of war or plague, when individual candles simply aren't enough."

Suddenly, the candle seems very heavy.

"Oh. I'll take it. Along with these two," I reply, holding out the maroon and blue candles. "How much?"

The woman shakes her head as she wraps the candles in a piece of cream cloth. "There is no charge."

"But—"

She ties the package with a piece of twine and hands it to me with a gentle smile. "I know who you are, and I cannot in good conscience charge you. I have heard of you, Prince Ehren. You are a good man who strives to do the best for your people. I am only happy to help you in the grief you bear."

Tears threaten to break free as I incline my head in gratitude. "Thank you. I do not know that I am necessarily a great man, but I strive to be one."

"And that is one of the reasons you are indeed a great man."

Unsure of how to respond, I offer her one last parting nod before escaping into the street where Cal waits for me. He pushes off the wall of the larger building he's leaning on, his brow furrowed with concern.

"Are you okay?"

I swallow and nod, looking into his eyes.

"Are you sure?" he asks. "Because you don't look okay."

"Why do you love me?"

Cal starts, his eyebrows knitting together. "What?"

"You said you loved me." Cal nods once in affirmation. "Why?"

His eyes scan my face. "I love you because you are the most amazing, caring person I know. I've seen you literally give someone the shirt off your back without a moment of hesitation."

He reaches up and runs his knuckles down my cheek. I close my eyes under his soothing touch and step closer on instinct. He places his hands on my hips and draws me closer, pressing a kiss to my temple.

"I love you because you don't judge people, but you give them a chance to prove themselves. You don't care about things like class and rank. Everyone is equal in your eyes. I love you because you always think of others first and yourself second. I love you because you are true to yourself, and that's not always easy to do. I love you because you fight. You don't just give up or give in."

He pulls back and I meet his eyes. "Do you need more reasons? Because I have plenty more."

I shake my head, forcing a smile. "No, that will do for now."

I take a deep breath and one of the tears brimming in my eyes breaks free, sliding down my cheek. Cal shakes his head.

"No, my prince," he says, his voice low and rough, making my heart race uncontrollably. "We can't have you crying."

He leans forward and kisses the tear away, sending warm shivers down my spine. His lips drop to mine, and I return the kiss with fervor, pressing Cal against the wall behind him. He gasps against my mouth as he wraps his arms around me, flipping our positions so I'm the one pinned up against the wall. My breath catches as he eyes me with heat, slowly easing his lips to mine. I moan softly as his lips trail along my jaw and down my neck.

"I feel like we should probably resume this off the street," Cal whispers, his breath hot on my ear before he draws back, the tips of his ears reddening as he glances around.

I laugh and nod, though I very much want to continue our previous activity. "You're probably right. I have my candles, so unless you want to browse some more, we can go back to the castle and relax until it's time for the candle ceremony."

Cal nods, patting his pocket. "I purchased a candle while you were in that shop, so I'm done here as well."

My eyes glint with mischief as I glance down. "Ah, so that's a candle in your pocket. I thought you were just excited to have me near."

Cal chokes on a laugh as he flushes. He glances around, leaning in and nipping my ear before whispering, "I think we both know the candle doesn't even begin to compare."

My own cheeks heat with color as my imagination races. "Hmm, I may need a reminder," I mumble, grabbing his shirt and pulling him back for one last passionate kiss.

Cal grins wickedly and takes a step back, glancing toward the street. "Should we find Lorrell and Pascal?"

I shake my head, slipping my free hand into Cal's as we weave back into the crowd of people. "They'll find their way back. Honestly, I want to head back to our suite and relax for a bit."

Cal brushes a quick kiss to my cheek. "Me too."

Despite our actions in the street, Cal and I do indeed rest, spending a couple leisurely hours in our sitting room reading. I lie stretched across one of the couches, my head in his lap, as I prop my book on my chest with one hand and turn the pages with the other. Cal leans against the corner of the couch, his left arm slung over the armrest holding his book. In between turning pages, his right hand plays with my hair. It's peaceful and perfect.

Lorrell and Pascal return an hour into our reading. Cal tenses, watching them warily, but he doesn't move away or remove his hand from my tresses. I barely look up from my book, struggling to hide my grin. Lorrell stares for a moment, mouth gaping, but Pascal pushes him toward his room muttering something about him needing to learn to mind his own business. As soon as they're locked away, Cal relaxes with a soft sigh, pressing a quick kiss to my forehead before resuming his reading.

When it's time for La Prière aux Saints, we all dress in black tunics, mine sewn with silver thread. We gather our candles and head to a lake just outside the palace and village walls. Everyone is in attendance, their faces drawn and solemn. We push through the crowd, making our way to the sides of Prince Luc and Princesse Nicolette. Shortly after our arrival, the minster from earlier takes a small rowboat to the center of the lake.

"We gather here in memory of those we have lost," he says, his voice clear, carrying across the water like a song.

"Our memories tether them to this earth, though their souls reside with the gods. Today, we light their paths so that they may find us before returning among the stars." He pauses, raising his palms to the sky, his eyes closed as he recites a prayer.

The prayer is ancient and in dialect or language I do not know. A few of those around us chime in, their voices rising like a chant. Once the prayer has ended, Prince Luc lights a few small, long white candles and passes them through the crowd. He saves one and uses it to light a small sky-blue candle, which he places on the water. He passes the thin candle to us and we each light ours before passing it on. The smaller candles we place directly onto the surface of the water, letting them float away. The larger candles, like the one I have with the gold and black flecks, we place on rafts. Cal lights a small green candle and sets it on the water. His gaze is fixed on it as it floats away.

I grab Cal's hand, weaving my fingers between his. He glances toward me, his eyes heavy with tears. My heart breaks at the sight. I press a gentle kiss to his cheek before we both turn our attention back to the floating candles.

Side-by-side, hand-in-hand we stand, watching the flames reflect off the silver water. Together, we say goodbye to our ghosts.

CHAPTER THIRTY-ONE

ASTRA

With Kai gone, I throw myself wholeheartedly into my research, Ronan by my side night and day. The day after Kai leaves, more books from Athiedor arrive. It's a frustrating, slow process to comb through all the texts, but it's a good distraction. With Ronan's help, I'm able to learn a few key words and phrases in Yallik so I can work independently from him. Not that it's much help. The majority of references to the Fae share little to nothing about contacting them, and the ones that do bridge the subject offer no details.

The second afternoon Kai is gone, another batch of books arrive from the personal library of Lord Dughlas, accompanied by a note.

Dear Lord McDullun and the Court Sorceress,
*   I have no idea why you need these books, but I hope you can find them useful. Clan Dughlas prides itself on maintaining our histories. Other Clans tend to fail in this*

*regard. Nestled among these books is sure to be the infor-
mation you seek.*

*Wishing you well in your attempts to save a lost
kingdom,*

Lord Dughlas

"Well, he's a pretentious arse," Ronan mumbles, reading
the note over my shoulder.

"Let's hope he actually sent some new information with
details." I sigh, setting the note to the side as I scan the books
and scrolls piled on the table.

Ronan chuckles. "As much as I want to find the information you need, I almost hope there's nothing in the texts he
sent just to spite him."

I laugh, shaking my head. "Let's dive in, shall we?"

Ronan groans as he plops down into a chair. "Fine, but in
a few minutes I'm ringing for mead."

"Mead is not the solution to every problem," I chide,
picking up one of the books and thumbing through.

"True," Ronan concedes with a nod, "but you can't deny
it makes this seem less tedious."

I lift my eyes from the book in front of me to look at
Ronan. "You know, you don't have to stay in here with me.
You can go do other things."

"Like what?" Ronan asks, grabbing another book.

I shrug. "Whatever it is you like to do."

Ronan lifts his eyes to meet mine, a wry grin curling on
his lips. "I like spending time in the library." He glances back
down to the book in his hand, turning the page. "Besides, I
told you I've always wanted to have a handsome Fae warrior
fall in love with me. How am I supposed to accomplish that

task without even knowing how to bridge the worlds? It's all very self-serving really."

He lifts his eyes for a moment and waggles his eyebrows. I laugh and toss a book at him. He chuckles, easily ducking out of its path before it can hit him.

After a few minutes, he does indeed ring for mead and snacks. We drink and munch away as we scan the texts and, admittedly, the mead helps. It's nearly time to leave for dinner when I stumble across an entry in an old journal that mentions the Fae. I expect it to veer off and avoid any details like previous texts, but it doesn't. I sight up straighter, leaning forward to examine the page in the flickering candlelight.

"What is it?" Ronan asks, rising to come peer over my shoulder. "Did you find something?"

I nod, not speaking as my eyes scan the text. It's not quite straightforward but it's more than we've had before.

> *Alaric and I returned to the forest, where we met the Fae on their blessed ground. We aligned the stones in the appropriate order, the summoning symbols facing inwards. Together we spoke the ancient words given to us by our father. At first, we assumed we had failed, but just as we were about to leave, we were greeted by a cold wind. A single strand of light shot up from the ground and a Fae male stepped through.*

I barely breathe as I read it through again, Ronan letting out a low whistle.

"So," Ronan muses, leaning his back against the table and crossing his arms across his chest. "There is a blessed ground, symbols, and a special chant. That still leaves us with a lot to find."

I nod, my eyes bright. "We have the recipe, though. Now, we need to find the ingredients."

"We're not going to dinner, are we?" Ronan sighs.

"You can do whatever you want." I grin up at him. "I, however, will be staying in the library."

Ronan shakes his head, pushing away from the table and grabbing his cane. "I'll go see what I can scrounge up."

"You don't have—"

Ronan waves me off. "Don't bother arguing. I'll be back in a few minutes."

While Ronan is off hunting down dinner, I organize the remaining books according to how likely I think they are to contain the information we need. Ronan returns with servants bearing plates of roast meat and vegetables and, of course, more mead. We eat while we read, but we don't find any more details. Though we do discover the ceremony and blessed ground referenced multiple times. Eventually, we decide to rest our eyes, reinforcing the wards before heading to bed.

The next day we dive in bright and early. The day starts out frustrating and fruitless until things turn in our favor around mid-afternoon when Ronan stumbles across something scribbled in the margins of one of the Fae accounts.

"Look," he says, passing the books across the table. "Are those—"

"Fae runes," I mutter in awe, tracing the runes with the tip of my finger. I tap the Yallik above the runes. "What does this say?"

Ronan pulls the book back to him, tilting his head as he translates. "North to the Northwest." He raises his eyes to mine. "I'm assuming that's the order they must be written in."

I nod, licking my lips. "Seems likely. Let's see if we can find more."

Finding the new information energizes me, but the elation soon wears off when we find nothing new. When I start absentmindedly sketching the runes on the edges of papers, Ronan pushes his chair back.

"All right, we're taking a walk," he insists. "Grab your cloak."

I scowl up at him. "But it's not time to reinforce the wards."

"You know, I heard a rumor that you're allowed outside the walls of the castle even if you aren't putting up wards."

I laugh, shaking my head at him as I stand, pulling on my cloak. "Fine, but we can't take long."

"You're the boss." Ronan grins.

We wander aimlessly through the gardens until night falls. Even then, we linger outside for a bit, relishing the fresh air. For dinner we join the joyful clamor in the dining hall. Ronan seems very at home among the others, but every so often he catches my eye and winks. After dinner, we return to the library, but neither of us as are really ready to dive back into pointless texts. Instead, we settle around the fire and Ronan reads to me. His voice combined with the crackling warmth of the fire nearly lulls me to sleep. I'm only saved when Felixe appears, a note in his mouth. I sit up abruptly from where I'd been leaning against Ronan's chair as I accept the note.

"What is it?" Ronan asks, startled by my sudden movement. He leans forward. "Oh, it's the little fox."

I arch my neck back to look up at Ronan. "You've met Felixe?"

Ronan chuckles. "Aye, love. I met him when I met Alak back in Athiedor."

I nod, unfolding the letter. "I suppose that makes sense."

My Most Beloved Astra,

I apologize for not having written sooner. Things here have been incredibly busy, yet I have very little to share. Though my concern lies with Bram and his mental health. I think we may be losing him. Bram has said at least two nice things about me this week, and I'm not sure how to take that. You know him better. Is he planning to murder me in my sleep or is his attitude toward me really changing? Please advise.

As far as our mission for the salvation of the kingdom goes, things are progressing. Your friend has done a good job preparing these soldiers. If all goes as planned, we will be leaving in the next couple of days to head to the fortress. We'll be bringing 150 men. Well, not men, exactly. Boys, girls, women—it's a very inclusive group of talented individuals. Honestly, at first I had my doubts about this army composed of refugees, but things are coming together. We may actually be able to build a competent army. Even Bram seems to agree.

I love you and I miss you so much it hurts. I cannot wait until I can hold you in my arms again.

Yours Until the Stars Fade,
Alak

"Good news?" Ronan asks as I fold the letter, tucking it into my pocket.

I sigh and lean back against the chair. "I suppose. He says they're almost ready to bring the army, so I guess that's good."

"You really miss him, don't you?" Ronan asks, his voice so low I barely hear it over the crackling fire.

"I do. And it's not just because of the soul bond, though that is a part of it. Alak completes me in practically every way and without him, I feel lacking," I confess, staring into the fire.

"Now, I don't quite believe that," Ronan scoffs.

I jerk my eyes to him. "What do you mean?"

"I believe you two are truly a unique pair. Don't get me wrong, you complement each other in ways that I envy, but you are strong and independent without him. You are in no way lacking, I can promise you."

I smile softly and nod. "I guess you're right. It's simply nice to have someone, you know?"

"No," Ronan says with a dramatic sigh. "Alas, I do not know, for I have yet to charm me a young man of my own."

I chuckle as he grins down at me.

"Why don't you write him back?"

"And say what? That I've read a bunch of dusty books? It's not like I've really accomplished all that much here."

Ronan chuckles. "Come now, love. You just poured your heart out telling *me* how much you miss Alak. Tell *him*."

I shake my head at myself as I push up from the floor. "You're right."

"Course I am, love," Ronan says, pushing up from his chair with his cane and following me to the desk.

I roll my eyes as I pull out the supplies and write a quick note, straight to the point. When I'm done, I call out to

Felixe, who curled up in front of the fire while I wrote. He glances up at me with disdain.

"Come on, Felixe. Just one more little letter," I coax, kneeling next to him. "Please? You can come back and snuggle by the fire when you're done. I'll even find you a snack."

Felixe grumbles but accepts the letter, disappearing in a blink. When he returns a moment later, I hold true to my promise and offer him a tea biscuit.

"Well, love, shall we check those wards and then turn in for the night?"

"I suppose," I say, suppressing a yawn.

We make quick work of the wards and by the time we make it to bed, I'm already half asleep.

The next morning, I have little desire to read more, but I force myself to dive in. I struggle to focus on any of the words, especially the ones I have to translate from Yallik. A little before noon, another messenger from Athiedor arrives with a small collection of books. Unlike the other texts we've received, these are spell books and grimoires preserved from the time of magic. The dialects are ancient, even for me, but I'm fascinated.

"Shite," Ronan mutters, his eyes wide as he stares down at a black book with yellowed pages. "These seem a bit dark."

I lean forward, eagerly peering into his book. "What are they?"

Ronan shakes his head, "I'm not entirely sure, but I have feeling this is bordering on dark magic."

He turns the book toward me and I flip through, examining a few of the spells. He's right. This definitely pushes the limits. We set the book aside and focus on books that have promise, hoping to find a summoning spell for the Fae.

Despite spending our entire day in the library, eating both lunch and dinner within its walls, we only get through a little over half of the new spell books, largely thanks to the language barrier. With a sigh of resignation, we leave our exploring to another day. I take my sleeping tonic and slide into a familiar glade from my childhood. Kato is there, but he's younger. Eight, maybe nine years old.

"Look at this beetle," he crows as I approach. "I caught him myself."

I kneel down next to him, a child myself, to examine the shiny blue beetle in his hand. I shriek as the beetle takes flight.

"Aw! You scared him away!" Kato bemoans. He plops down onto the ground, grabbing a stick. "I'm going to draw him."

"I can draw him better," I challenge, sitting down next to him and grabbing my own stick.

After a moment, I hear footsteps. I turn my head and it takes my brain a second to catch up and make sense of the sight before me. Ehren. Time to dream walk with my dear friend.

CHAPTER THIRTY-TWO

EHREN

After La Prière aux Saints, we all head back to our rooms, somber and silent. Without prompting, Cal follows me into my room. The ceremony of La Prière aux Saints weighs on us. I'm not sure how Cal will react once we are alone, so when he gathers me into his arms, his lips finding mine in the dark, I give as much as he does. We both crave comfort, and that need drives us. I keep half-expecting Cal to change his mind, to withdraw and leave, but he never does.

At some point in the night, we finally cave to sleep. I wake after only a couple hours, my heart racing from a nightmare I can't remember. I glance over at Cal, who lies next to me, his bare torso illuminated by the moonlight streaming through our window. I smile to myself. I tuck my hand behind my head and watch Cal sleep for a minute. Then I realize how creepy I feel watching him, and I make myself look away. For the first time in months I feel truly happy, and I really want to share with someone. Once the thought strikes, I can't shake it.

I rise quietly, careful not to wake Cal, and pad across the room to my bag. I gather the ingredients I need for the dream walking spell and climb back into bed with Cal. I slip away and I'm in a forest. I look around for Astra and am startled when my eyes fall on two children, no more than eight years old. They sit in the dirt, drawing with sticks. The boy has raven-black hair and the girl long, white braids. I approach slowly, almost afraid I'll disturb them. The little girl stops abruptly and turns to look up at me with bright amethyst eyes.

"Ehren?" she says.

Suddenly, she's not a little girl anymore—she's the Astra I know. The little boy has disappeared. Astra smiles softly, tilting her head.

"Why are you so happy?"

I laugh, shaking my head. "What makes you think I'm happy?"

"You're practically glowing." She pauses, furrowing her brow. "You are dream walking, right? This isn't my imagination?"

I nod. "Yes. It's really me. Is my happiness so unrealistic you believe it can only be obtained in a dream form?"

"No." She laughs. "I just want you to be happy so badly, I was afraid I was imagining it."

I smile softly. "I miss you, Ash."

"I miss you, too, Ehren. How are things going? Will you be back soon?"

I sigh and run my hand through my hair. "I think they're going well. I should have a definitive answer in a couple days."

Astra nods, weighing my words. "That's good, then.

Bram and Alak have had good success, as well. By the time you return, we should have an army."

"That's definitely good news."

"Oh!" She declares, her eyes brightening. "And I think I'm close to figuring out how to contact the Fae. I've found the runes I need and now just need to find the right location and possibly a spell."

"Really? That's amazing! How?"

She grins. "Research, of course."

I reach out and take her hands in mine as my eyes meet hers. "We'll have a fighting chance if we can contact the Fae. You realize that, right?"

She nods, her grin growing. "Everything is falling into place." She cocks her head and pulls her hands back, crossing her arms. "So, if you're unsure of your negotiations in Ascaria and didn't know about my progress, why are you happy?"

I laugh, my cheeks flushing.

"Ehren," she prods, bouncing on the balls of her feet like an excited child. "Tell me!"

I sigh, still grinning. "I just . . . Gods, Ash, I'm in love."

She gets a knowing look on her face. "With Cal?"

My mouth drops open. "How . . . ?"

"I'm observant," she says with a dismissive wave. "Besides, you two belong together."

I shake my head. "If you say so."

"Well, I do say so." She pauses, a wicked, mischievous grin on her lips. "So, how in love are you exactly?"

"I don't kiss and tell."

"So, there's kissing . . . ."

"I'm not telling you any more."

"So, there's more than kissing . . . ."

I playfully push her shoulder and she giggles.

"Sorry."

I pause as pieces start clicking into place.

"What?" Astra asks, her voice growing serious. "That's your plan face. What are you planning?"

I arch an eyebrow. "I have a plan face?"

"Yes. A very distinctive plan face. But what is the plan? We don't have much longer."

I nod, licking my lips. "Right. Do you know about La Prière aux Saints?"

Astra squints her eyes in concentration for a moment before nodding. "Yes. It's part of the festival of one of the gods—Visc maybe?"

"Yes. According to tradition, the veil between spirits of the dead and the living are the closest tomorrow—or perhaps today, depending on what time it is." Astra nods along, trying to follow where I'm going. "Prince Luc told me that necromancers in Ascaria used to do some sort of ritual to communicate with the dead when the veil was thin. Do you think you can find anything out about their magic?"

Astra nods thoughtfully. "Maybe. The resources here aren't vast when it comes to magic, but . . . Yes, I think I know where to look. Who do you want me to contact?"

I shake my head. "I'm not entirely sure. Just someone who might know what we're dealing with or who can help fill in the blanks. Someone who was alive before when the Dragkonians wreaked havoc. I wish I had thought of this sooner, done more research, so I could have a better suggestion."

"I think I can work with that," Astra says, nodding thoughtfully.

I feel the dream weaken around me. "I wish I had more time," I sigh.

"Don't worry. I can find what we need, and you'll be back soon. Just be careful, okay?"

I nod, offering Astra a parting smile. "I'll try, but life's no fun if you're not a little reckless."

Astra laughs, her eyes shining. "I'm happy you're doing well and that you have Cal. I really am."

I smile, but she fades before I can respond. I'm back in my bed, Cal inches away, still sleeping peacefully. I lean over and kiss his shoulder. He shifts in his sleep, turning toward me. I sigh with contentment and snuggle closer to his warmth as I fall back to sleep.

The next morning I wake to Cal sprawled across my chest. If happiness could kill you, I would welcome death to keep this feeling. I run my hand over his shoulder blades, tracing the muscles along his back. He shifts with a soft moan, pressing closer.

"Good morning," I whisper as he kisses my bare chest. "Did you sleep well?"

He rolls his head back and looks up at me, grinning. "Best sleep I've had in my life. Did you sleep well?"

I shrug. "Off and on. I dream walked and checked in with Astra."

"Is everything okay with her?" he asks, pushing up onto his elbow to look down at me.

I nod. "Yes. Things are finally going in our direction. Now, if we can just secure this Ascarian alliance and stay one step ahead of Kato." I sigh. "There's still so much to do, so much that could go wrong."

"You're right," Cal says, "but let's choose to focus on the good."

I nod, lifting up to brush a quick kiss across his lips before collapsing back onto my pillow with a sigh. "All right." I close my eyes, tucking a hand behind my head. "Can we stay in bed all day?"

Cal laughs, sitting up. "No. We have the lighting of the pyre this morning, remember?"

I groan. "I forgot about that." I open my eyes and glance toward the window. "I hope we're not too late."

Cal shakes his head as he rises from the bed. "I think we're fine, but we shouldn't dawdle."

I groan again and crawl from the bed. We dress quickly before dragging Pascal and Lorrell from their beds. We meet Prince Luc and Princesse Nicolette as we leave the palace. I fall into stride next to Prince Luc, but Cal drops back, walking with Lorrell and Pascal. I fight the urge to reach back and pull him next to me, choosing to distract myself by talking to Luc.

"Remind me what the pyre lighting means?" I ask as we cross the courtyard toward a large pyre constructed of white-washed stone.

"When we light the fire, we are letting the spirits and the saints know that we accept their presence," Prince Luc replies.

I nod, staring up at the pyre as we come to a halt close to its base. It stretches at least two stories high, reaching toward the sky. I've never been one to hold to religion much, but something in me really wants to believe that the spirits can be beckoned by this fire. I want to believe in an afterlife. I want to believe that happiness can extend beyond life. That way, I don't need to feel as guilty. I can hold to the idea that they didn't die in vain—that they're really in a better place.

My chest tightens at the thought of all those who have

died—my father, his soldiers, innocents in Embervein, Makin. I close my eyes, bowing my head, fists clenched by my side. I can't breathe. I can't think. I need . . . I need . . .

A warm hand slides down the wrist of my left hand, forcing my fist open, fingers weaving between mine. My eyes fly open as I jerk my head to look at Cal. He stands by my side, eyeing me with concern. He offers me a small smile and I take a deep breath, exhaling slowly. I give his hand a squeeze as Prince Luc steps up onto a small dais, turning to face the gathering crowd.

"Today, we gather to light La Flamme Sacrée, so that the spirits of our loved ones may find peace."

I expect his speech to go on longer, but he stops, nodding to someone in the crowd. A man steps forward, handing Prince Luc a long stick lit on the end. Prince Luc turns, lifting the small flame to the top of the pyre. It immediately incinerates, a large flame licking the air. Everyone bows their heads as Prince Luc turns back to face the crowd, his own head bowed in reverence. I follow his lead.

"We pray to the saints and the gods to bless those who have passed on before us. We are thankful for their sacrifices. May we take what they taught us and learn to live wisely. May we learn to love stronger and better, serving not our own purposes, but rather those around us. May their souls rest in peace."

He ends by making a religious motion across his chest, most of those in attendance following suit. With a smile and nod, Prince Luc descends the dais and the crowd begins to slowly disperse. Cal releases my hand but stays by my side as I turn to face Luc.

"That was a lovely prayer."

He nods. "It is one of my favorites to recite. This holiday

is both somber and festive. I do not believe the dead would want us to live forever in mourning, do you?"

I shake my head. "No, I don't."

"That is why we will end this day with a grand feast. We will celebrate the lives they lived and the bonds we shared. I hope you will be attending?"

"Of course." I pause, my lips turning up into a smile. "I seldom turn down the opportunity for food."

Luc's laugh is rich and full. "Indeed. I can't say I turn down many such opportunities myself. And perhaps tonight we will have more to celebrate than just this holiday."

"Oh?" I say, arching an eyebrow.

"I believe my sister and I have discussed everything thoroughly enough with our councilors that we can present a formal treaty. Perhaps we can meet this afternoon?"

I nod, trying not to seem too eager. "Of course. If you feel you have had enough time."

"We have, I believe. I will send for you when we are ready. Until then, please enjoy your day. There will be much celebrating throughout the village today," Luc says, giving us a parting nod before he turns back toward the castle.

I turn to Lorrell, Pascal, and Cal with a grin. "Let's go explore, shall we?"

I'm a little surprised at how festive everything is, especially given that this holiday is one that celebrates the dead. However, it seems to be going in the same tune as the pyre lighting ceremony. Everyone is simply celebrating life, eager to remember the good part of the lives they shared with those that have passed on. We decide to stay together as a group as we weave through the crowd. Ribbons and banners flutter in the breeze. I am surprised when I see a cart with people passing out masks to small children. These masks aren't nearly as ornate as the ones we wore in Koshima, but they are still fun and festive. The children tie them over their faces, running around in circles, pretending to be different animals and creatures. I'm so caught up in watching the children play, I don't notice Princesse Nicolette come up behind me until she speaks.

"It's lovely to see to the children so delighted, no?"

I startle and turn my head to look at her. "I suppose. I didn't realize that there was so much fun to be had during a festival that celebrates the dead."

"Well, children should be free of the burdens that weigh us down as adults," Nicolette says, her gaze fixed on the children. "Their joy is a good reminder. The dead may have passed from this life but, if you believe the holy texts, they watch us. I have not lost many people in my life, but I know that those who have left me behind would want me to live and find happiness in life. If the spirits and saints are truly looking through the veil this day, we should show them that, while we miss them, we have not forgotten what it is to be alive."

I muse on her words, watching a child with a lion mask chasing the other children, who run away, screeching with glee. I smile.

"Why the masks?" I ask, not taking my eyes from the children. "How do they work into the holiday?"

"Ah," Nicolette smiles, "those go back to darker traditions, but we make light of them for the children. It was once believed that dark spirits would return on this day. People would craft masks to hide from those dark spirits, as if they could be so easily fooled. Now, the children wear masks as part of the fun."

The children race toward us, cutting between me and

Cal. I step back, grinning as I watch them. When I look at Cal, I find him smiling as well, watching the children's delight. He meets my eyes and his smile grows. Nicolette clears her throat and Cal's smile falters. Determined not to let Nicolette make Cal feel any shame, I shift closer to him, taking his hand. Pascal and Lorrell share a look, grinning.

Nicolette's gaze drops to our hands, a sharp grin curving on her lips.

"It was clever of you to parade your relationship," she says.

I scowl, tightening my grip on Cal's hand. "What do you mean?"

"Many of the councilmen and nobles were . . . impressed by your open affection," Nicolette answers, glancing between me and Cal.

"Impressed?"

"Indeed. They figure that a prince who could so shamelessly court not only a man but also a lowly member of his own Guard is a prince who is not afraid to be open and honest about other aspects of his life."

Her words strike something that irritates me to my core.

"My relationship with Cal is not a show I've put on to garner support. I genuinely care for him."

"Oh, I have no doubt," Nicolette says, a little too flippantly for my tastes. "However, it was well-timed, no?"

"Our relationship has been building for some time," Cal says, his low voice startling me. "Ehren means the world to me, and I will not let you belittle what we have."

I glance over at him. His face is hard with determination, his eyes flashing. I tighten my grip on his hand. He swallows, glancing over at me, his gaze softening slightly.

"Well, then," Nicolette says, clearly just as surprised at

Cal's reaction as I. "I do apologize if my assessment was out of place. I can assure you that I did not mean it negatively. I admire you both, and hope that I can have such courage to love without hinderance, should I ever choose to give my heart away."

Cal relaxes and I smile, pulling him closer so our arms touch. He leans over, brushing a kiss to my cheek, making me blush. I'm still not used to his open affection, but it thrills me. Nicolette grins, but it's a gentler smile than I usually see curling on her lips.

"Anyone with any sense can see you two are meant for one another." She pauses, letting her gaze wander from us and over the crowded, busy streets. "I will allow you your peace to enjoy the day." She brings her eyes back to mine, tilting her head. "I suppose my brother told you about the impending meeting?"

"Yes, he did," I reply with a sharp nod.

She nods, her eyes drifting again. "Good. I suppose I will see you later, then."

Without another word she disappears into the crowd. I release a long breath and turn to face Lorrell and Pascal, who watch me and Cal with wide grins.

"Do you have something you wanted to say?" I ask, perhaps a bit too sharply.

Lorrell shakes his head, his grin growing. "Nothing much. We suspected something was going on between you two, so it's nice to be right."

Pascal elbows his brother. "What he means to say is that we are very happy for you two."

Cal tries to hide his smile as I reply, "Thank you, I suppose, but let's not waste this day. We should enjoy as much of the festival as possible before the feast tonight."

Everyone agrees and we dissolve into the crowd. Several different vendors offer a variety of foods, and we are eager to try them all. A selection of snails gives us some pause, but Cal sucks his down with little hesitation, declaring them chewy but tasty. His description is enough to make me back away.

"Come on, Ehren," he grins, holding one out between two of his fingers. "They're not bad."

Lorrell chokes on a snail behind me, gagging as Pascal pounds on his back.

"Are you trying to kill me?" I ask, narrowing my eyes.

Cal laughs and I melt. "Just try one."

I sigh and hold out my hand. "Fine. I'll try *one*."

"Open your mouth," Cal instructs, his eyes meeting mine.

I cock my head, a grin fluttering on my lips. "What?"

In response, Cal holds up the snail. "Open your mouth."

This time I oblige, parting my lips and leaning forward. Cal slips the snail in my mouth, his fingertips lingering on my lips a moment longer than necessary. His touch sets me on fire. I don't even care that the food in my mouth is less than pleasant.

"Want another one?" Cal asks.

I shake my head, forcing myself to swallow the snail I already have. "No, but you can feed me anything else you want."

Cal arches his eyebrows, the tips of his ears reddening as his eyes darken with lust. "Anything?"

Heat rises in my own cheeks as I lean closer to him, wrapping an arm around his waist to tug him closer so he's flush against me. He inhales sharply but doesn't resist.

"What did you have in mind?" I ask, my mouth a mere breath from Cal's.

Cal's lips turn up into a wry smile. "Oh, I have a list," he murmurs, slowly pressing his lips to mine.

"Um, you do realize we're in the middle of a street," Lorrell whispers, his eyes darting around.

I exhale slowly, dropping my hand from Cal's waist to grab his hand as Cal takes a step back, glancing away but still grinning.

"Fine." I lean closer to Cal and whisper so only he can hear, "We'll finish that later."

The red on the tips of Cal's ears darkens and hints of red tinge the top of cheeks.

"I look forward to it," he replies, his voice deep and low, sending shivers down my spine.

As much as I want to duck behind one of the vendors' carts and finish the moment now, I force myself to focus on the festival around us. It's much more carefree than I expected, and I make a note to incorporate a similar day of celebration into Callenian tradition. Perhaps a shared holiday could help to mend the broken ties between Ascaria and Callenia.

It's nearly sunset and time for the feast when a messenger finds us in the crowd, letting us know that Prince Luc and Princesse Nicolette are ready for us. We follow the messenger through the swelling crowd back into the palace. We stop outside the same room we met in previously, but this time the councilors are not present. Luc and Nicolette sit on the long sides of the table instead of the thrones, two documents on the table in front of them. A man dressed in formal attire stands glowering in the corner, his sharp eyes falling on me as I enter the room. Pascal and Lorrell take a guard position on either side of the door, but I pull Cal into the room with me.

"This meeting is only for those—" the man in corner starts, taking a brisk step forward.

I grit my teeth as Cal starts to draw back, but before I speak Luc waves his hand, cutting the man short.

"It is quite fine if your Guard joins us. This meeting is less formal and more tying up of loose ends. Besides," he says, his eyes shifting to the man, "it would be beneficial to have a witness from Callenia present to the proceedings, no?"

The man looks like he has many objections, but he inclines his head anyway. "As you wish."

"Please, take your seats," Luc says with a smile, gesturing to the two chairs across from him and his sister as the man retreats to his corner. "I am sure you are as eager to finalize things as we are."

I nod, Cal and I crossing the room and easing down into the chairs. "Very much."

Luc pushes the two documents my direction. I scan them and realize with a start that they are copies of the same document, each translated into both Callenian and Ascarian.

"We wanted to be quite thorough," Princesse Nicolette says, noting my surprise. "You will take one copy with you and we will retain one here. Well, not *here* here, but in our records in Beaurac."

"The terms are quite simple," Prince Luc says, nodding to the papers. "The first section simply reiterates what our fathers agreed on during their last treaty. We will continue to honor the current borders, maintain a peaceful existence, and keep trade open and honest. The following sections address our current situation."

"We will give you what resources we can spare," Nicolette jumps in. "We need to retain a certain amount of force around our borders to keep our country secure and, of course, we need part of our army within Ascaria to defend our own people, but all remaining soldiers will be sent to Callenia to aid your cause. It will take a few weeks to send word and gather the soldiers necessary, but we will act with haste."

My eyes widen as I quickly scan the treaty in front of me, verifying their words. When I raise my eyes to Luc, he meets them with a gentle smile.

"We do not wish to see you suffer. Our countries have been allies for many decades, but it has been a tenuous peace. We hope to rectify that now. We want to be friends as well as allies if you will allow."

"Of course," Nicolette cuts in, "we do expect those actions to be reciprocated, should we ever need aid against a foe."

I nod, licking my lips. "Naturally. Callenia would be willing to aid you whenever we can. However, we will be a country of magic. I know you want to repair the damage done by previous generations, but are your councilors and people at peace with such an alliance?"

Luc and Nicolette exchange a wary glance that makes my stomach twist in knots. Cal reaches under the table and places his palm on my knee. I take a deep breath and release it slowly, placing my hand over his.

"We will not lie," Luc says at length. "There are many on our council and amongst our nobles who are less than pleased with our actions concerning magic, but we care about the best interests of our people more than their petty, outdated politics."

Nicolette nods, adding, "We are not so easily swayed by the ideas of men who think themselves wiser just because they've lived longer. Wisdom is not gained by years alone, but by seeking knowledge and having an open mind. They think we are making a mistake, but we will prove them wrong by changing the world."

I smile, pulling my hand from Cal's and folding my hands on top of the treaties. "Very well. Shall we sign, then? Seal this alliance once and for all?"

Luc smiles, his eyes bright. "Indeed. Armand, bring the quill."

The man from the corner steps forward, bringing with him ink and a large plume. He sets them next to me and I dip the quill in the ink, signing my name on both copies of the treaty with a flourish. I pass the documents and quill across to Luc and he and his sister add their names.

"Now," Luc says, raising his eyes to Cal, "your Guard and Armand will sign as witnesses beneath our signatures. That way, no one can have any doubts of our intent."

Cal's hands almost tremble as he signs before passing the quill to Armand, who accepts it with a huff. Once Armand has resumed his spot in the corner, Nicolette stands, grinning.

"Well, I say this was a very successful first treaty—a good step for both our nations—but there is a feast calling to us. Shall we go?"

I laugh and stand. "Yes, of course."

Luc pushes back from the table. "I assume you will want to leave first thing in the morning. Please, let me know what you require for your journey, and I will make sure you have it."

"The only supplies that were truly depleted were our

404

food rations and a few ingredients I use for spellwork," I reply.

"The food is easy enough, and I will send word to the kitchen. Let me know what additional ingredients you need for your spells and, if we have them, they are yours. I will also send a few of my soldiers to accompany you to the mountains to make sure your journey is as smooth as possible."

I incline my head. "Thank you, Prince Luc. We truly appreciate your kindness."

"It is the least I can do," he says, walking toward the door, Nicolette on his heels. "Will you be at the feast?"

"Yes, we will be along shortly."

Luc gives us a parting nod and Nicolette flashes me a grin and a wink before they stride through the door, Armand following behind with Ascaria's copy of the treaty. Once they are gone, I release a long breath that feels like I've been holding for days. Cal slips his arms around my waist and turns me to face him.

"You did it," he whispers, his eyes shining. "You secured an alliance with our most tenuous ally."

"I did, didn't I?" I reply, looping my arms around Cal's waist, drawing him closer.

"Yes, my prince, you did." Cal notices my very physical response to his words and he leans forward, his lips brushing my ear as he whispers, "You like it when I call you 'my prince,' don't you?"

"Very much," I reply, my lips grazing the warmth of his neck.

"So, I take it the treaty went well?" Pascal interrupts.

I pull back enough from Cal to glare at Pascal over my shoulder. Pascal has the decency to look apologetic. Cal laughs and releases me, stepping toward the table to gather up our copy of the treaty.

"Yes, everything is official," I reply, unable to hide my grin. "Ascaria has promised to send armies and aid. We will return home tomorrow, bearing good news for once."

Pascal and Lorrell grin.

"We knew you could do it," Lorrell says. "We never doubted you for a second."

"Really?" I ask, my voice betraying my genuine surprise.

"Of course," Pascal replies, clapping a hand to my shoulder. "We knew when we agreed to be members of your Guard that you would go on to do great and amazing things."

"But I've failed you all so much," I mutter in disbelief.

Lorrell shakes his head. "You haven't failed us once. You're the strongest man I know. You may have gotten knocked down, but you got back up. I know if I had to go through what you have, had to suffer in the same way, I wouldn't have been able to recover as quickly as you did."

"You are our prince and king," Pascal adds. "Even if you hadn't moved on as quickly as you did, we would still believe in you. You will be a great king. You already are."

I can't manage more than a nod, their words swirling through my brain.

We agree to go back to our rooms before the feast and pack our things. I'm shoving the last of my things into my pack when Cal slips into my room.

"Pascal and Lorrell were right, you know," he says, his eyes meeting mine. "You're stronger than you give yourself credit for."

I shake my head. "I don't know what you all see in me, but it really makes me want to try to live up to your expectations." I take a deep breath and look down at my hands clenched in front of me. "I'm afraid of what will happen when—if—I fail you all."

"Ehren," Cal says gently, crossing the room in two strides and gathering my hands into his. "You will never fail me—us." I lift my eyes to his. "You are far too stubborn for that."

Despite myself, I laugh, pressing my forehead against his. "I suppose you're right."

His lips hover barely a breath from mine as he whispers, his voice low, "Of course, I'm right . . . my prince."

We don't make it to the feast.

CHAPTER THIRTY-THREE

ASTRA

I wake the morning after my dream with Ehren feeling motivated. I check in quickly with Cook, but nothing has changed. Nothing good, anyway. My brother still sits on his throne, the people calling him "The Fire King" in terrified whispers.

I'm in the library, already searching for a spell to reach the dead when Ronan finds me.

"You seem a little more enthusiastic today," he muses, sauntering over to see what book I'm combing through. His smile turns to a frown. "Astra, love, why are you looking through this book? It's dark spells."

I grimace and meet his eyes. "I think I need a spell that's a bit a darker."

"Why?"

I sigh, tucking a strand of hair behind my ear as I lean over the book. "I don't think I can really explain. Ehren dream walked with me last night and I think there's a solution to our problems in this book."

Ronan doesn't look entirely convinced, but he nods. "All

408

right. I trust you. But right now, we need to reinforce the wards."

I nod, marking my place in the book with a scrap of paper. A light drizzle assaults us the entire time, so we don't dawdle. Once back in the library, Ronan sinks into his own collection of books, still looking for the spell to summon the Fae or a hint to their location. I look for a spell to raise the dead.

My heart nearly stops when I find what I'm looking for. I scan the ingredients, expecting something odd or dangerous, but most of them are commonplace enough. I quickly scribble down the spell and ingredients and excuse myself. Ronan arches a curious eyebrow but doesn't question me as I scurry from the library. It only takes a few minutes to gather everything I need. If something goes wrong, I don't want Ronan to get hurt, so instead of going back to the library, I head up to my room.

Once inside, I lock the door behind me and I say a quick prayer to the gods that the spell I found is what I need. I quickly mix the ingredients and trace the required six symbols on the floor with a spare piece of charcoal. I place six candles six inches apart in a circle around the symbols, lighting them one by one. I stand at the edge of the circle, the paper with the spell in my trembling hands, and I read the words aloud, my voice echoing off the walls. My heart races as smoky tendrils rise from the symbols, filling the room with the scent of ash and death. The smoke shifts, creating a swirling deep gray portal of sorts, blurry figures moving within it.

"Spirits of the dead come forth!" I repeat, my heart thrumming so hard I'm afraid it's going to burst free. This is no normal magic. Maybe I should have asked Ronan to be present.

"Who are you to ask questions of the dead?" a harsh voice calls back from the darkness.

I take a steadying breath. "I am Astra Downs and I hold the spirit of the goddess Aoibhinn."

"What business have you with the spirits?" the voice asks again.

"My kingdom is in danger from an evil race called the Dragkonians. They were defeated once before. I hope to find those who locked them away the first time and seek knowledge from their experience."

Silence echoes back.

"Please," I beg. "I need answers. I need—"

"You're asking the wrong spirits. These are being dreadfully unhelpful," a light, familiar voice responds.

My breath catches in my throat as a figure comes into focus, stepping from the portal but remaining within the charcoal circle, smoke curling around him. His body looks like a foggy mirror image of his former self—there in front of me but not fully corporeal.

"Makin?"

He grins, his hazel eyes shining. "The one and only."

Tears burn my eyes as I stare at him in disbelief. He cocks his head.

"I was going to ask if you missed me, but I think your response is answer enough," he teases with a wink.

I give short laugh, shaking my head. "You have no idea how much we miss you."

His gaze softens as he sticks his hands in pockets. "That boring without me around, eh?" His grin fades entirely as he adds, "How is he?"

"He's doing his best to live," I reply, offering Makin's spirit a weak smile.

Makin nods, licking his lips. "Good. I worry about him. I can see him from this side sometimes, but it's different here." He shakes his head and forces a grin. "Anyway, you're seeking a spirit to help lock the Dragkonians away?"

I nod. "Yes. Or someone who knows how to open a direct line to the Fae so they can help us. You don't know any spirits that old do you?"

Makin shrugs, shaking his head. "Not really. They're not exactly chatty. We spend most of our time asleep or . . . Actually, I'm not sure I can say. But we're not together. The exception is today when we're drawn back toward the mortal realm."

Chills rush across my flesh as Makin speaks so casually about the afterlife. I swallow and force myself to focus.

"I'll do what I can to find out if any spirits hovering nearby have any information, but it could take some time, which I know you don't have much of," he continues.

I nod. "Yes, time is short but I can perform the spell again in a few hours."

Makin nods, his face falling as his eyes meet mine. "At least I can be useful now."

"Makin," I start, my voice breaking. "You were always useful."

His smile is sad as he says, "I always tried. And I'll continue trying. I'll see you again in a few hours."

Makin steps back, smoky tendrils pulling him from view. I use magic to extinguish the candles with a wave of my hand, and the spirit world fades away. For a few moments I stare mindlessly at the smoke swirling through the air, but

411

then I fall to my knees, sobbing. I didn't realize how much I missed him until now.

I decide to distract myself with books and texts, heading back to the library, but I can't concentrate. Too much is riding on what Makin finds. Makin. I shake my head. I still can't believe I saw him, spoke to him. My heart seizes and I feel the tears well in my eyes.

Ronan watches me for a while before leaving and returning with a tea tray.

"You don't look well, love," Ronan says.

I try to force a smile but it doesn't really take. I sit straighter and nod to the tea tray as he sets it on the nearest table. "Is it time for tea?"

Ronan flashes me a grin. "It's always time for tea."

"I thought it was always time for mead."

Ronan chuckles. "I like to mix it up sometimes."

I manage a real smile as he pours the steaming amber liquid in a cup, handing it to me. I take the tea and take a sip. It's different.

"What's in this?" I ask, taking another tentative sip.

"It's a special concoction of my own making," Ronan replies, sinking down into the chair next to me. "It has lavender as well as few other herbs and flowers. It's not quite a spell, but I've found that helps to brighten one's mood and open your mind."

I nod, the effects of the tea already taking hold. By the time I'm nearly halfway done, I already feel less stressed. Ronan watches me, grinning over the edge of his cup.

"What?"

He laughs. "You look brighter."

I blush, focusing on my tea. "Well, talking to the dead does dim one a bit."

"Ah," Ronan says setting his tea cup down as his expression darkens. "So that's the spell you were looking for in that dreadful book. Why didn't you ask me to join you? I would have happily helped."

I shake my head. "It was too risky. The spell came with warnings that other . . . things might be summoned. I didn't want to put anyone at risk beyond myself."

"Astra, love, dear heart, just because you are a mighty and powerful sorceress doesn't mean that you need to put yourself in danger alone." Ronan frowns. "Please, don't feel like you're doing me any favors by shoving me aside when you need my help."

"I was fine. The spell worked well."

Ronan straightens. "Did you find an answer?"

I shake my head. "Not yet, but I found a lead. I'm checking back in with the spirit world in a couple hours to get a final answer. At least, I hope he'll have a final answer."

"He?" Realization flashes across Ronan's face. "Oh, Astra. You talked to a spirit you know, didn't you?"

I nod, biting my lip in an attempt to hold back the tears that burn my eyes.

"Oh, love," Ronan says, reaching out and taking my hands in his. "Why didn't you say? Ghosts haunt our memories and minds enough without us having to actually stare into their eyes. You shouldn't have gone through that alone."

"I didn't mind. Not really," I reply, my voice barely a whisper as a tear breaks free. "In a way it was good to see him again."

"May I ask who it was?"

"His name was Makin. He was one of Ehren's Guard and a good friend. He died in the battle at Embervein."

My voice breaks with a small sob. Ronan leaps from his

seat and pulls me from the chair, gathering me in his arms. He sits on the floor while I cry into his chest. I'm not sure exactly why I'm reacting this way. I feel weak. Ronan doesn't seem to care. He just holds me firmly, stroking my back. When I finally regain my senses, I sit up, wiping away my tears.

"I'm sorry," I mumble, standing to my feet.

"You never have to apologize to me for feeling things. Emotions make us stronger. They make us human," Ronan replies, smiling softly. "Do you want me to be with you when you summon him again?"

I meet his eyes and consider his offer. In some ways, it might be easier to have him there. Part of me doesn't want to face Makin alone. On the other hand, meeting Makin feels far too intimate to share with Ronan.

"No, I think I need to do it on my own," I say quietly, shaking my head.

"You're sure?" I nod. "Would you like me nearby? Maybe the next room over or the hall? That way if you need me, I can be there quickly."

I tilt my head, considering his offer. "Yes, I think I would like that."

Ronan smiles. "Good. Let me know when."

"Two hours. I want to perform the summoning spell in two hours. You can help me prepare the spell and then wait outside the room."

"What shall we do until then?"

I grin. "Drink tea, of course. And maybe some mead."

Ronan laughs. "Excellent plan."

The next couple hours pass quickly, Ronan and I lost in light conversation. When the time comes for the spell, he helps me as agreed, pausing in the hall outside my room as I slip inside.

"Remember, I'm only a yell away if you need me," he says.

"I know," I say, smiling softly as I close the door.

I take a deep breath to clear my mind before I begin the spell. As before, smoke fills the circle of candles. This time, however, it seems darker, more dangerous. I can't shake the feeling that something is off.

"Spirits of the dead come forth!" I call out. "Makin Parelli, are you there?"

I hold my breath as I stare in the swirls of blacks and grays. Something deep within the realm of the dead growls, sending shivers down my spine. I'm tempted to extinguish the spell but, no, I need to talk to Makin. Even if he has no information, I need to see him again.

"Makin Parelli, are you among the spirits of the dead? Come forth!"

Only silence echoes back. I'm about to give up when a figure forms against the shadows.

"Makin?" I ask, my voice trembling.

"The one and only," Makin says, stepping into the light of the flickering candles.

I release a long breath of relief. "Thank the gods."

He winks. "You must miss me a lot." His face sobers. "We should make this quick. Things are stirring in the dark-ness that have no place in the world of the living."

I frown. "Are you okay?"

Makin grins. "Yes, I am more than fine. What prowls this realm is only dangerous to the living. I swear. It's actually quite a nice place to spend eternity."

"Did you find out anything?" I ask, my eyes shifting nervously to the darkness swelling behind him.

Makin's spirit nods. "I did. Well, at least I know how to contact the Fae and bring them to our—your—realm. It appears that the only things anyone is willing to share or can remember is that without the Fae, it's a pointless cause. You'll need Fae runes and a Faerie ring. The older the better."

"I have the runes, but a Faerie ring?" I repeat with a scowl. "Where could I even find one?"

Makin shrugs. "I'm not sure. The spirit I spoke with said something about it being hidden in stories and tales to keep the knowledge hidden but available to those who seek." Something growls behind him, and he glances nervously over this shoulder. "You'll need to close this soon, so listen carefully. The spirit I spoke to was an old mage. He said there are ancient summoning spells meant to bridge realms. They need to be used with the Faerie ring and runes. You need to trace the runes around the edges of the Faerie ring while chanting the spell. Space them as evenly apart as possible. It will create a bridge between worlds."

I nod, committing everything to memory. Makin pauses, a grin spreading across his face.

"What?"

Makin shakes his head. "The mage kept repeating that only someone with strong magic could perform such a spell. I insisted that it was no problem, but he remained disbelieving."

I can't help but smile a little myself. "Let's hope I'm as strong as you think."

Makin's eyes meet mine. "You are. I've seen many spirits that claim they were powerful, but most of them don't even begin to compare to you, Astra. You can do this. You will find a way. You are going to save lives."

"If only I could have figured something out in time to save your life," I whisper, fighting back tears.

"None of that," Makin says firmly, shaking his head. "I lived a good life and I died saving my best friend. I have no regrets, and I can't stand the thought of any of you feeling guilt over my loss. Don't get me wrong, I'm glad I was significant enough in your lives to be missed, but I need you all to move forward without my death being a burden."

"I think we're trying, each of us in our own way."

Makin smiles smugly. "I peeked in on Cal and Ehren. It seems they're moving on together."

I bite my cheek to keep from grinning. "Oh?"

"Most definitely. And it's good." He winks but then sobers. "Can you pass a message on to them for me?"

"Of course."

"Tell Cal I'm happy for him. Really, truly happy for him. And tell Ehren it wasn't his fault. I don't blame him at all. I was happy to serve as his Guard and, even if I knew the outcome, I would make all the same choices."

I nod as a deeper growl rumbles around us, closer this time. Makin glances behind him briefly.

"I need to go. You're putting yourself at risk."

My chest tightens. I don't want him to leave. Not yet. But I nod.

"You have no idea how much you've helped me. Goodbye, Makin."

"Goodbye, Astra," he says with a sad smile.

He turns to leave but I call out to him. He pauses, turning back to me.

"Yes?"

"You really are missed. So much."

A tear slides down my cheek as he nods.

"I know. Can you do one thing for me? One thing I can't do?"

"Anything."

Makin smiles, taking a step backward. "Live."

He's swallowed in smoke, his shining eyes and smile the last thing I see. A roar rumbles through the air and I quickly end the spell. I exhale slowly. Live. I can do that. But first, I have to summon some Faeries and I think I know exactly who can help me. And he's standing right outside my door.

CHAPTER THIRTY-FOUR
JESSALYNN

We end up staying in Heldonia for three full days. Cadewynn spends most of that time viewing the vast array of weapons and, as much as I love looking at weapons, I'm bored out of my mind. If I could actually touch the weapons and play with them, that would be different. But if I so much as breathe near one, Kiera or one of her dogs goes after me.

"What are these?" Cadewynn asks, lifting a small metal disc.

Sure. It's fine if she touches the weapons.

Kiera grins. "Throwing stars."

She takes it from Cadewynn and whispers a word. I jump back as the small circular disc makes a whispering sound, shifting from a smooth circle to display four curved blades connected in the center. Cadewynn's eyes sparkle.

"I'd like to add as many as possible to our order."

Kiera nods, whispering another word that returns the throwing star to its previous form. "Very well. These are simpler to make than larger weapons so we should be able to provide a good supply."

"What are these?" I cut in, reaching toward some barbed darts on another table.

"Don't touch," Kiera snaps.

I scowl at her but pull my hand back. "Well, are they just normal darts?"

Kiera sighs and walks over to the table. "These," she says picking one up gingerly between her forefinger and thumb, "are silver darts made to hold poison."

"Posion?" Cadewynn asks, floating our way as she eyes the darts. "We'll need as many of these as possible."

Kiera arches an eyebrow. "These weapons are better for smaller interactions and may get lost in the chaos of battle."

"It doesn't matter," Cadewynn muses, picking up one of the darts to examine it. "Poison may be the key to winning this war."

Kiera frowns and glances at me but I shrug.

"Very well," Kiera concedes. "We'll add some of these to your order. Anything else you wish to inspect?"

Cadewynn sets the dart down and looks back up at Kiera. "I don't think so. Unless, of course, you think there's something beneficial we need to see."

Kiera flashes a grin. "I think we've covered everything quite well. We just need payment, and everything will be set."

"Naturally," Cadewynn says with a sickly sweet smile. "Send the final numbers to me and I'll make sure it's taken care of."

Kiera's eyes glint with something I don't like.

"And I'll be double-checking those numbers, so don't even try anything," I add, meeting Kiera's eyes.

Her grin falters into a harsh line. "I already expected you to meddle."

I open my mouth to respond, but Cadewynn catches my eyes and shakes her head. Instead, I sigh and roll my eyes.

"We should go pack," I say, turning to Cadewynn. "That way we can leave first thing in the morning for Gingtu."

Cadewynn nods, already turning toward the door. I fall into step behind her as we make our way back toward the inn where we're staying. As we we walk, I glance over at Cadewynn. She's strangely unfocused, chewing on the side of her lip. We're nearly to the inn when I finally give in to my curiosity.

"All right. Out with it."

Cadewynn scowls, glancing over at me. "What?"

"Something is clearly bothering you, so what is it?"

Cadewynn sighs, coming to a stop. She glances around nervously before answering. "I'm a little concerned."

I fight the urge to roll my eyes. "Concerned about what? Just say what's bothering you."

Cadewynn's eyes dart around, making sure we're near no one else before she leans closer, whispering, "Everything is just so expensive."

"What do mean? I thought you anticipated this. You have the money fr—" I stop short as I realize what she's not saying. "You don't have all the funds you pretend to, do you?"

Cadewynn looks down at her wringing hands. "I have funds."

"But not enough. Gods, Princess," I hiss through clenched teeth. "Do you have any idea what they'll do if they find out you can't pay?"

Cadewynn's baby blues meet mine. "I do have funds, I'm

just not sure how far they'll go. And Ehren has more at the Summer Palace."

I shake my head, trying to quell my fury before I explode. "But you've been parading around like you have bottomless pockets, spending carelessly. You don't even know if Ehren is spending money. You're just assuming that it will be there when you get back. Do you have any idea the hole you're digging?"

Tears well in Cadewynn's eyes as she nods. "I know. I just . . . We need armor. We need weapons. They can change the tide of the war."

I release a long breath as I run my hand through my hair. "Show me what you have."

"What?" Cadewynn blinks at me.

"Show me what you have. Show me the funds you brought with you. I can help you figure out if it's enough. If it's not, I'll have Kaeya haggle it down. That woman can talk a fish from a hungry bear."

A small light shines in Cadewynn's eyes as she looks up at me. "You mean it? You'll really help me?"

I sigh and avoid her eyes, looking down the street. "I suppose. After all, your name is tied to mine now, so our reputations are linked."

Cadewynn nods eagerly. "I have the money up in my room."

I follow Cadewynn into her room, dreading the entire time that she'll dump a handful of coins on her bed and call it a day. However, her stash is quite a bit more impressive. She has three small boxes, each filled to capacity with jewels, gold, and other priceless items. This wealth could almost run the whole Valley for a year or two. But having seen the price list for the supplies, I understand Cadewynn's nerves. If this small hoard of jewels is enough, it will barely cover the costs, leaving her with no backup.

"Is it enough?" Cadewynn asks, eying me hopefully as I pick up a green gem and hold it up to catch the light coming in through the window.

"Possibly," I reply, tossing the gem back into its box before meeting her eyes. "But it will be close. Stop spending. Now. When the final amount comes in, I'll send Kaeya in and get it lower. But after this, no more promising funds. Got it?"

Cadewynn's head bobs up and down so frantically I almost expect it to pop off.

"Thank you, Jess. You have no idea."

I sigh and pinch the bridge of my nose. "Actually, I do have an idea. Things like this take time and experience to learn."

"Still, thank you."

I wave her off as I turn to leave the room. "Just watch it from now on."

I head down to the tavern in the base of the inn and order a round of drinks. A couple drinks in, Kaeya joins me, carefully nursing one large tankard. When the messenger brings the final numbers, it's even more than I imagined, but Kaeya agrees to help without hesitation. When she returns, she has a number significantly lower. I think Cadewynn could die from happiness as she passes the payment to Kiera, shaking on the deal. I'm just thrilled to be done in Heldonia so we can move on.

The next morning is bright and clear, but too cold for my taste. We wrap in our warmest cloaks and head out toward Gingtu. The capital city of Yomori is at the far corner from Heldonia. Gingtu is known for two things: a large gem mine and their rice paddies. With those two major exports, it's the wealthiest province in Gleador despite being one of the smallest, only beating out the Valley in size.

By midday, we're leaving the edges of Heldonia and entering Gingtu. It doesn't take long before we start seeing the rice fields flooded with workers. Cadewynn seems fascinated by the process. We stop for the night in a small town with only one room available at the inn. That might work, except when we get upstairs, we only find three beds.

"Shall we play Rochambeau?" Nyco asks with a wry grin. "Or just race and see who gets there first?"

"Rochambeau?" Cadewynn asks, arching an eyebrow. "What's that?"

Kaeya spins, Nila tumbling from her shoulder, and stares at the princess in disbelief. "You've never heard of Rochambeau?" Cadewynn shakes her head. "Janken, then?"

"Paper, Scissors, Rock," Sama offers.

"Oh!" Cadewynn says, her eyes brightening with recognition. "I suppose I have never heard those other names before, but I know now what you mean."

"I don't see the need, though." Cadewynn tilts her head as she looks toward the beds. "Sama and I can share one and I'm assuming you two won't mind sharing. That leaves the spare bed for Nyco. Unless Nyco would rather share with me and then Sama takes the spare. Or—"

I wave my hand, cutting her off as I take in the beds. They're not very wide, but two adults could share one easily enough, especially if they don't mind sleeping very close to the other person.

"We can double-up," I say with a shrug. "Kaeya and I will take the one closest to the door. You three can divide up however you like."

"As much as I love you two, I call dibs on the lone bed," Nyco volunteers with a grin as he waltzes into the room and claims the middle bed.

"Fine by me," Sama says with a grin as she sets her bags next to the bed farthest from the door, Ares hopping from his perch on her shoulder to sit on the windowsill near the bed. "You take up more space than Winnie anyway. She's clearly the better option."

Nyco laughs and sticks his tongue out playfully as Sama opens the window.

"Are you going to leave that open?" I ask with a frown as Ares soars out the window. "We'll all freeze."

"Only until he comes back. He needs to hunt," Sama replies. "He'll be back in plenty of time for us to shut the window before sleeping."

I narrow my eyes but decide not to press the issue. We head downstairs in search of dinner and find an offering of rice with various meats and vegetables. Once we've eaten our fill, we linger a little longer, absorbing the atmosphere before heading up to bed. I'm nearly asleep when Sama and Cadewynn start talking in low whispers. I can't quite make out what they're saying and that annoys me more than the fact that they're whispering. Eventually they quiet, and we all drift off to sleep.

The next morning, we're greeted by sharp winds bringing in dark, threatening clouds. Sama whispers prayers to the gods under her breath for the weather to hold. Whether it's by luck or actual divine intervention, we manage to make it to Yomori before the storm. Despite the impending threat of dark weather and the approach of night, the streets of Yomori are filled with commerce.

Yomori is positioned between two large rice fields, but

that doesn't keep the city small. Instead, the buildings are stacked high and close together, some roads so narrow there's barely room for two people to walk side by side.

We elbow our way through the crowded streets and find a place to keep our horses before seeking out an inn. The first inn we check has two rooms available, but I find another inn with another available room. Once we have our rooms arranged, we split up in pursuit of dinner. I wander the streets alone, holding my cloak tightly against the bracing wind. Night has fallen, but bright torches keep the streets well lit.

I find a stall selling bowls of noodles covered in soy sauce mixed with vegetables and fried eggs. I find a little place to sit and eat my dinner as I watch the bustle of the world around me. Sometimes, I miss cities like this. While Embervein was never quite this busy, it contained far more life than my quiet corner of the Hundan Valley. I could easily thrive in an environment like this. I realize with a start I almost long to go home to Embervein.

Home. I shake my head. When was the last time I thought of Embervein as home? It hasn't been my home for a long time. My home is the Hundan Valley, now. Isn't it?

I push such thoughts from my mind as I finish my dinner and dispose of the bowl. I wind through the crowd, pausing occasionally to examine some of the available merchandise. I pause at one vendor cart selling jewelry, an earring catching my eye. It's a single earring of a snake, its long curved tail made of several links of gold so it writhes with movement. It would be perfect for Brock.

The thought of Brock stabs my chest. Gods, I didn't even realize how much I missed him until now. My nights are most often spent with Kaeya as Brock spends most nights on guard duty. But we always find time for each other to satisfy every carnal need. But I miss more about Brock than mere tumbles in the bed. I miss his smile and his laugh, not so easily given but worth more than all the gems and jewels in Gleador.

I smile, recalling how I first met Brock shortly after Kaeya and I became lovers. He was her stoic childhood friend. Despite his constant solemn mood, I was smitten. I found my gaze drifting toward him often, and Kaeya noticed. After a careful discussion and laying of groundwork, she encouraged me to pursue a relationship with Brock as well. The rest is history. Over the years, a few others have tried to enter into our little cluster, but no one else stays. They either get too greedy or jealous or decide that our shared lifestyle isn't for them. In the end, they all leave, but Kaeya, Brock, and I have bonds stronger than any couple I know.

And without Brock, a piece of me is missing. I smile and purchase the earring, tucking it into my pocket for safekeeping. I'm nearly back to my inn when the torrent of rain finally breaks free. Even though I'm mere yards away, I'm still soaked through thanks to the thickness of the crowd slowing my path. Once inside my room, I shirk my clothes, carefully laying the earring on the bed as I change. Midway through pulling on dry clothes, Kaeya enters the room, completely dry, an equally dry Nila cradled in her arms.

"I see you also got caught in the rain," Kaeya says, her eyes shining.

I shake my head, rolling my eyes. "Don't even pretend the rain bothers you. You and your stupid water magic. Not a raindrop touches you unless you want it to."

Kaeya grins, sitting down on my bed. Nila leaps away and immediately finds the earring, batting at it playfully.

"I'm blessed by the gods and have no complaints." She pauses, noticing the earring. She slides it away from Nila and lifts it gingerly. "For Brock?"

I nod, taking a seat next to her. "Think he'll like it?"

"Of course," she says with a smile. "He always loves any gifts from you, *Jaanu*." Kaeya presses a kiss to my cheek as she places the earring in my palm. "You miss him terribly don't you?"

I nod, swallowing as I close my fist over the snake. "I do. I didn't even realize how much until a little while ago, but I'll be happy to see him in Koshima."

"Me too," Kaeya replies, placing her head on my shoulder. "Life seems off kilter without him, but in a few days we will all be together again."

I rest my head against hers and take her hand. "Together. Gods that sounds nice. I can't wait."

We sleep restlessly. I'm not sure if it's the thunder rattling the windows, the torrential downpour beating against the roof hour after hour without ceasing, or the anxious anticipation of meeting with Ichiro. When morning comes I'm an irritable ball of hate.

"Drink this," Kaeya says, offering me a cup of steaming liquid as I sit on the edge of the bed.

I take it and frown up at her. "This isn't coffee."

Kaeya smiles around her own cup as she takes a sip. "It's tea. Good strong tea."

I take a sip. It's strong all right, but still not coffee. I sigh and set the tea on the bedside table.

"Did you set up a meeting with Ichiro?"

"I tried," Kaeya replies, taking another sip of her tea. "Apparently he has a very busy schedule but will try to fit us in."

I clench my hands into fists. "Busy schedule my ass."

Kaeya grins and takes a seat next to me. "Don't worry. We'll get our audience."

I sigh and stare toward the door. "I know. We don't have much time."

"So, you are growing concerned about the fate of your home country after all."

I snap my eyes to hers. "It's not just Callenia. It's the whole world at risk. It may start with Callenia, but it won't stay there."

Kaeya nods thoughtfully as she sips her tea, but she doesn't reply. She knows as well as I do that while I am concerned about the effects this war will have on the continent as a whole, I am growing more and more aware of the devastation rocking my own country. The thought of my homeland being destroyed . . . I shake my head and stand.

"We should meet with the princess and let her know what to expect when she meets with Ichiro," I say, striding toward the door.

"You go on," Kaeya says with a wave. "I'll be along once I finish my tea."

I comply with a nod and go off in search of Cadewynn. Though the rain has stopped for now, heavy clouds still hang in the sky. The rain has left the city streets soaked and muddy, but commerce is up and going as usual. I weave through the crowd and find the princess and crew eating a breakfast of fried eggs at a cart outside their inn. Kaeya joins us a few minutes later.

We spend a good portion of the day wandering the city in frustration at being pushed aside by Ichiro. It's early afternoon when he finally deigns to send for us. A messenger arrives, guiding us to a stone building in the dead center of town. He leads us to a room with a low table set for tea. We take our seats, but our host in nowhere to be found as a young woman serves us tea. Our cups are nearly empty by the time Ichiro arrives.

"So sorry for keeping you waiting," he grins. "I had some last minute business to attend."

He takes a seat at the head of the table and assesses us quickly, something dark gleaming in his eyes. He settles his gaze on Cadewynn.

"It's not often I have the privilege of meeting visiting royalty," he says, inclining his head.

Cadewynn meets his gaze with a hard smile. "Perhaps that is why you kept us waiting for so long. You're too far out of practice."

Ichiro's smile falters only for a moment before he bursts out laughing. "You have bite. Can't say I was expecting that."

"Perhaps we should get straight to business," I cut in, offering Ichiro a warning smile of my own.

"Very well," Ichiro says with a shrug. "My answer is no."

Cadewynn blanches as she leans forward. "No to what exactly?"

"Everything," Ichiro says, motioning wide with his hands. "I will not provide soldiers or supplies. I am a businessman and as such I will not give away my wares for any less than full price. If you wish to purchase rice or other commodities, I will give you the same fair pricing I offer to everyone, but I will extend no discounts. There is nothing you can tempt me with to change my mind."

Cadewynn frowns as my blood boils. If he meant to send us away, he should have done so already instead of leaving us to wonder and wait.

"Are you sure there is nothing?" Cadewynn presses, desperation lining her voice.

A snakelike smile curls on Ichiro's lips as his eyes scan the princess. "How desperate are you, Princess? What exactly you willing to offer that goes beyond shiny gems and pathetic promises?"

Cadewynn blinks, confusion clouding her features. Nyco shifts closer to her, but his hard expression is set on Ichiro.

"I'm not sure what you want me to offer when you've already declared you're not willing to negotiate."

"Winnie . . ." Nyco whispers, his voice low and full of warning.

Cadewynn glances at him then back to Ichiro. "We can offer some money off course, but—"

Ichiro cuts her off with a throaty chuckle that makes me want to stab him. The only thing stopping me is the sudden weight of Kaeya's hand on my thigh.

"You are so much more naive than even I thought. Perhaps you are no more than a pretty face with more bark than actual bite. And I thought you might have some use, but alas, you're just another pitiful display of a little girl playing at things far beyond—"

"You will not speak to my sister in such a manner!" I yell, slamming my palms down on the table so hard the teacups rattle and tip, tea spilling onto the table.

Ichiro seems startled, tearing his gaze from Cadewynn, whose cheeks are a bright crimson.

"Oh?" he says with a casual flick of hand. "And why not?"

I laugh, standing to look down at the man. "Clearly you've never met our brother. He would have your head for

431

such words. Who will run your little rice empire if you are dead?"

Ichiro pales slightly but only straightens his shoulders in defiance. "I am a man of forty-seven. It takes more than casual threats to intimidate me. Your brother is a discarded prince with no power. If I desired, I think even I could take his kingdom."

I laugh, shaking my head as I whisk my dagger from its sheath. It takes barely a second to cross to him. His eyes widen as I press it to his throat. His eyes dart to his attendants standing along the edge of the room.

"Stop her!"

I hold up my free hand. "Make a move toward me and I slit his throat." I meet Ichiro's wide eyes and grin. "Now that I have your attention, listen carefully. We will make do without your services, but if you ever disrespect any member of my family again, you will not live to make any further comments. Understood?"

I press my blade closer to his skin and he nods. "Understood."

"Now," I say, pulling back and sheathing my dagger. "We won't take up another moment of your time."

I turn and stride from the room, Cadewynn stumbling to her feet to follow. Once outside, I pause, still seething as I wait for the others to catch up.

"You called me your sister," Cadewynn breathes in awe as she steps to my side.

I wave her off. "I meant nothing by it. I only wanted to to remind that despicable man—"

I stop short as Cadewynn places her hand on my arm. I look down into her crystal blue eyes.

"Thank you," she whispers.

I open my mouth to answer, but snap it shut as Nyco approaches with a stout, sweaty man.

"Your Majesty," the man says, inclining his head to Cadewynn. "I apologize for my master's attitude. He was very much wrong in his actions."

"I would say so," I say, glaring at the man as I cross my arms. "Who are you and what do you want?"

The man bows. "Sorry for my rudeness. You may call me Yoon. I am the chief of trade under Master Ichiro. I oversee all the business aspects. Not one bit of trade happens without my knowing."

"That's all well and good, but why did you seek us out?" I demand.

Yoon offers me a weak smile. "I came to offer you a deal —a reasonable one. I can arrange for rice to be sent to your armies for a quarter of the usual asking price."

Cadewynn raises her eyebrows. "But Ichiro said—"

"It matters not," Yoon insists with a wave of his hand. "I can cover the books so he will never know. We have large shipments of rice being prepared now. I will take a little from each and send them your way."

"Why?" I demand, narrowing my eyes at Yoon.

Yoon licks his lips. "Because I am not as foolish as Ichiro. He may be forty-seven and well versed in putting money in his pocket, but I am a good many years older and know that money will not save us from destruction should it come knocking on our door. I also know that his attitude does not please the gods, and as I am likely to meet them before he does, I would rather have them look favorably upon me for what actions and sides I take in this war." He looks back to Cadewynn. "Do we have a deal?"

Cadewynn nods slowly as I add, "Have the numbers sent

to our rooms and we will continue negations. Nyco will provide you with the information."

Nyco straightens as Yoon eyes him, nodding. "Very well. I will have it to you within the hour."

Yoon turns and heads back toward the building, Nyco trailing behind as the rest of us head into the city. We don't speak until we find a somewhat quiet corner alley to step into.

"Do you think he's sincere?" Cadewynn asks, wringing her hands.

"That man is afraid and fear can be a very good motivator," Kaeya answers.

"So, where do we go from here?" Cadewynn asks, glancing toward the busy street. "Koshima?"

I nod. "Yes. Brock will be there with our army and likely a few other armies will have arrived by now. I should also have correspondence from the other provinces waiting for me. Once we arrive in Koshima, we can assess our position and make plans to move into Callenia." I clap a hand to Cadewynn's shoulder. "You've done it princess. You've gathered armies and supplies. It may be a few weeks before we reach the warfront, but you did it."

Cadewynn smiles weakly, but her eyes shine. "Will it be enough?"

I smile. "Only time will tell, but I have a feeling you may have turned the tide in this war."

Cadewynn ducks her head. She's so humble. Who would have thought such a girl could hold the power she does? For once, I'm glad to call her my sister and I can't wait to see what we can do together to win back her kingdom—our kingdom, my home of Callenia. Hopefully, we can arrive before it's too late.

CHAPTER THIRTY-FIVE

JESSALYNN

I t's late evening when we ride into Koshima, but the marketplace is still flooded with merchants and thick crowds. A few people cast glances our way, whispering under their breath, but most ignore us. After all, our small traveling band is nothing to the armies gathering outside the city walls.

The moment we enter the palace courtyard a guard stumbles forward, ready to usher us before the king. We weave through the ornate halls to the throne room where King Naimon sits on his throne, a tall man in a sweeping mage cloak standing behind him to his right. My eyes linger on the Mage only a moment before they fall to the man already standing before the king, his own eyes turned to me. A smile quirks on the corners of Brock's lips and I fight back a smile of my own.

"Jessalynn," the king's voice booms, drawing my sharp gaze back to him. "I've been discussing the . . . advancements with your lieutenant, but perhaps you could fill me in on the finer details?"

I bow my head in show of respect, stepping forward. "Of course, my king." When I lift my eyes back to him his gaze is sharp and cutting. "I suppose you are familiar with my sister, Princess Cadewynn of Callenia?"

I motion to Cadewynn and she steps to my side, her head held high. King Naimon nods, barely bothering to glance at the princess.

"We are acquainted."

"Then you well know the plight she has brought before us. You know that her kingdom is falling and they require our aid."

I didn't think the king's gaze could get any colder, but somehow it does. Nervous needles rise in my chest but I refuse to back down or avert my eyes.

"Of course I am aware. I was aware when Prince Ehren and his Sorceress came before me, and I was equally aware when the queen and princess returned requesting shelter from the evil that plagues their land. I have given aid to Prince Ehren in the form of gems, coins, and priceless artifacts. I have supported their cause."

I sense more than see Cadewynn tense next to me but she, thank the gods, holds her tongue.

"And I'm sure they appreciate your outflowing of generosity," I say, inclining my head. "Unfortunately, however, it seems things have advanced beyond what funds can easily mend. If troops are not sent to Callenia, it will fall and the inky black of evil will surely invade our own border."

King Naimon's jaw tightens, and his eyes darken. "Are you suggesting that I am unable to defend my own kingdom?"

Kaeya's whispered "Careful Jess" is so quiet I barely catch it, but I refuse to back down now. Cadewynn risked her life and reputation to secure these troops for her—our—brother and hell if I don't have at least the same amount of courage. Hell if I'm going to go back to the Valley defeated and useless. I take a bold step forward, King's Naimon's eyes narrowing almost imperceptibly at my borderline insolence.

"I am suggesting, Your Majesty, that the evil that has risen in recent months is something that no king can stand against. The longer their evil is allowed to reign, the more power they gain, the more difficult they will be to defeat. If Callenia falls, it is only a matter of time before the rest of the continent falls with it." I take another step forward and even Brock shoots me a warning glance. "The troops that have gathered outside have answered the call of Princess Cadewynn. They have chosen to join the fight. You have always allowed the provinces some decision in which wars to fight and we have chosen to back Prince Ehren. Surely you will not ask us to retreat only to rise again in the near future when our fates are less secure."

I hold the king's gaze while he studies me, his face unreadable. I barely even dare to breathe as I await his decision.

"So be it," he says at length and I nearly gasp in relief. It takes every ounce of willpower I have not to break out into a grin. "I will allow these assembled armies to march to Callenia. I will even provide the necessary supplies and funds, but I will not require any more to join this cause."

I nod, my heart pounding against my ribcage. "Of course, Your Majesty." I drop to my knees, my head bowed in true appreciation and respect. "And that is why you are a most just king whom I am pleased to serve."

"Rise." I stand to my feet and look back to the king's cold gaze. "You and your armies are welcome to reside in

Koshima as long as necessary while you regroup. Whatever supplies you need, simply request."

"I will. Thank you, Your Majesty."

He eyes me with something akin to distaste before waving his hand and glancing away. "You are dismissed. Your lieutenant, I assume, will be able to show you your room, and your additional guests"—he glances to Cadewynn, Sama, and Nyco—"will be shown to their rooms."

With a final bow, I spin on my heel and march from the throne room, retaining as much dignity as possible. Brock and Kaeya follow closely. Brock takes the lead a few steps out of the throne room, showing us the way to the suite we've been assigned while a servant steps forward and guides Cadewynn and crew to another suite of rooms near ours. I hold my head high until the door of our suite closes behind us.

"One day your tongue will get you in trouble," Brock says, turning to face me.

A grin curls on my lips. "I thought you liked the things my tongue can do."

Brock tries hard to fight his smile but his eyes shine, giving him away. "You need to take this seriously, Jess."

I wave my hand and stride past him to collapse on one of the many ornate couches. "I knew he wouldn't be upset with my decisions. He had already given permission in a way. It was only a matter of standing my ground."

"You still played a bit of a risk," Kaeya interjects, shaking her head. "But I expected nothing less of you."

I grin, tilting my head as Brock settles on the couch next to me. "Did you miss me?"

Brock's grin finally breaks free as he rolls his eyes. "Of course I did."

I lean forward and pull him into a kiss. It was meant to be a simple greeting, but when his hand slides around my waist and pulls me into his lap, it's anything but simple.

"I'll go make sure the princess is settled," Kaeya says, reaching for the door handle. "I'll also check on the armies."

I pull back from Brock and glance at Kaeya. "I know you're tired. There's no need to run off if you need to rest."

Brock nods. "This can wait."

Kaeya smiles softly. "No, it's fine. I still have a bit of energy racing through me from traveling. Might as well put it to our advantage."

I manage a quick nod before she sweeps from the room, leaving Brock and I alone.

"Now," Brock purrs, tracing a calloused finger down my cheek, "I recall you saying something about what your tongue can do?"

I grin wickedly and pull him into a kiss, happy to refresh his memory.

KAEYA RETURNS ROUGHLY an hour later while Brock and I are casually lying about in the common area of our suite. She sinks down next to Brock and immediately leaps into conversation about the armies. I excuse myself to give them some time alone to chat and reconnect, making the excuse that I need some fresh air and food. At first I have no true purpose in my wanderings, but I find myself outside in a garden, drawn by light laughter. Nyco stands grinning next to a fountain while Sama sits cross-legged at his feet, Cadewynn's head resting in her lap as she braids the princess's golden locks. Even though I can't make out their words, I'm lost in their light banter. I'm not even sure how long I've been staring when Sama lifts her gaze and her eyes find mine. I clear my throat and walk their way.

"I wanted to make sure you are settling in well," I say to Princess Cadewynn as she pushes up into a sitting position.

The princess nods, her eyes shining. "Very well, thank you."

"Have you seen your mother since our return?"

Her face falls and Sama reaches and grabs her hand. "I have not yet visited her, though I'm sure she knows of my return."

Nyco straightens and steps almost protectively toward the princess. "I'm sure we'll make contact at the right moment."

I nod, glancing off. "Of course." I look back at the trio. "I suppose I'll leave you be."

I turn and begin walking off when Sama calls my name. I turn back to her as she rises, brushing bits of grass off her dress.

"I need to talk to you." She casts a glance over her shoulder at Nyco and Cadewynn and adds, "Maybe somewhere we can talk alone?"

I nod and lead the way to another part of the garden. We can still see Nyco and Cadewynn but we're far enough away for private conversation. Sama swallows and clasps her hands in front of her.

"Jess, I appreciate everything you've done for me, but—"

"You're not coming back to the Valley," I finish for her.

Her eyes widen as she nods.

I take a deep breath and release it slowly. "I can't say I'm shocked, if I'm honest."

"You're not?"

I laugh. "Sama, you're quite obviously smitten with Cadewynn or Nyco, or perhaps both. Either way, I wouldn't require you to leave them out of a sense of duty to me."

Red rises in her cheeks as she smiles. "I care for both of them."

She looks toward them as Cadewynn's laugh drifts across the garden. Nyco is now seated facing Cadewynn, and even from this distance I can tell his eyes are bright. He leans toward Cadewynn and says something that makes her laugh again. Sama's smile grows.

"I'm happy for you. I only hope they don't break your heart."

Sama turns her attention back to me. "They won't." She pauses, her expression growing thoughtful. "You know, I never expected to feel this way about anyone. I never had these kinds of desires before. And I was okay with that. But the closer I get to Nyco and Cadewynn . . . well, things changed. I want to be with them in ways I never imagined before."

I smile. "That's good. And they want to be with you?"

She nods, but pauses with a small shrug. "Well, Nyco is open to anything, and he's quite patient with me, waiting until I'm ready and letting me take the lead. Cadewynn doesn't want much of a physical relationship, just the occasional kiss or gentle affection, which is perfect for me."

"She's young. That could change."

Sama shrugs, her eyes drifting back to her partners. "Perhaps, but I don't think it will."

I swallow and watch as Cadewynn plucks up a flower and tucks it behind Nyco's ear. Nyco's cheek grows a soft shade of pink as he ducks his head, but he doesn't remove the flower. Sama smiles affectionately. I clear my throat and take a step back.

"Well, I'll let you be." Sama turns to me and nods. "If you stick with your decision not to return to the Valley, I respect it wholeheartedly. Thank you for letting me know. I wish you all the happiness."

Sama grins. "You know, Jess, I have a feeling neither of us will be returning the Valley."

I arch an eyebrow. "You're a Seer now?"

Sama laughs, shaking her head. "Hardly." Her expression sobers as a shadow crosses her features. "The world is changing, Jess, and we're all changing with it. The world we knew before, the future we expected, it will all be different. There's no avoiding it."

I grit my teeth and nod. She's right but I don't want to dwell on what that means.

"Perhaps."

Sama waves her hand like she's clearing the air and forces a smile. "Who knows. Maybe less will change than we think."

"I guess only time will tell." I look over my shoulder at the castle behind us. "I should probably seek out a few more allies and check the armies while I have the energy."

Sama nods, stepping toward her partners. "I'll see you later, Jess."

I watch for a moment as she rejoins Nyco and Cadewynn, their smiles growing with her approach. With a smile of my own, I return to the castle, an uncomfortable feeling swirling in my gut. I'm not ready for so much change, but ready or not, it's coming. I only wish I knew how to prepare.

CHAPTER THIRTY-SIX

EHREN

When I rise the morning following the treaty signing, I'm sore in the most wonderful ways. I sit up only to discover the bed next to me is empty. A brief moment of panic washes over me as I register Cal's absence, wondering if I somehow managed to screw everything up again. Gods, how did I mess everything up so quickly?

The door creaks open and I start, my eyes shooting to the door as Cal steps inside. A grin plays on my lips. He came back. Much to my chagrin, he's fully dressed in casual traveling clothes instead of how I last remember him before I fell asleep. Much to my delight, however, he's balancing a tray bearing coffee and food.

"Hmm," I muse, leaning back against the headboard. "Breakfast in bed. I could get used to this."

Cal laughs, shutting the door with his foot. "You're a prince, Ehren. Don't even bother pretending this is a first."

"Ah, but this is the first time I've been brought breakfast in bed by my lover," I grin with a wink, the tips of Cal's ears reddening slightly, much to my delight. "And such a handsome one at that."

Cal rolls his eyes as he sits on the bed, setting the tray between us. "I happen to know you've had many attractive lovers. I find it difficult to believe none of them brought you food in bed after the deed was done."

My heart plummets into my stomach. He would know. Gods, how many times did he stand guard while I . . . I shake my head, trying to push the thoughts away, but Cal knows me too well.

"Hey," he says, placing a hand over mine. "I'm not judging you or comparing myself to them."

I force a weak smile. "Good, because none of them compare to you. Not even slightly." I lace my fingers with his, squeezing his hand. "I love you, Cal. I never loved anyone else. I swear it. They all meant nothing. Gods, I regret every night I wasted on anyone who wasn't you. I—"

Cal cuts me short, leaning over and silencing my rambling with a firm but gentle kiss. When he pulls back, he meets my eyes.

"I know," he whispers. "And you were worth the wait."

I grin and clear my throat, glancing down to the tray. "Yes, well, I suppose we should eat before this gets cold."

Cal smiles, nodding as he pulls his hand from mine. We're about midway through our breakfast when someone knocks on the main door. Cal exchanges a curious look with me, but I shrug.

"Maybe it's just someone letting us know everything is prepared for our journey," I suggest.

The knock sounds again and Cal moves to rise from the bed. I reach out and place my hand on his arm.

"Lorrell or Pascal will answer."

As a third knock echoes through the suite, Cal turns to me and cocks an eyebrow. "You sure about that?"

I bite back a grin but am saved an answer as footsteps echo across the room and the door is finally opened. I lean forward, listening to the low voices, but am unable to make out anything. After a few moments, someone crosses to my bedroom and knocks.

"Your Majesty?" Lorrell says. "Are you awake?"

"I am," I reply, glancing over at Cal with a grin. "Come in."

Cal's eyes widen as he makes to move from the bed but my hand is still on his arm, keeping him in place. Lorrell has barely cracked open the door before his cheeks turn bright red, his eyes shifting quickly from my current state of undress—or as much as he can see that's not hidden by a blanket—to Cal next to me. He hurries to look away. Cal glances over at me, rolling his eyes, but I catch hints of a grin.

"You, uh, have a guest," Lorrell mutters, staring intently down at his boots.

"Who is it?" I ask.

"Noah."

Cal tenses beneath my touch and I slide my hand from his arm to his hand.

"Noah Greystone?"

Lorrell nods, finally looking up at me. "Yes. He said you had him stationed in Ascaria and he's come to report."

I nod and turn to Cal. He's staring down at our clasped hands, gnawing on his lip. Something is wrong, but I don't quite know what.

"Tell Noah I'll be just a minute," I reply, looking back to Lorrell.

Lorrell nods and leaves without another word, closing the door behind him.

"Are you okay?" I ask Cal, caressing his hand with my thumb. "Aren't you and Noah friends? I thought you were quite close."

Cal nods, still avoiding my eyes. "We used to be. We were very close for years." He slowly lifts his eyes to mine. "We had a small falling out a couple years ago. Nothing drastic—we're still friendly enough—but I'm not sure what he would say if he knew."

I frown. "Knew what? About us?"

Cal glances away, nodding. "Yes."

I reach out and cup my hand on his cheek, turning his face back to me. His eyes meet mine and I can see his fear and concern.

"Hey, I love you, Cal. Nothing is going to change that. I'm not going back on this, on us. You're my heart and life. I understand that it might be difficult for you, and we can take everything at your pace. If you don't want Noah to know yet, that's fine. You can stay in here while I go talk to him. But people will know eventually, unless . . ."

I drop off as I realize that maybe Cal can't do this. He hasn't been in a relationship for a reason. Maybe he's not comfortable enough to move forward with me. Maybe that was the falling out. What if . . . I take a deep breath and close my eyes.

"If you don't want to be in an open relationship with me we can end things before we go back to Callenia," I whisper, barely able to breathe. "Or keep it hidden. Alter our relationship to better fit—"

Cal's lips crash against mine so hard we topple back. His lips move desperately, and I wrap my arms around him, pulling him closer as I shift my body under his, knocking the coffee off the tray.

"Shit," Cal mutters, jerking back away from the spilt coffee.

I grin up at him, ignoring the mess we've made as I link my hands behind his neck. Cal looks down at me and a smile slowly spreads across his lips as he shakes his head.

"Ehren, I love you but if you ever even suggest ending or hiding this relationship again, I will stab you with my sword."

"Is 'sword' a euphemism for something else? Because I'd rather enjoy that," I grin.

Cal's lips part in shock before spreading into a wide grin. He lowers himself so his body is barely a breath from mine, his lips brushing my ear as he whispers, "Oh, my prince, if you think you deserve such firm punishment, who am I to disagree?"

Shivers run down my spine as I arch my body to press against his. He traces a line of sensual kisses along my jaw line. His lips are just meeting mine when Lorrell knocks on the door again.

"Um, You Majesty?" he calls through the door.

I growl in frustration as Cal sighs and pulls up, scooting off the bed.

"I should have him thrown in the dungeon. I'm the prince. I can do that."

Cal laughs, leaning down to press a quick kiss to my lips before whispering, "No."

I sigh and push up onto my elbows.

"Fine," I mutter before raising my voice to reply to Lorrell. "I'm dressing. I'll be out shortly."

With an overly dramatic exhale that makes Cal roll his

eyes, I crawl from the bed. While I dress, Cal attempts to clean up the mess we made. Once I'm ready, I stride to the door, glancing over at Cal.

"Do you want to come out with me? If you want to stay in here, you can. Tell Noah in your own way in your own time."

Cal smiles and shakes his head. "No, I'm going out there with you. I'm tired of hiding. After all, I don't want to hide this—you."

I smile, ducking my head as I extend my hand. Cal meets my eyes as he intertwines his fingers with mine. I take a rallying breath and open the door. Lorrell, Pascal, and Noah are spread out across the couches but leap to their feet as we enter the room. Pascal bites back a grin as his eyes fall on Cal, but Lorrell glances away, his cheeks flushing crimson as he no doubt recalls our earlier state. Noah's smile fades into a scowl of confusion, glancing from me to Cal to our hands.

"I wasn't expecting you to meet us here," I say, straightening but not releasing Cal's hand as his grip tightens. "You were in Beaurac, were you not?"

Noah nods. "Yes, Your Majesty, I was. Well, I was in a small town just outside the city. I heard you were here and thought to bring you my report in person." He raises his head, looking back at Cal. "I didn't mean to interrupt anything."

I tilt my head. "What makes you think you were interrupting something?"

Pascal hides a laugh with a cough as Noah's face turns bright red.

"I, uh, I wasn't sure. I mean, I just thought . . . this wasn't the plan."

I chuckle and look over at Cal to find him smiling, though his grip on my hand is as tight as ever.

"You're fine, Noah," I reply. "Relations with Ascaria are secure for now. We are leaving to head back to Callenia today. You're welcome to come with us."

Noah nods. "If you don't require me to remain here, I can return with you. I have all my own supplies and can be ready to go within the hour."

"First, give me your official report." I look past Noah to Lorrell and Pascal. "You two go make sure everything is ready for our departure."

The brothers nod and duck out of the room. I turn to Cal, taking his other hand in mine as he turns to face me.

"You should probably go with them since they don't speak a lick of Ascarian. Gods know what trouble they could get into."

Cal smiles and nods, hesitating only a moment before he leans forward to brush his lips across mine briefly—a motion that I know takes courage, making it all the more meaningful.

"As you order . . . my prince."

I inhale sharply as Cal grins and steps back with a bow, a knowing grin of mischievous intention curling on his perfect lips. He turns to Noah before he leaves.

"It's good to see you, Noah."

Noah manages a nod and a "You too, Cal" despite his obvious confusion and discomfort.

Once Cal is gone, Noah and I take seats on the couches across from one another. I can tell Noah is dying to bring up Cal, but I avoid any mention of him, diving directly into Noah's report. Thankfully, there's no bad news. Instead, Noah only confirms everything I've already discovered about the Ascarian court and the king's health. For once, things seem to be falling into place.

It doesn't even take the full hour before we're on the road. Luc escorts us to the gate along with a few of his personal guards he's sending with us to the mountain base.

"It was an honor and pleasure to meet with you," he says as I mount my horse.

I smile down at him. "I feel the same. Hopefully, we will be able to meet again soon in less dire circumstances."

"I will pray to the gods that it will be so."

With a final parting nod, we're on our way. We reach the mountains around dusk, the borrowed soldiers making camp with us. Using ingredients provided by Luc, I make a basic warding spell but we still take shifts, the Ascarians still wary of magic. In the morning, the spare guards leave and we take on the mountain terrain.

The first day of mountain travel goes smoothly. The wind is bitter cold, but our cloaks manage to hold against it. At night, we make camp—Cal and I in one tent, Lorrell and Pascal in another, and Noah in his own. Cal and I slip inside our tent early, leaving Lorrell, Pascal, and Noah talking and playing cards around the fire. As Cal sets out his bedroll his eyes constantly dart to the tent door.

"Cal, would you like to go out there with Noah?"

He shakes his head, swallowing as he concentrates on smoothing out his blanket. "No, I'm fine." He lifts his eyes and forces a smile, though his eyes are still shadowed. "I'd rather be in here with you."

To further prove his point, he stands and gathers me in his arms. He pulls me into a kiss that has an urgency I've never sensed from him before.

"Cal," I mumble against his lips, not quite possessing the will to pull away.

Cal silences me with another kiss, his hands sliding up under my shirt and pulling me closer. For a moment all other thoughts fly away and I lean into him, my owns fingers fumbling for the heat of his skin. When Cal begins drawing me toward the beds, I manage to clear my thoughts and force myself to step back.

"Cal," I manage, my voice hoarse. "What are you avoiding?"

Cal glances away, clenching his jaw. "Nothing."

I take his hands in mine and trace my thumb along his knuckles. He looks up at me and I can see the hurt shining in his eyes. My heart breaks at the sight, and I pull him flush against me in a tight embrace.

"Please, Cal," I whisper in his ear, the fingers of my left hand trailing up and down the back of his neck. "Something is wrong and I don't think I can fix it."

Cal wraps his arms around me and holds me tight. "No, it's something I need to deal with but have been avoiding for a couple years." He pulls back and looks at me. "But I really would rather stay with you tonight."

I press a quick kiss to his lips. "Okay. If you want to talk about it, I'm here."

Cal nods, brushing his lips across mine. "Thank you."

We finish setting up our bedrolls and settle down for the night. We share both blankets, and I curl up against Cal, resting my head on his chest, his arm wrapped around me. His hand traces slow circles on my back, lulling me to sleep. I'm on the verge of drifting off when Cal's low voice fills the darkness.

"Noah spread rumors about me loving men before I was ready to tell anyone."

I blink away my sleep and ease up onto my elbow to look at Cal. "What?"

Cal sighs and squeezes his eyes shut. "Noah talked about me behind my back and someone I did not care for—an enemy of sorts—found out about my . . . secret. That person used the knowledge against me, shouting it for the entire tavern." He opens his eyes and looks directly into mine. "It was one of the worst moments of my life, even if I did enjoy seeing Makin punch the asshole."

Something seizes in my chest. "Makin was there? He stood up for you?"

Cal swallows before nodding slowly. "Yes. It was the day he beat the trials. We were celebrating in The Gilded Goblet."

My jaw tightens as I nod, settling back down against Cal. I should have been there. Maybe I could have made a difference. Maybe I could have punched the asshole. Maybe I could have saved Cal some pain. Maybe . . .

"Noah and I were roommates at the time," Cal continues, "but I didn't like the idea of sharing a room with him anymore after that night. I simply didn't feel like I could trust him anymore. I moved in with Makin. Noah and I have barely spoken since."

"I'm sorry," I mumble.

Cal laughs softly but it's humorless. "It's not your fault, Ehren."

I turn my head and press a kiss to his cheek. "I know, but I'm sorry you suffered. And I'm sorry I wasn't there to help you. I feel like I should've been there for you. Even if I wasn't your lover, for lack of a better word, I was still your prince and your friend."

Cal pulls me closer and leans his head against mine. "You helped me significantly a couple weeks later when Makin and I had our falling out."

Memories tumble through my mind. I know exactly what time Cal is referring to. I remember it distinctly. It left me with questions I never had the courage to ask. Some questions linger still, though many others answered themselves.

"Whatever happened then?" I ask, curiosity getting the better of me.

Cal laughs again and I smile. "I . . . Well, I got very drunk and kissed Makin. It was a very awkward way to find out that he didn't feel the same about me."

"And here I was thinking you two had a lovers' quarrel," I mutter, making Cal burst into more laughter.

"A lovers' quarrel?" He laughs, pulling back and looking down at me. "Really?"

"What was I supposed to think?" I grin up at him. "You confessed to me that you loved men, and then he shows up, clearly apologetic. You two were obviously very close, despite not having known each other all that long. You were always together. It was a logical conclusion."

"Oh, Ehren," Cal whispers, tracing a finger down my cheek. "Makin and I were never together in that way. My heart was always waiting for you, even if I didn't fully realize it."

My own heart leaps in my chest. "And I was always waiting for you."

Cal eases his lips against mine, and I lose myself in the

warmth of his kiss. We shift so we're lying our sides, facing each other. Each kiss is soft and deliberate. When I finally pull back, I stare into his eyes, happy to drown in their depths.

"I love you, Cal," I whisper, tracing my thumb across his swollen lips.

Cal smiles, kissing my thumb before pulling me in for another kiss.

"I love you, too, Ehren," he whispers against my lips.

"I feel like we've been circling each other for years, and I never dreamed we'd finally find our way to each other," I confess, leaning my forehead against his. "When I think of all the years I wasted trying not to love you, running away from my feelings and trying to bury them . . ." I sigh, shaking my head. "We missed out on so much together because I was a coward, because I refused to let myself love you."

Cal presses a quick kiss against my lips. "You had good reason, and it's not like I ever did anything to encourage you. I forced myself to be content with how things were, even though I was far from being truly happy. I buried my true feelings as deeply as I could. I think Makin was the only one who ever really knew how I felt about you, and that was only because there was literally nothing I could keep hidden from him. He was the nosiest, most stubborn man I've ever met."

Cal chuckles softly and I smile, my hand finding his in the dark, our fingers weaving together on instinct.

"We're a pair of star-crossed fools, aren't we?"

Cal laughs. "I suppose we are but, thankfully, we found each other. And I think that perhaps the timing was perfect. That maybe things wouldn't have quite worked out the same if we had gotten together earlier. We had to wait for everything to fall into place."

I sigh, resting my head on Cal's chest as I snuggle closer.

"I think you're right. But when this war is over, I'm making up for lost time. I'm going to take you everywhere. We're going to see the world together. Now that I'm finally with you, I want this to last forever. I'm never going to let my fear get the best of me again. I love you, Cal, now and forever."

Cal looses a long breath and draws me closer. "I'd be a fool to disagree. You're my prince, and I'm the luckiest man alive. I love you and I will stay by your side for as long as you'll allow."

We fall back into silence, slowly drifting off in each other's embrace. Maybe the timing was perfect, but I will always wonder what could have been. At least we do have the rest of our lives to make up for it.

CHAPTER THIRTY-SEVEN

JESSALYNN

King Naimon keeps his word and provides any and all supplies we request. We remain at Koshima for nearly a week, waiting to leave as additional armies pour in from around the kingdom. Even the army with the magical weapons from Heldonia has arrived. With soldiers from every corner standing side-by-side, it's obvious that Gleador is made from what used to be many kingdoms filled with different cultures. We all speak the common tongue, but many different dialects and separate languages float around and the air is filled with the aroma of dozens of different delicacies representative of their corners.

Despite some of the differences in appearance, dialects, religions, and traditions, the armies seem to have no problems blending under one flag. There is no animosity. King Naimon has done well keeping his kingdom united, and I find myself developing a deep respect for him.

As the head of the Valley, I sit at a place of honor in the

grand dining hall, Cadewynn by my side. Kaeya, Brock, Nyco, and Sama are seated at a separate table nearby, which is also a show of respect. I'm midway through dinner one night when a sharp pain stabs at my temple. I gasp and clutch the stem of my wineglass tighter.

Cadewynn glances at me, leaning in to whisper, "Are you okay?"

I nod, lifting the wine to my lips, but the alcohol does little to subdue the pain. My hand shakes as I set the glass down, pushing away from the table.

"I just need a bit of fresh air," I mumble, standing to my feet.

Cadewynn nods, but her eyebrows are still knitted in concern. Brock, whose eyes have been trained on me since dinner started, immediately notices me walking away and makes to follow me, but I hold up a hand. He scowls but nods once, remaining in his seat.

I quickly make my way outside to a small, pebbled path trimmed in bushes. I follow the path to a garden and sink down onto a stone bench, the pain in my head easing with each breath.

"I'm sorry to disturb you," a voice says, making me jump as my eyes dart up sharply. An older woman with graying hair stands a few feet away.

"Who are you?" I snap, leaping to my feet, my head swimming with the sudden movement. I groan and press a finger to my temple.

"Ah," the woman says, waving her hand, the pain suddenly vanishing. "I do apologize for that as well."

I blink at her. Slowly, her actions register and my hand floats to the dagger strapped to my leg.

"I will ask again, who are you?" I grind out.

The woman smiles gently, seemingly unbothered. "My name is Ama. I am a Seer and I have a message for you."

I eye her skeptically. "A Seer?"

She nods. "Yes. You need to leave for Callenia or you'll be late. You may already be late. You're cutting it very close."

A snort escapes as I shake my head in disbelief, crossing my arms. "You came to warn me that war is brewing? I don't even need to be a Seer to know that."

The woman frowns. "It is more than that. The war has yet to truly begin, and it will be over before it even starts if you do not make it to Callenia—to your brother's side—in time. You must leave immediately or all is lost."

She speaks with such fervor I can feel it down to my bones, but I remain skeptical. "What will happen? What can I change?"

"I do not know. All I know is that you must go."

I scoff and start to take a step back, but the woman reaches out and grabs my forearm. I clench my teeth and try to jerk my arm from her grasp, but her hold is surprisingly strong.

"Let me go."

"Not until you listen."

I yank my arm again and am successful this time. I take a wide step back to put space between us.

"Look, Jessalynn," she says, her voice hard, "I know you have little reason to believe me, a simple old woman who has been a Seer for only a handful of months, but you should heed my warning. No, I do not know the details, but something dark is brewing—darker than you yet know. Your brother may very well die without you, and if he dies, hope dies. You must make it to Callenia in time. As I said already, it may be too late. The vision is hazy; it keeps changing. The future is not yet decided. You may be too late to stop what is to happen, but if you can arrive in time, there is a chance we can win this war."

I swallow and take a deep breath, releasing it slowly as I consider her words. Finally, after a moment, I nod once. "Very well." The woman visibly relaxes. "Mind you, I have no reason to trust you, but I already had plans to leave soon. We'll just leave a touch earlier.

The woman nods. "Thank you."

"Now if you'll excuse me," I reply, bushing past her, "I have things to do."

I make my way back inside, leaving the woman alone in the dark. When I reach the dining hall, the air has noticeably shifted. At the front of the hall stands a beautiful woman on the arm of a handsome man. They're both dressed in the finest clothes and the king seems delighted by their presence. I approach Kaeya and Brock.

"Who is that?" I ask, nodding toward the newcomers.

Kaeya glances up at me over her shoulder. "Princess Elaine."

My curiosity is piqued. I know little about the princess other than at one point she was set to be potentially betrothed to my brother and that she ended up marrying the prince of another kingdom. We met once when we were children and I still lived in the Callenian palace. She was younger than me and concerned more with keeping her dress clean than in building a friendship.

Princess Elaine takes her father's hand and he leads her around the table to where a place has been prepared for her and her husband. Not wishing to draw attention to myself, I squeeze in between Kaeya and Brock to finish my meal, but my eyes stay focused on Elaine. I nearly jump out of my skin when her eyes meet mine. She smiles and lifts her glass. I find myself returning the motion. Curious.

~

"First thing in the morning?" Kaeya clarifies. "Based on the word of a random Seer?"

I nod, glancing down the corridor to make sure no one is listening in.

"The Seer who apparently cast a spell on you to get you alone?" Brock presses, crossing his arms. "The one you didn't deign to mention until after dinner?"

"Yes, Brock." I sigh. "Look, I was weighing the options, and quite frankly Princess Elaine's arrival was a bit of a distraction. I know it's unusual to follow the word of a random Seer, but we were planning on leaving soon anyway. It won't hurt to err on the side of caution."

Brock shakes his head. "I don't like it, Jess. It could be a trap."

"And it could make the difference in winning this damn war. I'd rather take the risk."

Brock locks eyes with me but finally backs away, raising his hands in surrender. "Fine. You and Kaeya take our army and select few straight out in the morning, and I'll follow behind, guiding the rest of the armies."

"That sounds good."

"I'll spread the word. Perhaps I'll be able to keep our army from drinking themselves into a headache," Kaeya mumbles, glancing over her shoulder back toward the dining hall where many soldiers linger, drinking mead and wine and gods know what else.

"Not a bad idea." I turn to Brock. "And you'll—"

"Prepare everyone else? Yeah," he finishes for me, a smile playing on his lips.

I grin. He knows me too well. We split up, Kaeya and Brock going to their armies while I go back to the dining hall to talk to Princess Cadewynn. When I arrive, I find that she's already vacated the room. I sigh and step off to the side, leaning against the wall while I debate going off to find her.

"Jessalynn?"

I turn toward the gentle voice. Princess Elaine stands a few feet away, a cautious smile on her lips. Despite the fact she likely traveled all day, she's stunning and very put together. Her lips are a bright red, matching the red silk of her dress almost perfectly. Her ebony braid is woven with rubies and golden strands. Her fingers glitter with rings, bracelets adorn her wrists, and a delicate gold loop decorates her nose. She looks every part the regal princess.

"Your Majesty," I say, pushing away from the wall and inclining my head.

She smiles softly. "Thank you for your respect, but I feel that given our circumstances it might be easier to drop such formalities."

I cock my head, fighting back a frown. "What circumstances?" My eyes widen as her implication sinks in. "Surely you aren't joining us on the battlefield."

Her laugh is light. "Not quite. My husband, however, will be. He is the general of Oyrain's troops and he will lead them."

"And you'll be coming along?"

"Indeed. My husband wishes to keep me close." Her hands drift to her midsection almost subconsciously and settle there. My eyes dart from her hand to her face.

"You're . . . pregnant."

She smiles and nods. "Only barely, but yes."

I shake my head. "The battlefield is a dangerous place for anyone, but even more so for an expecting mother, even if you're only on the sidelines."

"I can assure you I will be well protected."

"Still."

Princess Elaine sighs and looks off to the side. "We were already on our way to Gleador when I confirmed I was with child. My husband suggested I return home, but when I insisted on remaining with him, he conceded."

"Why?"

She shifts her eyes back to me, tilting her head curiously. "Why?"

I swallow, trying to find a way to formulate my concerns. "Why did he not insist you go back?"

Elaine purses her lips as she considers me. "We did not bring a full army. King Marvello is not keen to enter the war fully, but once word reached us that Gleador was joining the war efforts there was no question that he would send some aid. Even then, he still was hesitant to send too many soldiers and leave his kingdom undefended. He has much to protect in his own kingdom."

"Surely there were still extra soldiers that could be spared to escort you back to safety."

She shrugs. "Perhaps, but I didn't want to deplete recourses from my husband. Besides, I have certain skills that may save lives."

I cock an eyebrow as she steps closer. She holds out her hand and closes her eyes. After a moment a soft hum of magic fills the air as her hand glows with a soft, warm yellow light.

"You're a Healer," I whisper in awe.

She smiles, dropping her hand as she opens her eyes. "A quite powerful Healer."

I take a deep breath and release it slowly. "You can save many lives indeed, but is it worth putting you and your unborn child at risk?"

A certain sadness shadows her eyes. "It is a difficult decision but I will take every precaution possible. Should my husband fall in battle and die because I was not there to heal him . . ." She trails off, shaking her head.

"You must love him dearly."

She meets my eyes with a certain fierceness. "I love him very much. It is not always so with marriages arranged in the way ours was, but I am very fortunate to have been matched to a good man." She pauses before adding, "He supports my decision to join the war. Will you?"

I nod. "Well, if you are willing there is nothing more for me to say, even if your husband wished for you to stay behind. The choice is yours alone to make, and it seems as if you are settled in your decision. I respect that."

"Still, to know that I have your support would mean something. You are strong, Jessalynn, and I rather admire you."

My eyes widen in surprise. "Why?"

The corner of her mouth turns up into a smile. "Not many can go through the fire like you have and come out so strong. You have a reputation, you know. You've risen from the ashes a way many envy. People in Gleador and beyond know of you and respect you. You would make a grand queen."

I stumble back a step, shaking my head. "I am no queen. For one, I have no kingdom."

"You have Callenia."

"My brother has Callenia."

"You are the firstborn."

I scoff, a laugh sneaking out. "The bastard, discarded firstborn."

"For some that will not matter."

I shake my head more firmly, setting my jaw. "Even then I will not steal my brother's kingdom. He was made to be king." As I speak I realize I truly believe my words.

Elaine notes my conviction and nods once. "You are loyal, Jessalynn. That is good. But there is a chance that your brother may not make it out alive, gods forbid. You may need to prepare yourself to take the crown should he fall. From what I've seen and heard, your sister is not prepared to take the crown herself. The responsibility may very well fall to you."

Her words are a punch to my gut and new, fresh fear twists in my gut. Now more than ever I feel the drive to heed the Seer's words. I *must* make it to Callenia in time. We *have* to win this war.

"Let us pray to the gods that doesn't happen," I manage, my voice quiet. "Now, if you'll excuse me, I do need to find my sis—Princess Cadewynn and let her know our departure plans."

Princess Elaine inclines her head. "Of course."

I start to step away, but she calls after me. I pause and look at her over my shoulder.

"If you would please keep my secret, I would appreciate it." She rubs her hand in a gentle circle over her stomach. "Not many know, my father included."

I manage a quick nod before I sweep away. I suddenly feel like the weight of responsibility may crush me at any moment. I'm not sure I'm strong enough for this, but I suppose I have to be. I've survived before and I'll find a way to survive again. If I don't—

No. There is no option for failure. I will come out of this. I have to.

CHAPTER THIRTY-EIGHT
EHREN

When morning comes, Cal pulls Noah to the side while the rest of us pack up the camp and ready the horses. I can't hear what they say, but when Cal joins me, he's smiling and seems lighter.

The day starts relatively clear but turns miserable within the first hour. If it's not raining, it's snowing. My eyelashes are frozen, my hands completely numb, and I can't stop shivering. Cal frequently asks if I'm okay, and I shrug his concerns off with a smile. He's riding side-by-side with Noah, chatting, and I don't want to get in their way.

On the second day, Cal insists on riding Dauntless with me, keeping me wrapped in his arms and cloak. The weather is still dreadful, but I care a little less, eager to lean into Cal's comforting warmth. We stop not long after nightfall, making camp. I set up wards so no one has to take a shift in the rain.

I wake midway through the night after a nightmare I can't quite remember. My heart is racing and I can't quite settle back down. Afraid I'll move around too much and wake Cal, I decide to dream walk and check on Astra. I quietly prepare the spell and slip into the dream world.

I'm immediately transported to a quiet forest glade. Astra sits in the center of a ring of flowers. As I approach, she looks up at me and smiles.

"Dream walking again?"

I nod, sitting cross-legged in front of her. "I figured it wouldn't hurt to check in. We're on our way back to the Summer Palace. If everything goes as planned, we should be there in the next few days."

Astra nods and plucks a flower, twirling it absentmindedly in her fingers.

"Not much to report on my end, except . . ." She pauses, looking up from the flower to meet my eyes, her face suddenly somber. "I found a way to contact the dead."

My heart stills. "You did? Were you able to glean any useful information?"

She glances off to the side, nodding. "I did. At least, I found the direction I need to go. I know what to do, now I just need to do it. It will require a trip to Athiedor. I'll wait until you return, however, before I leave."

There's something heavy in the way she refuses to meet my eyes.

"Ash, what aren't you saying?"

She lifts her gaze back to mine and I can almost feel her sorrow.

"Ash?"

"I spoke with Makin."

Her words fall like heavy iron.

"What?"

She nods, glancing away again. "I tried contacting other spirits, but Makin is the one who answered. He was able to find the information I needed." She looks back at me and smiles, though it's sadder than any smile has the right to be. "He told me to tell you that he doesn't blame you for his death."

My breath catches in my throat as tears sting my eyes. "Really?"

She nods. "Yes, and he said he would make the same choices again if he were given the chance. He also said he's happy for you and Cal."

I make a sound that sounds more like a sob than anything else.

"He knows?" I ask, my voice trembling.

"Yes," she replies, her smile growing. "And he more than approves."

I close my eyes and take a deep breath, holding it for a moment. He was Cal's closest and dearest friend. Merely knowing I have his approval means something. When I open my eyes, Astra is watching me with shining eyes.

"You're really happy with Cal, aren't you?"

"I really am, Ash. I don't think I deserve him at all, but I'm happy to have him."

Astra laughs and shakes her head. "Ehren, you deserve the world. I only wish you could see that."

The dream world flickers and I glance around. "I don't have much longer."

"Well, I suppose I'll see you in person in a few days."

I smile, but it's weak and likely doesn't reach my eyes. "I suppose."

The dreamworld flickers again and I'm back in a cold tent. I take a deep breath and snuggle closer to Cal, wrapping my arms around him. He shifts slightly, not waking, but moves closer to me on instinct. I smile and bury my face in the warmth of his neck. Slowly, I drift back to sleep.

The next morning we start out among a slight drizzle of ice-cold rain, but it thankfully lets up around noon. The air bites despite the clear blue sky and shining sun. The sunshine does help to brighten our moods, as well as the fact that we're heading downhill and should be leaving the mountains in the next day or so.

We're riding along the twisting downward path when a shadow passes overhead. At first, I don't think much of it, until the shadow passes over again and I realize that something feels very off. When I raise my eyes to the sky, my heart stills. Circling above us is a large, winged creature, mostly beast but even from this distance parts of it are strikingly human. A Dragkonian. I gasp and pull my sword from its sheath. Cal and Pascal are already doing the same, Noah and Lorrell immediately following our lead.

The creature dives, talons outstretched. I dodge the creature, tumbling from my horse just in time to avoid being caught, though it manages to snag my shoulder enough to tear my shirt but not my skin. Cal leaps from his horse, rushing to my side while the others dismount to take an offensive stance as the Dragkonian rears back into the sky to prepare another attack.

"Are you okay?" Cal asks, offering me his hand.

I nod, letting him help me up, but I don't have time to reply before the Dragkonian swoops in again, this time breathing black fire as he dives toward Lorrell, Pascal, and Noah. They press against the side of the mountain wall in an effort to avoid the blast. The fire misses them but the intense heat stings my eyes and prickles unpleasantly across my skin. The creature twists and dives toward me. Cal shoves me out of the way, blocking my body with his as he strikes the creature with his sword. His blade, of course, does nothing against the scaled armor of the beast.

Noah lunges from behind, striking with his sword and drawing the creature's attention. The Dragkonian rears around, swiping Noah's chest with its talon. Noah staggers back as Lorrell charges forward to block a second attack. The beast roars and sweeps into the sky, diving back down, spewing fire, altogether unaffected by the blows it has received.

"There!" Noah gasps, pointing a little ways down the path we're following to a wide crack in the mountain surface. He doesn't even need to say anything more. We know what he means. The small crevice is large enough for us, but small enough that the Dragkonian can't get at us, even with his fire. I meet Noah's eyes and nod.

"Go," I mouth, stepping into the center of the path, drawing the Dragkonian's attention.

Pascal, Lorrell, and Noah slide quickly along the mountainside toward safety, but Cal remains by my side as the Dragkonian attacks again. His talons stretch toward Cal and I spin between them, thrusting my sword forward. I knock the beast back, but don't do any damage to it. It, in return, catches my forehead with the tip of its talon, blood seeping from the wound into my eye.

"Cal, go," I say firmly, readying my sword as the Dragkonian arches back into the sky for another attack.

"Ehren, I'm not—"

"Go!" I yell, not taking my eyes off the circling beast. "That's an order!"

"Ehren—"

"Go!" I yell again, pushing Cal back with my right hand

as I ready my sword in my left. "Please, I need you out of danger. Go."

Cal hesitates but eventually runs off after the others as I ready for another attack. The time, I know my target. As the creature swoops down, I twirl away, thrusting my sword upward into its wing. It's thick and doesn't tear easily, but I'm determined. The creature rears back with a shriek and lunges again. I strike the wing in the same spot, tearing it through this time, black blood oozing from the wound. The Dragkonian makes a sound close enough to speech I'm positive he's swearing in some long-forgotten tongue. It staggers midair, struggling to rise. Its screech echoes over the mountain as it hovers above, debating its next move. In the end, it flies off to recover.

I turn, my gaze falling to where the horses retreated a little way down the path. My legs are shaking as I stumble to Dauntless and dig through my bag as the others leave their den of safety.

"That creature may come back," I say, pulling a spell book and assortment of ingredients from my bag as the others approach. "And he may bring friends. We need a spell to cover us."

I wipe blood from my eye with the back of my hand before flipping through the book, my hands trembling. I can feel Cal's eyes on me and I know he's not happy with my actions, but I don't have time to focus on that right now. Lorrell helps Noah bandage the scrape on his chest as I search. Thankfully, the wound on my head is shallow and already seems to be clotting, although it hurts like hell.

I find a spell that will keep us hidden, but I'm short the ingredients I need. Luckily, a few pages over, I find a spell that can be linked to objects that will make us undetectable. I quickly begin mixing the potion.

"I need a small item from each of you," I say as I mix. "I'll cover it in the potion, and as long as you're wearing it, we'll be invisible from further attackers." I raise my eyes and look up at the others standing over me. "Jewelry works the best since it will touch your skin and make the spell stronger."

Lorrell nods and pulls a leather strap from his neck, a metal emblem dangling from the end. Pascal has a matching one. They hand me their necklaces and I dip the charms in the potion, mumbling the sealing spell before passing them back. Noah offers me a cuff he wears on his left hand and I repeat the process. When I look up at Cal, he glances away.

"I don't have anything," he mutters.

I hesitate only a moment before I pull off my signet ring, placing it in the potion. "You can use my ring."

When I hand it up to him, he shakes his head. "I can't take that. You need it."

I offer him a weak smile. "Of course you can take it. I have other rings I can use."

Cal shakes his head again and I sigh. I slip a plain ring off another finger and dip in the potion. Cal extends his hand for the second ring, but I slip it back on my finger. I stand and meet Cal's eyes as I slide my signet ring onto his left ring finger.

"Please," I say quietly. "I would be honored if you would wear this one."

Cal swallows, clenching his hand into a fist as he looks away. "Fine."

Not willing to waste any more time, we quickly mount our horses and continue on our way. Despite the spell masking us from predators, we're all on high alert. I can tell Cal is still fuming quietly, but he doesn't say anything. When we stop for the night, I set up extra wards as we take guard shifts. Noah, Pascal, and Lorrell take the first shift and Cal and I agree to the second.

"Cal, what is it?" I ask once Cal and I slip inside our tent for the night. "I know you're mad at me."

"You put yourself at risk," Cal says, his voice cold. "You commanded me away from your side and—"

"I did what I had to do," I say, meeting and holding his gaze. "You were in danger, Cal. I wasn't going to let you—"

"You ordered me away!" he yells, his voice wrought with emotion. "I could have lost you. I—" His voice breaks off into a soft sob. "I can't lose you, Ehren."

"And you think I could live with losing you?"

"Ehren, you are the prince. Technically, you're the rightful king. It is my duty to protect you. I can't do that if I'm ordered away."

I shake my head, taking a step toward him. "Cal, things between us will never be as simple as a prince and his Guard. You are my world, and I will always do everything within my power to protect you."

Cal takes a shaky breath, his lips parting as if he wants to object, but nothing comes out. I take this as encouragement and close the distance between us.

"I felt more panic in that moment the beast lunged for you than I have ever felt before. A life without you is no life at all. The mere idea of losing you—"

My voice breaks and Cal gathers me in his arms, his lips crashing against mine. I kiss him hungrily, not even bothering to breathe. Finally, I pull back with a gasp, a wry grin curling on my lips.

"It seems you felt the same?"

Cal laughs, shaking his head as his hand cradles my neck. "If anything happened to you, I don't know that I could continue on. Please, never send me away again. If you have a death wish, at least let me die by your side trying to save you."

I sigh and press my forehead to his. "Well, then I suppose we'll have to always fight side-by-side as full equals. You and I, Cal, will fight as one, always having each other's backs. But more than that, you and I will be one heart and one soul. I love you, Cal. I never want to be parted from you in life or death."

Cal shifts, his lips finding mine. "Forever by your side. I like that," Cal mumbles, glancing down at my ring on his finger.

I follow his gaze and let my fingers trace around the ring.

"I wanted you to wear this ring not only so a piece of what is mine could protect you, but because this exact ring portrays my full devotion to you. I swear myself to you completely and I want the world to know that. When they see this ring on your finger, they will know that you are mine and I am yours. It is an open symbol that can leave no room for doubt in anyone's mind."

I pull back to look into his eyes and I'm nearly over-whelmed by the love I see there.

"What exactly are you saying?" he asks breathlessly.

"Cal, I know this world is mess and we're at war with the deadliest race ever known, but when it's all over, when it's done, will you marry me? Become the official prince consort?"

A soft sound escapes his lips that falls somewhere

between a sob and a laugh. "Of course I will. I would love nothing more. As long as you think I'm worthy—"

"There's no one more worthy or deserving," I whisper, pressing my mouth to his in a fierce kiss.

"You know," he says, his voice low. "This feels like something that should be sealed by a very specific activity."

"Hmm. Well, if the future prince consort thinks it's best, who am I to disagree?"

Cal leans in and kisses me with a fire I've never felt before. It quickly escalates into much more than a kiss. We don't get much sleep before our shift, but I have no regrets.

The next morning we're back on the road at dawn. A little before noon we leave the mountains, pushing forward at a fast pace. We can't get home quickly enough. We stop for the night, but I can hear home calling for me. I'm restless despite the fact Cal keeps me wrapped in his arms. I can't shake the feeling that something is off. I try to dream walk, but I can't reach Astra. She's either awake or she doesn't have the feather with her. I can't get back to sleep after the attempted contact, tossing and turning nonstop.

The next morning we're on the road even earlier, the first hints of morning light not even gracing the sky. We don't stop once, not even for lunch, eager to press onward. When night falls, we decide to continue riding. We're so close to home and I can't stop now. It's nearly midnight when we approach the wards. I fight the confusion that the wards send out meant to keep others from discovering the palace, keeping my mind focused so I can pass through. The others struggle as well, but they follow me without much difficultly.

"Who goes there?" a voice demands, a figure stepping out from the darkness with his sword drawn.

The moonlight washes over the figure and I recognize

him as Collin, a member of my Guard. As he recognizes me, his sword lowers. "Your Majesty?"

I offer Collin a tired smile. "Yes. I know it's late, but we're back."

Collin nods. "I'll escort you to the gates."

I thank him as we continue on our way. At the gate I turn back to Collin as I dismount.

"Can you make sure all our horses are taken to the stable and cared for? They had a long day."

Collin nods. "Of course."

"Also, can you make sure Astra knows we're back? I don't wish to wake her, but I don't know what time I'll be up in the morning."

Collin stays silent, frowning as he glances away.

"What is it?" I ask, afraid of his answer.

"The Court Sorceress isn't here."

My heart rate increases as panic swells through me. My chest feels tight and I struggle to breathe.

"What do you mean?" I manage, my voice a whisper against the night.

Cal steps forward and takes my hand in his as Collin lifts his eyes to mine.

"I don't know the details. All I know is that she had to leave suddenly a couple of days ago to aid Captain Bramfield."

I squeeze Cal's hand to keep from shaking. "Was there an attack?"

The guard shrugs. "I think there might have been, but I don't know anything beyond the rumors. Lord McDullun is still present, and I'm sure he can fill you in when morning comes."

I swallow and nod, trying to keep a mask of confidence. "Thank you."

Collin gives a final nod before leading our horses away. I barely register anything as we walk to our rooms. I'm floating in a haze of worry. Cal follows me into my room and gathers me into his arms the second the door closes behind us.

"I'm sure she's fine," he whispers, holding me close.

I wrap my arms around him and rest my head on his shoulder.

"But what if she's not. What if—" My voice breaks off with a shudder. "Cal, I can't lose anyone else."

"I know," he replies, pressing a kiss to my temple. "Astra is capable and powerful. She can take care of herself, and I'm sure this time is no exception. Stressing and worrying won't change anything. Let's get some rest and then in the morning we can get our answers. All right?"

I nod, drawing back to look into his eyes. "All right." I pause, glancing to my bed then back to Cal. "You'll stay here with me?"

He brushes his lips briefly against mine. "Of course. You couldn't keep me out."

Neither of us bother undressing before we climb beneath the covers. Despite my worries, I manage to find sleep in the comfort and warmth of Cal's embrace.

CHAPTER THIRTY-NINE

ASTRA

"S o, you think the answer to contacting the Fae has been in a book of children's stories the entire time?" Ronan asks, arching an eyebrow as he stirs honey into his tea.

"I know it probably sounds crazy," I admit. "A lot of children's stories, along with other myths and legends, were often told to share and preserve important information in less obvious ways. The Fae are very guarded, so it would make sense that they wouldn't want summoning rituals widely known. But the information would still need to be recorded in some way. Faerie stories would be a good way to hide the information in plain sight."

Ronan nods thoughtfully as he takes a sip of his tea. "It makes sense, but how will we be able to decipher what parts of the story are real and what parts are fictional embellishments?"

I sigh and stare into the fire flickering in the library fireplace. "I'm not sure. I think we need to read into every detail of every story and compare it to known interactions with the Fae."

"Ah." Ronan grins. "So, lots more work. Who knew one day the Faerie stories I loved for pure enjoyment would become a tedious task to save a kingdom?"

I chuckle, shaking my head. "If you'd rather not destroy the Faerie stories you love by tearing them into pieces looking for hidden clues, I can do it on my own."

"Ha! As if I would allow you to do something so fascinating without me, love. Besides, I know these stories inside and out, including other versions that may not be included the book I brought. Without my immense knowledge of Faerie stories, you'll never succeed."

I laugh. "Is that so?"

"Oh, that's so." Ronan grins. "When should we start?"

"I want to start right away, but honestly I think I need a little time to recover from talking with Makin. Not that it really drained my magic. I just . . ." I break off with a sigh, staring back into the fire.

"I understand," Ronan says with a nod. "I can only imagine how emotionally draining that would be. We can start tomorrow. In the meantime, I'll make a list of the stories that hold the most promise and maybe even try to track down a few additional books with different versions of the stories."

I meet Ronan's eyes and offer him a weak smile. "Thank you."

Ronan shrugs. "No problem. Honestly, I'm happy to help however I can."

"You've been a huge help lately in more ways than you know. I think having you around has helped keep me sane."

Ronan tilts his head. "Well, that's the first time my presence has had such a positive effect."

I shake my head, smiling. "I have hard time believing that." I glance at the clock in the corner of the library. "We should probably go reinforce the wards."

Ronan nods, setting his teacup down. "As you wish."

It doesn't take us long to secure the wards. Once back inside, we enjoy a round of tea and biscuits before I head to bed. I go into the quiet of my own room as Ronan works through the stacks of available books in the hopes of finding more Faerie stories.

By morning, Ronan has a comprehensive list of places to start so we dive right in. Put into historical context, some of the stories are suddenly much more serious than they first appeared. We switch between the Faerie stories and the historical records, managing to connect three of the stories to direct accounts with a couple more likely matches. A little after noon, more books arrive, including another book of various Faerie stories.

"Here," Ronan says, sliding a book toward me. "Could this be referring to a Faerie ring?"

I glance down at the page and find a simple poem.

> One, Two, Three, and Four,
> Faerie wishes settle the score.
> Five, Six, Seven, Eight,
> Meet me at the Faerie Gate.
> Nine, Ten, Eleven, Twelve,
> Whisper soft the Faerie spell,
> Thirteen, Fourteen, and Fifteen, too,
> Gather amongst the flowers blue,
> Sixteen and Seventeen hand in hand,
> Stand together on Faerie land,
> Eighteen and Nineteen seal the deal,

By the river known to heal.
And when Twenty comes around,
The Faerie secrets shall be bound.

I lift my eyes from the page to look at Ronan. "Do you know of a river that heals? I know there was a river in Brackenborough that had magical properties. Could that be it?"

Ronan frowns. "Many rivers on magical land are supposed to have magical properties but there are rumors and other Faerie stories about a specific river that had healing waters that could cure almost anything."

"Do you know where it might be?"

Ronan shakes his head, but he pulls his green Faerie stories book from the stack in front of him.

"There's a specific story that I loved as child about a young prince that was cursed by an evil Faerie," Ronan mumbles as he flips through the pages. "His parents broke a Faerie deal and the curse was the price of their betrayal. The curse made the prince sickly and marriage nearly impossible. There was no way to undo curse itself, but they were able to find healing waters that cured the sickness. Ah! Here it is."

Ronan turns the book so I can see. On the page is a sketch of a young boy with a tilted crown on his head. Next to him a young girl with ageless beauty is offering him something to drink from a cup made of leaves.

"And you think the water in that story is from this healing river?"

"It's possible," Ronan says with a shrug. "Growing up, my father used the story as a reminder for me to keep my promises, insisting that the story was true. He claimed it was based on a young prince of early Athiedor."

"Okay," I muse. "So if we can figure out who the prince

was, perhaps we can figure out where the river is. But the river is likely to be miles long. How do we find the exact location of the Faerie ring?"

Ronan shakes his head with a sigh. "I'm not sure. Maybe it's just a story after all to scare little boys. Though, I think the prince's name was Aidan or Adrian or something similar. I can look over the historical texts and see if I can find any reference to a prince with that name."

I sigh and look back down at the book. "I suppose it's better than nothing."

The hours tick by, yielding few results. I do find the story repeated in collections of other Faerie stories, with slightly different details. I'm able to confirm that the water used to heal the prince did indeed come from a river with magical properties, but there's no additional information about its location. I'm halfway through a journal of one of the Lords of Athiedor when a thought strikes me.

"I'll be right back," I say, pushing my chair back as I stand quickly.

"Find something?" Ronan asks arching an eyebrow.

"No, but I think there's somewhere else we can look. Someone unlikely who might be able to help." Ronan scowls in confusion and I laugh. "Just trust me. I'll be back in a minute."

"All right, love. Good luck," Ronan says, turning back to his book.

I hurry from the library, heading toward the healing quarters. When I enter, I find Healer Heora and Hanna mixing ointments while Pip sits on a nearby stool looking as bored as ever.

"Astra, dear. How may I help you? More sleeping tonic?" Healer Heora asks with soft smile.

"No, thank you. I still have enough for a couple more nights. I actually have a question for Hanna."

Hanna raises her eyes to me in surprise. "Me?"

I smile, nodding. "Yes. Do you remember when I was resting those days following the first time you helped your grandmother heal me and I read that book about healing plants?"

Hanna nods, her eyes bright. "Yes. You said your favorite of the plants was the White Eiyles."

"You have an excellent memory." Hanna grins as I continue. "I was wondering, do you happen to know things about other plants, ones that may not necessarily be magical but may grow in magical areas?"

Hanna furrows her brow in thought. "Maybe. What kind of plant are you looking for?"

"A blue flower. Possibly one that grows near a magical healing river."

Hanna chews on her lip for a moment as she thinks. "I don't know. Maybe—" She breaks off, her eyes going wide. "Wait! I think I know one! There's a flower that is supposed to only grow on magical ground that blooms all year long. Its petals have all sorts of magical properties."

I grin, hope blooming in my chest. "That sounds exactly like the flower I'm looking for. Do you know where it blooms?"

Hanna shakes her head as she hops down from her stool. "Not off the top of my head but it might say in the book."

She walks over to a stack of books in the corner and digs out a small, worn book with a burgundy cover. She turns the yellowed pages carefully until she comes to a page with a watercolor blue flower.

"This is it," she says, holding the book out to me. "The *Flos Nympharum*."

I gingerly accept the book and glance over the description.

Flos Nympharum

Blue Bud

Blooms Year-round on Magical Ground

Often forms Faerie rings

Common Healing Properties:

stem- pastes for healing open wounds

leaves- powders for pain control and numbing

bud- calming and healing teas

Commonly found in the Lachlin Province of Athiedor

I look up from the page, my face glowing.

"Did you find what you needed?" Hanna asks eagerly.

I nod, grinning at the girl. "I think so. Do you mind if I borrow this book for a bit?"

Hanna shakes her head, but glances briefly at Healer Heora. "We don't need it, do we Grandmother?"

Healer Heora smiles softly. "No. Take it."

I thank them before rushing back to the library. I practically run into the room and Ronan laughs at me as I nearly trip in my haste.

"I take it you found something of interest?" He grins.

"Look at this," I declare, placing the book in front of him.

His eyes scan the page, growing wider as he reads. When he's done he looks up at me, eyes sparkling.

"The blue flowers from the poem, they're these *Flos Nympharum?*"

I nod. "I think so. If we can find the river, then we just

have to find these flowers. Then, we have our Faerie ring and can contact the Fae." I pause, my smile fading. "Only, I'm not sure where the Lachlin Province is. Do you?"

Ronan shakes his head, looking back down at the book. "Not exactly, but I do know that the Clans are more or less divided according to how the provinces of Old Athiedor were assigned. I'm sure some of these old records will have the old province names. We simply need to find and match them to modern maps."

My smile returns as I resume my seat. "Well, at least now we have an exact focus that makes sense."

"True," Ronan says with a nod. "Good job, Astra. I must say, I'm glad I'm on your side."

I grin at him. "I'm glad you're on my side, too."

We start our search for every map we can find, but most either have no provinces or Clans labeled or they're only divided by Clans. By the time dinner time arrives, we're ready for a break. We agree to resume our search in the morning, opting to relax and let our brains refresh. However, as soon as the morning sun shines through our window, we're back in the library, searching the maps over tea and scones. We're about to take a break for lunch when we finally discover a map folded in the back of a record book.

"The lines are a bit faded," Ronan says, spreading the map out carefully, "but you can just make out the words. See," he says pointing to the top right corner. "This says the Gochland Province. That's my land." He scowls, tilting his head. "Though the borders aren't exactly the same, they're close."

I nod, licking my lips. "Okay, so where's the Lachlin Province?"

Ronan squints down at the map. After a moment he pauses, leaning in closer.

"It's hard to read," he mumbles, tapping his finger on a blurred word at the bottom left, "but I think it's here."

He slides the map to me and I squint down at the word. Sure enough, the smudged letters spell out "Lachlin Province" in curled script. I grin up at Ronan.

"So which Clan's land is this now?"

Ronan studies the map a moment before reaching for another text. "If I recall correctly it's a little of two Clans. Look here," he says, opening the text to a map and setting it above the older map for comparison. "It's a little Clan Dughlas and a little Clan Bashmore. Mostly the former."

"Okay, and where's the river?" I ask, tilting my head.

"Here's the most likely option," Ronan says, tapping the river. "Unfortunately it's rather long."

"So how do we narrow it down? It would take too long to search the full length."

"I suppose we could reach out to Lord Dughlas and Lord Bashmore and ask point blank if they know."

I nod but I don't really feel hopeful. "Alak is able to detect magic. If we can at least narrow it down to a few specific areas, Alak can probably find the exact location. We just have to wait until he gets back, which should be any day now."

"All right," Ronan muses, leaning back in his seat. "As the official representative for Athiedor, I shall reach out to my fellow Clan leaders requesting their assistance. Hopefully, we'll have an answer soon and we can find this Faerie ring and contact the Fae."

"What do we do while we wait?"

Ronan grins and somehow I know his answer before he speaks. "Drink tea and mead, of course. What else, love?"

Ronan prepares letters and sends them within the hour, but after that it's another waiting game. We have no idea exactly how helpful or forthcoming the Clan leaders may be, given the secretive nature of Faerie rings. We don't have much choice, however, so we simply hope for the best.

Without anything specific to research, I feel a little lost. The morning after our discovery, I write a quick letter to Alak, apprising him of my progress and checking in on him. He responds a couple hours later with a quick letter of his own.

My Most Beloved Astra,

I knew the salvation of the world had to lie in Athiedor. It only makes sense. When I return, I will happily assist you in finding the flowers you need. If everything goes as planned, Bram says we should be to the fortress within four or five days at the most, despite starting out a day later than expected. The fortress itself is slightly southwest of the Summer Palace but less than a day's travel. We'll be together again soon.

Gods. How wonderful that sounds. I can't wait to hold you in my arms again. I long to kiss you. I miss you so much, Astra. Once we're together, that's it. I'm never leaving your side again.

Yours Until the Stars Fade,
Alak

Hearing from Alak helps a little, but in some ways it makes me miss him more. My heart aches with longing. I spend a lot of time in the kitchen, chatting with Cook and helping to prepare meals. Ronan whisks me away to the village for a couple short adventures, but neither of us want to be away from the palace for long in case word reaches us from any of our sources. A couple nights after Alak's letter, Ehren visits me in a dream. I wake knowing that he will also be home in a few days. Now, I just need some sort of word from Kai.

It's odd to think a year ago, I didn't know the majority of the people who matter the most in my life now, but yet, life without them seems so impossible. And the person who was closest to me is now my enemy.

The morning after the dream, I wake ready to face the day. Knowing Alak and Ehren will be home soon gives me renewed strength. Ronan and I spend a good portion of the morning in Oxwatch. That afternoon, I'm having tea with Ronan in one of the gardens despite the chill of the day when I suddenly feel very uneasy. I gasp as the feeling overwhelms me.

"What's wrong?" Ronan asks, leaning across the table to take my hand.

"I don't know," I mumble. I feel another rush, a bit stronger and more distinct. I look up into Ronan's eyes. "Something is wrong with Alak."

I jerk to my feet, my heart beating wildly as I try to sort my thoughts. Ronan stands as I pace in a small circle.

"Can you tell what's wrong, love?" he asks, his voice filled with concern.

I pause in my pacing to look at Ronan as I shake my head. "No." My voice cracks as I struggle to breathe. "I can't tell. I think . . . I think I need to go to him. I think he needs my help."

Ronan nods, taking both my hands in his. "Okay. I'm

sure everything will be all right. Just breathe. Calm down and gather your wits."

I swallow and nod. "You're right." I take a deep breath and release it slowly. "I have to go to him."

I feel another rush of magic and I close my eyes. This time it's more than just magic. It's almost like Alak is calling to me down the bond. I open my eyes to a sharp bark. Felixe stands next to Ronan looking up at me with wide, panicked eyes.

"Go on, love," Ronan says, giving my hands a squeeze before releasing them. "I'll watch over things here. Do you have enough magic?"

I nod. "I think so." I raise my wrist, showing him the Syphon Stone bracelet. "I've been storing little bits of magic in here at random, so I have backup. It's become a bit of a habit."

Ronan holds out his hand palm up. "May I add some of my own magic?"

"Of course," I reply, placing my wrist in his hand.

He closes his fingers over the stone and I feel the trickle of magic as it transfers. Ronan's magic is far stronger that it appears.

I force a smile as he pulls his hand back. "I'll be back soon."

"I'll hold you to that, love," Ronan whispers.

Felixe leaps to my shoulder, and together we wisp away.

CHAPTER FORTY

ALAK

The morning after Bram and I create our plan, we fill Pax in on everything we've worked out and he agrees. He decides to put off his usual trip back to the refugee camp by a day or two so he can stay with us until we're ready to leave. He notifies Mara of the change with his whisper magic.

The sixth day of training everyone seems more focused. Probably because they all know what's at stake. Knowing that some of them could be seeing real battle very soon is definitely motivation. However, things don't go quite as planned. On the seventh day, we wake up to a torrential rainstorm. Even with some of the magic wielders making shields from the rain, it's too difficult to do anything, let alone judge performance accurately.

The next day, the rain finally subsides around noon. We do a few drills together before finally setting up the mock battle. We divide the soldiers into four teams. Each team includes twenty-five of the soldiers we've more or less decided to take and twenty-five of the ones we're considering, rounded out with the additional soldiers. Things go as expected, and by the end of the trial, we have our definitive list. We pass it on to Pax and he rounds up the soldiers.

"This does not mean that those of you who have been left behind are not worthy," Bram says, his voice ringing over the field. "I am sure you will all see battle soon but, when that day comes, you must be ready. Those of you that will stay get additional time to sharpen your skills. There is no shame in that. I look forward to fighting side-by-side with you all."

Murmurs of thanks and agreement spread throughout the crowd. Bram is good at this. He's meant to be a leader. Once everything is settled with the soldiers, I return to my tent. Felixe pops up next to me. I think he can sense my eagerness. I write quick letter to Astra, my heart longing for her.

I'm ready to go home.

I'm almost surprised by how eagerly I rise the next morning, but I want to be back with Astra so badly I'm even willing to get up before the sun. If that's not love, I don't know what is.

We get on the road bright and early, but moving with an army of 150 soldiers is slow. It doesn't help that we take a winding path through the mountain that likely adds at least a day to our travels, but we agree that the path is less likely to be under observation by Kato and his minions. Safety first and all that.

The second day we are greeted with rainy weather that further slows us, but we power on. The rain gives those with magic a good opportunity to use shielding techniques to keep the rain from soaking us through entirely. Mid-morning a letter from Astra arrives. I shield it from the rain with my magic and read while we ride.

My Dearest Alak,

Thanks to Ronan's help, I think we finally have a decent plan to contact the Fae. Thanks to a tip from Ehren, I was able to contact Makin on the other side and get some basic information about contacting the Fae through Faerie rings. Ronan has a few Faerie stories that he brought with him, and using clues hidden in the children's tales, we've discovered the general location of some of these Faerie rings to be in Athiedor. The rings are made of special, magical flowers that bloom year-round. We're working on narrowing down an exact location, but your ability to detect all things magical may come in very handy when we go to seek the ring.

I miss you so much and am counting the days until you return. How many days will it take? It almost doesn't matter. Even one day feels like an eternity without you. Just return to me safely as soon as you can.

Forever Yours,

Astra

I long to reply immediately, but writing from horseback while shielding from rain proves to be a difficult feat. Instead, I wait until we pause for lunch to write a brief response. As I watch Felixe disappear with my letter, I briefly consider going with him. After all, we're essentially done with our mission. What more of my assistance could Bram possibly need? By this point in our venture, I'm more useless baggage. I'd likely be doing him a favor. But as much as I want to go, I know I still have a duty to see through, so I grin and bear it. Well, I bear it. There's not much grinning due to the miserable rain.

The next day is our last in the mountains. Or so Bram promises. Whether it's true or not, the day drags on forever. At least the rain has moved on, though it's left behind a cloudy gray sky that hangs over us in ominous form.

On our fourth day of travel, we do leave the mountains behind as promised, but it's nearly midday. A landscape free of rocky hillsides is a welcome sight, especially knowing that every step puts me one step closer to Astra. I can feel the tug of the bond and I long for her. Even the sky seems to welcome us, a bright cloudless blue. Everything is going according to plan. Of course, as usual, that means everything will go horribly wrong soon.

An hour or two after we pause for lunch, something feels off. The magic around us is . . . wrong. I shift on Fawn and scan the small army. A few of the other magically inclined soldiers are also looking around. They sense it, too.

"What is it?" Bram asks, riding up next to me.

I shake my head. "I'm not sure, but it's not good."

Bram nods and turns toward the soldiers nearest him. "Stay alert."

The soldiers straighten, their eyes searching the area around us as they pass the message through the ranks. We're all tense, watching, waiting. A few of the soldiers have their weapons drawn while others have magic twirling at their fingertips. I call on my own magic as I scan our surroundings.

I'm beginning to think we overreacted, that I sensed

nothing, when shadows cross our path. I lift my eyes to the sky and my stomach turns at the sight I find. The sky is filled with dozens of Dragkonians. But they're not alone. A masking ward drops behind us to reveal hundreds of soldiers, all with magical abilities. We fell into an ambush and are completely surrounded.

The attack is in full swing before we even have a chance to set up any sort of defense. Thankfully, Bram is built for moments like this and snaps into full Captain Mode.

"Form your lines!" he yells, drawing his sword. "You've trained for this!"

He charges forward into the line of attackers, dodging their magical blows. Several soldiers follow him into the clash of battle.

"Shields up!" I yell to those with magic.

Fumbling half-formed shields flicker around our soldiers. I throw in a little of my own magic to strengthen them, but it's not enough. Not against an army full of magical soldiers trained for magical warfare and beasts that can't be harmed by human weapons.

"Use your magic to attack side-by-side with your weapons," I call out as I send a strike of my own. "But be careful not to drain yourself."

Magic swells in the air—some from our own army, but more from our attackers. Our army is valiant and we won't give up easily, but I see no way out of this. We're surrounded by soldiers and beasts with nothing to lose. We fell into the perfect trap. There's no way to win.

My heart sinks at the realization I won't see Astra again. I won't get to say goodbye. I simply don't see a way out. Unless maybe . . . No, I can't ask her to come. It would mean her death as surely as my own. Then again, it might be our only chance. Her magic is the closest thing in this mortal realm that can stand against a foe like this. I've seen her take on these beasts before and come out alive. Surely she can do it again. I believe in her.

I send a plea down the bond, praying that it finds her. That she understands. I leap back into battle, putting everything I have into saving as many lives as possible. I take a few blows, but I remain standing, determined to survive. Determined to once again fight the odds and come out alive. I call for Astra with all my heart again and again. I know she can sense me. Even amongst the chaos, I can feel her. I know she will come. I only hope I don't regret bringing her into this mess. I hope I didn't call her to her death.

When she appears, however, my heart stills with instant regret. What have I done? Her eyes meet mine before they look around at the carnage and chaos. She doesn't hesitate a moment before she calls the full force of her magic, glowing like a goddess. She sends out a blast that knocks our enemies back, many falling to the ground. With a rush of magic, she seals our army in a warded shield, using magic that I can sense is borrowed. Silver-blue lightning stretches from her fingertips, wrapping around the magic wielders who were cutting us down minutes before.

With renewed strength and hope, our army charges forward, but we're still severely outnumbered. Astra's magic can only hold out against the Dragkonians for so long, and once it fails, our chance of survival vanishes. She meets my eyes and I know what she plans to do. I sense her determination in our bond as much as her expression. She pulls her gaze away and wisps to Bram's side.

"No!" I scream, pushing Fawn forward, racing to her side.

I see Bram pale as he looks around, uncertain. Then he nods, looking back at Astra, his jaw set.

No. No. It would drain her far too much.

I leap from Fawn's back and rush to her side.

"Don't do it," I beg. "You can't."

She looks at me, sadness filling her eyes. "I have to, Alak. If we stay here, we die."

"No, you go. You get out. I never should've brought you here."

She shakes her head, smiling sadly. "You know I'm not going to abandon all these people to die, or worse be taken hostage and tortured."

I hold out my hand. "Here. At least take all my magic. Otherwise, there's no way you'll live."

She starts to protest, shaking her head. "Alak—"

"Take it!" I yell. I squeeze my eyes shut for a moment before meeting her gaze and whispering, "If you don't, you'll die, and I'll essentially die right along with you."

She holds my gaze before nodding and placing her hand in mine. I transfer as much of magic as I can as fast as possible before she jerks her hand away.

"That's enough. You need some for yourself."

The shield around us quivers as it starts to fail. I can feel Astra's terror down the bond as she turns to Bram.

"Just imagine the fortress as clearly as you can. I'll do the rest," she says in a voice far too even and calm for these circumstances.

Bram nods, but he looks unsure as he glances from Astra to me.

"Are you sure?"

"We don't have time to argue," Astra says firmly. "Just do it."

Bram takes a deep breath, closing his eyes. "Okay. I have it."

Astra takes his hand and I feel her magic reach out. It covers us like blanket—all of our people, those still fighting, the fallen, the wounded, even the horses we've brought along. The only ones left behind are our foes. The bloody battlefield fades around us as a fortress appears. The others look around in fascination, blinking wildly as they try to make sense of what happened. But I barely notice them. I'm focused on Astra. She meets my eyes.

"We did it," she says, her voice so quiet I'm not sure if she actually did more than mouth the words.

She wavers and I lunge to catch her as she collapses. I sink to the ground, cradling her body.

"Is she . . . ?" Bram whispers, his voice cracking.

"She's alive, but barely." I raise my eyes to his. "We need a Healer. Now. Or she won't make it."

Bram nods, turning abruptly to the soldiers.

"Everyone inside the fortress," he commands, his voice strong and full of authority. "Healers, come here. Everyone else inside for now. Sort out the dead and wounded. We—we will figure out our next move soon."

The army slowly shifts to enter the fortress, the Healers elbowing their way through the crowd. We brought two with us—one young man who has some experience working with non-magical healing who possesses a basic healing magic and a middle-aged woman with no formal training but great magical strength. They stop in front of us, staring at Astra in awe.

"Did she . . . ?" the young man begins, trailing off as he

shakes his head in disbelief.

"I didn't think such a thing was possible," the woman adds.

"It shouldn't be, and now she needs your help," I say, my voice edged with desperation.

The two exchange a quick look.

"I don't know what to do," the woman confesses.

I turn my attention to the young man who also shakes his head. "I've never dealt with this before."

My heart feels tight. "You have to help her," I plead.

The two exchange another look, the younger taking a step back.

"I'm sorry."

I squeeze my eyes shut, holding back the tears that burn my eyes. We need more time and a better Healer. There's only one solution. I take a deep breath and dive into my magic, pulling as much as I can forward. I don't have much left, but what I have is hers. It was always hers. *I* was always hers.

"Alak, no," Bram says sharply, grabbing my arm. "I promised her I would protect you. I won't let you kill yourself to save her."

I meet Bram's eyes and clench my jaw as a tear slides down my cheek. He can't feel her fading life-force. He doesn't know that her next breath could be her last. If he did, I know he would also give his life for her in an instant. He can't ask or expect me to react any differently.

"I don't have a choice," I mutter, shaking my head as another tear breaks free. I press a kiss to her forehead before looking back up at Bram. "Tell her I loved her. Make sure she knows that I—" I close my eyes before I look back at Bram. "Make sure she knows I tried everything."

Tears well in Bram's eyes, but he doesn't fight me. He merely nods. "I will."

I take a deep breath and give her every bit of magic I can. I drop to my knees as my body weakens. But I don't stop. I push forward until the world fades to black and everything goes numb and cold. With open arms I embrace death.

CHAPTER FORTY-ONE

EHREN

I wake in a state of panic, though I can't quite recall why. I jerk upright. I'm in my own bed at the Summer Palace. Cal lies next to me, stirring in his sleep to blink up at me. I should be calm. Why is my heart racing? Then I remember.

I leap from my bed, throwing my covers to the side as I race toward the door. Thank the gods I slept in my clothes last night.

"Ehren, wait," Cal calls after me, swinging his legs over the edge of the bed. "I'm coming with you. Whatever news there is, you aren't receiving it alone."

I swallow, nodding as I fight back the tears of frustration and worry building in my eyes. Cal strides to my side and takes my hand in his.

"Whatever happened, we will get through it together," he says, holding my gaze.

I nod, unable to form words. We walk silently down the halls. If it weren't for Cal by my side, holding my hand the entire way, I'm not sure I could make it. Darkness and doubt press against the corners of my mind, delving up the worst thoughts. Did I make a mistake leaving her alone? Is this my fault? Could I have changed it?

We check the Meeting Hall first but find it vacant. At Cal's suggestion, we go to the kitchen next. Cook is far too somber to give me any hope.

"Don't know the details, I'm afraid," she says with a shake of her head. "Lord McDullun is the one you need to speak to. He's likely in the come-and-go room down the way or out checking the wards. It's his job alone, now that Astra's gone."

"Thank you," I manage with a nod.

The come-and-go room is bustling with activity, the guards just having changed shifts. When we enter, everyone falls silent, their eyes watching me with something akin to pity. I struggle to breathe as Cal steps forward.

"Do any of you know where we could find Lord McDullun?" he asks.

"You just missed him," a young soldier says, stepping forward.

"I think he went to check the wards," a servant girl offers.

I open my mouth to offer thanks, but no words come out. Cal says it for me and guides me outside. Once we're away from the others, away from prying eyes, I sink to the ground, putting my head in my hands as the tears break free.

"Hey," Cal whispers, kneeling in front of me. "It will be okay."

I raise my tear-streaked face to his, shaking my head. "You don't know that."

Cal brushes a tear from my cheek with his thumb. "No, I don't, but I can promise you that no matter what has happened, you won't have to face any of it alone."

A sob catches in my throat as I nod. Cal wraps me in his arms and pulls me against his chest. After a moment I've regained a modicum of control and I stand on shaky feet. Cal takes my hand and presses a quick kiss to my lips.

"Ready?"

"No, but let's get it over with."

It doesn't take us long to find Lord McDullun as he's already walking back toward the palace.

"Ah, I heard you had returned," he says, offering us a weak smile. He scans my face and nods. "I take it you heard Astra isn't present?"

I nod once, unable to speak as worry consumes me.

"She's alive," he says.

Relief washes over me and I lean against Cal as my legs go weak. He wraps a strong arm around my waist, steadying me.

"Thank the gods," I mutter.

"But," Lord McDullun adds, drawing my attention back.

"But what?" I ask, terrified of the answer.

Lord McDullun glances off into the distance. "Perhaps we should take this discussion indoors?"

"No," I plead. "I can't take not knowing. Tell me whatever it is."

Lord McDullun eyes me for a moment before nodding. "Aye. It's only fair. Though what I have is mostly second-hand information, so bear that in mind." I nod and he continues. "A couple days ago, I was with Astra having tea when something went wrong with Alak."

"What? What went wrong?" I demand.

Lord McDullun shakes his head. "I don't entirely know. Astra only had a feeling that he needed her, so of course, she went to him immediately. I expected her to return shortly after, but as you can see, she's still gone."

I take a staggering breath and lean harder against Cal. He wraps an arm around me, keeping me upright.

"Yesterday, a messenger arrived from the fortress where they took the refugee soldiers. Apparently, they were attacked, completely outnumbered. The only way to escape was for someone to wisp them all."

My face pales as I stagger back, nearly taking both Cal and I down.

"She didn't . . . Astra didn't . . ." I stumble but Lord McDullun nods.

"Best I can tell she did. 150 soldiers, a few dozen horses with supplies, and of course Alak and your captain."

I shake my head as Cal's grip on me tightens. "That much magic would kill her."

"I gave her some of my own magic before she left to keep in her stone. I'd like to think that it helped. Either way, she's not dead, but she's not exactly alive either."

Words escape me as I struggle to breathe. My chest is tight and the world swims and blurs around me.

"What does that mean?" Cal growls for me.

"Once again, secondhand information, but I guess she and Alak are both in a deep, magic-induced sleep while they recover."

"Magic-induced sleep? So they're *both* alive?" I manage, my chest feeling a little less tight.

Lord McDullun nods. "Aye. I have no idea what state they're in now. Your captain requested a top Healer, and I sent Healer Heora and Hanna. I haven't heard anything more."

I take another deep breath, releasing it slowly as I pull

away from Cal but stay close enough that our arms brush. Now that I at least know she's alive the world is coming back into focus and I can function.

"I should go to the fortress as soon as possible," I say assertively, as if I wasn't having a full-blown panic attack a few seconds ago. "Do you mind watching over the palace a little longer while I settle things?"

"Of course not," Lord McDullun says, inclining his head. "I am happy to serve in any capacity possible."

"Thank you, Lord McDullun," I say, offering him a weak smile. "I know Astra has depended on you a good bit over the past couple of weeks and I cannot express my gratitude enough."

Lord McDullun waves me off. "It was a privilege. Astra is a delight and I'm honored to be held in such high esteem. Though, I would prefer you call me Ronan, if it pleases you."

I laugh slightly as I nod. "Of course. Ronan it is." I turn to Cal. "Well, it seems we're to be headed out again. Ready for another adventure?"

Cal smiles gently. "I'm ready for anything as long as I get to be by your side."

I grin and brush my lips against Cal's in what is meant to be a simple kiss, but when he leans in, lifting his hand to cradle my neck, it quickly turns into something a little more. I can taste his own relief. He pulls me in tighter and it's only the presence of Lord McDullun—Ronan, I suppose—that keeps me from pushing Cal to the ground and taking the kiss further. I force myself to pull back and look over to find Ronan grinning, eyes bright.

"I apologize," I mumble, my cheeks reddening as I step away from Cal.

"No need to apologize to me," Ronan grins. "Love is a

wonderful thing and it should always be expressed without hesitation."

"I agree," Cal says, glancing sideways at me as he grins.

I roll my eyes and laugh. "You would."

"There's your smile," Cal says, bumping me affectionately with his shoulder.

My smile grows and I shake my head.

"Well," Ronan cuts in, still grinning, "I suppose you'll want to be off soon, but let me know if you need anything else."

"We will," I reply. "Once again, thank you."

"My pleasure," Ronan replies with a wink before striding off.

Once he's gone, Cal turns to me. "Who do you want to take with us?"

"No one. Just me and you. That's it. Anyone else might slow us down."

Cal nods. "All right. Most of our things are still packed. Let's get some breakfast and then we can get on the road. Okay?"

"We can skip breakfast. Get on the road sooner."

"No," Cal says, shaking his head firmly. "You need to eat a proper meal. It'll take a few minutes to arrange everything anyway."

He reaches up and cups my cheek in his hand. I lean into his touch, inhaling slowly.

"I love you, Ehren, and I will do everything in my power to help you. That means making sure you eat and take care of yourself, even when the world is falling apart."

I smile. "I love you, Cal."

My lips brush against his, briefly this time because he pulls back, directing me inside. Despite my hesitations, breakfast is exactly what I needed. Sometimes, food is the best solution. Even with taking time for breakfast, we're on the road in less than an hour. We ride in complete silence, my heart drumming with each hoofbeat. When the fortress appears on the skyline my breath catches painfully in my chest.

"We're in this together," Cal reminds me as we continue on. "No matter what."

I swallow and nod, but I can't quite settle my worries.

When we reach the gate, the sentry calls down to us from a guard tower. "Who begs entrance?"

I look up at the young soldier, a boy no more than thirteen, and feign my most authoritative look.

"Your prince."

The boy's eyes widen as his mouth drops open.

"Your Majesty," he stammers. "I apologize. I didn't realize—"

"It's fine, soldier," I say, offering the boy a gentle smile. "But I would like to come inside."

"Of course! Of course!" the boy rambles, scurrying out of sight.

A few moments later the gate slowly lifts with a groan. Cal and I ride side-by-side into the main courtyard, several pairs of eyes falling on us as we dismount. We each take our bags from our horses as a young boy rushes forward, offering to take them to the stables they have prepared. Another soldier around sixteen or seventeen volunteers to take us to Bram.

"Actually," I say, offering the solider a tight smile, "I would prefer to be taken to the side of my Court Sorceress if at all possible."

"Yes, Your Majesty," the soldier says, inclining his head. "They are actually together. He's barely left their sides."

So, Alak and Astra are still unconscious. Worry blooms fresh in my chest as I exchange a worried glance with Cal. Cal smiles reassuringly as he takes my hand, but I can see there's worry shadowed in his eyes.

The soldier leads us down winding stone corridors that are cold and lonely. I suppose a fortress isn't supposed to be a welcoming place, really, but I wish it were a little less depressing. He stops abruptly outside a doorway, turning to face us.

"They're in there," he says, nodding to the room behind him.

"Thank you," I say, offering the boy a forced smile. "What's your name?"

"Tomas," the soldier replies, inclining his head in respect.

"Thank you, Tomas," I say.

Tomas looks up at me, eyes shining. "I'm happy to serve."

With one last parting nod, Tomas scurries back to his post. I take a rallying breath and turn to Cal.

"Now or never."

Cal reaches his free hand to my face and runs his thumb across my cheek. "Together."

I turn my face and kiss his palm. "Together."

He drops his hand to his side but doesn't release my hand as we walk into the room. At first, it's overwhelming. The healing room is wide with several tall windows cascading light across a room full of wounded soldiers. Most are propped up on their beds, their wounds bandaged, but some look much worse off. I don't recognize the young man who is checking the bandages of a soldier nearby or the woman mixing medicines in the corner. In fact, I don't recognize anyone here. Not until Healer Heora steps out from behind a curtain portioning off a section of the room along the back wall.

"Prince Ehren," she says, her eyes wrinkling at the corners as she smiles. "I figured you would be along soon."

I straighten and try to look like the prince I am, but I fear I fail miserably. My eyes dart to the curtained room, asking the question I can't find the words to voice.

Healer Heora nods. "You'll find all three back there."

"And their conditions?" I ask, my voice barely above a whisper as I hold my breath, terrified of her answer.

"Stable," she replies.

I release a sigh of relief and Cal squeezes my hand.

"Well, go on in there," Healer Heora insists, motioning toward the curtain.

Without arguing, I thank her and pull Cal toward the curtained room. Together, we pull back the curtain and step inside. Astra and Alak lie side-by-side on a bed dressed in white linens with a sleeping Felixe snuggled into a little ball between their heads. Bram sits in a chair by their bed, his eyes bloodshot and shadowed, every line of his face betraying his exhaustion as he watches over them. When Cal and I enter, he raises his gaze to us.

"Ehren," he mutters, blinking like he's clearing from the haze of a dream. "You came."

I smile. "Of course. Did you really think I would stay away?"

Bram shakes his head as he stands. "Of course not. I knew once word reached you that you would come. I just didn't expect you so soon."

I close the distance between us and clasp Bram's shoulder with my free hand. "I'm sorry I wasn't here sooner."

Bram smiles weakly. "You are here now, and that is what matters."

"What exactly happened?" I ask as I drop my hand and turn to face Alak and Astra. "I haven't been able to get many details."

Bram sighs and runs a hand through his tousled hair. "We were ambushed. Sorely outnumbered. We fought the best we could, but we didn't stand a chance. Not with our little army of freshly trained recruits. Not against the full force of magic."

Bram pauses, looking down at Astra with pained admiration. "I don't know exactly how she knew to come. I suppose it has something to do with their bond. However it worked, Astra came and unleashed her power, but even her magic wasn't enough to hold back the forces of evil that we battled. Our only solution was to run."

Bram raises his eyes back to me and smiles weakly. "She wisped us all, drawing on the memory I had of the fortress. It nearly killed her. Sh-she—" Bram's voice breaks but he quickly recovers, shaking his head. "She was dying. The Healers we had with us couldn't do anything. So Alak—he saved her. Gave her all his magic. Essentially killed himself doing it. Luckily for him, his Syphon powers work even if he is unconscious. In fact, it seems that on the brink of death, they increase to preserve his life. A few volunteers amongst the soldiers came forward and let him borrow some of their power. That little Fae Fox also stayed by his side and seemed to share some magic. I really don't understand how it all worked, to be honest."

His eyes shift back to Astra and Alak. "Now, Healer

Heora says it's up to them to recharge their magic and wake up."

"You know it's not your fault, Bram," I whisper.

Bram's eyes snap to mine. "I should have expected the ambush."

"No," I say, shaking my head. "There was no way you could have known. We were ambushed as well. The same day, I think. Kato was quiet for a while but he's making moves now. We're expendable pieces in his game for power. As much as we want to stay one step ahead, it will be hard. He's far too clever. But we'll manage. This was just one battle."

Bram nods. "I suppose you are right. Doesn't make it much easier, but—"

Bram breaks off suddenly, his brow knitting in confusion as his eyes fall on my hand clasped in Cal's. He lifts his gaze, his eyes darting wildly between me and Cal like he's desperately trying to fit together pieces of a puzzle. My eyes shine as I bite back a grin. Cal smiles, ducking his head.

"Wh-what is this?" Bram fumbles, nervously gesturing to our hands. "Why are you . . . ? What?"

I release a much-needed laugh, resting my head on Cal's shoulder as I grin at Bram.

"It seems like you're trying to ask something," I tease, pulling my hand from Cal's to wrap my arm around his waist.

Bram blinks rapidly and even Cal chuckles, pressing a quick kiss to the top of my head.

"You two? I thought . . . Ascaria?"

"We went to Ascaria," I drawl. "We had a very good discussion with Prince Luc and Princesse Nicolette."

Bram collapses back into his chair. "Who is Prince Luc?

And what the hell happened? I thought you might come back with some sort of engagement to someone in the Ascarian court. I never imagined . . ."

"I never imagined it either," I confess, my voice quiet as I look at Cal, meeting his eyes. "I still can't quite believe it's true and not just a dream."

Cal smiles and leans in to kiss me. When we pull apart I glance over at Bram. He's staring at us, mouth gaping in bewildered disbelief.

"So I am not reading into this?" he asks, looking from me to Cal. "You two are together? All these years, you've been dodging any sort of commitment to any relationship so you could marry diplomatically and now, when our country is at war, at its lowest, most desperate point, you decide to have an open relationship with a member of your personal Guard?"

My smile falters. I tighten my grip around Cal as he tenses, straightening almost protectively.

"It's not quite that simple," I say, my voice hard. As if anything in my life has ever been that simple, that cut and dry.

Bram shakes his head as he presses a finger to his temple. "I knew I should have gone with you to Ascaria."

I feel like my world is caving in. My emotions flicker between frustration, anger, and disappointment. I clench my fist by my side. The worst part of Bram's reaction isn't how he makes me feel. The part that infuriates me the most is how Cal feels. He shifts away from me slightly, glancing away as his jaw tightens.

"I'm not a child, Bram," I snap. "I can make my own decisions."

"But are they the right ones?" Bram challenges, meeting

my eyes. "You are not known for always thinking things through."

I rear back as if he slapped me across the face. He might as well have.

"How dare you question me on this? I know I've made mistakes and acted irresponsibly and impulsively before, but that's the past. I am a king now—or I would be if I could be properly crowned. If you think I made this choice lightly or rashly you—"

"Ehren," Cal whispers, his voice quivering slightly. I know he's trying to calm me, but the hurt in his voice only drives me further into my fury.

"No, I finally have some shred of happiness and light, and I will not let that be taken from me," I say through gritted teeth.

Tears sting my eyes as I fight to control my raging emotions. Bram stares at me like I'm a huge disappointment.

"I knew I would face many objections for my decision, but I never thought you, one of my oldest and dearest friends, would be on the opposing side."

Bram jumps to his feet, hands clenched by his sides. "I am not opposing you! I only . . ." He breaks off, dragging his hand down his face. "I am exhausted, Ehren. I haven't gotten more than couple hours of sleep in almost three days. I am obviously not in the right mind to be having this conversation. Maybe we can try again later after I have had a chance to rest?"

I nod, my jaw clenched tightly. Bram sighs, glancing over his shoulder at Astra.

"I suppose there is no point in both of us keeping vigil. I will be in my room if you need me." He looks back at me and attempts a smile before disappearing behind the curtain.

As soon as he's gone, I fall into Cal's arms, my tears breaking free. Cal wraps his arms around me, holding me close.

"It's okay," he whispers in my ear, pressing a quick kiss to my cheek.

"It's not though," I draw back enough to look into Cal's eyes. "Is it too much for me to want my friend to accept my decisions? To support me?"

Cal tilts his head as he raises his hand to brush the tears from my cheeks. "You knew some people would never accept me as your prince consort. I love you with everything I possess, but if even Bram can't accept us as a couple, maybe it's best if—"

"No," I cut him off sharply. "I don't care if the world turns against me. I would trade the world for you a million times over without hesitation."

Cal releases a long breath I suspect he's been holding the entire conversation.

"I love you, Ehren," he whispers, brushing his lips across mine. "I'm so thankful you chose me."

"Honestly, I don't think there ever was another choice for me besides you." I smile and pull Cal into another kiss. Cal smiles as he pulls back.

"I'll leave you alone with Astra and Alak," he says after a moment, glancing toward the nearby bed.

"You don't have to go," I reply but Cal shakes his head.

"I don't have to, but I feel like it's what you need. Don't worry, I'll always find my way back to you. "

I smile and give Cal one last quick kiss before he strides away. Somehow, once he's gone the room seems empty and cold. I gather my wits and settle down in the chair Bram

513

vacated. I reach out and take Astra's hand. It's cold. Too cold. Suddenly everything in me breaks free.

"I need you to wake up, Ash," I sob, squeezing her hand. "My kingdom has burned to ashes, but you are the stardust hidden in the rubble. You're the promise of a future, the chance we have to fight back. But it's more than that. I need you for entirely selfish reasons. Every time I think I've found a way to stay afloat, something tries to make me sink."

I break off as my tears take control, but after a minute or two, I manage to subdue them enough to speak.

"I love Cal and I'll trade my kingdom for him. He makes me feel complete in a way I didn't even realize I was lacking. Loving him is the only thing I'm sure of, and I need you here to support me. I need you so much. Please, *please* wake up. I need you to be okay. I can't do this without you, and knowing that I played any part in what you're going through destroys me. Come on, Ash. Wake up."

I stare down at her, barely breathing as I wait for her to move, to react in any way. I let my gaze trail over to Alak, but he remains equally still. My heart aches and I can feel the darkness edging in again.

But then, Astra's fingers twitch.

EPILOGUE
CAL

I leave Ehren as calmly as I can, but inside I'm a storm of fury. I've always looked up to and admired Bram, even though I'm older than him by two months, but now I'm wondering if all that admiration was misplaced.

"Ehren is going to stay with Astra and Alak for a bit, but I need to touch base a little more with Bram," I lie to Healer Heora with an easy smile. "Do you happen to know where his room is located?"

Healer Heora smiles softly. "I would assume his room is in the barracks."

"Do you happen to know which direction that would be?"

"I do," a voice pipes up behind me.

I turn to find one of Bram's new soldiers standing behind me. He's probably a few years older than me.

"Would you mind leading the way?" I ask, offering him my most charming smile.

"Not at all," the soldier says with a grin. "I was headed that way myself."

I thank him and follow him from the healing room.

"Name's Isaiah," he says as we wind through the fortress corridors.

"Cal," I reply with a nod.

"Nice to meet to you. You're one of Prince Ehren's personal Guard, aren't you?"

"Yes. I was lucky to be one of the first ones selected for his Guard."

Isaiah's head bobs as he marches along. "He's a good man, the prince. When everything started falling apart, a lot of people thought he fled the kingdom to save his own skin, but I knew better. He visited my village once a couple years ago. The man I saw that day cared too much about his kingdom to ever run and leave it behind to fend for itself. I knew he would come back, and I decided that I would be ready to fight for him when he returned."

My heart swells with pride for Ehren. That love for his kingdom is simply one of the many things that attracts me to him.

"I suppose that's not news to you." Isaiah grins, glancing over at me.

I chuckle. "I've known him since we were boys. He's always been kind and caring."

We round a corner and Isaiah pauses, gesturing to his left. "I believe the captain's quarters are down that hall. Not sure which room exactly. He hasn't been using it much, I don't think. He's hardly left the healing room."

"Thank you," I say, inclining my head.

I turn to walk away but Isaiah calls after me.

"You know Master Alak and the Court Sorceress, too, don't you?"

I turn back to him and nod once. "Yes. Why?"

Isaiah shrugs, glancing off. "No reason, I guess. They just saved my life—all our lives—out there on that battlefield. We'd all be dead without them. I want to tell them thanks, but I'm nobody. I was wondering if you could pass along the message?"

I smile and nod. "Of course. Though I can assure you in Astra and Alak's eyes, you're not a nobody."

He smiles tightly before giving one last nod and going down the opposite hall. I turn and focus on finding Bram's room. It doesn't take me long. When I open the door, he's sitting on the edge of his bed, kicking off a boot. He frowns up at me as I close the door.

"Cal? What are you doing here?"

All the anger I had managed to push aside on the walk here resurfaces as I stare Bram down. I tighten my hands into fists by my sides.

"I thought we should talk," I say, my voice hard and even.

Bram sighs as he stands, running a hand through his hair. "Look, Cal, I know I spoke harshly before, but—"

"But nothing," I snap.

Bram's eyes meet mine as his scowl deepens. "I only—"

"Do you have any idea the hell Ehren has gone through the past couple of months?" I yell, cutting Bram off. He opens his mouth to reply but I silence him with a wave of my hand. "No, I don't want you to answer. Not yet. Because whatever you say will fall short. Ehren puts on a brave face, but when the doors close, he falls apart. He is doing everything he can to hold himself together, and he doesn't need you to tear him apart."

"I know that, Cal," Bram says, standing to his full height, bringing us eye-to-eye. "I only want what is best for him."

"Who are you to decide that? You crushed him today.

You know that, right? I don't care if you don't approve of me. I don't care if you think I'm not good enough for Ehren. Believe you me, I have my own doubts, but I swear to the gods, I will not let you hurt Ehren like that again. He's been through enough."

Bram shakes his head. "It isn't that I don't think you are good enough for him. You are a good man, Cal. One of the best. But Ehren has responsibilities he needs to live up to. He tends to act rashly and bases decisions on emotions sometimes, which leads to mistakes. I don't want him to regret this decision."

"You're not his guide in life. Just because you spent time by his side as his closest friend for the past few years doesn't give you the right to belittle the choices he makes. If you think he gave in to his feelings overnight on a whim, you are a fool. I never took you for a fool, Bram. Ehren agonized over this. I agonized over this. The fact is the decision was made. It didn't include you then, and it doesn't include you now."

Bram clenches his teeth and his eyes flash fire. "You are out of line, Cal."

"Am I?" I challenge taking a step forward. "Because from where I'm standing, you're the one that's out of line."

Bram takes a deep breath, shaking his head as he scoffs. "You two need to reevaluate this before it gets out of hand. You are right. Ehren has been suffering the past couple of months, and it has torn me up. He is my *best friend*. I hate seeing him suffer. I never want that to happen again. But if you hang onto this ridiculous dream, he is going to end up hurt again. Ehren needs to focus on rebuilding his kingdom without worrying about who is warming his bed."

Before I even realize what I'm doing, my fist is flying through the air. I land my blow so hard on Bram's cheek he staggers back with a gasp. I flick my hand, shaking off the flash of pain before rubbing my stinging knuckles with my left hand. The discomfort is worth it, though Bram now looks like a cornered animal. In a sword fight Bram might win, but hand-to-hand I can take him, especially given the exhausted state he's currently in.

"How dare you?" he snarls, lunging toward me.

I brace myself for his attack, but it doesn't come. He freezes, his eyes locked on my left hand, focusing on Ehren's ring. He raises his eyes to mine, his mouth gaping open as he stumbles back a step.

"Is that Ehren's signet ring?"

I lift my hand, turning it so Bram can see the ring more clearly. I'd almost forgotten about it, having gotten used to the familiar weight on my finger.

"Yes. Why?"

Bram closes his eyes for a moment and blows out a low breath. "Shit."

"What?" I press, taking a step toward Bram.

Bram laughs, shaking his head as he runs a hand through his hair. "I can't believe this. All this time." He looks back at me and laughs again. "It was you. All this damn time."

I blink, thrown completely off-kilter by his sudden change in mood.

"I—I don't understand," I confess, knitting my eyebrows in confusion.

"It doesn't matter. It is a long story," he replies, waving me off. "Suffice it to say, I am sorry. You were right. I was out of line. And I apologize. Though it isn't really an excuse, I am exhausted beyond belief. I acted on impulse, and I was wrong."

I straighten, trying to pick up on whatever detail I've

missed. It has something to do with the ring on my finger, but I can't complete the puzzle. Too many pieces are missing.

With a sigh, Bram sinks down on the edge of his bed, rubbing his cheek where a bruise is already blooming. "Would you mind if we finished this later? I really need to rest. I am sure when I wake up, I will be a much more reasonable person."

I nod and back toward the exit. "Fine." I open the door, but pause halfway out. "I'm sorry I hit you."

Bram chuckles. "Don't be."

I smile as I shut the door. I'm not sure what caused the shift in Bram's attitude, but something about it makes me love Ehren even more.

View the Saga to See What Comes Next

Leave or Read Reviews

Support Amber D. Lewis on Patreon for Updates and Exclusive Bonus Stories

Leave a Book Review

ACKNOWLEDGMENTS

I acknowledge the fact that I am dreadful at writing acknowledgments. Alas, it seems part of this whole publishing process. Let's make this easy for all of us.

First I would like to thank the academy... No. Wait. *checks notes* Scratch that. Wrong acknowledgments. Let's start over.

I would like to thank the friends and family that have stuck with me throughout this process. Having you cheering in my corner has definitely helped me keep going.

I also need to give a shoutout to my Alpha and Beta Readers. Lana, girl, buddy, pal . . . what even to say? All the work we did getting those chapters in order? We deserve a prize. Like a big, BIG one. That was such a crazy experience and I'm glad I had your help. Megan, Shanti, and Karin—ya'll rock. And thanks to Alex for your feedback on those couple scenes. Like seriously. You all really helped to make the book smoother and your comments made my day. Thank you. Thank you. Thank you.

To my partner who will likely never read these acknowledgments: Thank you. I know I bugged you to make all the art and forced you to read my story, and you put up with that. So, thanks or whatever.

Andi, you know how commas work and I am eternally grateful. You also know how to spell "focused" when I clearly do not. Oh, and you know all that other editing stuff you did? Thanks. You really make all the difference in taking my book from good to great.

And I would be remiss if I left this section without a shoutout to you, dear reader. YOU keep me going. YOU inspire me. I write for YOU. I'm glad you enjoy my stories and I hope you'll stick around for the rest of the journey. We're just getting started, you and I. So whether you're one of my many internet friends or a complete stranger, thanks for your undying support. I can't even imagine doing this without you.

So cheers to us! We did it! We made another book. And you know what? We rock. We really do.

EXTENDED
AUTHOR NOTE

This book contains some of the following elements that may prove sensitive for some readers:

Mentions of Suicide

This is a continuation of the previously mentioned suicide and suicide attempts discussed in the first book (Chapter Seven). No suicide attempts are performed on the page. Another character struggling with depression struggles with brief suicidal thoughts (Heaviest in Chapter Twenty-Five).

PTSD & Past Trauma

This is a reoccurring thing throughout the book as Astra struggles with the guilt of having to kill off attacking enemies to survive and Alak battles with his past. Ehren also struggles to accept the losses he experienced previously.

Grief

Several characters grieve throughout the book as they relive previous traumas and experience new ones. This grief is especially strong in the first few chapters but is reoccurring.

Depression

One character struggles with heavy depression throughout the book but it is especially heavy in Chapters Two and Four.

Infertility

One character discovers that she may be unable to conceive children. This discussion takes place toward the end of Chapter Twenty-One and is briefly mentioned again in the following chapter.

ABOUT THE AUTHOR

AMBER D. LEWIS is a new adult fantasy author with a Bachelor's Degree in Publishing. She currently lives in Taylors, SC with her husband and three kids. When she's not reading or writing books, you'll probably find her wandering the aisles of Target.

The Fire and Starlight Saga is Amber's first series, though she plans to publish many more.

f facebook.com/amberdlewisofficialauthorpage

⊙ instagram.com/mugshots_n_bookthoughts

🐦 twitter.com/ADLewis_Author

BB bookbub.com/profile/amber-d-lewis

CPSIA information can be obtained
at www.ICGtesting.com
Printed in the USA
BVHW030406140223
658390BV00004B/88